RAVES FOR MICHAEL WEAVER'S

IMPULSE!

P9-DHS-112

"Michael Weaver shows promise . . . IMPULSE starts out like gangbusters. . . . What keeps one plowing through the steamy pages is the character of the demon developed by Weaver." —*Chicago Tribune*

"It is truly difficult to find a serial killer novel with a different twist, but Weaver has managed to write it. . . . There is enough suspense and good characterization to make this a first-rate novel."

—*Library Journal*

"First-rate . . . irresistible . . . Weaver has pulled off an assured and stunning debut."

—*Cleveland Plain Dealer*

"Merciless . . . terrifying . . . a powerful, mesmerizing psycho-thriller, the kind of book you just can't stop reading."

—*West Coast Review of Books*

more . . .

※

"Sex, violence, and action. . . . Don't read IMPULSE if you're home alone. Don't start to read this if there's anything you need to do in the next few hours—like get some sleep or go to work. Don't read this if you'r disgusted by such gripping books as *Along Came a Spider*. . . . Do read this if you really get into psycho-thrillers. It's guaranteed to give you some chilling goose bumps no matter how hot the summer day. . . . You're hooked for the entire book by page 3."

—*Oakland Press*

※

"A searing, craftily written suspense story that will likely haunt you as much as it engages your interest and admiration. . . . Michael Weaver is such a careful storyteller that the malignant progression of his protagonist's obsession becomes nearly as chilling as the killer's homicidal escapades . . . a sophisticated psychological thriller that deserves its place in the summer reading roster as readily as those by Ludlum, Grisham, and Turow."

—*Raleigh News & Observer*

※

✳

"If you think you've had your fill of psycho-rapist-killer books, think again. IMPULSE is a novel like none you've ever read before. It's as thrilling as *Silence of the Lambs*. . . . IMPULSE grabs you by the throat from the first chapter and scares the wits out of you at every page. Before you go to bed, make sure the windows are shut and the alarm is on." —*Providence Journal*

"Weaver writes well and thoughtfully, and Paul Garrett is an introspective and appealing hero. . . . I feel movie rights lurking. If a book can be visual, this is it. But the book itself is a quick, intense experience. An excellent choice for a quiet weekend."
—*Wisconsin State Journal*

"Weaver handles pace with the aplomb of a seasoned veteran. The novel is loaded with highly charged eroticism and smoldering characters, especially William Meade, a villain bad enough to keep the most jaded reader awake. Begin IMPULSE on a Friday night. That way you won't have to go to work bleary-eyed from lack of sleep."
—**Stephen Solomita, author of**
A Twist of the Knife* and *Forced Entry
✳

more . . .

❋

"Well written . . . It approaches the top of the genre and is a good, page-turning read."
—*Lincoln Journal-Star*

"Riveting . . . will keep readers awake and wondering long after the last page has been turned."
—*Ocala Star-Banner*

"Irresistible . . . IMPULSE manages to hold onto the reader . . . Weaver is a masterful storyteller and spins a plot full of detail and drama. Each of his three main characters is well drawn, as are several supporting ones, and the plot moves logically along the trail of terror."
—*Rockdale Citizen (GA)*

"Extremely well written and guaranteed to keep your mind racing, IMPULSE explores the depths of human depravity as few novels dare and kicks into high gear immediately . . . persistently balances the reader on a tightrope of suspense even beyond the end."
—*Somerset Commonwealth Journal (KY)*

"Haunting . . . You'll be fascinated from page one . . . IMPULSE will rivet you in your seat."
—*Macon Beacon*

❋

❋

❋

Michael Weaver

IMPULSE

WARNER BOOKS

A Time Warner Company

WARNER BOOKS EDITION

Copyright © 1993 by Michael Weaver
All rights reserved.

Cover design by Diane Luger and Mike Stromberg
Cover illustration by Edwin Herder
Hand lettering by James Lebbad

Warner Books, Inc.
1271 Avenue of the Americas
New York, NY 10020

A Time Warner Company

Printed in the United States of America

Originally published in hardcover by Warner Books.

First Printed in Paperback: July, 1994

10 9 8 7 6 5 4 3 2 1

For Arthur Pine, Nanscy Neiman, Rick Horgan . . .
respectively the kind of agent, publisher,
and editor that every author dreams about
but all too rarely finds.

IMPULSE

CHAPTER
1

Paul Garret first noticed the solitary figure when it was little more than a dark blur in the distance, a bare hint of movement in the yellow haze of the late-spring afternoon.

"I hope it isn't another visitor," he told his wife. "I hate those Sunday drop-ins when there's so much to do. People should be more sensitive than that. This makes the third interruption today."

"They're just trying to be neighborly," said Emily. "Not everyone is a time miser like you. Or has such a compulsive work ethic. Besides, it may only be a hiker."

The old Appalachian Trail ran across their property where it edged the lake, and there was always a scattering of backpackers passing through, particularly on weekends, which was about the only time the Garrets were there. They were native New Yorkers come late to the sylvan feast by way of a recently acquired vacation home, and they savored every moment. They loved the clarity of the days, and at dusk they heard thrushes, and there was a barn owl at night. When they stared up into the darkness, the stars looked closer than they had any reasonable right to look. Parts of the house were pre-Revolutionary and in need of repair, and the grounds were badly overgrown, and Paul and Emily were still at the stage where even the work was enjoyable.

The house itself, a white clapboard Colonial, was only about an hour-and-a-half's drive from Manhattan, yet it had a fine, solitary feel. Set on a deep, clear lake that eventually drained into the Hudson, the house looked down from a graceful knoll with a nice flow that carried the eye across thick grass and then over the water and up through the trees on the far shore. Whatever other houses were nearby couldn't be seen, and Garret had the sense, here, of being solidly situated in time and place. It was a feeling that his forty-one years of living in the city had never been able to match.

Taking a late break, he and Emily were having Bloody Marys and a snack on the porch overlooking the lake. Except for the earlier interruptions, they'd worked steadily for much of the day—Garret replacing a section of roof shingles, and Emily clanking through the high spring grass on the tractor with the cutting blades. It was the first cutting of the season and the slope still held the pale, delicate green that peaked out by the middle of June and wouldn't be seen again until next spring.

Garret felt the sun on his back and breathed the sweetness of the freshly mown grass. He'd grown up in sunless tenement apartments facing dark courtyards, and he never took days like this for granted. Nor, he knew, did Emmy. Sometimes, looking at her up here or catching a glimpse of his own face in a window or a mirror, he saw expressions that could only be described as tranquil. And yet, they were not tranquil people. They were interested in and deeply moved by almost everything. Ideas, things, happenings—all excited them, made them intensely happy or unhappy, angry or rapturous. The thing was, they were always *something*. Here, it seemed, they were mostly tranquil.

"I think you're right," he said. "It does look as though it's just a hiker."

Indeed, as the figure drew closer, Garret was able to see that it was a man with a pack on his back. It was perfect hiking weather, with a bright sun, a cooling breeze, and not a hint in the sky of the rain forecasted earlier. Garret suddenly envied the hiker his simple, unencumbered trek—the steady, regular placing of one foot in front of the other, the mind lying pleasantly fallow, the senses open to the perfection of the day. He even found the whole concept of the Appalachian Trail itself intriguing, a pre-Revolutionary path that extended more than two thousand miles from central Maine to northern Georgia.

On impulse Garret lifted an arm in greeting and the man waved in return.

"Poor guy," said Emily. "He looks so alone out there."

"That's probably how he wants it. That's why he's out there. Communing with nature, and all that. Not everyone is as addicted to people as you."

"Why don't we at least call him over and offer him something to drink."

Garret had to smile. A social worker who spent fifty-plus hours a week in the free-fire zones of New York's Welfare Department, Emily could never resist pulling in any human flotsam that happened to drift her way. It was her self-ordained mission in life, and in all their fourteen years together, Garret had yet to see her waver. "Relax, Mother Teresa. It's Sunday. You're off duty."

"Oh, don't be such a stick-in-the-mud. You could end up alone in the wilderness yourself someday."

"Are you planning to leave me?"

"Not yet. I still need you too much. Besides, who'd cure you of your cynicism?"

"I'm not cynical. I'm just not Mary Poppins."

If the hiker continued in his present direction, he'd pass less than two hundred yards from where the Garrets sat. But moments later he abruptly changed course and came directly toward the porch. He approached in silence, a young man of medium build who moved across the grassy knoll with an easy, graceful stride.

"Sorry to intrude on you folks," he said, "but my canteen is just about empty and I was wondering if I could bother you for a fill-up."

"No bother." Garret rose to greet him. "Been on the trail long?"

"Just since yesterday morning."

"After all the forecasts of rain," said Emmy, "you've certainly been lucky with the weather."

"Please don't jinx me, ma'am." His smile was broad and even, his boyish face almost startlingly handsome, with a friendly open quality that didn't seem to go with his eyes, which were pale gray and flat in expression. "I hate to tempt the gods when it comes to weather."

Garret offered his hand. "I'm Paul Garret. This is my wife, Emily."

"Tom Shea." He considered Garret with fresh interest as they shook hands. "Not *the* Paul Garret from *The New York Times*."

"The same."

Shea's expression took on a curious shyness as he stood staring at Garret. "You know, I always read your columns.

Haven't missed a piece in years. Though I don't always agree with you, of course."

"Neither do a lot of other people. And I've got a ton of letters to prove it."

"I once wrote you a letter. It was a long time ago and I didn't like what you said about hunting. I didn't think you understood what it was all about."

"Is that what you told me in your letter?"

"Pretty much."

"Did I answer you?"

"Sure did. You thanked me for writing and said that killing living creatures for fun wasn't something you ever wanted to understand."

Emily laughed. "That's my husband, all right. Why don't you take off your pack and have some cheese and crackers, Tom. It's the least we can offer an abused reader."

"Thank you, ma'am, but the water will do just fine. And I don't feel at all abused. It's a privilege to meet a distinguished journalist like Mr. Garret. It's also strange meeting someone you've read and known about for years and never even seen. You feel you really know him, yet he doesn't know you from Adam."

Shea swung off his pack and drew his canteen from its cover, which was attached to an old army-surplus web belt. Then using a hose that lay coiled beside the porch, he filled his canteen and took a long drink.

Watching, Garret was struck again by his extraordinary good looks, by his thick, cropped hair and sun-bronzed skin, by his Indian-like cheekbones and wide, sloping shoulders. Even his faded jeans and knit shirt carried the casual elegance that the more trendy designers were always striving for but could never achieve quite as well as this indifferent hiker.

"Great place you've got here," said Shea. He stepped back a few paces to squint up at the roofline, then the siding, then the fieldstone foundation that rose about four feet above ground level. "I love these old houses. I've even worked in a lot of them. I'll bet parts of this one go back to the seventeen hundreds."

"The earliest deed is 1743," said Garret.

"Awesome. How about the beams and flooring? Any of the originals left?"

"In the living room and bedrooms," said Emily. "Not a nail anywhere, just the wood pegs. And every adz cut still shows pure and clear."

The flat eyes glowed. It was the first hint of true expression that Garret had seen in them. Apparently old houses were what turned them on, adding a sense of life and purpose to what had been totally blank before. Too, the man was not nearly as young as Garret had at first thought. Up close, there were networks of fine lines and blue-purple hollows under his eyes and cheekbones that had to put him in his middle to late thirties. Time enough to have taken a few hits that even his deep tan couldn't hide.

"You're lucky," he told the Garrets. "There's not much of that very early stuff left. Most of what seems eighteenth century is faked. And people are so proud of it that when I'm working in their houses, I haven't the heart to tell them they've been taken."

"What sort of work do you do?"

"Carpentry, mostly. Cabinetmaking when I can get it."

Emily said, "You're beginning to worry me, Tom. Maybe we've been taken too."

"Oh, I doubt it. Not if your deed says 1743. But if you'd like, I could tell you fast enough."

"I wouldn't want to trouble you."

"No trouble, Mrs. Garret. It's my pleasure. I'm practically an addict when it comes to this stuff." Shea took a small, olive-green bag from his pack. "Even carry a few tools with me when I hike. Never know what I'll run into."

"In that case I'll certainly take you up on your offer," said Emily and led the carpenter inside.

Garret followed, amused as always by his wife's naïveté in certain areas. Shea obviously picked up a little work and a few dollars by going into old houses and uncovering things that needed to be done. There would always be something, of course, and why not give the work to a personable, well-spoken young man who happened to be right there on the scene and available. Especially when local craftsmen were hard to find, and not at all dependable when you did find them.

Still, as Garret watched Shea studying the beams, walls, and flooring, saw him poking and prying with one or another of his instruments, heard him explaining various points of technical or historical interest, he found himself fascinated. For there appeared to be a unique and genuine love felt by the carpenter—love for what was old and cared about by few, for what was crumbling and in need of care, for what had stood up against time and abuse simply because it was the best. Garret had occasionally known such solitary, single-minded people, those with so intense a sense of purpose that they had made it seem the only rational way to live.

Shea completed his examination of the Garrets' upstairs bedroom, a square, low-ceilinged room that faced the lake and caught the morning sun. "I envy you," he said. "Every beam, every board is original. There's work to be done, but you've got a real prize here." His slight bow was almost courtly. "And a lovely lady like you deserves no less."

Emily glowed. "How exciting. And we certainly appreciate your taking the time and trouble to look at everything."

"No big deal, ma'am. I told you. It's my pleasure."

Garret held out a pair of twenties. "We understand that. But I still hope you won't be insulted by at least a small, token payment."

"Money's no insult, Mr. Garret. Not to a professional. But if it's all the same to you, I'd just as soon settle for a half-hour or so with your wife."

Garret stood there with the two bills in his hand. For an instant he doubted that he had heard correctly. Then because Shea was half smiling, without a change in either his voice or expression, Garret thought the suggestion was intended as some sort of tasteless joke. He had known men with that kind of gross, locker-room humor—the perennial adolescents who somehow believed it's the ultimate compliment and height of gallantry to tell a man they fancy his wife.

Feeling himself flush, Garret crumpled the money into his pocket. "I don't think that's funny."

"I didn't mean it to be funny. I just think Mrs. Garret is a very beautiful woman. I'm strongly attracted to her. And at the moment I'd like nothing better than to take her to bed." Shea offered Emily his most disarming smile. "I promise, ma'am. You won't be sorry. I'm told I'm pretty accomplished at that sort of thing."

Emily just stared at him. Her face, like her husband's, was flushed deep pink. While her lips, slightly parted with shock, worked in silent disbelief.

"Get the hell out of here," said Garret, starting toward the carpenter.

But he'd taken only a step and a half when he saw the gun in Shea's hand and stopped in midstride. Garret had no idea how long the gun had been there or where it had come from, but it was there now—a 9-millimeter automatic with its blue steel muzzle pointing casually at the original eighteenth-century plank flooring, and Shea's right index finger resting just as carelessly on the trigger. Garret supposed it had been in the carpenter's olive-green kit all along, and that Shea had removed it when he replaced his last instrument. Garret slowly looked up from the automatic and their eyes met and stayed together. He saw a new look there, a raw look, and he was suddenly aware of a terrible coldness in his stomach.

"What do you want?" he said. "If it's money, there's a couple of hundred dollars in that top bureau drawer. There's also some credit cards. Don't touch my wife and I won't report the cards missing for a month. You can use them for whatever you want."

"I've already told you what I want."

"You sonofabitch! You'll have to shoot me first."

"You're a very intelligent man, Mr. Garret, so don't talk stupidly. If I shoot you, that means I'll also have to shoot your wife, and what good will that do anyone? If you and Mrs. Garret just do as I say, nobody gets hurt. I'm gone in an hour, and it's all over and done with."

Emily found a kind of voice. "I don't understand why you're doing this.... I mean, you're very attractive. You could have any number of women—you don't need me. And you certainly don't need the kind of trouble you'll be in if you"—her voice cracked—"if you continue this. Please. Just leave us alone, go on your way, and we'll forget the whole thing ever happened. Why risk ruining your whole life over something so unimportant?"

"Ah, but you're not unimportant," Shea replied. "Not to me. Not at this minute. Just standing here I want you so badly I... well, I guess you could call it a craving. I crave you, Mrs. Garret. Simple as that. So please talk some sense into your husband before he tries something foolishly heroic and gets you both killed."

Tensely following the exchange, Garret had heard Emily's quiet, reasoning tone, her calm, psychologically oriented social worker's logic trying to reach a kernel of rational control that no longer existed in Shea's brain. Judging from the man's speech and manner, he was neither stupid nor uneducated. But any thinking now going on was concentrated between his legs, and it was the kind of sick, twisted response that needed the gun, the force, the threat of violence and danger as a necessary part of it.

"What do you say, Mr. Garret? Are you going to be sensible about this?"

Garret looked at Shea and felt himself in a cold, empty place where deaths were stored. He took a step toward the man and saw the automatic rise until its muzzle was pointed at his chest. Garret had no idea what he was going to do, but it felt right to take that step. He stared at the small, deadly hole, and it was like standing at the top of a high building with your eyes looking downward and your stomach sucking out of you. Then there was an instant when he remembered taking a couple of machine-gun hits in Vietnam, and his legs all but went on him. Still, something in his nerves was pushing him and he began another step.

"Don't!" Emily shrieked.

He stopped and turned toward his wife. Her face was pale and her eyes had a washed-out look.

"Please," she begged. "He means it. He'll kill us both."

Shea pushed forward a straight, wooden chair. "Better sit down, Mr. Garret. It'll be easier on us all if you just relax. There have to be worse things in this world than watching your wife have sex with another man. As a matter of fact, a lot of husbands actually get off by fantasizing such things. Maybe you're even one of them."

Garret slowly sat down. He felt near to being ill. He gazed

past and above the pointing gun, and a beast appeared to peer back at him. The carpenter's even, white teeth showed, the point of light in his eye was violent, and his open mouth was a cave where dark, crawling things lived. Listening, Garret was sure he could hear a wind whistling up from the cellars of the earth.

"Now here's how it's going to be," said Shea, a stage director preparing his cast for the big scene. "Whatever else is happening, this gun will always be aimed at one or the other of you. So please. Just remember. People die from bullets, not from intercourse."

"All right," said Garret. "What will you take to stop this insanity and leave us alone? How much do you want?"

"You mean how much money?"

"What else?"

Shea's flat eyes had turned curious. "What is it worth to you?"

"You're the one holding the gun."

The carpenter appeared faintly amused. "What do you propose to do? Write me a check?"

"I'll call my lawyer and have him go to the bank in the morning. Then he'll send me the cash by bonded messenger. Just tell me how much?"

"How about fifty thousand?"

Garret took a moment to think it through. "I'll have to liquidate some time deposits, but I can do it."

Shea stood there for a long period, silent and unmoving, a cautious hunter in the midnight of some jungle. When he finally spoke, it was to Emily. "I'm afraid your husband doesn't really understand. But you do. *You* know it has nothing to do with money, don't you, ma'am?"

He waited with deliberate politeness for Emily to answer.

When she failed to respond, he shrugged. "Please take off your clothes, Mrs. Garret."

It was said in precisely the same soft, easy, well-spoken tone as the rest, so that Garret didn't absorb it all at once, but rather in small fragments, tiny shards, sharp edged, cutting as they went in. Then he was out of his chair with a hoarse cry, his body packed so solid with fury that he was seeing with his pores. He went for the carpenter in a flat, all-out dive, hands reaching, fingers wanting to pry this creature open because there had to be a soft spot where he could be split and killed. Then there was an explosion and lightning went off somewhere behind his eyes, before everything went blank, as he fell toward it.

He drifted in and out of consciousness, the periods between each state being no more than a minute or two and sometimes just seconds, but seeming longer. Even when he was conscious it was hard to see because blood was spurting past his eyes onto the floor-planking where he lay. There also was blood in his mouth as well as in the sinus cavities around his nose. The sensation was not too different from getting water in your mouth and nose while swimming—except that now, in this extremity, he couldn't seem to move or speak.

Garret had long had his personal vision of hell—red walls and ceiling, a floor of hot coals, and a single giant candle burning in the middle. All wrong. He saw now that it looked no different from his own country bedroom, with an etched image of his wife's beloved face, turned to grief, staring wide-eyed from their bed, Shea's bare ass pumping between her pale, equally bare thighs, and her cries searing his brain. *This is what hell is really like for you,* said a dim voice, and

Garret waited—waited for what seemed like centuries—for smoke and flame to come through the floor.

He felt a new pitch of pain, as if fangs had dug into him. There was a different sound now in his head and something violent was loose inside. But he held it with a delicate calm and made himself look once more at her face. Suddenly it seemed he had never seen her more lovely. Her hair was alive, her skin aglow, and her eyes keyholes to a gate that opened into a palace. But most of all she had splendor at a time when few could have managed it. And for that alone, he could have loved her.

Then silently, feeling himself a long way off and drifting farther, he told her good-bye.

CHAPTER
2

Garret's first conscious sighting was of a pale green ceiling that showed hairline cracks and a few bits of peeling paint. He thought at first it was part of some terrible nightmare, with plastic tubes connected to his arms, nose, and body; his head, face, and neck bandaged; fluids flowing in and out of him; and the feeling that he was unable to breathe and was suffocating.

Then, increasingly, he began to sense that it was all real, and that the nurses sticking hypodermics into him also were real, along with the pain in his face, neck, and head, and the blinking lights of the monitoring equipment, and the doctors in white coats peering at him, and God only knew what else. Everything was real. But most real of all was the sudden terrible awareness of what had happened and why he was there.

"Emmy!" he croaked.

But his mouth was not moving right and the word came out in an idiot's mumble.

Instantly he heard footsteps and saw shapes hurrying to his

side. He swung wildly at them, tearing a tube out of his arm and sending blood shooting in a bright red fall. A nurse pressed the vein shut and stuck the tube back into his arm while someone else gave him a shot.

"Where's my wife?" He yelled the words loudly and more carefully this time so they would understand what he was saying.

Two nurses were struggling to hold on to his arms. One of them said, "Just relax, Mr. Garret. You're doing OK. Everything's going to be fine."

"Where's my wife?"

Then the morphine took hold and he floated away from his thoughts and fears, finally closing them out along with everything else.

When he next came out of it, there were three men wearing sterile masks and street clothes sitting against a far wall. Two of the men were strangers to him. The third man was Henry Berringer, managing editor of the *Times* and his closest friend.

"Hank," he whispered.

Berringer came over to the bed and took Garret's hand. He smiled behind his sterile mask, a thin, generally sober-faced man who did not smile easily and was working very hard at it now. "Welcome back. You had us worried."

"How long—how long has it been?" It was finally coming to him that his speech difficulty stemmed from whatever the bullet had done to his face.

"You've been here at Poughkeepsie General for five days."

"Where's Emmy?"

Berringer just looked at him. His smile was gone, and

small hidden failures were taking place where it had once been.

Garret gripped his friend's wrist, holding on with whatever strength he could muster. Berringer made no effort to pull away, nor did he say anything. There was no need. All he had to do was let Garret see his eyes.

"Aaaa..." It was a curious sound for someone entering the farthest reaches of grief—no more, really, than the softest of sighs. Yet it somehow managed to hold it all.

Garret closed his eyes. He felt as though something terrible, some deadly acid was flowing into his bloodstream through the attached tubes and searing his veins and flesh. He prayed that he might die instantly of it and never have to know more, never have to think about any part of the horror again. But he knew he was not about to be that lucky.

"Paul..." Berringer's voice choked itself off. He was still in the grip of Garret's hand. Leaning against the hospital bed, he rocked gently. The bed, Garret, his tubes, all swayed to the editor's mournful rhythm.

Sweat ran down Garret's face, mixing with tears he didn't even know were there. He was suffocating again, his breath stifled, as if the valves of his heart weren't closing and the blood was rushing back into his lungs. *Maybe I'm going to die after all*. But it was only a forlorn hope, and when he finally was able to face opening his eyes, Hank was still there, with the two strangers now standing beside him. One of the men was bulky, the other lean, and they both wore dark gray suits with the kind of rumpled indifference that instantly marked them as cops to anyone who had the slightest knowledge of such things.

The bulky man said, "I'm Lieutenant Canderro of the Poughkeepsie Police, and this is Detective Baldwin. We're sorry to—"

"Did you at least get the sonofabitch?" Garret cut in dully.

"We haven't gotten anybody yet, Mr. Garret. We've been waiting for you to be able to tell us something. All we know so far is that your wife was shot dead and you were shot and evidently left for dead. Which you would have been quick enough if your electrician hadn't come by when he did and rushed you here to emergency." Looking uncomfortable, the lieutenant paused. "There also was evidence of rape. We've been hoping you might have known the perpetrator."

His head bolstered by two pillows, Garret seemed to see the detective in parts—dark, thinning hair; shadowed, prying eyes; broad cheeks above the sterile mask.

There also was evidence of rape. A fresh flood of anguish swept through him, along with suddenly recalled images.

"I hate to press you like this, Mr. Garret, but time could be important and we've already lost five days. Did you know the man? Or was there more than one?"

Garret sucked air and felt it come in cold and cutting. "There was only one. I never saw him before. He was a backpacker who stopped by to fill his canteen. He said his name was Shea—Tom Shea. White, young, medium build . . . very good-looking."

The short speech had exhausted him and he lay gasping as the two detectives conferred. Baldwin, the lean one, seemed to have an angry ulcer, for he spoke and moved in short irritable bursts. Canderro seemed more stolid, almost sluggish. Hank Berringer, standing silently beside him, still clutched Garret's hand, as if to let go might cause his friend to slip away forever. All three men suddenly looked red to Garret, then green, then red again, and he wondered if he were close to passing out.

"We don't know about any Tom Shea," said Baldwin.

"We'll try sticking it in the computer. It's probably a fake name anyway."

"Maybe not," said Garret in his strange new mumble. "Maybe he didn't know what was going to happen when he gave us his name."

"You think it was all just impulse?" asked the lieutenant.

Garret didn't answer.

"Would you know him from a picture?"

Garret could feel himself soar out on a rush of anger so intense it threatened to burst his heart. "How—how in God's name could I not?"

He looked deep into his friend's eyes, met the full reality of what was there, and quietly fainted.

While he drifted in drugged sleep, his wife came to visit him—Emmy, with her gentle smile and solemn eyes, her voice soft yet urgent, her hair made golden by the morning sun. Garret reached for her with miraculously tubeless arms and she was gone.

Still, it was her presence that had wakened him. And through this break in her death, small bits of her floated free—her supple warmth curled in sleep, a vagrant wisp of perfumed air, her faint off-key whistle. Images of her came to punish him. He should have spent more time with her, taken more days off, not been so compulsive about his writing. Work wasn't what made you human and whole. It was those you loved and how you cared for them. He had cheated them both. Grief lay on his chest like a two-ton rock.

A doctor came to explain things, a plump-faced man with a jovial, confident manner who raised the blinds and let the sun pour onto his white coat and the bed and the pale green walls.

"You're doing very well," he said. "You happen to be an extraordinarily lucky man."

Garret peered at him through two slits surrounded by swollen, discolored flesh. He felt himself to be many things at that moment, but extraordinarily lucky was not one of them.

"By all odds you should have died on the spot," said the doctor. "You had no blood pressure when you were brought in. You were shot twice. One bullet took away small pieces of your forehead and skull. The other went through the soft tissue of your face and came out of your neck. Either bullet could have finished you had it gone just a hairsbreadth in another direction."

"Why do I talk so strangely?" Garret mumbled.

"Because you've had a hole shot through your face and there's some slight, localized paralysis. In time it should straighten itself out. Or you'll adjust. You're a very lucky man, Mr. Garret."

Thinking about Emily was absolutely too much for him, so he thought about Tom Shea, letting his anger build, feeling it cold and solid in his stomach. He had fantasies of tracking the monster down, confronting him, and tearing him to bits—slowly, piece by piece. Then he imagined throwing his bleeding remains into a fire, watching the parts go up in smoke, and finally pissing on the ashes. None of it helped. He just wanted to dissolve into tears, just wanted to listen to the cries of his heart. His mouth begged to open wide and let them out, but they stayed silent inside him, giving him a whole new schooling in grief.

Lieutenant Canderro returned. This time he was alone and carried a worn leather briefcase.

"You're looking better," he said.

"Don't start off by lying. What have you got on Shea?"

"He gave you a fake name. The computers had nothing. We even did a national check with the FBI."

"What about fingerprints? He should have left a whole mess of them around the house."

"He should have but he didn't," said Canderro. "Everything was wiped clean. Which means he's probably had experience with these things and it was not an impulsive act. He was thinking from the minute he gave you the name Tom Shea."

Garret was silent. A part of him knew it was irrational, but he couldn't help scolding himself for not recognizing the warning signs the minute he'd laid eyes on Shea. There must have been something he'd missed.

"I've brought some pictures to show you," Canderro said, opening his briefcase and taking out several large albums. "I've got mug shots here of everyone from this part of the state who's done time for this kind of crime and is no longer incarcerated. It's a hell of a long shot but you should check them out. Who knows? We might get lucky."

"I'm already lucky. Ask my doctor."

Without much hope Garret began studying the pictures. It wasn't easy. One eye was swollen completely shut and the other seemed out of focus. As he searched in vain for Shea's face, the nausea slowly crept over him again. All those benighted faces, with their angry eyes and bitter mouths. So many terrible histories, recorded and preserved for all to see. Dear God! Who were these creatures? Yet they undoubtedly considered themselves human, too, as their victims screamed, clung, begged for mercy. . . .

It was too much. Garret had an acrid fluid in his mouth that had to be swallowed. A pair of pale, vacuous eyes stared at him and he returned their stare. Then he moved on to the next page, and the one after that. Suddenly, in a delayed, half-abstracted reaction, he stopped, went back, and looked once more at the flat, expressionless eyes.

"Jesus Christ," he whispered.

Canderro was instantly beside him, leaning over to see. "Which one?"

Garret's lips moved but no sound came out. Seemingly struck dumb, he could only point a trembling finger.

"You're sure?"

The handsome, even-featured face was younger, thinner, and unsmiling. The thick hair was cut shorter. But it was unmistakably the man who'd called himself Tom Shea. Garret stared dully at the police photo with the number inscribed across the front. He felt the picture, his bed, Canderro, the room and everything in it begin that now-familiar whirl. Only a supreme effort of will kept his stomach where it belonged.

"I'm sure," he said.

Lieutenant Canderro took the album from him. "His name is William Meade. I've got to report in, but I'll be back in an hour with a full printout. Don't go away."

Garret closed his eyes and did his best to think of nothing. He felt himself torn, then torn again. He imagined he heard his wife's voice calling out to him. And as if in answer, he whispered the name.

"William Meade."

Canderro was back in the room in less than forty minutes. He took out a pack of cigarettes, remembered where he was, and returned them to his pocket. Then he pulled a chair up to Garret's bed and sat down, a strong man with hands like meat cleavers. He was holding a sheet of computer paper and a large photograph. He showed the photograph to Garret.

"This is a blowup of the man you identified before. Look at it carefully. It's a lot clearer than the first picture you saw. Do you still feel this is the person who attacked you?"

"Yes."

"OK," said the detective. "But it's important that you understand a few things. It's only on the basis of your word, nothing more, that William Meade is about to be listed as wanted for rape, assault, and murder. Which means that any of three things can happen. He can surrender peacefully at his home or wherever else he may be found. He can resist arrest and maybe get himself and a couple of cops killed. Or having read in the papers that you're not nearly as dead as he thought you were, and figuring that you've probably identified him as your assailant, he'll have already run off and disappeared."

Canderro shook his head. "Too bad you're so famous. Otherwise we could have reported you dead, fooled Meade into thinking he was safe, and picked him up without any trouble. As it is, we're left with only the three possibilities. So I want to hear again that you're sure this is the man we want. Because once the warrant is issued, he and others could die from it."

"I'm sure, damn it! I've told you three times. What does it take to convince you?"

"It's nothing personal, Mr. Garret. Just doing my job."

Garret nodded grudgingly.

"All right, then let me tell you what we know," said Canderro, glancing at his printout. "The guy's full name is William Jayson Meade, and this isn't his first offense. In February of 1983 he was convicted of rape and murder in Brookeville, New York. The sentence was plea-bargained down to twenty to forty years in Attica, and when he showed up there, he was automatically granted nine and a half years of good time credit, which he held on to by keeping his nose clean. Add another two-year reduction in sentence because of New York's Prison Overcrowding Emergency Powers Act, and—bingo—he gets paroled to a halfway house in July 1991, after only serving eight and a half years of his original minimum sentence. He was released six months later, and showed up at your place four months after that."

Canderro folded the paper and wearily stuffed it into his jacket pocket. Despite the casual recitation of facts, the journalist saw in the lieutenant's eyes a look that conveyed deep frustration. He suddenly felt a new respect for the big, gruff cop.

In a minute's time, though, Garret seemed to lose all awareness of Canderro. Lying there, he might have been rendered permanently deaf, dumb, and blind. He just stared up intently at the ceiling, struggling to make sense of a system that could give a man like Meade a mere slap on the wrist and send him back out to kill.

They were gradually taking him off the drugs, which made it harder for him to find refuge in sleep. He lay awake in the night, studying the pink and white glow of the monitors on the ceiling. The same murky fire still burned inside his chest. He had scattered moments of calm, but they were very delicately balanced and he was unable to sustain them for long. Sometimes he wondered what it would be like to join his wife's soul in whatever sweet and tender place it might finally be resting. *Goodness and mercy shall follow her ... and she will dwell in the house of the Lord forever*. Her body, he had been informed, was awaiting disposition in a local funeral home. When he recovered sufficiently, he would see to her burial. *When he recovered sufficiently*.

• • •

Hank Berringer appeared one evening with a huge sack of mail. "Just a small sampling of how your readers feel," he said. "And there are stacks more piling up by the day. Not to mention the hundreds of calls. One of which, incidentally, was from the White House press secretary. We've even been running daily bulletins on your condition. A lot of people care. You're not alone, Paul."

Garret gave the editor his glassy, hundred-mile stare. "What about Meade?"

"He's vanished. But his picture has been on every front page in the country, and there's not a cop who doesn't know what he looks like. Sooner or later he'll have to surface. And when he does, they'll get him."

Garret was silent. At times just the effort of speech was too much. Yet his body, being a small functioning part of the greater human miracle, continued to heal. They had disconnected most of the tubes and deposited him in a chair for several hours a day, where he sat like a propped-up corpse. A barber came in daily to shave him, and once to cut his hair. Proud of his work, the barber had held up a mirror and Garret saw a death's head staring back at him, a portrait painted by Goya at the end, when he was close to madness, with red-rimmed eyes, a stitched-together hole in his face, and flesh of yellow parchment. "Beautiful," he told the barber.

"Listen," said Berringer. "I'm—we're *all* so sorry about Emily. If there's anyone who didn't deserve—" His voice cracked and he broke off. "That's stupid. Who deserves something like that?"

Garret looked at his friend and saw that his eyes were drowning. Berringer's words were the first expression of condolence that anyone who really knew Emily had offered

Garret, and he was not prepared to deal with it. A dark cloud of sorrow, imprisoned for days inside his head, suddenly burst loose and he wept. Hank knelt and embraced him where he sat, a powerful, bewildering embrace, for Berringer had never done more than shake Garret's hand for all the years of their friendship.

Then, the embrace finished, Garret hugged his friend again for a moment—his presence, the warm, solid feel of his body more real to him as an incarnation of Emily than of Hank himself.

"It didn't have to be," Garret said. "They had the crazy animal safely locked in Attica. They could have kept him there for another thirty-two years. That was his goddamned sentence. So what did they do?" Garret stared fiercely into Berringer's eyes. "They sent him out to rape and murder my wife."

He took his first tentative step outside his room and was surprised to discover a uniformed policeman sitting in the corridor reading a newspaper. The cop grinned at him, a pink-cheeked kid who looked to be no more than eighteen.

"Glad to see you up and around, Mr. Garret."

"You're here to protect me?"

"Yes, sir."

"How long has this been going on?"

"About a week, sir. Right around the clock."

"On whose orders?"

"Lieutenant Canderro's."

Garret shuffled along the polished floor of the hospital corridor, coldly aware of the young officer's eyes on his back, but aware, too, of himself, this poor human husk, suddenly in need of protection.

• • •

Canderro appeared in his room several hours later. "Congratulations," said the detective. "I hear you've begun testing your motor functions."

"What else do you hear?"

The lieutenant looked around for a place to sit. Since Garret was occupying the only chair in the room, he settled for the edge of the bed. This time he actually went so far as to place a cigarette in his mouth before remembering he was in a hospital. He left it there, unlighted.

"I'm afraid I haven't heard much. If I had, you'd have known."

"So why am I being protected?"

"As an outside precaution."

"Then you don't really believe Meade is still somewhere nearby?"

"It's possible, but unlikely. I'm sure he knows big cities are always easier to get lost in than areas like this."

Garret fingered the taped bandages on his face and neck. The small action was fast becoming a tic, a compulsive need to physically confirm their existence. Did he really still hope it had all been just a nightmare?

"A point of information, Lieutenant. Suppose Meade did somehow manage to double back, get past your guards, and finish me off right this time? What would happen then?"

"How do you mean?"

"Let's say I had officially identified him, giving a sworn deposition that he was the man who shot and murdered my wife. Would that be enough to convict him if I weren't alive to testify in court?"

Canderro shook his head and frowned. "Your statement would be thrown out as hearsay. Which is evidence by someone not actually appearing in court. Also, you're not being present would deprive our boy of his legal right to cross-examination, and that's not allowable either."

"Now I understand why you've got cops outside my door."

"You don't have to worry."

Garret looked vaguely surprised. "Do you really think I'm worried?"

The detective said nothing and the two men sat in suddenly heavy silence. Even now, talking to Canderro, Garret felt himself alone, isolated, a man whose only true state had become inconsolability. He could sit unmoving, in an enclosed room, and feel like a vagrant. The swelling and discoloration about his eyes were lessening by the day, but all that was visible in his irises was a stinging desolation.

"I do have one small request, though," said Garret. "I'd appreciate it if you'd get me a handgun. A nine-millimeter automatic would do nicely. Considering the circumstances, I don't think there should be any problem about a permit. Would you do that for me, please, Lieutenant?"

"Why do you want a gun?"

"I'd say that's pretty obvious."

"Not when you've got twenty-four-hour police protection."

"But I don't plan on having twenty-four-hour police protection once I leave the hospital. It doesn't fit in at all with my concept of living. And as I understand it, neither you nor anyone else can force it on me against my will."

Looking at Garret, the detective seemed to give off the strong physical communion usually given by an interested woman. In fact, Canderro appeared to have a sudden fresh awareness of Garret, as if some subtle instinct in him had been stirred to attention and was only now beginning to offer a whole new range of possibilities.

"You surprise me," he said.

"Why?"

Canderro shifted uncomfortably on the bed. "I just never expected that macho stuff from a guy like you."

"You consider it macho to take responsibility for my own survival?"

"I do when there's obviously a better way to handle it. What the hell do you know about the proper care and handling of firearms?"

"Enough to get me through one bitch of a war—albeit an unpopular one." Garret dug fitfully at his bandages. "And exactly what did you mean by not expecting that sort of thing from *a guy like me?*"

"Well, you're an intellectual, aren't you? A heavy hitter at the *Times*. In my mind I don't associate you with guns."

"Do you associate me with one nine-millimeter bullet through my face, another chipping away my skull, and my wife raped and murdered?"

Canderro sucked at his unlighted cigarette and said nothing, but Garret could tell that the comment had struck home.

"Let me tell you something about my intellectual, thinking-man's current state of being," Paul continued. "It's all been reduced to four basic facts: my wife is dead, I've been almost dead, the man responsible is still out there someplace, and all I'm praying for is one lousy shot at him. So please, Lieutenant. Just get me the gun and the permit. It will save us both a lot of time and argument."

When the detective was gone, Garret had plenty of time to think, so he thought. Canderro had described him as an intellectual—which meant exactly what? Aldous Huxley had once defined an intellectual as someone who'd found something more interesting than sex. Garret himself had once said, only half-mockingly, that a consistent disregard for truth, and a preference for ideas over people, were what characterized the true intellectual. Except that Garret had never really thought of himself as an intellectual in the first place. What he felt himself to be, at his best, was a writer, a journalist, with a certain feeling for the world around him and the creatures who populated it.

The thing was, he cared. In fact, over the past several decades he had—at one time or another—cared deeply about the abused Vietnamese, the starving Ethiopians, the disenfranchised of South Africa and Central America, the vanishing whales and butchered sea pups, battered wives and mistreated children, civil and economic rights for minorities and women, gun control, and the wanton denuding of the Amazonian jungle, whose final disappearance would surely destroy (he had been assured by ecologists) the planet's entire ecosystem.

Too, he had cared about finding a cure for cancer and heart disease, getting shelters for the urban homeless, saving runaway kids and stray dogs and cats, and making the world safe from nuclear cataclysms. Having evidently found his way onto some secret international suckers' list, he'd made donations to and written heartfelt pieces about every humanist cause under the sun. He had even—God help him—spoken out for prison reform, prisoner rehabilitation, and the elimination of the death penalty. And look what had happened. A released killer had murdered his wife, and none of the rest of it meant a goddamned thing anymore.

The doctor was his usual jovial, confident self, which Garret had come to resent the moment he entered his room. Worst of all, he never seemed to tire of telling him how lucky he was. In addition, Garret had decided he didn't like the doctor's face. It looked too much like the face of a small-town businessman, growing fat and overcomfortable, yet always alert to the chance for better profit margins. Given a choice, Garret would have preferred a more ascetic, self-denying face for his doctor, one that reflected disciplined, scientific contemplation. Or else he should have looked like a haunted character out of a nineteenth-century Russian novel, with a face marked by visions of suffering and death. *My doctor,* thought Garret, *always looks as though he's got a great buy for me in a new stereo or air conditioner.*

"I think we're very close to getting rid of you," said the doctor. He probed and considered the bullet marks on Garret's neck, cheek, and forehead, newly raw-looking with the last of their bandages removed. "You're healing quickly and well."

"I guess I'm lucky."

"You certainly are," said the doctor, either missing or ignoring the intended irony. "Your speech is much better too. How does it feel when you talk? As though you've got someone else's tongue in your mouth?"

"Pretty much."

"It should improve in a few months. So will the scars. If they bother you then, you can always have some plastic work done. But you're a writer, not a movie star, and no one ever said writers have to be beautiful." The doctor laughed as though he had just said something excruciatingly funny. "Judging from much of the stuff I've been reading lately, they don't even have to be very smart."

When Hank Berringer next visited, he brought a bottle of Napoleon, the good wishes of everyone at the newspaper, and the wryly expressed hope that Garret was finally about to put an end to his shameless malingering and get back to work.

"I'm not coming back just yet, Hank."

The editor's eyes were dark, cautious. "What do you mean by 'just yet'?"

"I don't know. Maybe six months. Maybe a year. I'm not even sure of that. The only thing I'm sure of is that I can't just pick up my life where I left it before all this happened."

"I understand how you feel. But once you get back, I'm sure you'll be able to—"

"I said that incorrectly," Garret cut in. "It has nothing to do with being *able* to. I don't *want* to pick up my life where I left it. It's not just a question of burying Emmy, healing my wounds, and getting on with things. Whatever I was before, I'll never be again. I don't *want* to be that again. There had to be something dangerously wrong with what I was."

"Paul..."

Garret didn't seem to hear Berringer. His eyes stared off somewhere, blankly.

"Worst of all," he said, "it never occurred to me that any such thing could happen to us. Sometimes I worried about where Emmy had to work in the city, but never up here. It's my fault. I should have known."

"You're not making sense. You should have *known* what? That some sociopathic nut was going to wander in out of the woods and suddenly go ape?"

"That wasn't just *some* sociopathic nut," Paul said, anger suddenly in his voice. "That was a particular sociopath. That was a creature who'd done the same thing before, been sent to prison for up to forty years, then was paroled after only eight to do it again."

"And you blame yourself for that? That's *your* fault?"

"Damn right it is," Garret said. "I took up arms for all the wrong causes. I should have known more about this kind of official lunacy. I'm forty-one years old and alone and the only woman I've ever loved is dead and all I ever did was stick my head in the sand and beat my breast about a whole collection of noble causes that never really touched either one of us. This horror has been going on for years, and I never gave it more than a passing thought. And when I did, I cared more about justice for the fucking criminals than about their victims' wasted lives."

Garret stopped and stared fiercely at his friend. He was sweating now and the salt was in his eyes and he had to rub them to see Berringer clearly. Berringer—to most he was the stout-hearted, respected editor of a great newspaper who, in war and peace, unfailingly chose for his readers all the news that was fit to print. Except that Garret knew he, too, sometimes made the wrong choices, played a little too much politics, took a few too many evasive actions, collected a less-than-admirable sack of compromises and shortcuts that may well have been the lifeblood of any money-making enterprise but had little to do with the truth as it was generally understood.

"There was nothing you could have done," said Berringer.

"Like hell there wasn't! I could have made speeches on street corners, and grabbed people in restaurants and airports, and written columns and screamed at politicians. I could have told them killers are being sent to walk among us and murder us in our homes. I could have driven from New York to California, warning people. I could have done a lot. But I didn't. I stayed at home and loved my wife and believed everything was in place for us. But it wasn't. It was like a mirror getting ready to shatter."

                    • • •

On the day Garret was due to leave the hospital, Lieutenant Canderro brought him a handgun and a permit to carry it. He also brought two holsters—one belt, one shoulder—and showed Garret how to wear them. The piece was, as Garret had requested, a 9-millimeter automatic, fully loaded. He hefted the weapon, feeling it solid and comfortable in his hand. He had not held a gun since his discharge from the army, but the mixture of dread and power it carried was the same, and instantly familiar.

"When did you last fire one of these things?" Canderro asked.

"About twenty years ago."

"Want to come down to the range and try it out?"

"I'll remember."

Garret was dressed in the same clothes he'd been brought to the hospital in, but with the blood washed out. He'd lost a great deal of weight and everything hung on him. His legs and body still felt strange and there were occasional spots floating in front of his eyes. The doctor had said that both conditions would eventually pass. But of course so would everything else.

"Are you heading back to New York?" Canderro asked when Garret was fully checked out and prepared to go.

"Not right away. There are things to take care of first at my house."

The detective appeared doubtful. "You really think this is such a great time to go back there?"

"I can handle it. Besides, I want to pick up my car, if I can get it started. I've been diddling around in this place for more than five weeks."

"At least you're leaving under your own power."

Garret looked at the detective. His strong, homely, honest face had become a solid constant to him in an otherwise amorphous world. In an odd sort of way, Garret was going to miss it.

"I'll drive you," said Canderro.

"I can get a cab."

"Sure you can. But isn't it nice you don't have to."

The floor nurses made a big fuss over his leaving. They embraced him and several asked for his autograph. Garret responded with a dryness in his throat and a sudden, insane welling of tears. Walking down the corridor beside Canderro, his jaws were clenched and the muscles in them stood out like pieces of cord. With his shirt draped loosely over the automatic on his hip, he felt like an overaged scholar who has finally graduated from a special university of the damned.

CHAPTER
3

He wasn't nearly as prepared as he had thought. The thing was, how did you prepare?

They went around to the back, and it hit Garret even before he entered the house. The tractor was exactly where Emmy had left it when they stopped for a swim and lunch, with the grass she had cut already grown back and the uncut sections almost six inches taller. There were the asphalt shingles, still waiting to go on the roof, and the coiled water hose from which William Meade, aka Tom Shea, had filled his canteen. On the terrace Garret stared dimly at the remains of their five-week-old lunch, their two Bloody Mary glasses stained a faded red, their plates rendered clean by rain, birds, and squirrels.

He stood there in the sun, pretending to himself that he was searching for some specific object. Really, though, he was gasping in the brilliant light, drowning in a sudden flood of remembrance. He swayed with a touch of his recurring dizziness and wondered if, should he fall, he'd land on the gray slate of the terrace or keep falling through the earth itself.

A powerful hand gripped his arm. "You OK?"

Garret nodded.

"Let's check out your car battery," said Canderro. "If she's out of juice, I've got some booster cables in my trunk."

It took some effort, but Garret's car finally started without help.

"Want me to go inside the house with you?" Canderro asked.

"No. That's something I have to get through alone."

They stood considering one another. Above them the house rose, bright in its own yellow haze. A squirrel dashed across the graveled driveway and up a tree.

"There's still nothing on Meade," said the detective. "Not even a hint. I don't know what to tell you. He's either burrowed in somewhere or left the country. Unless he's just been . . ." Canderro hesitated.

"Just been what? Waiting for me to leave the hospital?"

Canderro lit a fresh cigarette from a one-inch butt and was silent.

"I don't think so," said Garret.

"Why not?"

"Just a gut feeling really, but I don't think this is a personal thing for Meade. Right now he's invisible and living free. I can't see him risking his life, his freedom, everything, just to kill me when he doesn't have to."

"That's because you're thinking rationally. Not like a homicidal psychopath."

"Is that what you think he is?"

"Don't you?"

"Not really. Not unless rape and murder automatically stamp you as a psychotic. And since he was paroled from a prison, not from a mental institution, I have to assume he's officially considered sane."

"I still say you should have police protection. But since you refuse, do yourself a favor. Don't take a thing for granted. Sane or not, don't forget for a second that he's out there someplace and wants you dead. Maybe then you'll have a chance."

"You're not very hopeful, are you?"

"I've been a cop for twenty-two years, Garret. You might start out hopeful, but you don't end up that way." Canderro held out his hand. "I'm around if you need me."

Garret watched the detective walk back to his car, a chunky, powerful man who lumbered without grace. As he drove off, Garret experienced a curious sense of loss. Then he took a deep breath, let it out in a sigh, and entered the house he'd once loved but which now only filled him with dread.

For an instant, standing in the entrance hall, he was tempted to turn around, leave, have a real estate agent sell the house and everything in it, and never see or set foot in the place again. Who needed this? *I do*, he thought, and closed the door behind him.

For a few moments he found some small comfort in the silence. But then the quiet became dark and threatening, like a bowl filling with a strange, possibly dangerous fluid, and he said, "Hey, come on." His voice startled him, and he went into the kitchen, made some instant coffee just to have something to do, and poured it into the sink without tasting it. One of Emmy's plants on the windowsill caught his eye, wilted and dead from five weeks without water. He picked up the pot, stared at it, and smashed it against the floor in a sudden blind rage. Then he spent the next ten minutes cleaning up the mess with a dustpan and brush.

He took the first floor slowly, in sections, walking from the kitchen to the dining room, to the living room, pleased by the almost human sounds of the flooring beneath his feet. From the center of the living room, he considered the possible directions he could take. He stood there for a while, feeling again the silence of the house about him, picturing its separate parts—that is, all but the master bedroom, which he was not quite ready to deal with.

Finally, with something like courage, Garret went into the foyer and forced himself to climb the stairs. The door to the master bedroom was closed, with a stenciled police placard proclaiming CRIME SCENE—DO NOT DISTURB. Feeling as if he was about to go over a high cliff, literally experiencing the fall deep in his stomach, Garret opened the door and let the room leap at him in full nightmare reality. He saw the chalk outlines of his body on the floor where he evidently had fallen, and the massive bloodstains surrounding the area of his head, and the delicate tendrils leaking from the dark core of the center. Then moving as if in spasm, he turned and faced the big double bed, which, he knew, would bear the worst of it.

There were chalk marks and bloodstains there, too, but this time they outlined the form of Emily's body on the rumpled bedsheets, giving the feeling of a giant, poorly stretched canvas upon which the artist, a purveyor of three-dimensional illusions on two-dimensional surfaces, had painted his own horror story. Garret stared as though in personal atonement. He was looking at things he needed to explain to himself, that he needed to make a statement about, and yet could come up with no satisfactory way of doing it. He was a writer, and a writer was supposed to be an explaining creature—the roots of this, the causes of that, the sources of human behavior, the structure and reasons for what people did. Yet for what he was considering at this moment, for what an alleged fellow human had, without provocation, done to a gentle, well-intentioned woman, Garret had no explanation. And if the soul had its own natural knowledge of such things, it had so far refused to share its insight.

William Meade, he thought, and thus primed, waited for the expected rush of loathing. Yet somehow now, in the precise place where the act had taken place, it didn't come. All he was able to generate in his mind was a lean, good-looking young man in jeans and polo shirt, who spoke with love of old houses. And that love had been genuine. Garret was sure of at least that much. Just as he was also beginning to realize that he lacked a bona fide monster to star in his fantasies of revenge. Current villains were marked by no unsightly scars, carried no bloody sword, breathed no visible fire. Most often they appeared quite ordinary and harmless, making them that much more dangerous because you had no advance warning, no chance to prepare.

There was just one thing left to do.

Moving with slow deliberation, Garret climbed onto the bed. He lay down on his back, over the bloodstains and the red-chalk outlines of his wife's body. Closing his eyes, he remained very still in the silence of the empty house. There seemed to be a faint scent of perfume, the intimate, distinctive fragrance of his wife, clinging to the sheets. His body stayed rigid and an intolerable fatigue crawled through him. *Ah, love,* he thought, and thought it again and kept thinking it because there was nothing else. He imagined her face, seeing it on the pillow beside him as he had seen it on the mornings when he was the first to waken and tried to will her out of sleep so he wouldn't have to be awake alone. And sometimes, through her sleep, she would feel it and smile, her eyes still closed.

Once, smiling just that way, she had said, "Good morning, darling."

"How did you know I was up?" he had asked.

"I felt you."

"But I didn't even move."

"I felt you inside."

"Did you really?"

"If I were *dead*, I would feel you," she had said.

He had held her then, this person that was like a part of him, with the early sun splashing her scented flesh, still warm with sleep.

But not now. There was no way he could hold her now. And as he considered the abject truth of that statement, felt its tangibility as if it were an object he could grasp, he began to swear. He swore carefully, almost fastidiously, in a low, even voice, hurling epithets at William Meade, at the anonymous parole commissioners who'd set him free, and at the entire insane system of justice that had made Emmy's murder possible in the first place.

A ringing telephone jarred Garret out of his bitter recital. The phone was on a night table beside him and he instinctively picked it up and said hello.

"Welcome home, Mr. Garret."

Garret heard the deep, quietly controlled voice and knew at once who it was. Yet a part of him didn't know, because there was no logic attached to such knowledge and he was still a believer in logic. His throat suddenly dry, he tried to swallow and couldn't.

"I don't know how you're still alive, Mr. Garret. Nobody lives with two bullets in his head. But since you've obviously managed to, maybe there's a reason for it. Maybe you've been touched by the hand of God. Maybe you've even been able to work out some new kind of deal with Him."

There was a soft, mocking laugh. "Please forgive the blasphemy, Mr. Garret. Not being a true believer myself, I sometimes tend to forget that others may be. Are you able to hear me all right?"

Garret moistened his lips and ventured a kind of sound. It came out as nothing intelligible.

"I understand," said Meade. "You can't talk to me yet, can you? In your mind it would be obscene to engage in any sort of civilized conversation with the subhuman creature that raped and murdered your wife. Which is all right. But please listen carefully because this is important. What I'm calling to say is that you don't have to worry about me. I have no reason to hurt you now. You've already identified me and that's all the damage you can do."

There was another pause and Garret could hear Meade's breathing. Or was it his own? At this point he was gripping the receiver so hard that his fingers were cramping. Yet he remained aware enough to have noted the subtle change in Meade's speech. Gone was the plainspoken demeanor of the carpenter who'd possessed such love for eighteenth-century houses; in its place, a coolly controlled urbanity and sophistication.

"I had no plans to shoot you when I did, Mr. Garret. You forced that when you attacked me. My original intention was just to have you watch me make love to your wife, to trap you in the dichotomy of an unbearable anger mixed with the inescapable lust aroused by the eroticism of the sexual act itself. You see, Mr. Garret, despite our intellectualized repugnance of the whole concept of rape, it still remains the ultimate pornographic turn-on for the observer. And that holds even when someone we love happens to be the victim."

The soft, mocking laugh again came over the wire. "Does such a thought disgust you, Mr. Garret? It shouldn't. Because it's the truth. And as a writer you must know better than most that the truth, regardless of the paths it sometimes takes, should never be compromised.

"In any case, I'd still have had to shoot you when it was all over to prevent your identifying me. So you're certainly better off this way, aren't you? Even though I'm not. Or do you sometimes wish you hadn't lived? In thinking about your wife, I'm sure, you must have such moments. If so, try not to. Whatever pain you may experience, alive is still alive, and dead is still nothing. Good-bye, Mr. Garret."

There was a click and the line went dead.

Garret was unmoving on the edge of his bed. When he finally tried to hang up, his hand was shaking so badly that the receiver clattered to the floor.

In considering it later, he decided not to tell Canderro or anyone else about the call. At least not for now. At that moment he had no rational reason for his decision.

CHAPTER
4

Canderro arrived in Manhasset about a half-hour too early for his appointment with William Meade's family pastor, so he drove slowly about the historic Long Island town in the pale morning light, passing the elementary and high schools that Meade had attended, and the athletic fields where he'd played ball, and the movie theater and pizza parlor where he'd probably taken girls on dates. Finally, too, he parked for a while in front of the stately Georgian home on Eldersfield Road where the young killer-to-be had lived during the years of his growing up.

This was it, this was where it all began, he thought, and was once again reminded that evil takes root in soil that is all too often quite ordinary.

"Please understand, Lieutenant, I still suffer a sense of unreality about all this. I know these terrible things have happened. How couldn't I? I read newspapers, listen to the radio, watch television. Yet I still can't reconcile them with the William Meade I once knew."

So said the Reverend Morgan Cantwell, a frail, elderly man who looked, with his thin parchment face and long white hair, like an old musician, too lost in sonatas and etudes to remember to go to the barber. Sitting amidst the somber, medieval-looking furniture of his rectory, he gazed soberly at Canderro, his eyes pouched in waxen wrinkles.

"You can't imagine the kind of boy William was," said the minister. "Loving? Gentle? He'd take infinite pains not to step on an ant. Such was his reverence for life. When he was little more than a child, I taught him that we must love our neighbor as ourself and our enemy as our brother. And until he was convicted of rape and murder, I never knew him to forget a single one of those words."

The minister paused. He had a low, old man's voice, almost lost in the rush of sound from a faulty air conditioner. Canderro liked it. He thought it a truly religious and unchurchly voice, without pretense or cant. The kind you heard all too rarely from a pulpit.

"What about his mother?" said the detective. "When did you last see or speak to her?"

"I can't even remember. Not in years. When William went to prison, she sold her home and disappeared without a word. There was no comforting her. She absolutely rejected Christ. And me as His messenger. People react to tragedy and grief in different ways, Lieutenant. Adele Meade was an intense, prideful woman. Most parents love their children, of course. But William was everything to her. When he went to prison, she simply couldn't face it. This was her second major tragedy in two years. The first took her husband."

"How?"

"He was flying an airplane. A senseless loss. Richard

Meade was a most unusual man and William adored him. Looking back, I sometimes wonder how much the loss of his father had to do with pushing the boy into the awful things he's done since."

The old man sighed, then smiled sadly. "How you and your colleagues must despise someone like William . . . a rapist and murderer. But please. Try not to let it blind you. Hate is such an ugly, destructive thing."

Canderro said nothing. He had the feeling that the minister had not been too far off when he confessed, earlier, to suffering from a sense of unreality, that in his vaguely misted mind William was still attending his Sunday school and singing in his choir.

"I know a lot of people are hunting for William," said the Reverend Mr. Cantwell. "Who knows? Perhaps you may even be the one to find and finish him if that's what he finally forces you to do. But if it does come to that, do it sadly. Do it with a bit of sorrow for what he once was and might still have been."

Amen, thought Canderro.

The minister slowly rose from his chair. Standing, he appeared very old, very frail.

"I'd like to show you something," he said and led the detective into his study, a large, wood-paneled room with three entire walls covered by framed photographs. Squinting nearsightedly at the pictures, he shook his head. "I've been in this place more than half my life. Sometimes, preaching to my congregation, I see faces that have been gone for years. Many of them are on these walls. The pictures help my eyes remember what my mind is beginning to forget. But these over here are the ones I wanted you to see."

The pictures that the Reverend Mr. Cantwell indicated were all of William Meade, shown here at a range of ages that ran from early youth to young manhood, and looking more shining eyed and handsome at each successive stage. The minister offered Canderro a running commentary. Here was William helping the handicapped and tutoring the underprivileged. There he was preparing meals for and even feeding the elderly. At fifteen he was teaching classes in Sunday school, leading interracial study groups, and lecturing against drug and alcohol abuse. At sixteen he was working with autistic children and teaching sign language to the newly hearing-impaired. At seventeen he was pictured publicly rejecting a community service award from a major veterans' organization because he disapproved of some of their far-right political views.

Canderro looked and listened without comment until the minister's guided tour of William Meade's formative years was through. *Saint William*, he thought. Still, there were no lies here. He had done all these things. This was what he had been. Canderro supposed that one day young William just decided he'd had a bellyful of playing the white knight.

"What about the girl?"

The old man stared at him.

"She's with Meade in just about every one of those photographs. The one always looking at him like he's Prince Charming."

"Ah, you mean little Jenny. Of course. Whatever William did, wherever he went, you could always count on her being there. She used to follow him around like a puppy. For years the two of them were utterly inseparable. Her name was Jenny Angelo. Some people called her Angel."

She looked like one, a blond blue-eyed girl with delicate features and a soft inner glow. The two kids were like Ken and Barbie, Canderro thought to himself. He was almost afraid to ask what had happened to her. "How long were they together?"

"All through school. I always had the feeling they'd marry one day." The minister stared at his wall of pictures but his eyes were blank. "Sometimes I like to imagine that things might have worked out differently for William if they had. But that's only the foolish dreaming of an old man. More likely, William would simply have dragged Jenny down right along with him."

"Did she ever marry?"

"I believe so," the minister said, furrowing his brow. "It seems to me I even heard talk of *two* marriages." He shook his head. "I don't understand the forces at work with young people today. There's simply no permanence. If it's not new, it's not good."

"Any idea where I could find her?" Canderro asked.

The Reverend rubbed his chin. "Well, you might try here in town. They usually come home when things don't work out."

The Long Island Health Club was in a trendy, upscale shopping mall on Northern Boulevard about a mile east of the First Episcopal Church. After making a few hurried phone calls from the rectory, Canderro drove over there and was greeted by a loud rock beat and a smiling receptionist in a designer warm-up suit who told him that Jenny Angelo was leading an aerobics class in studio B and would be free in about ten minutes.

He found the studio. Through a glass partition he recognized her instantly from her pictures. Her hair was still blond and worn in a pony tail, her body trim in a bright-colored leotard, and her face as beautiful as ever from a distance of thirty feet. It was probably close to seventeen years since the most recent of her pictures in the rectory had been taken, but she in no way looked the age that time and logic said she had to be.

Saint William's girl.

The music ended. A few minutes later the class straggled out and the detective walked up to her as she was toweling off.

"Miss Angelo?"

She looked at him and her face was a complexity of images. Light reflected on her skin, little glints of perspiration as bright as sun on wet snow.

"Yes? Did you want to talk to me about the class?"

"I want to talk to you but not about the class."

"What then?"

"William Meade," he said.

There was a total closing down of expression, as if an opaque shade had been drawn. It covered her not so much in anger as with a cold, remote little air.

"Are you a cop?"

"Yes." He flashed her his shield and identification.

Her face remained the same but her eyes widened at their cores. "I don't understand."

"What don't you understand?"

"How you found out about me and William. How you even knew I existed in that connection."

"I was with Reverend Cantwell in his study. I saw all those pictures of you and Meade. You were always looking at *him*, never the camera."

She studied Canderro for a moment, seemed to waver, then came to a decision.

"All right, we'll talk, but I'll need to take a shower. I'll be in the reception area in fifteen minutes."

• • •

It was a jewel of a day and she said she was starving, so Canderro picked up some sandwiches and followed her directions to a nearby pond. Once there, he parked beneath a giant willow and watched her wolf down her food.

"Do you always eat like that?" he asked.

"You mean, pig out?" She shrugged. "Only when I'm nervous."

"Why are you nervous?"

"Because I know the kind of questions you're going to be asking."

Canderro watched a young mother showing her two toddlers how to feed bread to a bunch of ducks, and he wondered if Meade's mother might have at one time brought her son here for the same purpose.

"Let's walk," said Jenny, reaching for the door handle. "I think I can probably do this better if we're in motion."

There was a path that wandered along the edge of the pond and they followed it with an easy, casual stride that was really neither easy nor casual. Sensitive to her mood, Canderro remained silent, letting her work it through at her own pace. But he did glance at her from time to time, and he realized she was crying.

"I'm sorry about Mr. Garret and his wife, Lieutenant." Her voice was soft and controlled, as if speaking through tears was something she was accustomed to doing. "When I found out it was William who did it, I felt sick—as if I'd had some part in it myself." She gave a short sigh. "You see, as far back as fifteen years ago, William was sending me very clear signals."

"What kind of signals?"

Jenny didn't seem to hear him. She licked the tears at the corner of her mouth.

"Please understand," she said. "I loved that boy from the

time I was nine years old, and I never wavered and never stopped. Even now, despite everything, I think I still love him."

The path veered away from the pond and into a patch of woods that cut off the sun. It was very soft underfoot, with pine needles and twigs cracking in the stillness. A primitive world with the traffic of Northern Boulevard just minutes away.

"You said William was sending clear signals," Canderro prompted again. "Like what?"

"Like the things he would think of to do," she said dully. "He wanted everything and was afraid of nothing. It was like he'd invented this wild, new way to live, and if you spent some time with him, after a while you wanted to live that way yourself."

"What way?"

"Oh, you know . . . looking for turn-ons, I guess. But it was more than that. It hooked you. Believe me, Lieutenant. It hooked you as much as any controlled substance ever invented."

"You're talking sexually?"

She nodded. Then she went into herself again, and Canderro once more had the feeling she was slipping away from him.

"I know how hard this must be for you," he said.

"Hard?" Her laugh had an edge of wildness. "In a way, yes. But don't let me fool you. Talking about it is still kind of . . . well, satisfying. It stirs me to just think about it."

Canderro was silent.

"You ask if I'm talking sexually?" she said. "Damn right, I am. And sexually it was everything I'd ever carried around inside myself but didn't even know was there until it was pointed out."

"But there was more?" Canderro felt he was setting outlines of bait for the wildest, most unpredictable of creatures. "That wasn't enough for William?"

"Nothing was ever enough for William. And it wasn't too long before I was into all that kinky far-out stuff as well. Only I didn't really know that it was that far-out. It was just something more he wanted, and somehow it always seemed to take us to another level. Do you know what I mean?"

Canderro wasn't sure he did. "Did it go beyond the sex?" he asked.

"Of course. Sex may have been at the core of everything, but there were still other areas William wanted to explore. Other turn-ons. There was the thrill of breaking the law, of stealing and burglarizing, of doing things that could bring you punishment."

Jenny stopped walking and they stood facing each other on the sunlight-spotted path.

"Then finally there was the ultimate," she said, "the feeling of pointing a loaded gun at someone's head with the safety off and your finger tightening on the trigger and knowing you had the power of life and death. You know the feeling, Lieutenant?"

Canderro left that one alone.

"The first time I saw William like that," Jenny said, "saw his eyes at that moment, I knew that sooner or later he was going to have to make it happen."

"Is that what finally made you break away?"

Jenny started them walking again. "No. Not even that. So you can see how far gone I was by then. That was too abstract, still too far in the future. What did it for me was something much more personal and immediate."

Her cheeks were flushed, her eyes a bright celestial blue.

"One night William just threw another man at me. A big,

coarse brute he'd picked up in a bar. He had the guy stick it to me while he watched. Then he joined in himself until the three of us were no more than a pile of twisting flesh on a king-sized bed. And if I die senile and mumbling, I'll remember every minute of it to my last breath."

Canderro was silent as they walked into a stand of tall pine through which the sun flashed in moments of brilliant light and green darkness. He saw her eyes and although they still held tears at the edge, they also seemed coldly mocking, even prideful. Jesus, she *was* actually enjoying the telling. And in one form or another she *had* told it before, too.

"Sounds pretty awful, doesn't it?" she said. "Well, I must tell you, Lieutenant, it wasn't. To be perfectly honest, it was the single most exciting sexual event of my life. Anything else I've experienced pales by comparison. I loved every second of it. I wanted more, then still more, then more again. I wanted it so much that at a certain point I realized it would finally bury me. I knew that if I didn't get away from William then, I never would. So I cut it clean. It was my final chance and I took it."

"When did you last see him?"

"Seventeen years ago. When he went off to MIT and I decided to finish school in England. I was still very shaky about the whole thing. I felt much more comfortable with the Atlantic Ocean between us."

"And how have you been since?"

She'd stopped crying but her eyes still glinted wetly when flashes of light caught them. "Well, I've been up and I've certainly been down. I've married and divorced two decent, caring men I didn't love and shouldn't have married at all. And now I've come back here where it all began, crawled into a cocoon. These days I teach these classes at the club so I'll be tired and empty enough to sleep at night."

"How long have you been back?"

"Ten or eleven months."

"You mean, since just about the time William happened to be coming out of prison?"

Her face was a collection of separate emotions, but she refused the bait. She had some real toughness, Canderro thought, the hard, practical look of a good wife and mother who gets the kids off to school, does the laundry and marketing, plays some bridge, and still manages to spend an hour or so in bed with someone else's husband before preparing dinner for the family.

"Has he contacted you yet?" Canderro asked.

"No."

"Do you think he will?"

"He has no reason to. I haven't seen or spoken to him in seventeen years. And the last time we did meet, I said I never wanted him anyplace within a hundred miles of me again."

"I didn't ask what you said to him seventeen years ago. I asked whether you thought he would contact you."

"No," she said. "I don't think he'll contact me."

"Then why did you bother to come back to Manhasset after all these years?"

"I was born and raised here. It's the only place I've ever really considered home."

Once more Jenny stopped walking and faced Canderro on the narrow path. "Understand this, Lieutenant. If I did have some pipe dream that William would arrive on my doorstep when he was let out of prison, it died a quick death when this latest..." Unable to say the word, she simply drew her arms across her chest. "Now I just want him to be caught."

"Do you think that's how his mother feels about it?"

Suddenly moving on, she seemed to walk in shadow. "Why don't you ask her?"

"I would if I knew where she was."

Her gaze crossed his and there was a flash, as when light catches on glass. But she said nothing.

"I don't suppose you have any idea where she might have gone from here," he said.

"I'd be the last to know something like that, I was never her favorite person. Just the reverse. I'm sure she still thinks it was I who seduced her baby boy at the age of twelve and sent him straight to hell. I used to call her Madame Oedipus—she was a real piece of work, that one. I mean, she grabbed onto William's balls the day he was born, and she's been wearing them on a chain around her neck ever since."

The light left her eyes. "I think I'd better be getting back, Lieutenant. I don't want to be late for my next class."

After he left Jenny Angelo at the health club, Canderro called the Nassau County PD and arranged for them to have her placed under twenty-four-hour surveillance. Then he drove over to the Manhasset Library on Onnerdonk Road and checked through the microfiche records of the *Times* for Richard Meade's obituary and possible news accounts of his death. There turned out to be more material than he might have expected. William Meade's father had obviously been a man of note and achievement. In addition, there was the manner of his death. Not many people died by crashing their own planes into the Atlantic Ocean.

The news accounts themselves carried elements of suspense and impending tragedy that stretched over more than seventy-two hours. The first day's reports simply announced that a Lear jet, piloted by Richard Meade, a Long Island investment banker, was several hours overdue on a business flight from New York to Palm Beach, Florida. Meade's last recorded radio contact with traffic control at Palm Beach

Airport indicated no problems of any sort. But there had been heavy electrical storms reported in the area and considerable concern was expressed for the banker's safety. On the second day Coast Guard and navy planes were being sent out to search hundreds of square miles of ocean in the hope of spotting some of the flotation equipment with which the plane would normally be equipped. On the third day scattered bits of wreckage were located and picked up without trace of a survivor. According to an FAA spokesman, the nature and wide-ranging distribution of the wreckage indicated that the plane had in all probability been struck by lightning.

Several days later, the *Times* obituary read:

Richard W. Meade, an investment banker and chairman of the firm bearing his name, died three days ago when the private plane he was piloting was struck by lightning off the coast of Florida. He was 49 years old and lived in Manhasset, New York.

A living Horatio Alger story, Mr. Meade began life in a series of orphanages and foster homes, worked his way through school, and single-handedly started and built one of the most successful investment companies on Wall Street. He attributed his success to a belief in the so-called verities, which he found all too often lacking in a society increasingly given to greed, shoddy performance, and a lack of personal pride and standards. A memorial service in Lincoln Center is being planned for next Sunday at 10:00 A.M.

Mr. Meade is survived by his wife, Adele, and his son, William, both of whom live in Manhasset.

His next stop was surrogate court on Old Country Road in Mineola, where he went into the record room, filled out the required form, and for a modest fee received a photocopy of the late Richard W. Meade's probated will.

Canderro hated wills, hated all the hundreds of dry legal phrases and sly, money-saving financial devices. A will, he thought, should contain a few words about what you'd learned in life and, in as upbeat a manner as possible, dole out the paltry things you'd accumulated to the people you'd left behind. Not this one, though.

Richard W. Meade had evolved into a man of considerable means, and this carried with it certain responsibilities. Pushing through page after page of typewritten legalese, Canderro learned that Meade had left the bulk of his estate to his wife, Adele, a large amount in trust for his son, William, and most of the rest to the Meade Foundation, an administrative shell for the continued funding of various philanthropic efforts. The only other specific bequest mentioned was to something called the Phoenix Children's Shelter. He'd never heard of the shelter, and wondered why, if all the other philanthropies were being funded through the Meade Foundation, it had been granted a specific bequest of its own?

Hungry for outside air, Canderro slipped the copy of the will into his jacket pocket and hurried out of Nassau County's hall of the dead.

CHAPTER
5

If Garret had indulged his own feelings, he would have allowed no public announcement of the funeral and limited it to just a few friends. Emily's parents were dead, she had no brothers or sisters, and Garret despised the fatuous performances these occasions were frequently turned into by those officiating. But he knew his wife would have preferred it otherwise. Emmy had always tried to share as much as possible with others. She would have said that if people cared enough to want to pay their last respects, why not let them? Garret had rarely argued with his wife when she was alive. Dead, he didn't even try.

Many hundreds of mourners filled the large, midtown church, most of whom had been part of Emily's working life and were strangers to Garret. The minister was deep voiced and impressive, and he had sharp, pale eyes that missed no one of importance among the mourners. When he spoke of Emily's work, of her years of effort on behalf of the poor, the homeless, the handicapped of the city, Garret had the feeling he was hoping to ennoble himself by the magic of association. The minister had talked privately with him before the ceremony, wanting to know if there were any personal thoughts he cared to have included in the eulogy. Garret was polite but gave him nothing. As if he could share what he felt with several hundred strangers. Still, he was not untouched by the sight of so many of New York's obviously disenfranchised among the mourners, dozens of whom came over to him after the ceremony to offer tearful condolences and say how much his wife had contributed to their lives. They were all there, all colors and creeds, Emily's rainbow brigade.

There, too, was William Meade. Indeed, at one point Garret had seemed to look directly at him. Then Garret had passed so close that Meade was actually able to reach out a tentative hand and touch his arm in what might also have been a small gesture of condolence.

Meade could all but feel each hair bristling on the back of his neck. There was an exquisite excitement in being this close, a sense of walking a high wire in a wind. One wrong move, a single instant of carelessness, and it could all be over. Having already picked out the considerable police presence in the crowd, he knew this was a patently foolish thing for him to be doing. Yet he still indulged himself. It had to be part curiosity, part ego food, and probably part death wish. Which the police undoubtedly knew as well as he, since they all read the same overly simplistic criminal psychology manuals on the expected behavioral patterns of compulsive killers.

But they would have to recognize and pick him out of seven or eight hundred people first. And this stolid, paunchy business type that he had made himself up to be, this deeply middle-aged man with iron-gray hair and mustache, who squinted through thick, horn-rimmed glasses above an ultra-conservative pin-striped suit, bore not the slightest resemblance to the lean, youthful William Meade whose glossy mug shot currently graced the walls of uncounted precinct houses across the country.

His eternal playacting. For as long as he could remember—as a child, all through school, even in college—he had been irresistibly drawn to drama, to the altering of character and appearance, to the chance to briefly become anyone or anything he might choose to be. He apparently had a talent, even a gift, for such deception. And now, in this, it was finally offering its own practical rewards.

Meade sought out and focused on what he could see of Paul Garret's face. The raw, pink bullet scars fascinated him. They seemed to carry their own mystic sign, a kind of personalized, if wrongly placed, stigmata. Imagine his being alive!

He was still trying to work it through, still trying to deal logically with so supremely illogical a survival. It was more than just an academic exercise for him. It was his life. Or whatever remained of his life since he had been identified as a wanted criminal, his face splashed all over the media, his once reasonably human status reduced to that of a hunted animal. And all because this one man had taken a pair of 9-millimeter rounds in the head and insanely refused to give up the ghost.

Yet there was a curious lack of bitterness in the thought. He could hardly blame Garret for refusing to die as ordained. There was even something wryly appealing in the whole concept of his miraculous survival, a bit of added complexity and excitement to the game that would otherwise have been missing. A good man had dived flat-out at certain death to save the woman he loved and failed to save her. Now he was alive to think about it for as long as he lived. It could end up being a greater punishment than dying. God's little joke.

Meade considered the hundreds of mourners crowding the great church. Grief, expressed in such numbers, impressed him. Emily Garret had to have been an exceptional woman to have touched so many lives. Sometimes it humbled and abased his soul to know there really were people like that. But maybe it helps make up just the slightest bit, he thought, for people like me. The thought was oddly without remorse.

In a few minutes the service was over and he shuffled out of the church into the glare of the midday sun. The crowd moved slowly, grudgingly, seemingly reluctant to leave, held by a pack sense of loss.

Meade groped for his cigarettes. He lingered with the others on the broad stone steps.

Look what I've caused, he thought, and felt it coming, felt the warm, sweet aftertaste, the soaring sense of exultation. They were all here because of him. The hundreds of·mourners, the police, the reporters and photographers, the minicam units would all be someplace else, doing other things, if he had not brought them together. He'd stirred the thoughts and emotions of millions. Excitement bumped his chest with a steady beat. Then the inside shivering started and his hands and knees felt like those of an old man with Parkinson's.

He raised his face to the sun for warmth and it was better after a few minutes. The shivering stopped and the feeling of calm and control returned. He glanced around but no one appeared to have noticed his brief lapse. How could they? It was all interior. Although someday it might not be. Not that it worried him. When the time came, he knew he could handle that, too.

Starting down the church steps, Meade recognized Lieutenant Canderro from his news photos and television interviews. He was lighting a cigarette as he scanned the crowd breaking up and leaving. The detective might have been a tank, his eyes two gun muzzles. Physically, he projected that same sort of solid menace, although Meade in no way felt threatened by him. Behind his bulk he was nothing but an old-line hack, a paid paranoid thinking ill of everyone and mired in bureaucratic routine. He was too obvious, too predictable, to be truly dangerous. He lacked the subtlety and imagination of the superior hunter. Or so Meade believed from listening to his statements and reading his interviews. And since Meade was the quarry, who was in a better position to know?

On impulse, suddenly feeling a fresh surge of blood pumping, Meade approached the lieutenant where he stood smoking while trying not to look too much like a cop.

"Got a light?"

Busy with his crowd scanning, Canderro barely glanced at him as he held out a book of matches. "Keep them," he said.

Meade thanked him.

The sun warmed his face and turned his hair a bright, shimmering silver. As he walked away, he was humming. *I'm untouchable. I can't be stopped. I can do anything.*

CHAPTER
6

Garret had dreaded going back to the apartment. He'd known it would be bad, and it was. Yet he actually welcomed the solitude. People called, wrote, asked to come over to visit, but he received no one, not even Hank Berringer. There were things he needed to resolve and he wanted no distractions. He sat alone in rooms once shared, thoughts drifting, searching, hands touching the fabric of chairs and couches. He spent hours staring down at the streets below, watching cars and delivery trucks arrive and depart.

Sometimes he opened his wife's drawers and closets, touched her things, breathed the ghosts of her fragrance. He prepared endless pots of coffee and drank cup after cup. He sent out for meals, carefully ate everything that was delivered, and slowly built up his weight and strength. Occasionally he sat at his typewriter, wrote words and sentences he didn't believe, and tore them up. At night he walked from one room to another, switching lights on and off, looking for what? He passed through the foyer, the living room, the dining room, the bedroom, the study where he worked—a man in transit with no place to light. For a few hours at a time each night, he lay stiffly in the middle of the big king-size bed. By morning a deadly fatigue filled him, and he forced himself up anyway, showered, shaved, then dressed as though he were going out—except that he never left the apartment.

On the third day after the funeral, Canderro called. "How are you doing?" said the detective. "I figure you should be starting to miss me a little by now."

It was not all that far from the truth. At intervals Garret had begun thinking of Canderro with something strangely akin to expectation. Even now, just hearing his words at the other end of the line brought its own uniquely positive reaction. Or was it just an unreasonable rush of hope at a time when there was nothing else? "Any news on Meade?"

"At last count he's been reported in about a dozen cities— all the way from Portland, Maine, to Fargo, North Dakota. Which means he probably hasn't been seen at all." There was a pause, then the sound of a match being struck. "What about you? Have you seen or heard anything?"

"I've barely been out of my apartment."

"That's nothing. Sometimes they like to sniff around a little. They like to call up, make contact, get some kind of relationship going. There are all sorts of psychos around. I figure our boy could be one of them."

"Why?" asked Garret, making a mental note not to underestimate the detective, who always seemed to be one step ahead of him.

"What he did, for one thing. People think of rape as a sex crime, but there's really a lot more violence and psychosis in it than sex. Also, it's not his first. He's a repeater. So there's this compulsion there. I don't believe he was out looking for another victim. I think he just stumbled into an appealing situation, got caught up, and couldn't resist it. And now that he knows you're alive, he can add to the original excitement by keeping in touch. So don't be too surprised if he calls you one of these days."

"And if he does?"

"Play along. See what he wants. It could be a break for us. But if it does happen, let me know. Don't be cute and try to handle it yourself. It could prove fatal."

Garret was silent and the wire hummed between them. Unaccountably, he still felt the need to keep Meade's call to himself.

"You feeling any better?" asked Canderro.

"No."

"This kind of thing takes time."

"You an expert on that, too?"

"Not really. But I know how you feel."

"No, you don't."

"Seven years ago my wife and little girl were blown to bits by a car bomb meant for me. So I've had a little schooling in that, too."

Garret's throat began closing on him. "When does it start getting better?"

"I'm still waiting to find out."

Garret waited for the suffocation to pass. "I'd like to ask a favor. I want the names and addresses of the parole commissioners who decided Meade could be set free."

Canderro failed to answer.

"You don't have to worry, Lieutenant. I'm not going to shoot them."

"Then what *are* you going to do?"

"Talk to them. Look at their faces. Sit in the same room

with them. Try to understand why they made it necessary for me to bury my wife."

"That's not going to help anyone."

"Wrong. It's going to help *me*."

"It can't bring back your wife."

"No. But it might give me reasons I haven't even begun to imagine."

"What can reasons do?"

"A lot," said Garret quietly. "They can keep me from sitting here screaming at the walls, and from resenting every living thing I see, and from believing there's no true order or purpose to anything, just the random insanity of sudden death. But mostly, Lieutenant, reasons can keep me from feeling my wife wasn't just casually swept out with the garbage somewhere between lunch and martini time."

It took Canderro several moments to answer. "Okay. I'll get you what you want."

"Thanks. And I'd also appreciate all you can give me on Meade. Background, criminal record, where he grew up, any close family. In fact I'll take anything the computer can offer me."

"You planning to write his biography?"

"He's the element of chance in all this. He's the one who squeezed the trigger. I need reasons for that, too."

Canderro sighed. "I really think you should go back to work, Mr. Garret."

The material arrived early the next morning by Federal Express. It came in a large manila envelope stamped with the return address of the Poughkeepsie Police Department and Lieutenant Frank Canderro's name hand-printed on top. Garret carried the envelope into his study, placed it on his desk, unopened, and sat down before it. He felt a trickle of sweat run down his back and a minute trembling in his stomach.

What am I getting into here? he thought, and was shaken by a sudden, reasonless terror of the envelope and what it might contain.

Then not liking what was happening, Garret gazed out the window and took in the familiar forms of the city, the brick and the limestone buildings across the street, the windows reflecting the morning light, the traffic crawling bumper to bumper. This was his home territory and he sought its assurances. What was he afraid of discovering? What could be worse than the nothingness he had now?

He opened the envelope, sorted out the various summaries and printouts, and began going through them.

There were three commissioners on the parole board that had set Meade free. They were two men and a woman, and Garret wrote their names and addresses on a clean sheet of paper. The woman, Martha Benton, lived in Manhattan, Martin Reilly in Brooklyn, and Dwight Johnson in Queens. Garret sat considering the three names. From their names alone he knew that one commissioner was, of course, female, that Reilly had to be an Irish Catholic, and that the third member of the board, Dwight Johnson, was probably black. By itself all this meant little to Garret, but it did, at least, start personalizing the three. Not that he even came close to tumbling into the traditional pitfalls of stereotyping. He had lived and worked all his life with minorities of one kind or another, was Jewish himself, and knew only too well the blatant falsity of group labels. Still, everyone remained a prisoner within his own skin, and who ever totally escaped his origins? In any case, the three commissioners were no longer blank holes in Garret's brain.

He approached his wife's killer. According to Canderro's

computer printout, William Meade not only was born and raised in the prosperous Long Island community of Manhasset, but went on a full academic scholarship to MIT, where he made a reputation for himself as an actor, picked up a master of science degree in electrical engineering, and graduated first in his class before going out into the world to rape and murder. The crime for which he was imprisoned and later paroled—and which, he steadfastly maintained, even after his conviction, had been completely unpremeditated and accidental—involved a young woman he strangled during a violent sexual assault. The jury hadn't believed him. The parole board, thought Garret coldly, evidently had. Meade's last known address was listed as White Plains, New York, where he reported punctually, once a week, to his appointed parole officer, before absconding four months later after being charged with rape, murder, and assault with a deadly weapon.

When Garret finished reading through all the material once, he read through it twice more. He did it slowly, deliberately, with the same attention to fact, detail, and innuendo that he might have brought to the preparation of a particularly important column for the *Times*. It was so quiet now that he became aware of his own breathing, each breath coming in slowly and going out quickly in a kind of offbeat rhythm that left a break between breaths, which made him wonder whether he was breathing at all.

That night he saw Emmy again. She stood naked at a window, her body slender, her breasts still girlish and undeveloped, having never nursed a child. She came and caressed him where he lay and he felt the small miracle created by her touch. He heard her voice, heard certain expressions she used echo through his brain, but he was not yet ready to receive them. Having awakened him, she left, and he pressed his face to her pillow, still faintly fragrant with her perfume. Then with parched throat and burning eyes, he turned away.

Lester, the doorman, brought up a package at 9:05 A.M. He said a man had apparently paid some kid five bucks to deliver it.

It was a small, square packet wrapped in brown paper. There was no return address and Garret's name was neatly printed on one side with a blue, felt-tipped pen. Knowing no more than this, no more than what he could see before him in his right hand, he was absolutely certain it was William Meade who had sent it. The very real possibility that it might blow up in his face occurred to him only sometime later.

Garret opened it on the kitchen table and took out a folded sheet of pale blue notepaper. On it were just four handwritten lines.

> *For each poor session of sad silent*
> *thought*
> *I summon a dear remembrance of*
> *sweet things past.*

He read it three times. But what *dear remembrance* was the crazy sonofabitch summoning?

Then, looking in the box, he saw it lying on some cotton batting. And even then he needed several moments to figure out exactly what he was looking at, to know that the tiny, round, glistening object was definitely a pearl, and that the pearl had to be part of an earring, and that what the earring itself was still attached to was simply a small, dried-up piece of human earlobe that had been pierced to receive it, and that all of the aforementioned had at one time belonged to Emmy.

The fire was all through him by then and he literally could feel it curling his skin. But it took a fair amount of time before it came to him that the sound—the shrill, keening cry that had filled and echoed through the kitchen—had been his.

It was an additional half-hour before he felt himself ready to deal with it. Then he called Poughkeepsie Police Headquarters and asked for Lieutenant Canderro.

"Canderro," said the detective.

"You never mentioned a damn thing about my wife's earlobe."

The line was silent for a full ten seconds. Then Canderro swore softly. "What dumb bastard had to tell you?"

"No one told me. It just came by messenger in a little box, complete with Emmy's earring and some poetry."

"What kind of poetry?"

Garret recited the few lines for the detective. He had every word memorized.

"You calling from home?"

"Yes."

"I'll be there in an hour and fifteen minutes. And don't touch any of the stuff. Not a thing. Leave every piece exactly where it is this second."

Lieutenant Canderro sat mopping his face. He was in Garret's kitchen, cigarette dangling from his lips, half-empty coffee mug on the table. His skin was moist and florid and he looked as if he had run a great distance. It was the first time Garret had ever seen the detective appear affected by the heat or anything else. Using tweezers and wearing white rubber surgical gloves, he had just finished putting everything in separate, sealed plastiline bags—box, wrappings, string, notepaper, cotton batting, earlobe and earring.

Garret stared at the small, uninspiring collection. "So what do you do with it all now?"

"Fly it down to the FBI labs in Washington. They're the best in the world and I've got an old buddy runs the Scientific Analysis Section. Instead of the stuff sitting around for weeks, waiting its turn, maybe I can get Rick to let me walk it right through."

"I don't understand all this fuss about clues. Why are we playing Sherlock Holmes? There's no mystery. We know who the goddamn killer is."

"Yeah, but we don't know where he's holed up. And the forensics guys are *better* than Sherlock Holmes. These are the first bits Meade's given us, and I want to really squeeze everything out of them that I can."

Canderro squinted, red eyed, at Garret through his own smoke. "You know anything about that bit of poetry?"

"It's a misquoted piece of a Shakespeare sonnet."

"Any idea why he'd send it to you?"

"Sure. Because he's probably got the twisted idea that it makes his ugly brutality seem more of a class act. But he really sent it for the same reason he'd send me a piece of my wife's ear. Because he's a sadistic, murdering crazy."

"*Crazy*, eh? So you've revised your opinion. Maybe now you'll consider some police protection."

Garret shook his head. "No, it's better this way. It's better to keep him 'sniffing around,' as you say. Maybe he'll make a mistake."

Or maybe you'll make a mistake, the lieutenant thought.

"Thanks for keeping Emmy's... mutilation... from me," Garret said, barely getting the word out. "I appreciate it."

Canderro looked vaguely uncomfortable. "Hell, you've had enough. You didn't need to have that, too."

"I guess Meade thought I did."

Garret poured them both more coffee, then laced it with some good Irish.

"Hey, I'm on duty," said the detective.

"This'll just make you work better. Speed you up a bit."

Canderro leaned back in his chair and folded his hands. It was an effort at repose. "You're handling this OK, Garret."

Garret sat wordless.

"Are you really this tough a guy?"

"Is that a real question?"

"I'm a cop. It's the only kind of question I know how to ask. Or even want to ask."

Canderro smiled, his eyes suddenly full of Italian good cheer. "Anyway, you interest me."

"Why?"

"Because I watched you come back from the dead and made close to five grand because you did."

Garret looked across the table at him.

"The betting at headquarters was ten to one you wouldn't make it, and I picked up as much action as I could get."

"You're all heart, Lieutenant."

"Hey, I had faith in you," Canderro said, lighting up a fresh cigarette. He gave it a few puffs, then suddenly turned serious. "Losing something valuable can fill you with a lot of hate," he said, his gaze fixing on the ceiling. Slowly, it became more focused, intent—as if a movie were playing itself out on the tiles. "It's hard for the body to quit on you when you have that pissed-off feeling inside, willing you to go on. In those circumstances the body doesn't stand a chance, the rage just takes over." His eyes dropped back down to Garret. "You know what I mean."

Garret nodded, felt a sudden rash of affection for the big cop. "About your wife and kid, Canderro—I . . . well, I'm sorry."

The lieutenant stubbed out his cigarette. "Yeah," he said, "me too."

CHAPTER
7

C anderro called the FBI's Washington headquarters from his car phone. Moments later he was put through to Special Agent Richard Falanga, chief of the Scientific Analysis Section.

"Rick, I've got to ask a big one."

"You can at least say hello and ask how I am first, you big, ugly wop."

"Hello, Mr. Falanga. How are you doing today?"

"Awful. I'm up to my ears in shit."

"That's why I didn't ask."

"You've got to learn to kiss a little ass, Frankie."

"Doesn't suit me."

"That's for sure." Falanga sighed. "So what's this big favor you have to ask?"

"I've got some stuff that our number one sicko just sent Garret. I need you to give it the full treatment—fast."

"How fast?"

"I'd like to fly it down this afternoon."

"Give me a break, Frankie. We're dealing with a thirty-day backup here."

"Rick, humor me. My balls are starting to itch, and you know what that means."

"The sicko's about to get sicker?"

No answer from Canderro.

Falanga swore. "All right, all right. Bring the stuff down."

The lieutenant hung up, drove straight to La Guardia, and just managed to catch the 1:00 P.M. shuttle.

His cab dropped him at the J. Edgar Hoover Building in the middle of a summer shower.

Falanga met him at the escort desk near the underground driveway entrance and helped him pick up the required credentials and magnetically encoded tag. As always, Canderro found it harder getting in and out of here than Attica. Still, the place did have an air, even if it was just the cold sterility of a maximum security prison.

Leading Canderro down a long white corridor, the FBI agent nodded at the small brown paper bag in his hand. "That's the whole bit?"

"Yeah. It's not that much but it's all we've got from him so far. And at least it's current."

"You think he's still holed up in your area?"

"He was about eight-thirty this morning. Which was when he paid some kid to deliver this stuff to Garret."

Falanga looked at his friend. They'd been born on the same Poughkeepsie block, played cops and robbers and even double-dated together. Then Canderro went straight from school into the local police, while Falanga traveled on to law school and his current ranking in the Bureau. He'd always maintained, though, that the lieutenant was by far the smarter of the two. It was a judgment Canderro tended to dismiss as pure fly shit.

"So how does it feel having first crack at what's shaping up as the hottest, most talked-about case in the country?"

Canderro walked looking straight ahead at the endless corridor. He wanted a cigarette so badly he could feel his lips puckering. He shrugged, gave a little grunt.

"Come on, Frankie. This one reads like a Hollywood script. Angelic protector of the homeless gets raped and murdered, big-deal journalist has half his head blown off and walks away from it, and the perp is an MIT valedictorian no less. Shit."

"You want the case?"

"You kidding? We're all sticking voodoo pins in William Meade dolls. We're trying to get him to commit some high-profile federal crime so the Bureau can move in and take over from you locals."

"Good luck. You're welcome to the sonofabitch."

Falanga stopped at an unmarked door, slipped the magnetically encoded tag he wore into a lock slot, and led Canderro into the Scientific Analysis Section. Then he left him alone while he went to collect the required people.

The lieutenant stood waiting, fascinated and a trifle awed, as usual, by what was routinely accomplished here. Closest to him now was the Hair and Fiber Section, where cartons of evidence from dozens of police departments around the country stood in rows, awaiting examination and analysis. There were lengths of rope that had strangled people, bloodied articles of clothing, sheets and towels with bullet holes in them, newly arrived body parts packed in dry ice—all the assorted, secret angers of a curiously violent society.

Falanga came up from behind and took Canderro's arm. "Let's go. I've got the team briefed and set up in an empty lab."

There were two men and a woman. Canderro had met them all several times before, but Falanga reintroduced them: Tess Murphy of Latent Prints, Larry Endel from Hair and Fiber, and Jack Rule, who worked in Documents.

In less than a minute, using white surgical gloves and tweezers, Larry Endel had the lieutenant's tiny collection spread out on a brightly lit examining table.

"That's everything?" he asked, a thin man whose quick, birdlike movements made him appear in a hurry to get to other things.

"The whole show," said Canderro.

"When did Garret get the package?"

"About nine this morning."

"As far as you know, whose prints can we expect to pick up besides Meade's and Garret's?" asked Falanga.

"The messenger's and the doorman's. But those would only be on the outside wrapping."

Tess Murphy, a buxom, motherly type with glasses, looked at Canderro with sad eyes. "What's your best guess on where Meade might be staying?"

"I'd say somewhere inside a fifty-mile radius of Pough-keepsie."

"What about close family?" asked Jack Rule. "Are there any living in that area?"

"There doesn't seem to be any family living in *any* area. The guy grew up in Manhasset, Long Island. There are no brothers and sisters, the father's dead, and the mother disappeared years ago and may also be dead." Canderro paused. "The mother's the only real hope we have of getting a fix on him. We're still trying to turn her up."

There were no more questions.

"OK, let's do it," said Falanga.

• • •

After the three agents dispersed to their separate work areas, Falanga was called to the director's office, and Canderro drifted from one area of the lab to the other, observing, asking and answering questions, trying not to build any false hopes. The FBI's technology was awesome, but it still couldn't manufacture what wasn't there.

He watched Tess Murphy operating the helium-cadmium laser as she searched out fingerprints on the pale blue notepaper and made them fluoresce. Peering through a window, he saw glowing smudges appear. Some were nothing but oil stains, but others were actual prints. Murphy examined everything through a powerful glass, then photographed the better possibilities under high magnification.

Larry Endel was gathering hair and fiber samples from the box and from the cotton batting inside it. He showed Canderro which grains were probably particles of dried cereal and which, under high magnification and photo enlarging, seemed to indicate a particular kind of powder. Later he'd go through the same procedures on the string, with a deeper, more specific chemical analysis to follow.

In the Documents Section, Jack Rule was taking his turn with the notepaper, making the blue sheet appear to glow under his assortment of lights. He put a different filter on a small but powerful television camera and focused it on the paper. Then he darkened the examining room, leaving only the muted glow of an infrared bulb and the pale green of a television monitor screen. Watching the screen, Canderro saw colorless, previously invisible impressions on the paper slowly take the form of writing. They were the deeper pressure points of words written on the sheet above that had passed through and left their marks on this one. "Later," said Rule when he motioned Canderro to come inside, "we should be able to find out what he was writing. And if we get really lucky, we might even learn whom he was writing to."

Canderro found everyone in the section warm and friendly, eager to explain what he might not understand, willing to answer all questions. But it was more than just politeness, more than his being an old friend of their boss's and heading an investigation that was drawing national attention. They were simply nice people. Also, they loved what they did, loved their high-tech labs and their instruments and the dazzling array of forensic wonders they routinely produced.

Yet the longer he hung around the section, the more anxious he became to leave. He'd had enough of this place of the dead, the maimed, the missing, and the misbegotten; enough of their secrets; enough of the hair, blood, and semen samples; enough of the severed body parts packed in dry ice that were the section's stock in trade.

When he finally left to make the 8:00 P.M. shuttle back to La Guardia, all he really wanted was to get out. He needed something to replace the nameless dread that was flowering in his chest. *What I need,* he thought, *is William Meade, smiling at me as he stands very still, waiting, in the sharp V of my rear gunsight.*

What he settled for, some five hours later, was Kate Venturi.

Having his own key, he silently let himself into her apartment. It was close to one o'clock and she was asleep. He showered without waking her, drank a fair-sized tumbler of bourbon, and slipped naked into her bed. Lying as still as he was able, he kept himself separate from her flesh.

But moments later she turned, felt his presence, and nuzzled against him, kissing his neck.

"Go back to sleep," he said softly, hating to wake her.

She mumbled something, then sensing the rigidity of his body, shook herself awake.

"What is it?" she said. "What's happened?" They were not new questions for her. He was in a line of work in which the dark underside of things was always tearing loose.

"Aah..." he said, turning finally and breathing softly against her breast.

"Frankie..."

He rolled apart from her and lit a cigarette. "It's nothing. It's just...ah, I'm afraid I'm getting too old for this shit. I was in Rick Falanga's butcher shop and ended up just wanting to puke."

She sighed, whispered, "Sweet Mary." The words were instinctive, out of her childhood. She hadn't been to church in twenty years. Though nearing forty, she had a round child's face, innocent blue eyes, and a softly voluptuous body that seemed to have stopped aging on her twentieth birthday. Canderro, sometimes teasing, called it a terminal case of arrested development. Still, he was pleased to accept its rewards.

"It's this Meade thing that's getting to you, isn't it?"

"The bastard's sitting on my chest, chewing away. I can't get rid of him. And he's going to do it again. Soon. I know it. That's why he's hanging around, fooling with Garret. I keep waiting for the next body to fall."

"OK. I have the perfect solution for you. Quit."

"Sure."

"Why not? You've got your twenty years in. You've got a decent pension waiting. How long do you have to go on bleeding? You just said yourself you're getting too old for this. What are you waiting for, a captain's funeral?"

It was a characteristic exchange for them. So much so that it almost seemed to have taken on ritual form. He said, then she said, then he said. Kate knew about ritual. She was a guidance counselor in the Poughkeepsie school system, where everything was reduced to ritual. And there, as here, she played her expected role. She believed that more people should do that. In time of trouble it could keep you from flying apart.

"You know I can't just walk away from this," he said.

Of course she knew. He would die a cop. That's if he was lucky. If he was unlucky, they would retire him so he could sit staring off at nothing.

He ground out his cigarette and reached for the sweet warmth that finally had come to be his single acknowledged refuge. He spoke into a scented cave at the side of her throat. "He's close, Kate. I keep feeling him. It's funny, I can't explain it, but I feel like if I get this guy, that'll be the end of it. Like he's the last of the breed or something." He sighed. "Geez, I feel stupid even saying it."

And yet something *was* different this time. He felt that if he could just track down Meade, nail the sonofabitch, a giant weight would be lifted.

He fell asleep dreaming of his little girl.

CHAPTER
8

Martha Benton was tall, had dark eyes, fair skin, and brown hair, and carried herself as straight as a dancer or a marine—depending upon whether your feeling about her was friendly or hostile. She was standing at that moment before a Rembrandt self-portrait, her head tilted slightly, her stillness remarkably like that of the photograph. And because she was young, beautiful, and exuded life, Garret had resented her doubly on sight.

It was a bright, pleasant Sunday in July, and Garret had, successively, waited across the street from the East Side brownstone where Benton lived, followed as she strolled west to Fifth Avenue and north to the Metropolitan Museum, then trailed after her through the French Impressionist and nineteenth-century American genre collections, before finally settling in with Rembrandt, who, judging from the time and attention she was lavishing on him, had to be one of her particular favorites.

The gallery was crowded and Garret was standing a fair

distance behind Benton. But as if the parole commissioner felt his eyes, she suddenly looked toward him, and her gaze gave Garret the sense of being briefly illuminated. Then she turned and left the room.

He caught up with her as she approached the main staircase.

"Miss Benton?"

She stopped.

"Yes, can I help you?" She had a low voice rounded by the remains of what might have once been a touch of the south.

Instead of answering, Garret gave her a chance to look at him. He saw himself right along with her, saw the raw pink of his new scars, the slight facial pull of the remaining paralysis, the hospital pallor and dark stains of insomnia. Then he let her enter him through his eyes. *Take a good, hard look,* he thought. *Feel what I feel. Nibble on my loss. See what the pain feels like.*

"You're Paul Garret," she said.

She showed a flicker of uncertainty, as though she were checking possible avenues of escape. Briefly, there was even a hint of panic. Then with an obvious effort of will, she appeared to gain control.

"I'm not going to hurt you," said Garret. "You needn't worry."

"I'm not worried."

"Yes, you are. You're scared stiff. And you have every right to be. I could easily have turned out to be another nut with a gun. But all I want is a few minutes of your time."

"Why?"

"So I can talk to you."

"I really don't see much point to that, Mr. Garret. I know the tragedy you've suffered, and you have my deepest sympathy. I also know the part I'm sure you feel Mr. Reilly, Mr. Johnson, and I played in it. But a few minutes of talk isn't going to help either one of us." She paused, a shapely, graceful woman with the color just now returning to her face. "In fact, I can only see conversation between us making things worse."

"How can things be made worse? My wife is dead. I've been almost dead, and a killer with a gun is running loose somewhere. What further damage can you possibly expect from our talking?"

Martha Benton said nothing and they stood two feet apart on the marble floor as streams of art lovers eddied about them.

"People talk, Miss Benton. When there's pain and trouble, when there's a need for understanding, people speak to one another. They hear each other out. That's what men and women do. They don't just turn their backs and walk away."

"I didn't—"

"I don't know what you came out of," said Garret. "I don't know a thing about your family and background. But I can't imagine it being so empty of grace and kindness that it can let you close your eyes to tragedy and pretend it's not there."

"You're being unfair."

"And you're not? All I'm asking is to *talk!*"

Benton stepped closer so that they were almost touching. Her cheeks were flushed and she seemed near to an angry retort. Then as she stared at Garret's face, it suddenly appeared to drain out of her.

"All right," she said. "If it's so important for you to talk, let's talk."

They took a corner table in the museum restaurant, ordered coffee to keep things civilized, and sat considering one another. There was a little blood on the ground between them now, and Benton's head was up and her arms were folded tight as a locked gate as she awaited Garret's next assault. Then she decided not to wait.

"I'm not unfeeling, Mr. Garret. Nor am I a fool. I know perfectly well why you're here and where you're coming from. I knew the minute you identified one of our parolees as your wife's killer. It's our recurrent nightmare in this business. And instead of getting better, it gets worse. Because after a while you know it's not just a question of *if* something like this is going to happen, but *when* and how often."

"What are you telling me? That you actually take this kind of thing for granted?"

Her gaze caught his across the table and there was a flash, like light caught on water. "We take nothing for granted. We work hard at what we do. But since none of us can see into the future, we learn to accept our occasional disasters and hope to do better next time."

"You make it all sound so reasonable. But since I had only one wife, I can't seem to accept your disasters nearly as well as you. The fact is, I don't even want to."

"Exactly what *do* you want, Mr. Garret?"

He looked at her as she drank her coffee, an intelligent and attractive woman whom, had she been a great horned toad sitting opposite him at that moment, he could not have found more loathsome.

"I want my wife back."

Benton said nothing, but a tiny blue vein began to pulse in her temple.

"Failing that," said Garret, "I want to at least hold on to the anger I feel at this moment."

"Why?"

"Because I find it easier to live with than despair. Also, because without it I might be lulled into accepting your occasional disasters as reasonable, and that's something I refuse to do."

"Accept it or not, those are the facts."

"So you tell me."

"You can check it yourself. At last count the National Council on Crime and Delinquency reported nine percent of paroled offenders went back to prison with new major convictions. The statistics, unfortunately, are irrefutable."

"You people buried my wife, not a statistic."

"That's as cruel as it is untrue, Mr. Garret."

"Meade may have squeezed the trigger, but it was you, Reilly, and Johnson who put the gun in his hand. I blame you three almost more than I blame him. He'd already shown you he could rape and murder. That was a given. Yet you deliberately sent him out to do it again, and to me that's criminal."

They sat confronting one another across the table. Garret, suddenly aware of the polite, urbane voices about them discussing such things as Manet, broken color, and chiaroscuro, felt as though he were undergoing an hallucinogenic experience.

"You told me you wanted to talk," she said, "but this isn't talk. It's pure indictment. You're not interested in what I have to say. You just want scapegoats for a tragedy that couldn't be helped."

Benton picked up her bag and rose. "What this has done to you is nearly as sad as your wife's death. I'm sorry for both of you."

Garret watched as she threaded her way among the tables. Her head was bent and her body seemed tired. Then halfway across the room, she suddenly quickened her pace and walked out with the erect, almost arrogant bearing that Garret remembered from his first sight of her.

• • •

Martin Reilly lived on a tree-lined street of modest homes in the Bay Ridge section of Brooklyn, with only the width of a driveway separating the houses and a small patch of neatly tended lawn in front of each. The houses themselves were of brick veneer, which, thought Garret, undoubtedly conveyed a sense of security and permanence to those who lived in them. At best, a forlorn hope. Reilly's house also boasted a front porch, white shutters, and ivy climbing the walls, and Garret had been parked a short distance down the street, watching it, for the better part of an hour.

Reilly came home at about seven, a man of medium build who was just starting to go to paunch. His wife and children were inside by this time, and Garret watched him open the screen door and enter the house. Garret allowed him a full hour for dinner with his family. Then he left his car, walked over to Reilly's porch, and rang the bell.

Reilly himself came to the door. Peering through the screening, he recognized Garret at once. "Please wait here," he said. "I'll be out in a minute. I don't want my wife to know who you are."

Garret stood there, feeling like a malevolent spirit. When Reilly reappeared, his face was calm and he seemed to have settled on something. Still, there were beads of perspiration on his upper lip and he kept clearing his throat as he led Garret to a group of chairs at the far end of the porch.

"I've been expecting you ever since you spoke with Martha," he said. "I just wish I had something more to tell you than you already know."

"What I know isn't enough."

"It's all I have. I'll be honest, Mr. Garret. We carry an impossible load. We average twenty minutes an interview. *Twenty minutes!* Then something like this happens and—"

"You mean my wife's life hung on twenty minutes of conversation with Meade?"

"Not just that, of course. We have our prescribed guidelines as well. Obviously they didn't work in Meade's case. But none of us are villains, Mr. Garret. We don't set out to cause tragedy. We're just three rather ordinary people doing our best in a hopeless job. We get pressure from all sides and up the middle. The prisons are overcrowded and no one wants to spend money for more. The liberals scream for easier parole, the hard-liners yell just as loud for tougher decisions, and we're squeezed somewhere in between. In the end, all we can do is trust our instincts."

"Some instincts," Garret said, the bitterness rolling off of him.

"There's an old Irish saying," Reilly half murmured. "It says no matter which way you place a sick person, you can't make him comfortable. I'm afraid it's the same with you, Mr. Garret. No matter what any of us tells you, your wife's still going to be dead."

The screen door opened and Mrs. Reilly appeared with a tray of iced tea and cookies. Her husband frowned, obviously upset that she'd come out. Garret stood up as she placed the tray on a table and smiled, a pretty woman with intense eyes and the type of small, perfect nose that seems so characteristic of the Irish.

"I apologize for my husband," she said. "He's usually too good a host not to offer a guest—" She stopped as she had her first clear look at Garret's face. "My God, it's you!"

"It's all right, Mary," said Reilly. "Mr. Garret and I are just talking."

"I can see how you're talking. Your face is green and you're dripping perspiration. The only thing this kind of talk can get you is a heart attack."

Mary Reilly turned furiously on Garret. "How dare you come to our home like this? What do you want, my husband's blood? He hasn't slept through a night since this thing happened. You don't know how he agonizes over every case, every decision. Then you have the gall to come here and—"

"Please, Mary—"

"Don't you 'please, Mary' me! I despise this job of yours. One way or another it's going to widow me. If it doesn't finish you with a stroke, then some maniac with a gun will do it because he doesn't like one of your decisions."

Still politely standing there, Garret looked at Mary Reilly hazily, as though she were far away, obscured in mist. *Virtue,* he thought, *everyone is so damned sure of his virtue. No one is ever wrong, guilty, or ever makes a mistake. Or if an error is finally admitted, it's unfailingly on the side of the angels.*

"Leave my husband alone," said the parole commissioner's wife. "He can't help you. And don't ever come to this house again. If you do, so help me, I'll call the police."

There was no need for Garret to seek out the third member of the board. Dwight Johnson was waiting for him in the lobby of his apartment building when he arrived home later that night. Garret saw the parole commissioner sitting on a couch against a far wall and knew instantly who he was, a big, broad-shouldered man in an elegantly tailored summer suit, with skin so dark it had a bluish cast. Reilly had to have called him immediately.

Johnson rose. There was no pretense in his face. He was angry and it showed. "I figured it's time we met," he said.

The doorman approached, looking concerned. "This gentleman said he was a friend of yours, Mr. Garret."

"It's OK, Tom." Garret motioned Johnson toward the elevator. "Come upstairs."

They rode up in silence, barely looking at one another. Still, Garret felt the impact of the man's presence. It wasn't simply his size, which in itself was imposing. It was the mood of fortified certainty he seemed to exude, which is often found in the presence of successful politicians and ranking military officers. He gave the impression he could handle just about anything.

There were no amenities. Garret led the parole commissioner directly into his study, switched on a lamp, and turned to face him. This was the room where he usually was most comfortable, where he lived and worked. But just seeing Johnson standing in it brought a turn of mood akin to entering a dark cave.

Johnson sat himself in a straight-backed chair, lit a cigarette, blew a cloud of smoke in Garret's direction, and began without preamble. "I've busted my ass to get where I am, Garret. I came out of the sewers, worked two shit jobs around the clock, slept in a chair for seven years with a book in each hand, and ended up with three solid degrees. I'm not rich or famous, but I take pride in what I do and feel it's important. Then I wake up one morning, turn on the radio, and find I'm in the worst fucking trouble of my life."

He looked coldly at Garret, his eyes steady and baleful. "But I don't run from trouble. I'd rather meet it head-on than have it get me in the back. I'm different from Benton and Reilly. Martha is a gentle, Southern-bred lady who rides the subways on principle, contributes to the Negro College Fund, and feels like the Great Emancipator himself each time she sets an offender free. Marty's a sweet guy who goes to confession regularly and suffers over the Irish cops who troop into St. Patrick's to get their thirty-eights blessed before shooting up the spic and nigger drug dealers in Harlem and the Bronx. They're both climbing walls this minute. Not only because of what Meade did to you and your wife, but because of your less-than-charitable attitude toward us."

"And you're not disturbed by my lack of charity?"

"I stopped expecting charity when I was five and watched my daddy take six fat police slugs in the chest when one would have done just fine," he said. "And I sure as shit have stopped looking for reasons why. In this world you make the best of the deal you get. You best be learning that or there won't be any hope for you at all."

With Johnson finally gone, Garret poured himself half a snifter of brandy and sat with it far into the night. A heavy rain was pouring down, and at one point he rose, pressed his face to the cool window, and watched sheets of water whip across the streets below. His face left a print of forehead, nose, and chin on the glass. He didn't recognize himself.

Something was very wrong with him.

What was he trying to do to these people? Punish them for his pain? Might as well die and try to rise slowly, like a feather. But even that couldn't help Emmy. Even that could in no way bring her back.

Face it.

He had sought them out, met them, looked into their eyes, listened to their voices, and uncovered no shimmering nest of snakes. They were just two men and a woman, with their own stricken souls, trapped in an impossible system. He had seen and recognized their soreness of heart. It was little different from his own. *How sad*, he thought, *what a tragedy that we have only each other*.

He closed his eyes and stared into his darkness until he

saw William Meade. Now there were just the two of them. And, of course, the system.

He had his blessed anger again.

It made the edges of his darkness come alight.

Garret called Lieutenant Canderro and told him he was going up to Attica early the next morning to talk to William Meade's former cellmate.

"I've already tried squeezing Stover," said the detective. "So did Warden Gemson. It was a waste of time."

Garret phrased it carefully. "I know. But I do have certain advantages over you two when it comes to talking to convicts."

"Yeah? How's that?"

"I'm not a police officer and I'm not a warden."

It was a long trip, but it was something positive to do and Garret welcomed it. He took a taxi to La Guardia, boarded an 8:00 A.M. flight to Rochester, rented a Mustang at the airport, and drove southwest for about thirty miles to the New York State Correctional Facility at Attica.

He had been preparing for two days. Warden Gemson had faxed him Stover's background material and he had studied and acted on it. So he knew more than a little about the man with whom Meade had shared a cell during his last seven years in prison. Man was not born criminal, but a fair proportion of the species managed to fall into the pit early. Harry Stover, for example, had started falling at the age of nine, when he cracked open a couple of kids' heads with a baseball bat, and didn't stop his descent until he was put away permanently seventeen years later for killing a cop and two armed guards during a series of holdups. Now he was serving a mandatory life term without the possibility of parole, and this alone narrowed Garret's options as to what he could offer Stover as a sweetener.

Warden Gemson greeted Garret in his office. An enlightened penologist whom Garret had praised in several columns over the years, the warden was now ready to pay off his markers. In addition, he was living with the unhappy knowledge that William Meade would not have been paroled at all without his endorsement.

His face showed it as he shook Garret's hand. "My sincere condolences." He groped for more, but what else was there?

"Thanks for the material on Harry Stover," said Garret.

"I wish there was something else I could do. But with a mandatory lifer it's all hard time. Still, I've tried to prepare him, tried to soften him up a little for you."

The warden made a helpless gesture. "Exactly how much do you know about long-term prison cellmates? About what they can often be and mean to each other?"

"Not as much as you."

"Just remember. Stover and Meade lived together twenty-four hours a day for seven years. That can be closer than a marriage when it's good, and theirs was good. That's sexually, too. Which is no stigma here. So you can probably be sure of at least one thing. By the time Meade left here, there was nothing about him that Harry Stover didn't know in full detail. Which in no way means he's going to share it with *you*."

Harry Stover was a surprise to Garret. Or were all killers ultimately a surprise unless observed in the act? Physically, he was a youthful, slender man of medium height, with even features and fair, thinning hair combed straight back from his forehead. His eyes, when they met Garret's, were dark, curious, and soft as a doe's. Entering the room and sitting down, he exhibited the delicate grace of a fine figurine. And with no more to go on than that and the warden's words, Garret was almost sure that he and Meade had been lovers.

Gemson had set up a small cubicle for them. There was a table, two chairs, and little else. A fluorescent light flickered and hummed softly overhead. Two guards watched, unseen, from behind a one-way glass window.

"Thanks for seeing me," said Garret. "I know you didn't have to."

Stover shrugged. "Billy did your wife and almost did you. I was curious." His eyes never left Garret's face. "That's some piece of work he did."

His voice was quiet, even, with a pleasant lilt. He hardly seemed to open his mouth or move his lips as he spoke, yet each word was clear.

"I'm really here to talk about your mother," said Garret. "I spent a nice piece of time with her the other day. Wonderful woman. She sends you her love."

Stover was silent. He blinked twice. That was the full extent of his reaction.

"Ever think about her, Harry?"

Stover took out a pack of Camels, lit one, and left the pack on the table. Each move was slow, deliberate. Smoke drifted from his mouth, his nostrils. He didn't answer Garret's question and didn't stop looking at his face.

"Well, she sure thinks about *you*," said Garret. "Just about every minute of every day. Never stops. You're her life, Harry. Without you, all she's got is the pain. Her arthritis keeps getting worse, you know. It's all through her now . . . hands, knees, hips, back. Some cold, damp mornings it can take her a good half-hour just to get out of bed and straighten up. Not that she complains. She says she can handle the pain. What worries her is how much longer she'll be able to work. And she's got to work. Because all she's got in the bank is a hundred and thirty-eight dollars and forty-two cents."

The convict's lips were pressed into a thin, dark line and muscles worked in his jaw. Whatever color had been in his cheeks before appeared to have drained off. His face looked as gray as the smoke from his cigarette.

"Mr. Garret, you are one mean fuck," he said softly.

"What your mother needs is a nice warm, dry climate, Harry. Her doctor says Arizona would be perfect. But of course she has no money to move and you've got none to give her. Also, at her age and in her condition, there's little hope of her finding a job even if she did get there. But worst of all, she'd have to give up her visits to you each week, and that would be as good as giving up the rest of her life."

Stover leaned forward in his chair, his body and limbs so slender that the move hardly seemed to disturb his clothes. But there was a first, faint stirring of interest in his eyes.

"I guess you're really not giving me all these needles just for kicks, are you?"

"No."

"What then?"

"A deal."

"Let's hear it."

"Your mother gets a good job in Arizona, fifteen thousand in cash to move and carry her for a while, and you'll be transferred to a nearby facility out there. She won't have to miss a single visit."

Stover's brows went up. "You can really do all that shit?"

Garret nodded, although at this point he had no guarantees from anyone.

"And *your* end?" said Stover.

"You know what I want."

"Say it for me."

"I want your friend, Billy."

"Who for? You or the cops?"

"Either way," said Garret. "It doesn't matter."

"It fucking matters to me. I wouldn't want Billy ending up with a bunch of bullets in his pretty head."

"I don't need him dead."

Harry Stover sat with it, and Garret could almost pick up a whiff of the thoughts and feelings that flowed from his own bane-filled life. Meade and Stover. What kind of dark communion had these two shared? But perhaps there had been a kind of caring there, too.

"If any of this got out, I'd be dead," said Stover.

"You'll be protected."

"Bullshit. You can't be protected on the inside. Who'd know about this besides you and the warden?"

"The cop who paid you a visit last month—Lieutenant Canderro."

Stover sat with it again. Then he looked at Garret and Garret saw the decision in his eyes before he spoke. The lids seemed to lift in the light. Garret had seen much the same expression in pre-Renaissance paintings of early Christian martyrs.

"What the hell," said Stover in his soft voice. "At least my old lady'll be out where it's warm and have fifteen big ones. Even if I'm dead. But it's gotta be my way."

"What do you want?"

"I need to figure a few things."

There was a yellow legal pad and a pencil on the table and Stover spent a few minutes thinking and scribbling some notes. To Garret, watching, it might have been the Magna Carta.

"OK, here's how it is," said Stover. "I can't give no guarantees you're gonna find Billy. But my mom still has to get the fifteen big ones up front—and no refunds."

"And what do I get?"

"You can ask me questions. I'll tell you whatever I know."

"How do I know you won't be lying, making things up?"

"Why would I lie when you've still got my transfer and my old lady's job in your pocket?"

"So your mother can at least end up with fifteen thousand she doesn't have now."

Stover crushed out the remains of his cigarette, lit a fresh one, and blew smoke. They looked at each other through the gray haze.

"How's this?" said Stover. "Before Billy was sent up, he did two women nobody knew about. You can check them out."

"You mean he told you where they are?"

"Yeah."

Garret felt his pulses suddenly going like a fluttering of wings. "I don't understand. If you talked, he'd never have gotten his parole. Why would he tell you something like that?"

"To show trust. We do stuff like that. What else have we got? Besides, if I did talk while he was still here, I'd have had my throat cut in a week."

"What did *you* do for *him?*"

"That's not part of our deal."

"Didn't it ever hit you that your buddy might have been lying about the two women?"

"Sure. I'm not stupid." Sitting there, Stover's bearing lent a special grace to each fold of his uniform. "So let's try it this way. Just to show good faith and make sure nobody gets screwed, you write my mother a check for the fifteen Gs and I'll draw you a little map of where the two ladies are supposed to be. If you find them, you can come back for another visit and we'll take it from there. If Billy was lying, you can stop your check and maybe we can try something different."

Garret wanted to stand up and cheer. "You should have been a union arbitrator, Harry. You missed your calling."

"Shit, Mr. Garret. I missed my whole fucking life."

They were in Lieutenant Canderro's car, with the detective driving, Garret beside him, and three plainclothesmen in coveralls following in an unmarked van. Stover's sketch lay flat across Garret's knees. The convict had taken pains to draw a neat map of the area, detail it with roads and distances, and mark off the two side-by-side burial sites.

"How did you remember it so exactly?" Garret had asked.

"By carefully memorizing it."

"Why would you do that?"

"Because I thought it might come in handy someday." The soft doe eyes were all innocence. "Why else?"

Heading west on Route 52 in the vicinity of Loch Sheldrake, they were in the same general area where Meade's attack on the Garrets had taken place. Right now they were watching for a bridge over a narrow stream, immediately followed by a cut off to the right. It was a gray morning without shadows, the ground fog still drifting in low spots.

Canderro drove leaning forward over the wheel, as if physically urging the car on. "I wish I'd have had fifteen thousand bucks here and there when I needed it," he said. "I'd have been chief of police by now."

They rode in silence, watching for the bridge. Garret rolled down a window, felt a soft mist on his face, and breathed deeply.

"You think this'll be anything?" he asked.

"It's a long shot. All cons are liars, and lifers are the

worst. But even if Stover's playing it straight, Meade may have lied to *him*. That's what bothers me. I can't quite buy Meade exposing himself with something like this."

Garret pointed ahead. "There's the bridge."

A hundred yards past the crossing, they turned right onto a rutted excuse for a road that ran alongside the stream. According to Stover's sketch their next landmark would be a large outcropping of rock about a mile ahead. Garret glanced at his side-view mirror and saw the police van turn in behind them.

"Just to keep you up on things," said the detective. "I was in Meade's hometown the other day and picked up a few possible threads."

He briefly filled Garret in on his talks with Reverend Cantwell and Jenny Angelo, and on his particular interest in Richard Meade's bequest to the Phoenix Children's Shelter. "But his mother's the one I really want. If we find her, we might have something. Nobody disappears like that without a reason."

A huge glacial rock suddenly showed through the trees and the lieutenant pulled over beside it. The van stopped behind them.

Garret led the way and did the pacing. Starting from the far side of the rock, he measured off exactly fifty normal strides in a straight line going due west. It brought him a short distance into a meadow. He kicked out a divot. "Right around here."

They brought pickaxes and shovels from the van and started digging. Garret stripped off his shirt and worked with the others. They went no deeper than two feet in any one spot. Garret leaned into it, feeling the sweat break, welcoming the mindless physical effort. Until he remembered what they were looking for. Then each shovelful of earth trembled. It complained as he dug into it. It grumbled and growled as if trying to tell its secrets. Or didn't it have any secrets? It was beginning to seem so. Garret swore softly while a cloud of gnats swarmed, entered his nose and ears, fluttered his eyes. At one point he began feeling himself back in 'Nam, digging in as the rockets and mortars exploded, the earth shaking and trying to rip itself up and him with it. Then his shovel rang against something hard. "Hey!" But it was only a rock.

Garret leaned on his shovel and stared at the ground. The sun had broken through, and a caterpillar crawled along the underside of a weed in the yellow haze. Around him the meadow was becoming a growing cluster of small, round holes and mounds of dark earth. A graveyard waiting for tiny dead things, Garret thought.

He squatted at the edge of his latest pit and drew a mood out of the cool, damp loam, a sense of earthy odor, faintly unpleasant and soft with rot. It was an air, circling on itself, that seemed curiously alive. For no reason that he knew, he reached down, grabbed a handful of dirt and kneeled there, staring at it, studying it. It was almost as though something was trying to tell him he had never truly understood what earth was all about, that this would be the only moment he would ever be offered in which to learn, and that if he didn't learn it now, the loss would prove fatal.

Then trying to escape this latest touch of madness, he gazed down into that same hole and saw it.

It seemed no more than a fragment of dirty gray stone that his last handful of soil had uncovered. But as Garret carefully worked a few additional inches of earth aside with his fingers, it became something other than stone.

"Over here," he said.

It came out no louder than a hoarse whisper, but it instantly brought everyone huddling around him.

Canderro took immediate charge. Using the tips of his fingers and a handkerchief, he gently brushed aside only enough earth to expose a human skull with a small, round hole puncturing its crown. Then he stood up and lit a cigarette.

"Go back to the van and call the chief," he told a detective. "Tell him I want a forensics team out here right away. Quietly. No sirens and flashing lights. And no reporters. That's important. I don't want one fucking word of this getting out."

He turned to Garret. "If Meade hears what we've found, nothing Stover tells you after this'll be worth shit."

Garret said nothing. He thought the war had made him immune to the flotsam of violent death. He had walked across ground red with blood and littered with body parts. Then an eyeless and faceless head stared up at him from a hole and he felt as though he was experiencing the central moment of his life. But of course there had been one other moment . . . .

They started digging for the second body. The first one was to be left for the forensics team and its *in situ* specialists to fully uncover.

Twenty minutes later, Canderro himself scooped away some earth and revealed the ribs of Meade's other victim. Less than six feet from the first, the bones were strung together by strings of rotted fabric and mummified flesh. Meade had been sent to prison nine years before, which meant these two victims had spent at least that much time in the ground. Not much was left. The earth had reclaimed its own. Even the smell was gone.

Poor souls, thought Garret. Or was his commiseration more for their loved ones? Imagine waiting, hoping and praying all these years for a missing wife or daughter to one day come home, stubbornly denying the logic and finality of death, then winding up with a cop and a set of dental X rays at your door?

It was too much.

The heart rebelled.

Garret made his second trip to Attica the next day, sensing there would be more to follow. The familiarity, the feeling of routine, already was there. It lay solid and comfortable inside him. He had something to do.

He and Canderro had discussed the possibility of their seeing Harry Stover together but had decided against it. A police presence would have been too negative a factor, too great a source of distrust for the lifer. But Garret had agreed to go into the meeting wired, which would allow the lieutenant to review everything that was said and help him make suggestions for possible future meetings.

Stover was patiently waiting at the table, smoking one of his Camels and doodling on the yellow pad as Garret entered the cubicle.

"I didn't expect you back so fast," he said. "Is that good or bad?"

Garret sat down opposite him. "Bad for the dead. Good for you."

"Then you found them?"

"Right where you said."

"So you didn't stop the check."

"No. The money is your mother's."

Harry Stover took the check out of his pocket and held it at arm's length to the light. "She's coming up tomorrow.

This'll freak her out. In her whole life she's hardly had two nickels to rub together."

Garret waited. Stover couldn't seem to stop looking at the check. Emotion warped his features. Then it passed and there was only the cold blankness.

"Now I'd like to know who the two girls were," said Garret.

"Billy never told me their names."

"What *did* he tell you?"

"Just that he picked them up one night in a shopping mall, bought them a lot of bracelets and booze, and drove them into the woods for a little party."

"Did he say which mall?"

"No. But it couldn't have been too far from where he buried them."

The table had evidently been waxed and polished that morning, and the odor made Garret think of every mean governmental institution he had ever visited in his life. This one was the worst yet. Just breathing its smell filled him with dread.

"What about Meade's mother?" he said. "Did he talk much about her? Did he ever mention where she was living?"

Stover slowly shook his head. "Now that old lady bit's one thing that never added up."

"How so?"

"I mean, she never came to see him—not that Billy let on anyway. It was weird, too, because to hear Billy tell it, he and his old lady were always real close."

"Did Meade ever mention any old girlfriends?" Garret asked, remembering that the warden had told him Meade had received visits from a few women over the years.

"Well, there was one. Some broad named Jenny. They

were nuts about each other when they were kids. Grew up to-gether on Long Island."

"Manhasset?"

"Yeah. That's the place. But Billy said she dumped him when he went off to college, and he hasn't heard a word from her since."

It all checked with what Canderro had told him the day before. Garret continued to probe. "So who *did* pay Meade a visit?"

Stover gave a shrug. "It didn't happen but a few times. Once Billy talked about a friend from college. Other than that I can't tell you."

They sat in silence.

"Where do you think he's holed up, Harry?"

"Could be anyplace."

"I know. But what do you *think?*"

Stover sat doodling on the yellow pad. He drew five-pointed stars. That was all. Over and over. Big, small, all sizes. He drew them with great care.

"Beats me," he finally said.

"You guys talked for seven years. Think, for Christ's sake! Didn't he ever talk about some favorite place he might have had or gone to? Maybe someplace with good memories that would be nice to see again when he got out?"

Harry Stover glanced up from his stars and the air between them suddenly seemed hazy with thought.

"Yeah. When he was a kid, I guess he had a place like that. Anyway, that's how he sometimes talked about it."

"What did he say?"

"It wasn't all that much. Just that there was this little log cabin up in the Catskills that him and his old man used to go to and have these great times together."

"Did he say where in the Catskills it was?"

"Only that it was right on a lake where they caught some of the sweetest fish he ever tasted."

"A big or a small lake?"

"Don't know that."

"No town? Didn't he ever mention some town it might be near?"

Stover doodled three complete stars while he thought about it.

"Liberty," he said. "I don't know how near it was, but Billy said they sometimes went into Liberty for stuff they needed, or maybe to catch a movie."

There was just enough uncertainty and reluctance in his voice to set Garret's pulses racing. *Liberty.* It even had the right sound.

"So what do I tell my old lady?" Stover asked. "I mean about Arizona and all."

"I'll start moving on it right away. But better figure on at least four or six weeks."

"That long?"

"I've got two state governments to hustle, Harry. That's a lot of red tape to cut."

Stover's gaze was steady. "You wouldn't fuck us on this, would you, Mr. Garret?"

"Not unless you tried to fuck me first, Harry."

Canderro was waiting at the gate when Garret's flight from Rochester came into La Guardia half an hour late. It was 7:26 P.M.

"How did it go?" asked the detective.

"I'm not sure. I think pretty fair. You'll hear the tape."

"You still wearing the wire?"

Garret nodded.

"Don't take it off till I get you home."

• • •

Two hours and three double bourbons later, they had just finished listening to the recording in Garret's study, a quiet, book-lined room with the drapes drawn, the air-conditioning on, and not even the perennial sirens able to intrude from below.

"Well, it's a start," said the detective. "At least we know he's given us the truth on the two bodies and Jenny Angelo. With a couple of strong doubtfuls on Meade's mother and the log cabin story."

"You think he's holding back?"

"Of course. All you've given him so far is the fifteen thousand. So the bodies were just to make sure you didn't stop payment on the check. You still owe him the two most important parts of his deal, his mother's job in Arizona and his transfer out there. Stover's a crook and a killer but he's not stupid. In his world you're either the fucker or the fuckee. So he's got to keep some insurance while he sees how things go."

"What's the cabin story worth?"

Canderro shook a cigarette out of his pack and lit it from the butt in his mouth. "Very little. Remember, it was you who came up with the whole idea of a possible favorite place for Meade. Stover could have taken it from there just to toss you another bone. It's an old trick cons use in interrogations. Especially when something's almost impossible to check on."

"You're probably right." Garret's budding hope faded. "I feel like an idiot."

"Don't. The story could be absolutely true. But even if it is, the odds against Meade's hiding out in an old Catskill Mountain cabin he once shared with his father would have to run a thousand to one."

"Then I guess you're forgetting the whole thing."

"The hell I am. I'm treating it exactly as if I believed Meade was sitting there in that cabin right this minute, reading his goddamn press notices and playing with himself."

Garret just sipped his drink and looked at him.

"First," said Canderro, "I'm getting a large-scale map and marking off every lake inside a fifty-mile circle of Liberty. Then I'm sending an innocent-looking sightseeing chopper over the whole area to pin-flag anything that looks even a little bit like a log cabin. And finally, I'm getting a team of plainclothesmen to follow up leads on the ground."

"What about Harry Stover?"

"What about him?"

"Should I keep pressing?"

"No. Give the prick a rest. Let him start worrying about his old lady's deal. When he gets worried enough, he'll get in touch and throw you some of his better goodies."

"You're that sure he's got them?"

"Sure I'm sure."

Canderro took a solid belt of bourbon and wiped his mouth with the back of his hand. "And I'm also sure that if Meade hits again and we still don't have him, Stover's gonna up the ante on you."

"You mean he'll ask for more money?"

"More than that. My guess is he'll go for broke. That means parole, or maybe even a pardon."

"He wouldn't be that crazy. He's a mandatory lifer."

The lieutenant's smile was coldly mocking. "You don't think so? I figure it depends on two things. First, how much real velvet your Harry's actually got to peddle, and second, whether Meade decides to increase his body count. If that happens, our good governor, struggling as he is to get himself reelected, may decide ole Harry's not such a bad guy after all."

CHAPTER
9

William Meade listened to the muffled sounds of sex coming from the backseat of the convertible and found less passion than pain in them. Groans, whisperings, breathless cries. The audible residue of lust. They might have been the ululations of small animals. Yet no sounds on earth came anywhere near to being as exciting for him. At that moment there was nothing else.

He had felt it coming for days, a slow pressure building without the relief of climax. Knowing how it finally was going to have to be, he had not slept for the past two nights. Even the lovely summer days oppressed him. He was not fooled by their beauty—the cloudless azure skies, the lacy greens, the paths of sunlight through the trees. He knew what was hidden just below their paltry dazzle and glitter. The dead turning to dust.

The convertible was red, its top was down, and it was parked at the edge of a rutted track in a wooded glade that sometimes served the locals as a lovers' lane. It was late, almost midnight, with a waning moon directly overhead and a light fog drifting off an adjacent lake. The night was warm. Meade wore only a T-shirt and jeans. He stood in the total darkness of shadow, unseen against the trunk of a broad maple. He was less than twenty feet from the lovers. Watching them perform, hearing the fever in their voices, he felt his own heat rising.

It didn't come all at once, but moment by moment, without any rules of time or planning. There was just the instant itself and the sense of what was taking place, which was how he preferred it.

Meade's heart raced.

When it neared its peak, when it seemed to become too much to bear for even one second, he left his shadowed place and approached the open car.

Up close, the scent of heated sex mixed with the girl's perfume. They were young, in their early to middle twenties, their lovemaking really more athletic than sensual and erotic. Naked only below the waist, they appeared to have deliberately kept their upper bodies clothed, as if the exigencies of time, interest, and convenience had limited them to just the basics. At best, a shameful waste. Youth and instinct alone, thought Meade, could take you only so far. The artistry, the fine tuning, were sadly lacking. They had a lot to learn.

It was the girl who noticed Meade first.

Shifting her eyes at one point, she suddenly saw him over her lover's shoulder and cried out.

"Oh, God!"

Mistaking her cry for one of passion, her partner responded with a joke. "You can call me Tommy."

Then seeing her expression and where her eyes were focused, he quickly turned. His face congealed. It seemed on the edge of dividing in two—one that belonged to a macho prince of love certain of his powers; the other, that of a frightened little boy caught in a dirty act.

He tried to brazen it out. "You goddamn creep! Get your ass out of here or I'll—"

He stopped as he saw the gun and attached silencer pointing at his head.

"Or you'll what?" asked Meade softly. "Punch me out? What would that prove? That you're a tough guy? What would be the point of that?"

The young man who called himself Tommy licked suddenly dry lips and said nothing.

"Please don't hurt us," begged the girl, her eyes wide, her voice hoarse with fear. "There's no reason for you to hurt us."

Meade looked at her. She was pretty in an open, vacuous sort of way, with dark curly hair framing an oval face. She lay on her back across the car seat, Tommy seemingly forgotten between her legs. Meade offered her his sweetest, most reassuring smile. He saw that neither of them recognized him, which made it simpler all around. He didn't want them paralyzed with fright. Although his disguise tonight was limited to nothing more than a full mustache and longer and darker hair than displayed on his media shots.

"What's your name?" he asked her.

"Nancy."

"Well, you don't have to worry, Nancy. The gun doesn't mean anything. It's just to keep Tommy from having to be a hero and beat me up. I'm not here to hurt anyone."

"Then what the hell *are* you here for?" said Tommy, still trying to sound tougher and less frightened than he knew himself to be.

"Nothing terrible. Just a little partying. The same as you two. Only I'm going to make it a lot more fun for everyone."

They stared at him with the vague beginnings of hope.

Still, neither of them dared move. Nor did the air or the surrounding wood.

"Not that you weren't doing great without me," Meade said. "That's what turned me on. There's nothing more exciting to watch. But right now I'm going to offer you something even better. The ultimate sexual fantasy. With the three of us going at it together until the devil himself comes up to join us and our heads pop off."

His eyes found the girl's and held them. He was the quintessential pitchman now, the pure snake-oil salesman, and loving every second of it. "The truth, little Nancy. Haven't you ever wondered what it would be like to make it with two men at once. Haven't you ever thought about it?"

She stared at him for several seconds but then turned her eyes away. High in the dark of a tree, an owl made its sound.

"Hmmmm, just as I thought."

He looked at the man, who was half turned now, watching him. "And what do you think of all this?"

Tommy was amazed. He looked at the woman he thought he knew, sensed her guilty anticipation.

"Jesus, I think you should get rid of the gun and sell rugs. You'd be rich in a week."

"Have I sold *you?*"

"Hey, give us a break. Listen. I've never fucked under a gun. I'm not even sure I could do it. So if I've got any kind of choice, I'd just as soon skip your little party, your 'ultimate sexual fantasy.'" He managed a weak smile and tried a joke. "Maybe some other time."

"I appreciate your honesty, Tommy. But I'm afraid you don't really have any kind of choice."

Gently, William Meade drew up the ends of his net.

• • •

Many years ago, as a small boy, he had been brought up to believe in such things as the hand of God and the swish of the devil's tail, in the bright light of a true state of grace and the fetid darkness that surrounds its absence. That was gone now. Yet from time to time some small, barely acknowledged part of him still believed that it was infinitely better to be in tune with the forces of darkness while making love. And tonight he and they were totally, exquisitely in tune, he thought, as the convertible rocked and swelled with their combined sexual energy. They were all part of it now, the three of them, along with whatever other maleficent spirits might have been coaxed out of hell—a bubbling stew of two victims and one oppressor, with that all-powerful gun never out of sight, never leaving his hand.

In the moon's silvery light he glanced at the man and saw glazed eyes seeking their own jeweled cities. But his odor was carnal, that of a carnivorous beast, and Meade felt himself deep inside an overheated zoo. As for Nancy, she was running through a gamut of expressions ranging from fear to self-loathing to helpless sexual excitement.

"Come on, you crazy fucking bastard," she whispered, "come on," as if it were a race, a contest, some sort of sexual round-robin for bedeviled lunatics, and the three of them its leading contenders.

Meade half closed his eyes. Then he went into the girl with the sense of deliverance of someone who has had to cross an ocean to get there. *I'm an icy midnight darkness. I can do anything.*

Seconds later he heard Tommy cry out, his voice soon followed by Nancy's own high-pitched wail.

There was a long, slow sorting out.

Nancy seemed to be stricken, sprawled alone in a field of cold gases. She looked at neither one of them.

• • •

Tommy's mood had taken a sullen turn. He got out of the car and began putting on his clothes. "OK, you've had your party. Now can we go home?"

Still lying naked beside the girl, Meade considered him. "Is this your car?"

"No. It's hers. Mine's down the trail."

"Do you always go on dates in separate cars?"

"It depends."

Meade thought about it. "Are both of you married, or just you?"

"What's it to you?"

Meade looked at him without expression.

"Just me," said Tommy resignedly.

"Fine. Then just you can take a nice little walk to your car and go home to your wife."

"What about Nancy?"

"*She* has no one waiting for her." Meade's smile was warm, gentle. "It's all right, Tommy. You don't have to worry about her. I'll see that she gets home OK."

"What if that's not what she wants?"

"Ask her."

Tommy finished tucking in his shirt. His eyes were uncertain and his feet shuffled nervously. "Let's go, Nancy," he said, motioning with his head down the trail. "We really should go."

She brushed the grass off her thighs, sighed, then looked expectantly at this stranger who'd just taken her.

"I can go if I want?" she asked.

"Suit yourself," Meade replied, his eyes boyish and bright. He flashed a smile that was full of promises.

A few moments passed, but Nancy made no effort to rise.

"Oh, go home, Tommy," Meade said at last. "Your wife will be getting worried about you."

After Tommy had reluctantly stumbled off, Meade and the girl moved to the backseat of the car and said nothing. Words were tepid after the heat that had passed between them.

Finally Nancy broke the silence. "You do know how to look at a woman," she said.

"How am I looking?"

"As though I were edible."

"But you are edible. The sweetness of you is in your genes."

The compliment seemed to embarrass her. In an odd sort of way it robbed her of worldliness, made her appear very young.

"Just say things like that and you can probably have any woman you want. Why did you need that crazy gun before?"

"I'm insecure."

"I'll bet," she said, and Meade wondered why it was that on the rare occasions when he spoke the truth, people thought he was joking.

It was Meade who began the actual lovemaking, not rushing, simply caressing and nibbling at her as though that in itself was so satisfying, so exciting, he would be content to continue that way and go no further.

"What are you trying to do to me?" she said, half-annoyed with herself but still aroused. "Drive me out of my mind?"

"Yes. That's exactly what I'm trying to do."

And saying it, Meade reached out, placed a hand on each side of her waist, and lifted her astride him where he sat. He entered her as quickly and easily as that, with no sound coming from her except a soft "Oh," and then again, "Oh," as if she had never experienced anything quite like this before.

Then they were really into it, with Meade's hands grasping the perfect valentine heart of her bottom, and she picking up his rhythm and working smoothly against it until all the small ceremonies of possession were performed.

He closed his eyes, hearing the girl's whispers of pleasure, her soft sounds of encouragement. Meade's own sounds were more primitive. There was no great joy here, only a quiet moan of lamentation. This could have been the voice of a man carrying an iron safe up a mountain.

A moment later he heard her cry out as she began her run, and he increased their cadence, picking it up even further and reaching some shuddering panic of movement that ended in a series of shrill, rising cries from the girl.

But it had not yet ended for Meade. He felt himself just seconds behind as he went into his own slide, his breathing quicker and heavier, his voice reduced to a tortured groan.

When he knew for certain it was going to happen, that there was nothing this side of heaven to keep it from happening, he reached for his gun.

Then the full heat rose and everything hit together and he knew that in the next instant they would break apart. It was the right moment. And so he did the only thing on God's earth that could make it more exciting for him. . . .

CHAPTER
10

The man who had called himself Tommy, but whose full name was Thomas Lukens, sat in his car nervously smoking a cigarette. It was his fifth in less than forty minutes. He'd walked the quarter mile to get here, but he had not gone home to his wife. For one thing, his wife was not home. She and the kids were spending the night with her folks in Providence. But he was still too much on edge to have gone right home anyway.

Imagine having to screw with a gun six inches from your head? The wonder of it was that he'd been able to do it at all. Yet when he did finally manage that part, when he found it actually was possible, it was like a goddamn Fourth of July. *Wild!*

Lukens looked at his watch in a sliver of moonlight. It was 2:14 A.M. He'd been waiting for Nancy's car to pass for almost an hour. Where the hell were they? And when they did finally come? What then? Lukens had no idea.

The truth was, he felt like shit leaving her back there with

Don Juan. True, except for the pistol, the guy didn't come across as a nut. Still . . .

A shadow crossed Thomas Lukens' face as he thought about how he'd shuffled off, dragging his tail between his legs.

So I'm no hero, he thought. *But what should I have done? Take a chance on dying just to impress a horny college kid? And what was I to her anyway but one more married asshole out cheating on his wife?*

Then what was he waiting here for?

Groping for a fresh cigarette, his hand suddenly went stiff. Distant headlights were approaching through the trees. Moments later he heard the motor. But when the convertible finally passed the cluster of brush behind which he was parked, its top was up and he was unable to see who was driving, or even whether there were one or two people in the car.

Lukens swore softly. Then acting on impulse, he turned the key in his ignition and followed.

He drove with his lights off and staying a good distance back. But there was enough moon to keep the trail visible, and Nancy's headlights could be seen from a long way off.

After only a few minutes Lukens saw the headlights angle sharply to the right, stop moving, and go off. He braked his own car and waited. A moment later he heard a motor start and saw a different pair of headlights go on. Then the new lights began moving along the trail and Lukens went after them. When he reached the convertible and got out to investigate, he found the car empty.

Suddenly he felt nauseous. He pressed his head with both hands and walked a tight circle on the grass. *Oh, Jesus,* he thought, and started after the other car.

Keeping his own lights off, he picked up speed to close the gap. When the dirt trail hit Route 684's service road, the headlights turned right, onto it, and a mile down the road, they swung onto the parkway.

Now there was enough traffic moving to let him turn on his lights without being noticed. As he drew closer, he saw that he was tailing a white Honda with Connecticut plates. But he still couldn't see whether there were two people in the car.

After about three miles, the Honda exited 684 and Lukens followed. But now they were the only two cars on the road again, so he fell back still farther until he saw the Honda's taillights disappear off to the right. But when he turned at the next right, there was only darkness and he was afraid he'd lost the car for good. Still, he kept driving and finally spotted the Honda parked about a mile east of where it made its last turn.

He drove past it twice to be sure it was empty. Then he drew up beside it, tried the doors, and found them locked. There were no houses in sight and the last one he remembered passing had been about a mile away.

Sonofabitch, he thought, and wrote down the Honda's plate number. The bad feeling was all through him as he headed back the way he'd come.

He searched for the spot where they'd been parked in Nancy's convertible. Then he saw the opening in the trees and the tire tracks leading into the glade, and he stopped his car and got out. There was a heavy dew and the grass felt wet against his ankles. Some clouds had covered the moon and it was hard to make anything out.

"Nancy?"

His voice sounded shrill, not like his own. What was he doing here? What did he expect to find? If the bastard had left her here instead of taking her home, she wouldn't just be sitting here, waiting. She'd have walked to 684.

If she could walk.

Lukens got a flashlight from his glove compartment and began going over the area. His palms were wet and sweat was running into his eyes. He kept telling himself she wasn't there, yet he couldn't stop looking.

It took almost twenty minutes, but he finally found her.

CHAPTER
11

arret's phone rang at exactly 4:23 A.M. and he picked it up, instantly awake. With the clarity of someone jolted from a deep sleep, he saw everything around him—the bureau opposite his bed, the faint reflections in a closet mirror, his clothes thrown over the back of a chair, a patch of moonlight on the floor. Knowing who was on the other end, he didn't even bother to say hello.

"I'm afraid I've gone and done it again, Mr. Garret."

This time Garret was prepared to take Lieutenant Canderro's advice and just play along. "Done what again?"

"Indulged myself. Followed that same destructive impulse."

"What are you trying to say? That you've killed somebody."

"Yes."

"Congratulations. But why tell me?"

"Who else can I tell?"

Garret was silent. He felt as if he'd slipped off the edge of all sanity and was still falling.

"You don't believe me, do you?" said Meade.

"No."

"Why would I lie?"

"I have no idea," said Garret, who thought, *I'm talking to him. I'm actually lying in my bed in the middle of the night and carrying on a conversation with the butcher who murdered my wife.*

"What you don't seem to realize," said Meade, "is that you're probably the one person in the world I *don't* have to lie to anymore. You've stared deep into what passes for my soul and seen the absolute worst. That's why you're so valuable to me. For the first time there's someone I don't have to pretend with."

"I still say you're lying."

Meade allowed a full ten seconds to go by. "All right," he said at last. "Since you obviously need convincing, I'll do my best to convince you. Take Route Six Eighty-four to exit six. Go north on the service road for about a mile until you come to an old ruined barn. Turn right past the barn on a dirt trail and you'll see some brush and a stand of pine. If you're willing and foolish enough to go to all this trouble, you'll find what I'm talking about a hundred yards behind the brush. Good night, Mr. Garret."

He left the garage before dawn and was well on his way by first light. It had started to drizzle during the night, and there were few things drearier, Garret thought, than country roads in the rain. Without the cover of darkness, the past few hours had lost all reality. Still, with decisions to be made, he had made them. Tempted at first to call Canderro and let him handle the whole thing, he'd chosen to do it himself. This was still his. And if it proved to be the baited trap he expected it to be, then this would be his, too. All he wanted was for Meade to be there waiting for him.

He drove past open fields, an occasional house, and patches of forest. At times he could almost feel the steering wheel quiver like a dowsing rod in his hands, while some hidden sense of direction urged him on. He had the sensation of traveling through a tunnel rather than a wet, mist-covered countryside, with something deadly waiting at the far end. Then he thought of Emmy and had a moment of panic because he suddenly couldn't remember her face. His stomach, if it *was* his stomach, felt severed from him as in those first nights after she was gone.

He turned off the parkway at exit 6 and followed the service road north. There was little traffic at this hour and he hadn't seen a house for several miles. Spotting the remains of a barn directly ahead, Garret made a sharp right turn onto the dirt trail that ran past it. When he came to the stand of pine Meade had described, he drove a short way into the wood and parked behind some brush. Then he took the automatic from his belt holster under his shirt, released the safety, and slid quietly out of the car.

He stood very still, listening to the forest sounds—the summer hum of insects, the call of birds in the upper branches, the drip of moisture from the trees. It had stopped raining and a streak of pale sunlight broke the overcast. The air was cool but Garret suddenly felt himself sweating. And it was less, he knew, from fear or tension than because there was a fair chance he was going to kill a man. Then with the gun in his hand and his shirt wet against his back, he started through the heavy undergrowth. He circled around to the left, stepping carefully and lightly, and trying to think only of what lay immediately ahead. He didn't really expect to find a woman's body. That particular piece of fiction was just the bait Meade was using to get him out here so he could finish him properly this time.

There was a flicker in the branches ahead and Garret instantly swung his automatic toward it. But it was only a bird and he continued on. His finger was on the trigger now, and he walked crouched over, stopping often behind the trunks of trees to listen. His heart was going very fast and he kept yawning nervously. He imagined Meade stretched out in the brush, and had visions of tiny insects setting off delicate warning systems in his path. *Easy*, he told himself.

Then rounding a cluster of brush, he saw a flash of bright blue in the grass between two trees.

He thought at first it was a bird or a patch of wild flowers. Then edging closer, he saw it was some sort of fabric. For the second time he checked the automatic's safety and started circling more to the left, carefully scanning everything—trees, brush, grass, for some sign of Meade. He had a sudden, terrible horror of being forced to do exactly what Meade wanted him to do, as if the mood of the wood itself, even the air, were enemies.

Dropping flat, Garret slowly crawled forward. He moved in a wide, closing arc that would, if he'd figured correctly, bring him to the patch of blue from the opposite side of his original sighting. He breathed as though there was hardly any air left in the wood, and what was left carried some godawful stench. Then he broke through a veil of the most verdant green and saw a naked woman with a bright blue T-shirt bunched about her neck lying just a few yards from his face.

Oh, Jesus.

Garret moistened his lips and tasted his own sickness. He looked at the dead, staring eyes and felt suddenly fresh memories clutch his heart. Wanting only to turn away, he forced himself not to. She was a young woman, probably in her twenties, with dark, curly hair and a slender, sun-tanned body marked by bikini-and-bra–shaped patches of gray-white flesh. Alive, she undoubtedly had been beautiful. Dead, she was merely grotesque, an oversized doll that had been used and tossed aside. Having to force himself, he lifted the hair at the right side of her face. The tip of her ear was missing.

Just beyond the girl's head, a small, clear, plastic bag was lying partly visible under a rock. There was a note in it. Written in pencil on a sheet of lined paper, it said:

> Merely to establish two important
> points, Mr. Garret. I don't lie to you
> and I intend you no harm.

Garret rocked gently on his knees on the wet ground. As seconds passed and the dampness began to seep through, a vision came to him of endless calls in the night, the tortured faces of once-beautiful women, and Meade's face above it all, laughing.

Twenty minutes later, having reached a gas station off Route 684, he put through a call to Lieutenant Canderro.

CHAPTER
12

anderro met Garret at the ruins of the old barn less than half an hour after receiving his call. Garret had told the detective nothing on the phone other than that he needed to see him. He wanted to do his explaining in person and alone, not surrounded by cops and reporters.

They shook hands. Then they stood silently in the wet grass as Garret groped for some sort of rational-sounding beginning. A cloud drifted over the sun, graying them both. The lieutenant lit a cigarette, blew smoke and waited, looking as though he could wait that way forever. Garret envied him his patience. Or was it simply a carefully projected illusion?

"I've lied to you," he finally said. "You told me that Meade might call, and he did. Twice. The first time was the day I left the hospital. Then a few hours ago he called to say that he'd killed someone else. When I refused to believe him, he told me exactly where to find her body. It was no lie.

She's about half a mile from here, in those woods off to the right."

Canderro's face had lost its calm. "You actually went in there alone?"

"I know. I thought it was a setup too. But that's just what I was hoping for. I figured he'd be waiting for me and I'd finally get my shot at him. I told you that's what I wanted. Except that all I found was a dead girl and this note."

Studying the few penciled lines that Garret handed him, the detective's jaw muscles worked like wires between skin and bone. "Of course."

"It doesn't surprise you?"

"I told you I expected you to be a new source of excitement for him. This just confirms it." Canderro folded the note along its original lines. "OK, let's go see the lady."

They drove to the edge of the woods in Canderro's car. Then with their guns ready, they worked cautiously through the brush on foot. But if Meade did lie watching somewhere, he offered no sign. Still, Garret's lungs burned with his presence. Suddenly, there was the girl. Garret turned away as Canderro knelt to examine her.

"Did you touch anything?" the lieutenant asked.

"Just the note."

"Where was it?"

"Beside the body. In a plastic bag. Under that white stone."

"What did you do with the bag?"

Garret found it under a bush and gave it to the lieutenant—a clear, plastic bag without lettering or other identifying features.

"I suppose you saw the ear," said the detective.

Garret nodded.

"I wouldn't be too surprised if he sends it to you."

"Sonofabitch" was all Garret said.

Canderro rose from his knees with a sigh. "Come on. I have to get a team out here. In fifteen minutes you and this girl are going to be onstage, under the lights."

"I suppose there's no way for me to avoid all that?"

"It was you who got the call, spoke to the killer, and found the body. Without you there's no story."

Back at his car, the lieutenant sat in the front seat and spoke at length on the radio-phone. Then he stepped out, cursing, and slammed the door.

"We'd better get a few things straight before everyone gets here, Garret. I asked you to let me know if Meade ever contacted you, but you decided not to. If you'd listened to me, there's a fair chance we could have traced this latest call and got the bastard. We can't change any of that, but I'd like your word right now that it won't happen again. And another thing: don't mention this to my crew, the press, or anyone else. The story I plan on using is that Meade called you for the first time last night, and that you contacted me immediately. OK?"

Garret nodded. Drained and depressed, he felt his respect growing for this chunky, graceless cop. Everything in Canderro's world could be dealt with, was somehow manageable. There was nothing, not even the bottomless depravity of a homicidal sociopath, that could not be handled with the honest common sense of a decent workman. *I could never do his job,* Garret thought dully.

The wail of a siren sounded faintly in the distance. Then others joined in and Garret saw the first of a line of flashing lights. They came in a loose convoy of police cars and vans, trailed by the media. Birds of carrion.

The lieutenant, taking instant control, kept it all very workmanlike and efficient. The crime scene was cordoned off. Police photographers snapped pictures in brilliant flashes of light. The homicide team's *in situ* specialist made a brief, preliminary examination of the victim's body. Plain-clothes detectives combed the area for possible clues. A biologist took blood samples. Warned in advance by Canderro, the newspeople stayed quietly in the background as they waited to be briefed. They all recognized Garret but had no idea why he was there or what connection he had to the case.

Although he tried to avoid looking at the dead girl, Garret's eyes kept being drawn to her. The fatal bullet had entered under her jaw, taking an upward path, and exited at the back of her head. There was very little blood on the ground, so she evidently had been shot somewhere else, then dumped here. Still, her naked thighs were deliberately spread wide, brutally exposing her. Garret stared, glassy eyed. Was this the way Emmy had been found? The ultimate indignity. Finally, they left you nothing.

One of the younger cops had recognized the girl as a local college student he'd once dated, who worked nights as a waitress in Wappinger Falls. Obviously shaken, he kept mumbling "Jesus, I can't believe it's Nancy" until Canderro sent him home.

With Garret at his side, the lieutenant held an impromptu news conference. He offered the cluster of reporters his carefully edited story, making no mention of Meade's earlier call or of the personal note the killer had left behind or of the missing earlobe. In the questioning that followed, a newsman asked Canderro what he supposed Meade's purpose was in calling the husband of a previous victim to tell him about his latest killing.

"I'm just a country cop," said the lieutenant. "For an answer to that one, you'd better search out some big-city shrink."

False humility, thought Garret. *Or more likely, a sensible reluctance to find himself quoted in tomorrow's news with a facile answer to a complex psychological question.* When they were briefly alone together later, Garret pressed him on it.

"What's your theory, Lieutenant? I'm sure you must have one."

"I doubt that I'd go so far as to call it a theory."

"What would you call it?"

"A hunch maybe."

After a few moments the detective expounded. "There's something special going on here. Meade never expected you to live with two bullets in your head. It's not natural. He sees it as trying to tell him something—a message from God maybe. He was religious when he was a kid, and that superstitious stuff tends to stick. Also, it's sexy as hell. Like sharing a woman with her own husband—the fantasy he was playing out with you. Now that you've turned up alive, you've suddenly doubled his pleasure, given him two hard-ons at once. And he's loving every minute of it."

"Then you think he's going to do the same thing again?"

"I know he will. And he'll call you again, too. So whether you like it or not, I'm getting a court order for a tap on your phone."

Standing there, Garret listened in obedient silence as Canderro gave him detailed instructions on how to handle any future calls from Meade. Most important, he was to keep him on the phone as long as possible, using such stall tactics as talking a great deal, asking questions, and faking sudden fits of sneezing or coughing.

Garret wondered how well he would be able to handle what was being asked of him. Right now, feeling reasonably in control, it all seemed simple enough. Yet even as he gazed off at his wife's killer's latest victim, he could feel his composure leaking away. He became aware of the girl's face as if for the first time, and it struck him as frightful. Her eyes were wide, desperately staring, her mouth gaped in a soundless scream, and suddenly, without comprehension, he was absolutely certain she was screaming at *him*.

CHAPTER
13

Garret was in Berringer's office at eight-thirty the next morning, at least half an hour before the managing editor usually arrived at work. The idea had come to him in the middle of the night, smothered any hope of further sleep, and kept him walking the streets for the past two hours. This was his first trip back to the *Times* since Emily's death, and he'd worked his way through the ordeal of return with careful composure, accepting greetings and condolences with quiet appreciation, and even managing traces of a smile along the way.

"Paul! What a happy surprise."

The surprise was evident enough, but Hank Berringer did not really look happy as he entered his office and shook Garret's hand. As one who'd spent a lifetime dealing almost exclusively with bad news, Berringer wore lines and ridges in his face that reflected the sad knowledge that most things were not going to improve.

"I hope this means you're coming back to work."

"That depends."

"On what?"

"On whether you'll accept my conditions."

Berringer settled himself behind his desk. "Try me."

Garret allowed himself a moment. The whole concept was new to him and he was still thinking it through. That morning's *Times* lay in front of the editor, and Garret nodded toward the front page coverage of William Meade's latest performance.

"How did that affect you?" he asked.

"Like a kick in the gut. I can imagine what it must have done to *you*."

"That's why I'm here. Suddenly, it's not just Emily anymore. The horror is open-ended. I've decided to do something. I can't just sit and wait for others. I have a voice, a certain force and reputation as a writer. Whatever weight it carries, I want to begin using it."

Berringer was staring at the newspaper on his desk. It might have been a snake. "I'm glad you feel that way. At least it's positive. But you mentioned conditions."

"I want no set routine, no deadlines, nothing like that. Maybe I'll do only a column or two a week, or just whenever it feels right. I want to shove this whole mess in the public eye like a sharp rock and keep it there. I don't want anyone forgetting about it. And I don't mean just Meade himself. I want to go after the whole system that made Meade and his crimes possible. That's all I want to dig into and write about. Nothing else."

Garret paused. He was breathing heavily and the floating spots were back before his eyes. "Do you think the paper could live with that?"

"Could *you*?"

"What does that mean?"

"You're already burning at a white heat. How long do you

think you'd last with the kind of all-out vendetta you're talking about?"

"As long as I have to."

"You're obsessing, Paul."

"You're damn right I am. But can you think of a better reason?"

The editor's eyes appeared dead at their centers, a sure sign that he was troubled.

"What if I reject your conditions?"

"Is that what you're going to do?"

"I might."

"Why?"

"To keep you from destroying yourself in a futile crusade. But if you need more practical reasons, we do tend to frown on our staff writers using the paper for personal blood feuds. Also, we're not paying you to be a police reporter but to comment on the varying elements of the contemporary scene."

"To hell with the varying elements of the contemporary scene."

"You haven't answered my question," said Berringer. "What if I reject your conditions?"

"I'll go to another paper."

"Your contract still runs for another two years."

"Then sue me."

"Be reasonable, Paul."

"Be *reasonable?*" Garret felt his hands begin twitching in his lap. Gripping one with the other, he forced them still. "Emmy and a young girl are lying dead at the hand of a man the system once had safely locked up, and you tell me to be reasonable?"

The editor was silent.

"Why are you fighting me on this?" said Garret.

"Because I care about you."

"Then please care about me a little less and just help me do what I have to do."

Berringer gazed tiredly at his friend. *How could I not?* said the dead centers of the editor's eyes.

Garret went directly from Hank Berringer's office to his own and closed the door. He felt driven to start at once, as if the compulsion itself would give his commentary added force, weight.

He kept a new word processor and an old Royal portable sitting side by side in his office. The processor was mostly for show and self-defense. It beat having to explain why he didn't have one. The typewriter remained his true friend and sword. Today, responding to the continued reflex of uncounted years, he went straight to the Royal. Seated before the old machine, just slipping a clean sheet of paper onto the roller and positioning it, Garret felt a physical high as potent as any he'd experienced.

But he found himself groping for the right approach. Despite his bravado in Berringer's office, he felt curiously uncertain. At his best he was a visceral writer. He wrote more from feeling than from plan or technique, so he had few literary conceits to fall back on. This time, too, emotion could render him maudlin. Which meant he had to be careful.

All right, quit stalling, he told himself, and finally got on with it.

I'm thankful to be back. I'm grateful, too, for all the warm expressions of sympathy and encouragement I received while in the hospital. Each one touched me. And it was at a time when I deeply needed to be touched. Now I have things to say.

In the early spring of this year, my wife, Emily, was raped and murdered by a paroled convict named William Meade. This was not

Meade's first such offense. About nine years ago he was convicted of a similar crime and sentenced to prison for a term of from 20 to 40 years.

After serving a bit more than eight years of his sentence, Meade was paroled and sent out into a free society. Four months after his release, he raped and murdered my wife and left me with two bullet holes in my head and presumably dead. Two days ago he raped and murdered once more. At this writing he remains at large, leaving me with one very important question. How could such a thing happen?

It's not a new question. It's been asked all too many times before by all too many other surviving victims. The major difference this time is that I'm the victim and I'm the one asking the question. And I promise this. I won't stop asking until I get an answer I can live with.

This will in no way be a witch-hunt. I'm not looking to place blame on individuals. I believe that those involved in William Meade's release acted in all good conscience and well within the parameters of the system they serve. I believe that if the blame for this and other, similar tragedies lies anywhere, it's with the system itself. This is what I intend to address.

Garret read what he had put down so far. There were no fireworks exploding off the page, but it said what he wanted to say. He pushed the column further.

With few fixed notions he worked it through for the rest of the day, slowly letting it build on itself. This was just his opening shot and he kept it general, impersonal. He made no mention of the three parole commissioners whose decision it had been to set Meade free, nor did he intend to later on. He'd already gotten that particular monkey off his back. If anything, he felt sorry for them. Because once the media, the public, and the politicians began working up a full head of steam on this, it was likely they'd be scapegoated. Too bad. Three more victims for Meade.

• • •

Anxious for some word from Poughkeepsie, Garret put through a call to Lieutenant Canderro the moment he arrived home that evening.

"Anything new?" he asked the detective.

"Nothing definitive," said Canderro. He took a long, slow breath. "I've sent the note and plastic bag to Washington for analysis. It'll take a few days."

"What about the girl, Nancy Palewski?"

"I can't tell you much more than you read in the paper this morning. She was in her third year at Putnam College, waited tables three nights a week at a local diner, and turned out to have been two and a half months pregnant. Her boyfriend said they were planning to get married in a few weeks. We found her car parked behind some brush about a quarter mile from where her body was left."

Garret had no idea what he'd expected, but suddenly he had a throbbing in his head.

"There were a few not so delicate details," said Canderro. "Pathology came up with something curious. How much do you want to hear?"

"As much as you've got."

"She had male fluid in all three cavities—oral, rectal, vaginal. Which is fairly standard in such cases. What's strange is that the semen came from two different males."

"Had she been with her boyfriend earlier?"

"I questioned him. He swore they hadn't had sex in nearly a week. Also, the pathologist said both sperm types were deposited during approximately the same time period."

Garret closed his eyes as the throbbing in his head grew worse. "So she was making it with another guy?"

"Maybe," said the detective. "But there's always the possibility that it was forced on her."

"I don't follow you."

"Meade's sexual tastes aren't exactly conventional. We know that he was fond of threesomes in the past. If that's the case here, we could either have a living witness wandering around somewhere, or another corpse—male gender. I have people digging up the area right now."

Garret sighed. "How are you able to sleep at night, Lieutenant?"

"By making a very great effort."

"I don't understand about this other guy. If he was part of Meade's syndrome, why didn't he mention him when he told me about Nancy Palewski?"

"The next time he calls, you can ask him."

The wire hummed through a long, strained silence.

"So how are you doing, Garret?"

The sudden softness in the detective's voice caught Garret off guard, made him vulnerable. "I went back to my office today." He stopped. What was he trying to say?

"That's great. Work's the best thing you can do."

There was another pause.

"What about the stuff Harry Stover gave us?" asked Garret, suddenly wanting to hold onto the detective's voice as long as possible. "Have you spotted any likely cabins yet?"

Canderro's grunt was pure disgust. "That's gonna be even more of a ball-breaker than I thought. There turns out to be no less than nineteen lakes in the fifty-mile loop around Liberty, and our aerial shots picked up a grand total of three hundred and forty-two log cabins scattered around them. And that's not counting Christ only knows how many more that could be hidden under trees. But what the hell. Tomorrow I'm sending out some men to start beating the bushes anyway. Who knows? Maybe in seven or eight months somebody'll get lucky and stumble over something."

"And the remains of the two girls?"

"I've got the FBI labs and computers working teeth and missing persons. It's another tough go. Meade could have planted them anywhere from nine to sixteen years ago, so that's a lot of missing girls. And even if we do get an x-ray matchup, we can't go to their families because it has to be kept quiet."

"Maybe I should go back up to Attica and push Stover some more."

The line hummed as Canderro thought about it.

"No," he said. "Better wait. I figure he'll be getting word to you in a few days. Let Nancy Palewski lie on his chest for a while. Let her sink in on him. Now that he knows his Billy-Boy's back in production, he'll be all excited. He'll see his own star rising. I'm sure he's already got visions of freedom fairies dancing in front of his eyes. You've got yourself a nice fat fish on the line. Play him right. Be patient."

Be patient.

And would all good things come to him if he were? Garret wondered how long it took to hunt down a man. A year? Ten years? How many calls in the night would he receive before it was done? He smiled gently as he reflected that, by the end of it, he might be crazier than Meade.

It was wildly erotic and mad, one of those crazy dreams in which you know it's a dream and yet don't know it, with mounting pleasure that asserts its own control over the body and forces you awake, gasping and feeling the telltale wetness on your inner thighs.

Oh, God, he thought, and lay very still in the darkness, not wanting to move because his wife had come so vividly alive for him and he was trying to preserve at least that part of the sensation. But there had been more to it than that, and eventually he had to accept Meade along with the rest—accept that handsome, hated face flickering in and out among their twisting, thrusting bodies, the three of them drenched in each other's lust. He sought and touched the semen on his upper leg and felt betrayed by his own body, felt a terrible disgust break loose in him.

Idiot, it was only a dream! he told himself.

Yes, he thought. *But it was* my *dream, not Meade's.*

CHAPTER
14

Wall Street law offices were all pretty much the same to Lieutenant Canderro—hushed elegance, the distinct odor of money, and nose meters to charge you for breathing. Sharett, Belding, Ryan's twenty-second–floor perch high above the New York harbor might have been the prototype.

Mr. Ryan, whose signature was on Richard Meade's last will and testament, had died some years before, so Canderro was passed along to a current partner, Charles Epstein, who was evidently impressed enough with the detective's recent media celebrity to handle his inquiry personally. Epstein was young, probably not yet forty, with a sincere manner backed by obvious intelligence. He also had a corner office with one of the largest Persian rugs Canderro had ever seen, and an inspiring view of the Statue of Liberty. At the moment Canderro's copy of Richard Meade's probated will was before him on his desk, along with a thick file folder from which he had removed some papers.

"The Phoenix Children's Shelter is easy," he said. "Our firm still administers the trust that was set up for it. We have the current address right here on file."

"Why haven't I been able to find it listed anywhere?" asked Canderro.

"They've apparently changed locations several times over the years. Their most recent move was to Stamford, Connecticut."

Epstein scrawled the address on a sheet of yellow legal paper. "Mr. Meade's widow appears to be more of a problem. We ceased to represent her soon after the estate was closed, and the only address we have listed is her old one in Manhasset. But let me check further."

He leafed through half a dozen papers while Canderro stared at his face for his own clues. It was an occupational reflex conditioned by two decades of police work. Finally you abandoned all normal trust and civility and just kept trying to dive beneath the surface of things.

"Here's what I was hoping for," said Epstein. "Sometimes after an estate is closed, there are a few months of drag correspondence, mail still coming in for beneficiaries. In Adele Meade's case she left us instructions to forward anything for her to a law firm up in Kingston, New York. Its name is Gaynor, Price. Maybe they'll be able to help you."

Epstein wrote the name and address under those of the Phoenix Children's Shelter and handed the paper to Canderro. His eyes were a dull yellow-gray, about the color of a clam, but sharply alive and interested.

"I hope this will be of some help, Lieutenant," he said. "What else can I do for you?"

"Forget you ever gave this to me."

The lawyer's face was blank. "Did I give you something?"

Imagine. From a Wall Street lawyer.

• • •

Two hours later Canderro was certain that Epstein had made a mistake.

The Stamford address that the lawyer had given him for the Phoenix Children's Shelter was occupied by a modest, split-shingle Colonial on a tree-lined suburban street. Or did he simply suffer an old-fashioned stereotypical view of what a children's shelter should be? In any case, he was there. So he parked in the driveway and rang the bell.

A fairly young black woman in jeans and cotton blouse opened the door. She was very attractive and had gleaming dark eyes that held you in their gaze.

"Yes?"

"I'm sorry to disturb you," said Canderro. "I may have been given the wrong address. I was looking for the Phoenix Children's Shelter."

The woman considered him with a quiet, remote little air. "May I ask who gave you this address?"

"Someone at a New York law firm."

"Which firm?"

"Sharett, Belding, Ryan."

"And what is your name?"

"Lieutenant Canderro." He showed her his badge and ID.

"You weren't given the wrong address," she said, and led him into a skylighted den that had as little of the institutional about it as he had seen on the outside. Indeed it was a warm, comfortably furnished room with a fireplace, scattered paintings, and an aura of quiet well-being. He picked up no sound of children in other rooms, although there were several framed photographs of young boys and girls arranged on a breakfront and end tables. Curiously, all the children appeared to carry a mix of black and white racial characteristics, and all were quite attractive.

"What can I do for you, Lieutenant?"

"Forgive me, but I don't know your name."

"Bingham," she said. "Natalie Bingham."

"Mrs.?"

"No. I'm not married."

"Are you the director of the Phoenix Shelter?"

"Yes."

They sat facing one another on bright, flowered print chairs, static electricity seeming to pass between them.

"Uh, Miss Bingham," Canderro began uncertainly, "I'm the officer in charge of the William Meade investigation, and . . . well, I'm trying to determine if there is a possible link, some sort of connection between William Meade and the Phoenix Children's Shelter."

"I'm afraid I don't understand," she said. "Why on earth would you expect to find a connection between a murderer and a home for children?"

"Because the killer's father happens to have been Richard Meade."

Canderro paused, hoping she would pick it up and push him along from there. But she just sat looking at him with her dark eyes until the room itself seemed to darken.

"You're not going to make this any easier for me, are you?" he said.

"Why should I?"

"Because all I'm trying to do is find a killer before he kills again."

"You'll never find him."

"How do you know?"

"I just know. What's the difference?"

"The difference could be a few more wasted lives. Or doesn't that matter to you?"

She went silent again, and Canderro felt as though he were sitting with a hunting rifle, waiting for a wary animal to come within range. Her last answer had sparked a tiny flash of hope. *I just know*. What did she just know? He decided on a different approach.

"I'll tell you what brought me here," he said. "I had no place else to look so I looked at Richard Meade's will. I found that the Phoenix Children's Shelter was the only institutional bequest not funded through the Meade Foundation, and I wondered why. And now that I'm here, I'm wondering where the children are."

"They're at day camp."

"All of them?"

"Yes."

"How many are there?"

"Just four."

Canderro indicated the photographs on the tables. "I assume these are their pictures?"

She said nothing but suddenly appeared to be looking at him with new interest.

"I'm also wondering about some other things," he said slowly. "Such as why I didn't find Phoenix included in any listing of recognized charities, and why you seem to be its entire staff, and why your facilities are so much more home-like than institutional."

He gazed once more at the children's photographs. "And I'm especially wondering why every child here is apparently of racially mixed blood and bears so remarkable a resemblance to you and the other children."

He allowed himself a long moment. "I'm not your enemy, Miss Bingham. I promise you. I'm not here to do you or your children any harm."

Natalie Bingham sat stiffly in her chair, her expression set for a scornful protest. Then her face and body suddenly went slack and she seemed to diminish. When she spoke, her voice was not as certain as it had been before.

"I'm frightened, Lieutenant."

"Why?"

"Because William is out there someplace and Jesus only knows what he's going to do next. Look at my eyes. I haven't had a decent night's sleep since they set him free. When I do sleep, it's with a loaded shotgun under my bed."

"I don't understand."

"That's because I haven't told you anything yet."

She brought out a bottle of Canadian Club, poured herself a long drink without offering one to Canderro, and took a couple of swallows. When she looked at him again, it was as if she'd reconstituted herself out of alcohol and sheer will.

"Richard Meade and I were lovers for five years," she said. "These four children are ours. And this whole Phoenix Shelter bit was just his way of protecting our financial future in case his bitchy wife ever found out about us. Except she wasn't the one who found out. It was William."

"Did he tell his mother?"

"No. He said later he didn't want to hurt her. He loved her too much for that. So he decided it would be best for everyone if his father just flew off somewhere and didn't come back. And that's exactly what William made sure he did."

The room was so still that Canderro heard the silence ringing in his ears. "How do you know it was William who caused the crash?"

"Because he said so."

"And you never told this to anyone?"

"Who would have believed me? There was no evidence. Sometimes I didn't even believe it myself. This was almost two years before William was arrested for rape and murder.

He was still everyone's all-American dream boy. How was I to know he hadn't just made up the whole story?"

"Why would he make up something like that?"

"I'm sure now he didn't make it up." A flicker of sunlight broke through the window and added gold to the dark sienna of Natalie's cheeks. "But if he *had* lied about it, it would have been to show me what he was capable of doing, to let me know the lives of me and my children could be touched as easily as his father's if I didn't give him what he wanted."

"What did he want?"

"Me."

Her voice was soft, passionless, but Canderro could feel the stopped-up emotion in it.

"Don't mistake me, Lieutenant. William didn't blow up his daddy just to grab me. That was a whole different can of worms. But once Richard was out of the way, the idea of sharing his father's woman was irresistible to him. So he had me. I was that frightened and he was that sexy. And it lasted for almost four years. Until they finally put him away for rape and murder."

Canderro was incredulous. "You mean you actually slept with the man who'd killed the father of your children?"

The accusation was implicit, but Natalie's face, her expression, appeared seamless, without a visible break.

"I understand what you're saying," she told him, "but you don't know William. You can't imagine how appealing he can be. He has a way, a feeling, that can move something in you. It can twist your beliefs. I even convinced myself he *had* made up that whole story about putting a bomb on Richard's plane. He would go on about how much he'd idolized his father, how he'd tried endlessly to please him, how he constantly mourned him now that he was gone. He'd tell me how much he loved my children because they were his little brothers and sisters and part of his father, and how he'd sooner die than hurt any part of them or me."

"And you believed him?"

"I wanted to believe him. I had to believe him. Not to believe him would have been too horrible to consider. And remember, this was before he'd shown what he was, before he was under suspicion for murder."

Her tone had dropped so low that Canderro was finding himself leaning forward and straining to hear her words.

"The absolute truth of it, Lieutenant, is that I wanted him. There was something so sensual in the intensity of his needs that he seemed to turn the whole act of sex itself into a brand-new art form. I mean, he had a talent. I was young, only nineteen, when I started with his father. Actually, William's own age. And I hadn't had all that much experience. But William was a true revelation to me. I don't know what kind of craziness he has inside him that makes him have to rape and kill to get his highs. But believe me, it didn't get there because he couldn't do it straight."

Another unsolicited testimonial, thought Canderro, *to Meade's erotic genius.*

"Did he ever threaten you or your children?" he said. "Did he ever lay a hand on any of you?"

"Never. He loved my kids."

"Then why are you so afraid of him?"

She seemed to seek possible reasons from someplace outside the window. But when her eyes turned back to him, they were empty.

"I'm not sure," she said. "But whatever William is now, it's not what he was before."

"He's been out of Attica close to five months. Has he contacted you at all during this period?"

"No. But I have the feeling that sooner or later he will."

"Do you want him to?"

"Yes and no," she said.

"What does that mean?"

"It means, it's not all that simple. I have mixed emotions. I know the man. Sometimes I think how alone he is out there, and all I want to do is help him. Then at other times I think what an idiot I'd be to even want to get involved."

"Just one last question," Canderro said. "If Meade ever does contact you, will you call me?"

"I won't lie to you, Lieutenant. At this moment I honestly don't know."

He picked up Route 684 outside of Stamford, drove north to 84, and made good time all the way to the New York State Thruway. Then about five miles before New Paltz, a jack-knifed tractor-trailer tied up all traffic for more than an hour. When he finally reached Kingston and located the law offices of Gaynor, Price, it was after 6:00 P.M. and the firm was closed for the day. And since it was Friday, they'd undoubtedly remain closed until Monday.

Suddenly tired, and not caring a bit for his thoughts, Canderro started the long drive home. Halfway there, he remembered to call Chief Haggerty of the Stamford Police and officially request the same sort of covert surveillance on Natalie Bingham as he had gotten from the Nassau County PD for Jenny Angelo.

Moments later he put through another call, this one to Paul Garret. *My new friend.* The thought was faintly mocking, yet in a twisted sort of way Canderro believed they shared a sense of loss—that somehow getting this murdering son-ofabitch would at least partially avenge the deaths of his own wife and child. OK, so it was a little crazy. What else was new?

He heard Garret's voice answer.

"Canderro here, I've just picked up a few more choice bits on our boy," he said, and briefly filled him in on his meeting with Natalie Bingham.

It took Garret a moment to digest. "That's some bedtime story. Do you believe it?"

"Which part?"

"Killing his own father."

"Hey, look who we're talking about."

"Yes, but how many nineteen-year-olds would know how to blow up a plane in flight?"

"This one sure as hell did. According to a couple of his professors, he was a genius when it came to electronics. Won all sorts of prizes and awards. A clock in plastic would have been kindergarten stuff for him."

Garret was silent at the other end.

"Talk about bad seed," said the detective flatly. "Now I'm starting to wonder if the miserable prick went and made his poor mother disappear the same way."

CHAPTER
15

William Meade lay naked in the grass behind his cabin. He was enjoying the midday sun, feeling the warmth enter his pores. *Working on my carcinomas,* he thought, *wondering why all the things that were once supposed to be so good for you, such as eggs, beef, and sunlight, now simply killed you.*

Bright thoughts for a summer day.

Still, he was not unhappy. He loved just being here, loved making the most of what each moment offered. Sometimes he was able to do that, just letting the minutes wash over him. It was far easier to do it here, with the quiet, the solitude, and the memories the place still held for him. Now, in addition, it was his haven.

If the past ninety-three years had been spent in preparation for his current needs, it could not have worked out better. The cabin and its surrounding two thousand acres of unspoiled woodland had been in his mother's family for close to five generations, with the name of Meade bearing no discernible connection to them. Since neither electric nor telephone lines had ever been run in, there were no monthly bills to be paid. Which left only the annual taxes to be taken care of, and this had always been handled by an old-line firm of estate lawyers, whose collective names Meade did not even remember. Unless he started a forest fire, he could hide here and remain undiscovered until he was bones.

All his memories of the place were tied in with his father, who'd started bringing him here when he was little more than a toddler, and never stopped until his plane went down in the Atlantic. Occasionally his mother would come with them, but that was rare and mostly at the beginning, when he was very young. After that there was just his father and himself, the two of them cooking steaks over great fires, working on carpentry projects, taking hikes, and going fishing. His father knew all these terrific things—which mushrooms you could eat and which could kill you, which snakes made the best pets, and what the birds were saying to each other when they sang.

As a boy, Meade had no idea how his father had come by such wisdom. He'd never even been to college. Later on, though, he realized that there simply wasn't a thing his father was not interested in or didn't care about.

Meade slowly, lazily, rolled over on his stomach. He breathed deeply and smelled the sweetness of the grass against his face. That morning's *Times* lay beside him, and he'd just finished reading Paul Garret's first column since his return from the hospital. Part of him was still reacting to it. It felt strange to read about himself, to be referred to in print by a celebrated journalist for the benefit of millions of readers. Even the president read the *Times*, so it was not unlikely that the world's most powerful person had taken note of William Meade over his morning coffee. Heady stuff. Although to be granted celebrity by being labeled in print as somewhat less than human was hardly how he'd have chosen to make the big time.

Less than human, Meade sniffed. He was no less a man than that self-righteous Mr. Garret. The only difference was that he'd been able to throw off the repressive restraints of morality and experience the sense of exultation only killing could bring. Even Garret, who'd done his share of killing in Vietnam, was in the end just like all the rest of them. A hypocrite.

Sated, finally, by the sun, he dove into the small lake edging his grassy slope, swam briefly, and went inside the cabin.

It was just a large central room with a stone fireplace, a small kitchen area, and a sleeping loft that was reached by ladder. The furnishings were sparse, nothing more than an oak table, a scattering of chairs, and two walls of books with faded bindings. There was a sink but no faucets, and water had to be pumped by hand from a well at the side of the house. Two Coleman lanterns were on the table and a third stood on one of the bookshelves. Other than for some Audubon prints, the walls were bare.

Meade couldn't remember anything in the cabin ever being different. He would not have wanted a thing changed. Deviation of any sort would have been near to sacrilege. He knew every object, every inch of log wall, beamed ceiling, and plank flooring by heart. It was how he had always pictured them in prison.

When the air had dried his body, he put on a fresh T-shirt and khaki shorts and prepared a couple of tuna fish sandwiches. He had a hearty appetite and enjoyed eating, but food itself meant little to him. It certainly wasn't the passion or pretentious art form it appeared to have become to so many others.

Three news photos he'd clipped from yesterday's *Times* lay spread out on the table and he studied them as he ate. They were from a feature article entitled "The Victims of William Meade," and showed the smiling faces of Doris Baker, Emily Garret, and Nancy Palewski. It was one of those articles that tried to add background to a recent news event, as if in hope that some previously unnoticed pattern might be uncovered.

His gaze lingered over Emily Garret's picture—a portrait of a fair, gentle-eyed woman, who stared back at him with the absolute trust and kindness of the truly innocent. He touched the black-and-white picture with his fingers. But it was only newsprint and not even near to touching her flesh.

Flesh was what he needed now.

Allowing his thoughts to drift, Meade began thinking of another woman who'd had that special look of kindness. This one, bless her, still warmly, exquisitely alive.

In his mind he was soon reaching for the warm embrace of Jacqueline Wurzel, his former parole officer.

CHAPTER
16

The Westchester County Division of Parole was on the second floor of a stained brick building in White Plains, New York. Paul Garret arrived shortly after 5:00 P.M., gave his name to a receptionist, and asked to see Parole Officer Jacqueline Wurzel.

"Do you have an appointment, Mr. Garret?"

"Yes, but it's at five-thirty." As always, he'd allowed too much driving time.

"Please take a seat."

He sat down on one of a dozen plastic chairs, only three of which were occupied. The two men and a woman who were waiting stared vacantly at Garret. When he gazed back at them, they looked somewhere else as if self-conscious about their presence there.

Wurzel was the parole officer to whom William Meade had reported once each week during the approximately four months that elapsed between the winter morning he was released from Attica, and the spring afternoon he'd happened on the Garret house. Paul had checked out the parole officer in advance. She was a psychology major out of Hunter College who, to hear her colleagues tell it, projected a dedicated public-servant image with a no-nonsense approach to her work. Deceased parents were German Jews and Holocaust survivors, but Jacqueline was born here. She'd been married once and divorced, lost an only child—a son—to leukemia at the age of four.

At exactly 5:30 the receptionist directed Garret down a long corridor to room 238. By that time he was the only one waiting. He found the office, knocked once on an old-fashioned, frosted-glass door, and went in.

Wurzel came from behind her desk to shake his hand. "Sorry to keep you waiting, Mr. Garret."

"No problem at all. I was early."

She was slender, with fair skin, and eyes darker than her hair. Her look was neither friendly nor hostile. Mostly it was solemn. And her hip holster added its own note of seriousness. Somehow it had never occurred to Garret that parole officers would be armed. But of course they'd have to be. The men and women they worked with were still, technically, convicts under sentence.

Wurzel closed the door and returned to her desk. Garret sat himself a few feet away, giving her time to adjust to his face. His scars still gave him a special status.

"When you called and wanted to see me," she said, "my first instinct was to rush out and get myself a lawyer."

"Is that what you did?"

"No. My second reaction was to say to hell with you. I've done nothing wrong."

Garret considered her. In her white, short-sleeved blouse and navy skirt, she had the fresh, youthful look of a parochial schoolgirl in uniform. But the eyes that measured him were not those of a schoolgirl. They'd seen a lot.

"And then?" he asked.

"Then I began feeling guilty anyway."

"Why?"

Wurzel seemed to collect herself. "Understand this, Mr. Garret. I'm not naïve about my line of work. I know exactly what we can and can't do. But what happened to you and your wife, and to that girl the other day, well, it's really sticking in my throat."

"If it's any consolation," said Garret, "it's also sticking in the throats of the warden and guards at Attica, and of the three members of his parole board. I know. I've talked to them all."

Her expression registered a hint of sarcasm. "Is that why you're here? To offer me consolation?"

"No, Miss Wurzel. I'm here to find some answers."

"I'm sure you are. I've read your columns. But unless you can come up with a whole new set of questions, the only answers I have are those I've already given Lieutenant Canderro."

"When was Canderro here?"

"Months ago. Right at the beginning. The same day you identified Meade's mug shot."

"What did you tell the lieutenant?"

"The standard stuff."

"Please bear with me," said Garret. "I'm new at parole procedures. What do you mean by standard stuff?"

"Just that I never had a single problem with William. He did regular, honest work at a White Plains company that makes semiconductors. He had a nice apartment in a respectable neighborhood. To my knowledge he didn't drink, use drugs, or hang out with those who did. He came to this office every Thursday morning at nine o'clock sharp, never missed an appointment, and never was five seconds late. He showed no hint of bitterness toward me, the penal system, or society in general. He was repentant of the crime for which he was sentenced to prison, and grateful for the chance to make a new life for himself."

"What about friends?" asked Garret. "Was he going with any woman? Did he ever say anything about his family, his mother?"

"His mother apparently cut herself off from him when he was convicted, and she was the only family he had. As for friends and women, he told me he wasn't ready for any of that. He said he had to get his own head straight first, then maybe he'd be able to deal with others."

Wurzel lifted a hand and smoothed the back of her hair. It was so typically female a gesture that Garret somehow found himself surprised. It was a stupid way for him to react, he thought, because it had suddenly occurred to him that, gun or no gun, she was a very beautiful woman.

"For a newly paroled rapist-killer," she said, "William's response, his avoidance of relationships, was completely normal. He was understandably ashamed of what he'd done, and fearful that he might do it again."

"You called him William?"

"Yes. And he called me Jacqueline. I always try for warmth, trust, and at least the illusion of friendship. It's important to someone who's been nothing but a number for years." She paused, her eyes suddenly blank. "We try and we think we know. Then something like this happens and we find we know nothing."

Dully, remembering her background, Garret stared off at a framed photograph on the wall. It showed a thin, fragile-limbed Jacqueline Wurzel as a young girl, locked forever between her mother and father in a moment of summer sun.

The snapshot had been taken at the beach and the three wore brightly colored bathing suits. Yet they remain solemn faced and unsmiling, as though the day had turned out so badly that not even the camera could coax forth the usual obligatory grin.

Wurzel had followed his eyes. "That's me with my mother and father."

"I'd know you anywhere."

She laughed for the first time, and Garret thought it brought a whole new dimension to her face. It also made her look five years younger.

"I know it seems too personal and out of place here," she said. "But I feel it helps humanize me a little, makes me seem just a bit less formidable to those who have to deal with me."

"You don't strike me as especially formidable."

"Is that good or bad?"

"From where I'm sitting, good."

She hesitated. "I must say you're being a lot kinder to me than I expected."

"What were you expecting?"

"More of the anger I've been finding in your columns."

"My anger is at the system."

Wurzel nodded slightly, then seemed to retreat inside herself. "I should have known," she finally said.

"Why? Do you believe you have psychic powers of some sort?"

"No. But in William's case I should have had some intimation of what lay ahead."

Garret waited. This curious woman. She'd spoken lightly, but she wasn't smiling as she considered him.

"I'm going to show you something," she said. "It's a little

embarrassing for me because it's so utterly unprofessional. But I suddenly find myself wanting to show it to you."

Taking a key from her purse, Wurzel unlocked and opened the bottom drawer of her desk. Then she took out a small, brass picture frame and handed it to Garret.

Behind the glass was a time-yellowed newspaper clipping that showed the head and shoulders of a Nazi SS officer in uniform. The photo caption described the officer as Lt. Col. Heinrich Dieter, a convicted war criminal who'd just been sentenced to hang by a Nuremberg tribunal.

"It's more than forty-seven years old and faded," said Wurzel. "But look at the bone structure, the mouth, the line of the upper lip. Look especially at the eyes. Whatever feeling is there, it's always in the eyes. Look at all these things. Then tell me you don't see what I see."

Garret saw it all right. How could he not? The man could have been William Meade's brother.

"I literally grew up with that face," Wurzel said. "For as long as my mother and father lived, they kept it on the bureau in their bedroom. They were survivors of the camp Dieter administered. *Survivors* is the wrong word, actually. They never survived a thing. It just took them a little longer to die than most of the others."

Looking at Garret, her eyes were neutral.

"You might think it strange for them to keep such a picture constantly in sight, but it was a reminder that at rare intervals a tiny measure of justice can still be done. If not by God, then by flawed people like you and me, Mr. Garret."

Wurzel allowed herself a moment.

"Each Thursday morning, just before William was due to report, I'd take out the picture and look at it. 'Be careful,' I'd tell myself. 'There *could* be something there, behind the mask. Don't be fooled by his saying and doing all the right things.' This was what I told myself each Thursday morning, Mr. Garret, and yet I did nothing."

"What could you have done?"

"I don't know. But with that kind of truth lying in my bottom drawer, how could I not have done *something?*"

Parked in the municipal lot directly under Wurzel's window, William Meade was watching Jacqueline talk to Garret. And without hearing a word, he could all but sense what each was saying. This was his regular watching time. Garret was an unexpected intrusion. Or was he a bonus? Meade didn't know yet which he would prove to be.

My lovely Jacqueline.

He smiled, but the thought wasn't wholly sarcastic. A fair part of him did think of her as his. *His* personal cheering section. *His* keeper of the flame. *His* devout believer that the good in him would finally prevail. A foolish, utterly futile belief, yet how could she know? As for her loveliness, that was self-evident.

Thinking of her now, some small part of him that had once sung so sweetly sang no more.

They were some pair: a paroled rapist-murderer and a beautiful woman with the serenity of one of Raphael's more beatific Madonnas. Yet as ludicrous as the matchup seemed, it had been working. Because for that single hour each week, they sat together in that tacky second-floor office and talked and looked at each other as if they were friends. He knew, of course, that she was just doing her job, but that didn't matter to him. He simply enjoyed being with her, seeing the sheen of her hair, cut short and layered like the feathers of a bird, and under it the paleness of her cheeks and delicacy of her features.

He generally avoided too close a look at her body. It disturbed him too much. Yet he could picture it at will, clothed or unclothed, with its flesh almost milk-white, and the faintest, bluest of veins making delicate tracings on her inner thighs.

Wurzel suddenly changed her position in front of the window, and he had a better view of Paul Garret. The journalist was leaning forward slightly as he listened to whatever it was that Jacqueline was saying. Meade stared up at them. He felt the first stab of pain that came just from seeing the two of them together. Yet he felt, too, an almost instant sense of arousal.

Sweet God, he thought, and wondered how Garret felt being so close to her. Was he aware, this soon, of all she was? Could he breathe her scent and feel the warmth she gave off? Or was he still too absorbed in his loss to even notice the exquisite gift being offered to soothe his grief?

Meade gazed intensely, broodingly through the lighted window. His gaze remained fixed until, in his mind, the two figures assumed the naked shapes and erotic positions his increasingly aroused state was creating for them. Finally, when they'd coalesced into a single form, light as shadow on sand, he embraced them, and joined in their lovemaking. His first faint sense of betrayal did not arrive until much later.

When Garret returned from White Plains, he found a white envelope without a return address waiting for him with the rest of his mail. The envelope bulged slightly in the middle, and he knew what he'd find inside even before he opened it. Except that this time the tiny attached earring was made of silver, the notepaper was cream colored rather than pale blue, and the four lines of poetry were unfamiliar. Garret wondered whether Meade had written them himself.

So many I loved were not yet dead,
When I remember bygone days
I think how evening follows morn;
So many I loved were not yet dead,
So many I love were not yet born.

Lieutenant Canderro had left a pair of rubber surgical gloves for Garret to wear if and when Meade sent any more packages. But in his excitement Garret had completely forgotten to put them on.

CHAPTER
17

Charles Price, the surviving partner of Gaynor, Price, Attorneys at Law, was red faced and potbellied and projected the easy, homespun manner of what he enjoyed calling "a country lawyer's relaxed approach to the law." So too did his offices, a collection of dusty, book-lined rooms in a faded brick building on Kingston's main business street. To Canderro, the only things missing were wide suspenders for Price and brass cuspidors beside the chairs.

"The lady came up here to the office only once," Price told the detective, "and that must have been at least eight, nine years ago. But I remember her. Tall lady—very straight, very pretty, with a real no-nonsense manner. All business. No interest in pleasantries. But superb presence, if you know what I mean. Said she traveled a lot and would be wanting us to handle a few routine estate matters for her from time to time."

"What address did she give you?" asked Canderro.

"No address. That was the strange part. Gave us a post of-

fice box number in Newburgh where we could send her mail
and reach her if we had to. I remember wondering why Newburgh if she was going to deal with a Kingston law firm. Or
if she wanted her mail in Newburgh for some reason, then
why not a Newburgh lawyer? But there was nothing illegal
about it and it was none of my business. She had all the required identification as Mrs. Adele Meade, and she seemed a
person of considerable means. So that was it."

Price took a moment to relight his half a cigar, which had
gone out while he was talking. Then he puffed on it thoughtfully, an ample man giving himself to his small pleasure.

"You tell me she's William Meade's mother," he said,
"and I have no reason to doubt you, Lieutenant. But that's
still quite a shocker. I mean, a woman who looks like that?
Who carries herself like that?" He shook his head. "I guess
it's foolish, expecting the mother of a multiple killer to look
like Frankenstein's bride."

"Has anyone else questioned you about her?" asked Canderro. "Anyone at all?"

"No, sir."

"No phone calls either? No inquiries by mail? Was there
perhaps someone asking whether you had a client by the
name of Mrs. Richard Meade?"

"No, sir. Nothing like that." Price chewed at his cigar,
then sucked it like a pacifier. "Not so far as I know, anyway.
And if anyone ever asked my partner while he was alive, Bill
never mentioned it to me. As I said, we just did those few
routine things over the years, mailed them to the post office
box number she gave us, sent a bill for our services, and received payment by return mail."

"May I have the box number, please, Mr. Price?"

The lawyer wiped his red face with a gray handkerchief as
he considered the request. "I can't really think of any signifi-

cant reason why not," he said, and went over to a bank of files to retrieve it.

Using the New York Thruway, it took Canderro only forty-five minutes to reach Newburgh, a faded old town on the west bank of the Hudson that could still look quietly imposing when the light was right and you could see the river.

He found the main post office, learned that a John Riga was the assistant postmaster in charge of box rentals, and identified himself.

"I've seen you on television," Riga said.

Canderro nodded. The magic of celebrity. He was hoping to make some practical use of it.

"What can I do for you, Lieutenant?"

"There's a box number I have written here." Canderro glanced at the notepaper that the lawyer had given him. "Number eight forty-three. I need the name and address of the person who rented it."

"That's privileged information," Riga said. He was a big, thick-necked man with a fighter's broken nose and flared nostrils. "I'm afraid it's against United States postal regulations for me to give it to you."

Canderro was silent. He had been afraid of just that.

"It could cost me my job, Lieutenant."

"What if I got a court order?"

"Even that wouldn't be easy. You'd first have to show proof that the box was currently being used illegally, for fraudulent purposes."

Canderro felt frustration pump through him like boiling blood. *Nothing comes easy,* he thought, and was struck by the memory of his father saying those same three words, that same bitter lament, countless times over the years. The whining sound of defeat. It had depressed him in his father and it depressed him even more in himself.

"Then I have a serious problem, Mr. Riga," he said. "So I'm going to have to tell you something in confidence. When you hear it, you can either help me or not help me. But either way, I must have your word that what I tell you won't go any further."

His tough face solemn, the postmaster rose and closed his office door. "You've got my word."

Canderro looked evenly at him, summoned all his persuasiveness. "We think we may be close to finding William Meade's mother," the lieutenant said conspiratorially. "It could be a critical break in the case. Box eight forty-three belongs to her. She rented it under a pseudonym when she disappeared about nine years ago. If anyone knows where her son is, she does. And at this point in time, you're the only one who can tell me where to find her."

"How do you know for sure that this woman is really William Meade's mother?" said Riga. His voice showed a little more excitement now.

"I traced her to some lawyers through her husband's will. They gave me the box number. It's the only way they've communicated with her for nine years."

Riga's nostrils flared wider as he worked at it. "You've sure given me something."

The postmaster rose and paced the small room. His face seemed split into separate, conflicting sections. Forced into the unaccustomed role of decision maker, needing to do something that was not listed for him in any of the manuals lined up on shelves behind his desk, he was not a happy man. But when he finally sat down again, he appeared to have settled on something. And because the man's eyes did not quite meet his, Canderro had the feeling it was not going to be good.

Riga pointed to a gray metal file cabinet in the corner. "What you want is right over there in that cabinet, Lieutenant. Everything there is filed numerically, and it would be easy enough for me to walk over there, dig out the card on box number eight forty-three, and read off the name and address. Probably take me no more than thirty seconds from beginning to end. But I'm afraid I can't do it. You know why? Because if the lady ever took this to court, I'd have to testify under oath that I never told you who she was or where she lived, or be fired from my job. And I just won't lie in God's name."

He stood up and showed Canderro a key. "So easy. The file key is right here in my hand, and this whole thing is for such a good cause. But a man still has to live happily with himself and his God. I'm sure you can understand that, can't you, Lieutenant?"

"What I understand, Mr. Riga, is that while you're busy living happily with yourself and your God, any number of women could be getting raped and murdered."

The postmaster's shrug was sad, eloquently philosophical. "I'm afraid I'll just have to take that chance, sir. In the meantime, I have to take a leak so bad my eyeballs are floating. Swollen prostate, the doc calls it. Yet I'm only fifty years old, not seventy. So go figure it."

Riga tossed the file key on his desk. "Keep an eye on this till I get back, will you, Lieutenant? Then we'll talk some more when I can really concentrate."

He left the office, carefully closing the door behind him.

The name that Adele Meade had taken was Dorothy Lipton, and she was living at 36 Rosewood Lane on the outskirts of a town called Wallkill. It took Canderro no more than twenty-five minutes to drive there from the Newburgh post office and another ten minutes to locate the address.

The house itself was a traditional two-story—and—attic white clapboard, with a long, slanting roof, dormers, and black shutters. It had a pillared wraparound porch and a well-tended flower garden and, to a born and bred city-tenement dweller like Canderro, possessed the stereotypical aura of the American dream fulfilled. As a boy, he'd imagined only good things happening to those lucky enough to live in houses like this. He now knew better.

The detective drove slowly past the house without stopping. He planned a wiretap and a reasonable period of covert surveillance before he went in with a search warrant and a lot of questions. He didn't really expect to find Meade hiding in the attic or cellar. Yet neither did he believe it to be pure coincidence that Meade's mother had simply disappeared and taken another name soon after her son was sent to prison. Everything was obviously tied together. And there would be a far better chance of finding out how the strings were connected if Mrs. Meade still believed she was undiscovered.

Watching the house fade from sight in his rearview mirror, the detective felt a pleasant rush of excitement.

Yet he did have other things going. Despite the usual media hysterics he *had* managed to make some progress. He had his two round-the-clock surveillances started on Jenny Angelo and Natalie Bingham, his long-shot log cabin hunt, and people following up half a dozen leads based on the FBI's analysis of the two packages so far received from Meade. Ricky Falanga's specialists had come up with a sizable list of manufacturer's outlets in five surrounding counties that sold the exact types of string, note and wrapping paper, and cotton batting. There also were latent prints on the two boxes that had to be computer checked for possible matchups to fingerprints already on file.

Of course it was all just routine busywork, with little chance of hitting anything. But every part of it had to be done. Because if you were a cop, that was what you did.

Of greater interest to Canderro was the still unidentified semen specimen found in Nancy Palewski. The more he thought about it, the more certain he was that Meade had simply come across Nancy and the man parked in her car and done the job on them both. But if that were so, where was the guy's body? And if there was a body buried somewhere, why hadn't someone—a relative, a friend, a boss, or a coworker—reported the man missing?

It didn't feel right for Meade to have simply let the man walk away. Yet if he had, why hadn't the guy come forward to tell the police his story? The most logical answer to that was fear. But fear of what? Certainly of Meade. But inasmuch as clandestine sex was involved, it could also be fear of having to be publicly revealed. If the guy happened to be married himself, he'd *really* have a hard time coming forward.

Canderro had three detectives out focusing on just that angle. Two were interviewing Nancy's friends, relatives, people from the diner where she was a part-time waitress, and students at her college, trying to put together a list of men she might have been with that night. Another detective was talking to the designated men themselves and getting them to volunteer for blood and semen tests. Nancy's fiancé, the alleged father of her unborn child, had already been tested and cleared.

Poor bastard, thought Canderro. It wasn't enough for him to have his intended bride and unborn child murdered. He also had to find out that his dearly beloved had been making it with another man when it happened.

Police work. Some way to make a living. It wasn't any wonder that cops were all a little crazy. The wonder was that they didn't end up crazier than they were. *Thank God for Kate,* he thought. If he didn't have her . . .

Sometimes, lying beside Kate, he remembered his wife and what it had been like to have her in his arms. But the years were making it harder and harder to do that. There were times when he couldn't seem to recall his wife at all . . . not the way she'd looked or sounded or felt to his touch. It was almost as though she'd never been, and this turned him so cold inside that it usually took the better part of a bottle to make him warm again.

He was still excited about finding Meade's mother when he parked behind headquarters. But just entering the building cooled him at once. The place had the look and smell of an old elementary school he'd gone to, with dark, varnished wood trim, bruised hallways, and high ceilings studded with bits of flaking paint.

Canderro went straight to his main-floor office. His desk was a mess of used coffee cups, messages, and papers spilling out of wooden trays. Flimsy copies of the notes on all calls having anything to do with the William Meade case were stacked on a spindle. That day's collection went well over the fifty mark. Two flimsies were red-flagged and Canderro went over these first.

One note declared that four men had so far admitted to having engaged in sexual relations with Nancy Palewski at least once during the past several months, but none said he had been with her the night she was murdered. Two of the men had agreed to come to the pathology lab to have their blood and semen tested. The other two wanted to check with their lawyers first.

The second red-flagged flimsy said that the owner of a stationery store in Lake Mahopac thought he'd sold a package of Meade's exact pale-blue notepaper to a man who matched the killer's general description—except that the man had gray hair. That could have been a hairpiece of some sort. The reporting detective planned to check every store in town to find out whether anyone else remembered doing business with a lone shopper of Meade's height and build, who in all probability would be a stranger.

The lieutenant scribbled a note of his own. He wanted the photo lab to make up a batch of glossies of Mead with his hair retouched gray and have them distributed locally. Pushing the disguise concept further, he ordered another two sets of prints, the first with just a mustache added to the original, the second with both a mustache and beard sketched in.

He began going through the rest of the memos. Most were reports of people who were sure they'd seen Meade driving by in a car or on a motorcycle and were sending in the license numbers as confirmation. Canderro had a clerk tied up for three hours a day checking them out. Eight women had received threats from anonymous callers who said they were William Meade and who described in full salacious detail precisely what they planned to do to them. There were three accidental shootings by homeowners who mistook late-arriving family members or neighbors for prowlers. Fortunately no one was injured.

Mass paranoia was circulating like the Asian flu.

He barely glanced at the stack of surveillance reports forwarded by the Nassau County and Stamford police departments' stakeout teams on Jenny Angelo and Natalie Bingham. If they contained anything of importance, it would have been on a separate red-flagged memorandum.

Canderro pushed away from his desk and headed down the corridor to his chief's office. By the time he got there, his faded heat had revived.

"I've found Meade's mother."

Chief of Detectives Reagan glanced up from the copy of *The New York Times* he was reading. His face showed nothing. It rarely did. But Canderro picked up on the pulse suddenly going in his temple.

"Where?"

"Wallkill."

"Sonofabitch! Right under our noses. What name?"

"Dorothy Lipton."

"Does she know you've got her made?"

"No. I drove past the house once, just to have a look. That was it."

Reagan nodded. The slight movement of his head was the most extravagant sign of approval he allowed himself.

"I'll need a full stakeout and a wiretap," said Canderro.

"You've got them."

"And better come down heavy on no leaks. Not here, not at Paddy's Bar, and not at home. If even a hint of this gets out, we've blown our best shot."

"Don't worry about it."

Reagan rapped a huge knuckle on the op-ed page of the *Times* on his desk. "Talking about coming down heavy. Have you read your friend Garret today?"

"No."

"He's riding us like a bull with a rope on our balls."

Canderro picked up the paper and scanned Garret's column. It wasn't hard to see what Reagan meant. Without railing or going into specifics, Garret had somehow managed to dismiss the entire police effort to locate and apprehend

William Meade as a consummate exercise in futility. There was no discernible anger. The tone was cool. Yet this in itself just seemed to serve as a further indictment. It was as if the whole existing system of law enforcement was such a disaster, so utterly incapable of protecting the public from life-threatening criminal attack, that there was no point in getting emotional about it. You simply had to cut your losses and start over. As you also had to do, of course, with the current parole establishment. In fact, according to Garret, the two systems of justice were so tightly interwoven in their misconceptions, that the deficiencies of one actually compounded those of the other.

The lieutenant put the paper back on Reagan's desk. He liked and understood Garret too well by now to take this sort of thing personally or even seriously. It was no more, really, than a knee-jerk response to loss and frustration. He remembered his own reaction to losing his wife and child. He had been a madman with a loaded gun on a hair trigger. He should have been locked away. His survival and that of those in his path were miracles. There were no forts, no safe harbors in which to hide your loved ones. When you lost them, if you were lucky, you became merely grotesque.

"At least he didn't name any names," Canderro said.

"He didn't have to. Who in the country doesn't know he means us? And the man's *read*. You wouldn't believe the calls and mail coming in. It's getting to be an embarrassment at every level. Frankie, you know him better than any of us. What's with the guy?"

"He's got the idea he and his wife were murdered for no reason."

"Hell! *We* didn't fucking do it!"

Canderro gave a heavy sigh, shrugged. "I guess maybe he's not so sure we didn't."

The detective called Garret at home that evening and told him about finding Meade's mother.

"Terrific, Lieutenant! That's really great news."

The journalist sounded almost boyish in his excitement. It was the most positive response Canderro had ever heard from him. But then, what had there been for him to respond positively to during the past few months?

"What happens now?" Garret asked.

"We keep it quiet, we watch, and we pray."

"I appreciate your telling me."

"Glad to have something good to tell." Canderro paused. "I know it doesn't always seem that way to you, but we're really giving it our best shot."

Garret didn't let the innuendo pass. "Does my sounding off bother you that much?"

"It don't mean shit to me, Garret. I know where you're coming from. You just do what you have to."

The lieutenant lit a cigarette and blew smoke. "My chief might be hurting some, but to hell with him. A little fire in the hole helps get everyone's ass moving." He paused. "I guess you still haven't heard anything from Harry Stover at Attica."

"No."

"You will," said Canderro.

CHAPTER
18

It was late, nearly 9:00 P.M., but Garret was still in his office, brooding with clouded eyes over his old Royal. He was struggling through a piece that was in favor of the death penalty, and it was a battle all the way—pure emotion slugging it out with the ingrained liberalism of a lifetime. He fought the same battle all over again with each column he wrote.

He was finding himself becoming the eye of a spreading storm, partly because of who he was and his refusal to put his personal tragedy behind him. Mostly, though, it was the lurid nature of William Meade's crimes, and the killer's informing Garret of his latest bloodletting. As might be expected, the scandal sheets were milking the story for all it was worth. GARRET AND WIFE'S PAROLED SEX KILLER IN MYSTIC BONDING. Inspired journalism at its best.

But attention was not limited to the tabloids. The national media had leapt on the story too, and Garret saw his picture and read about himself in *Time* and *Newsweek*. An enterprising *Post* reporter, having somehow identified Benton, Reilly, and Johnson as the commissioners responsible for Meade's release, was pressing for their suspension pending an independent inquiry into their decision. Television minicam units waited outside Garret's apartment almost every morning, and suddenly his face was everywhere. He could no longer walk about his neighborhood or enter a store without being recognized, stared at, and sometimes even approached by those eager to express their opinion.

Everyone had a point, and right now Garret was struggling with his own. He sat back and regarded the two paragraphs he'd just knocked out:

> Contrary to popular belief, imposing the death penalty for an act of deliberate, cold-blooded murder places the highest possible value on human life. When a man, woman, or child is robbed of the greatest of all gifts, life itself, it demeans that stolen life to offer the killer anything less than death as punishment.
>
> This is not an act of revenge on the part of society. It's simply the moral and logical response to the destruction of what can never be replaced. It's also the only way we can be absolutely sure that the murderer never murders again.

He paused and stared dully at the rows of waiting keys. And what if it *were* an act of revenge? Would that be so terrible? Why did morality always have to carry the handicap of a higher code? Why did revenge have to be such an evil word? Damn it! He walked around with a loaded gun. He carried it everywhere. And at this particular point in his life, he could think of nothing that would give him greater pleasure than to aim it at the center of William Meade's heart and blow him away. Greater pleasure than seeing the police capture him? Yes. He had killed small, dark-eyed strangers in Vietnam and merely felt sick afterward. But to shoot this man would bring him nothing but joy. And if this diminished him in some way as a human being, made him a slave to his pain, so be it.

At 9:15 P.M. Hank Berringer came into his office carrying a quart of bourbon and two plastic cups.

"Party time," he said.

Garret was surprised. "What are you doing here so late?"

"Trying to spread a little oil on all the waters you've been troubling lately."

The editor poured two generous drinks. He handed one to Garret, dropped heavily into a chair, and held up his cup in a toast. *"L'chaim."*

They drank slowly and gravely.

"You seem to have hit a mass nerve," said Berringer. "Our mail and calls have tripled since you started, and they're running a good two to one in your favor."

Garret waited for the kicker. When it didn't come, he said, "But . . . ?"

"But we're not running a popularity contest. Also, there are people who think you're taking a lot of cheap shots."

"You mean people like the governor and the attorney general?"

"Yes. Among others."

"And what do *you* think?"

"They're not entirely wrong, Paulie."

"Neither are they anywhere near right. And they're the ones currently in charge of the whole disastrous system. Which I'd say makes their judgment slightly biased."

"And you're totally free of bias?"

Garret sipped his bourbon and felt the pleasant warming work its way down. It took effort, but he remained silent.

"Come on, Paulie. Let's be honest." Hank's voice was soft, his manner reluctant. "What the whole thing comes down to for you is that Emmy was murdered. If she were alive and well today, if it were just Nancy Palewski and some other unfortunate stranger that Meade had tangled with, do you really think you'd be carrying on this crusade against our entire criminal justice system?"

"Probably not. It's too bad but it often does take a personal calamity to get us to do what we should have done a long time ago. We see a dozen screaming malignancies a day. We can't fight them all. But this particular cancer has so far killed Emmy and another woman and almost killed me. So I don't think it's too hard to understand why this should be the one I've chosen to take on."

Garret looked hard at his friend. So many emotions were surging that he felt a kind of dizziness. "What's the matter, Hank? Has Scott Randal been on your back about me?"

"What do you think? He's the publisher. He feels you're becoming an embarrassment to both the paper and him personally. He sees those lining up with you in this. You've got the whole law-and-order, anti–gun-control crowd cheering you on. All the far-right wrong-heads. They're making you their new Messiah. He can't believe that's what you really want."

Garret laughed for the first time in months. "Poor Hank."

"You think it's funny?"

"Considering Scott, yes. I think it's funny."

He knew the *Times* publisher only too well, a supremely public man whose reputation meant everything to him and who was humorless about any threat to it. He thrived on the admiration of his peers, of those who dwelt on the same exalted plane. He'd never run for elective office, yet he suffered acutely of the political disease. He had to be thought well of, admired. And here Garret was tarnishing his noble reputation.

"The governor called Scott at home last night," said Berringer. "Conway's very upset. He feels you're unfairly scapegoating him, making him look little better than Meade's accomplice in the eyes of the public. Remember, Paulie. It's an election year with a close contest going. And we're supposed to be backing him."

"So the boss told you to feed me lots of bourbon and put the squeeze on?"

"The bourbon was my own idea. And all Scott really wants is for you to cut back on some of the damage you're doing."

"I'm not the one doing the damage. Just read a few of the letters coming in from families of those butchered by paroled killers. That'll give you a better idea of where the real damage is coming from."

Berringer said nothing and the office was suddenly as silent as the vacuum that follows an explosion. Garret looked at the editor's tired, aging face. The idealist grown old, weary, and cynical on the job. Issues and principles no longer carried their previous weight. Now it was mostly being practical, making accommodations, and surviving.

With some surprise Garret felt himself grinning. "Don't look so miserable, Hank. It's not the end of the world. You can always tell Scott to buy out my contract and get rid of both me and my embarrassment to him and the paper."

"He's already thought of that."

"And?"

"He's afraid of making a First Amendment martyr of you...turn you into our own personal Saint Paul. You've gone too far with this. You're too heroic, too sympathetic a figure to just cast out. Scott figures that would do him about as much good as you've already done the governor and his benighted criminal justice system."

CHAPTER
19

Warden Gemson called Garret early the next morning to say that Harry Stover was asking for another meeting. The Warden knew no more than that. Garret told him to set it up for 2:00 P.M. that day.

Don't expect too much, he warned himself.

But expectation stayed thick in his throat as he showered, taped the wire pack to his bare chest, and put on his clothes. By the time he phoned Canderro, he'd calmed down.

"You were right as usual," he told the detective. "Stover just asked Gemson for another meeting. I'm seeing him at two this afternoon. Any suggestions?"

"Yeah. Listen a lot and say as little as possible."

"I'm a reporter. That's how I make my living."

"Call me when you know what time you'll be coming back," said Canderro. "I'll meet your flight."

• • •

The warden came around his desk to shake Garret's hand. Just finishing his lunch, he poured the journalist some coffee from an electric pot he kept going.

"Stover's all set and waiting for you," Gemson said. "I tried to pump him a little, but he gave me nothing. He's impenetrable. In all the years he's been here, Meade, his mother and you are the only ones I've ever known to reach him."

"I haven't reached him. We're not even on the same planet. All we're doing so far is some fancy footwork." Garret took in some coffee but found it hard to swallow. "What do your psychologists say about him?"

"They say he's a sociopath, but that's only because they have to call him *something*. His electroencephalograms show normal patterns, he's never been cruel or sadistic in any of his crimes, and he's even expressed remorse and guilt."

"In other words, an all around great guy," Garret said, "except for his just happening to having shot three people dead."

Harry Stover watched Garret without expression as he entered the cubicle, walked to the highly polished wood table, and sat down in what had become his accustomed place. The lined, yellow pad full of freshly drawn, five-pointed stars was in front of Stover and he was smoking one of his Camels. The rest of the pack lay within easy reach. In prison, thought Garret, as in the army, orderliness to the point of ritual was another name for survival.

"Hello, Mr. Garret. My old lady sends her thanks and her blessings for the money and all. She says to tell you you're in her prayers every night."

"Please tell your mother it's my pleasure."

"My mom thinks you're a very smart man. She says maybe

if I hadn't goofed around so much and quit school, I could've been smart like you and not ended up in the shit house."

"You're smart enough, Harry. Smart's not your problem."

Stover nodded, a suddenly thoughtful man making a less than happy judgment. "I guess no luck yet with the log cabin on the lake."

"There are a lot of cabins on a lot of lakes around Liberty."

"I know. It's a real long shot. So I've come up with a better deal. Maybe this one even puts the odds in your favor a little. Interested?"

"That's why I'm here."

Harry Stover fidgeted in his chair. He seemed to be seeking a perfect point of balance.

"This one is all or nothing for us both, Mr. Garret. If you get Billy, I get what I ask. If you don't get Billy, I get nothing. And maybe even end up dead."

"What are you asking?"

"To get out of here."

Garret went empty, as if from a great loss. Unless it was just an opening gambit. Stover knew what was possible and what wasn't. Except that no less an authority on the criminal mind than Canderro had predicted precisely what Stover was asking.

"You know I can't promise anything like that, Harry."

"Sure. But the governor can."

"Why would he?"

"Because he's a politician." Stover's face was serene. It was as though his life to date had taught him to ignore any and all superficial impediments and cut straight to the heart of things. "Billy's just beginning his run. Nancy Palewski's only his second since he's out. Wait'll he really starts rolling. Your wife and Nancy'll seem like foreplay."

"How do you know?"

"Because I know Billy better than anyone living. I listened

to him talk nonstop for seven years. The guy's hooked. He's a bona fide murder junky."

"You mean like you?"

"No. Not like me. I was just a spaced-out kid who was into stickups. Every one of the three guys I killed had a gun in his hand and was trying to kill *me*. Billy kills because it's his high. It's how he gets his rocks off. And the more he gets, the more he needs."

Stover began a new star on his pad. "So you can tell the governor he'd be getting a damn good exchange—Billy back in here or dead, for me out there or dead. And all I really want is a chance to get lost somewhere with my old lady and start new."

"Why would you be dead?"

"Because I'd be the bait to get Billy. That means there's always the risk of Billy getting me before the cops get him."

Garret's eyes widened slightly, then returned to normal. "Go ahead."

"It's simple as one, two, three," Stover said, warming to his subject. "One. You write something in your paper that upsets Billy enough to want to wipe me out. Two. You put me someplace where he's got a chance to do it. Three. The cops get him instead of him getting me."

"Nothing's that simple."

"This is."

"Too much has to depend on Meade."

"Not if you know the right button to push."

"And *you* know?"

"I'm betting my ass on it."

Garret felt his palms sweating. All the moisture from his mouth seemed to have drained to his hands.

"OK, let's hear it. What do I write about that'll make him come after you?"

"Eleven more bodies."

Silence. Garret had to clamp his teeth together to keep from crying out.

"They're all on Long Island," said Stover. "Right around where Billy grew up. And all little kids. He did the first when he was only thirteen. How about that? *Thirteen* years old. Some are boys, some are girls. The sex thing didn't matter to him then. He was just starting out . . . getting the taste, learning. Before the kids, he said he practiced on dogs and cats."

Garret briefly closed his eyes and saw Stover's face swimming behind the lids. "How did you get him to tell you?"

"Straight tradeoffs. You tell me your shit, Billy-Boy, I'll tell you mine. You wouldn't believe some of the crap I dreamed up for him. Like it was a fucking blood-pissing contest."

"He believed you?"

"He knew *his* was true. Why shouldn't mine be? Hey, he *wanted* to believe me. I was giving him a blood brother. Suddenly, he wasn't alone anymore. He had *me*."

"And what did you have?"

"Something that one day might be able to keep me from having to die here."

Garret could do no more than stare across the table. Dig too deep into stuff like this and you struck madness.

"Listen," said Stover softly. "You've got plenty of time to think in this can, so I thought. And a lot of what I thought about was how one day Billy would get out on parole and I'd be left here to rot. So I just tried to figure out my best shot and plan for it."

"You couldn't have guessed everything that's happened since he got out."

"No, but I could guess he'd go right on doing the same crazy stuff he's done since he was thirteen years old. And I could guess that when there was finally enough bodies piled

up to scare hell out of everyone, I'd be in a good spot to talk
some kind of deal. What I *couldn't* guess is that someone like
you would live with two bullets in his head and identify Billy
right off from his mug shot. But that just made it easier. All I
had to do then was wait for the governor to start sweating."

"The governor won't buy your terms, Harry. Besides,
wouldn't Meade figure out you're nothing but bait?"

"Probably."

"Then why would he risk everything, neck included, just
to get a shot at you over eleven bodies out of his past?"

"Because in something like this he's got the blood code of
an old Sicilian don. I mean, he has this genius brain except
for where a few small parts are missing and this can make
him fucking crazy. Like, I've seen him cut throats of cons
over these little asshole things that didn't mean crap."

Stover lit a cigarette and averted his head as he blew
smoke. "But it was a lot more than that with these kids he
did. They were like the bottom of the barrel for him, as if
what he did to them made even him want to puke."

"Did he ever tell you what he did?"

"Sure he told me. He was never one to leave out details.
But you don't want to hear it."

"It was that bad?"

"Better believe it. And it still bothered him. He couldn't
stop thinking and talking about it."

"What did he say?"

"All kinds of flaky stuff. You know, about how the kids
screamed, or how it felt to hear it, or what their eyes looked
like, or the color of their blood in the sun, or the looks on
their faces afterward. It was like he was reciting poetry or
something. Like he almost *had* to, even though it made him
sick." He stared at the table. "The thing is, Billy told me to
make sure I never breathed a word of it or he'd feed me my

balls sliced in cereal. He always laughed when he said it, but I knew he wasn't joking."

Harry Stover's back was arched like a gymnast's. "So you don't have to worry about him not coming to do me. Just speak to the governor. If he says so, all you have to do is write in the *Times* how you heard some con was making a deal to take the cops to this old boneyard of Meade's on Long Island, and you can be damn sure Billy-Boy won't miss the party."

They sat quietly in the windowless cubicle under the bleak prison light.

"Just a couple more things," said Stover. "If it's done, it's gotta be done smart. No armies of cops. Maybe three or four state troopers and a few locals, that's all. Billy's crazy but not crazy enough to go up against fifty guns. He's gotta think there's at least a *chance* he can get me." Stover paused to study his collection of doodles. It seemed to please him. "If he does get me, Mr. Garret, my old lady gets a bonus of a hundred big ones. I want to make sure she lives nice out in Arizona."

"I don't have that kind of money, Harry."

"That's okay. I don't expect it from you. I figure the governor can always tap his campaign collection."

Five hours later, Lieutenant Canderro laughed at the comment when he heard it on Garret's recording pack. He agreed with Harry Stover. He considered the hundred thousand a legitimate political expenditure.

"My advice is to play the tape as is for the governor," he told Garret. "The whole thing couldn't be presented better. Even if Conway turns it down—as he probably will—he'll at least have it to think about on cold winter nights."

CHAPTER
20

New York governor Stephen Conway received Garret in his study, a walnut-paneled room in a somber, old-fashioned mansion. It was just after 10:00 P.M., and the governor, a big, once-handsome man who was not aging well, appeared worn and tired in rumpled shirtsleeves. His major problem was the dark, heavily ringed bags under his eyes that looked even worse on television and gave caricaturists a field day drawing him as a dissipated raccoon.

"Good to see you, Paul." He shook Garret's hand and lightly squeezed his shoulder. "So what are you bringing me tonight? Cancer?"

It was said with a smile, and Garret accepted the wry greeting as part of Conway's automatic bluff heartiness. The governor had sent a personal note of condolence at the time of Emily's death and Garret had responded to it. But they hadn't spoken until Garret called that morning and requested a meeting without saying why. It was a mark of their long and generally cordial relationship that Conway had not even asked for a reason.

"No cancer," said Garret. "But maybe a shot at a possible cure."

Conway looked directly at him. Unusual. More often his eyes didn't quite meet those of the person to whom he was speaking. "You've got something on Meade?"

"I've been up to Attica three times in less than two weeks. I've been talking to Meade's old cellmate, Harry Stover. A lifer. I'd like you to listen to a tape of yesterday's meeting."

Conway's broad features seemed to waver. "Is it going to add to my problems or cut them?"

"It depends on how you react. It could be either or both."

"I don't think I want to hear it." Conway sighed, poured some Napoleon into two large snifters, and handed one to Garret. "When I get a bit of this into me, you can start your dog and pony show."

The governor's congenital smile was back. It was how he negotiated, dealt with friends and enemies, handled either joys or sorrows. It was a mask that Garret had never seen completely moved. But it did start slipping a little as they sat drinking.

"I guess these aren't the best of days for you," said Garret. "I'm sorry if I seem to be making them worse. It's not deliberate."

"Don't you think I know that? I've started to call you a dozen times and always changed my mind. What could I say? 'I'm sorry as hell about Emily but get off my back'? Things have been a lot worse for you than for me. I don't know how you get through something like that. I doubt whether I could. I guess you've got to be strong."

"It's not a question of strength. You just do what you have to and try not to let it get you from the inside. At least that's what works best for me."

The governor took a deep swallow of brandy and leaned back in his chair. "I'm probably as ready as I'll ever be. Where's the tape?"

Garret picked up a leather case beside his chair and took out the tape.

"I haven't edited or cut anything. You'll be hearing our whole conversation just as it was. You may not understand some of the early references, but they're not that relevant and I'll explain anything you want to know later. The tape runs for just twenty-eight minutes so I'd rather you hear it straight through, without interruption. It sets a certain mood. It's better if it's not broken." Garret paused. "Any questions before we start?"

"Just one. Why am I so nervous?"

"Because you're the governor, you hold the power of life and death for more than a few people in this state, and nervous is pretty much what you should be."

Garret set the tape rolling and began what was to evolve into a twenty-eight–minute rite of passage for his audience of one. At the end, Conway certainly appeared to be something other than what he'd been at the beginning. His showcase smile was gone, he seemed to have aged years, and his usually florid expression had taken on the yellow-gray cast of the terminally ill.

He got up and refilled his snifter before he spoke.

"What are you trying to do to me, Paul? You know I can't sanction something like this."

"Why not?"

"Because it makes a mockery of our entire system of justice."

"Please, Stephen. Spare me the campaign rhetoric. Our

justice system is already a mockery. Our only consideration here is whether the thing will work."

"And you think it will?"

"It's wild, labyrinthian, but I think it has a chance."

"You want me to take this risk on the word of a stickup artist and three-time killer?"

"What kind of risk?" said Garret. "You're sending a prisoner out under guard to find eleven bodies and trap a multiple murderer. At worst, we end up with no bodies, no murderer, and the prisoner back in his cell. At best, we hit the jackpot and put a one-man killing machine out of business. Where's the downside for us?"

"Not for *us*. For *me*."

A man suddenly in motion, Conway swirled his brandy as he paced the room. "I'm the one who'll be setting loose a convicted killer."

"Only if we get William Meade. And if we do, it'll be the best deal of your life."

"Maybe."

"Why maybe?"

"Because today's best deal can end up as tomorrow's worst disaster." The governor stopped pacing and stood very still in the center of the room. "What if ten months from now Stover goes on one of his stickup sprees and blows away half a dozen people in the process? Who's going to think about William Meade while the blood's being mopped up? The only thing they'll remember is that I was the moron who turned Stover loose, and from then on I'm finished. And don't tell me we can keep it quiet because we both know we can't."

Garret was silent. There were no arguments against that, just a weighing of risks and rewards.

"I'm sorry, Paul," Conway said after a few moments. "I'm

sorry I can't do what I'm sure in your mind is the honorable thing. I guess I've been worrying about my political ass too long to go and stick it out now." He shrugged, the weight of the world on his shoulders. "I'm afraid I'll just have to play it safe."

"What's safe? Letting Meade go on raping and killing?" But the governor's eyes had already closed it out.

CHAPTER
21

CHAPTER
21

Tommy Lukens was doing his searching systematically. He'd drawn a rough map of the area to scale, marked the exact spot where he'd found the white Honda abandoned, and each time headed out from there in a different direction. This afternoon marked his fifth try in the past week, with the whole thing beginning to seem like some new strain of virus he'd caught and couldn't shake loose.

It had started for him the instant he went back and found poor Nancy lying all spread out there in the woods, eyes open and staring, and as dead as she was ever going to be. Although he hadn't cried in years, he'd cried then.

When the first news reports said the body had been discovered and that the killer was William Meade, it had put him into instant panic. So much so, that he'd actually started to drive toward the nearest police station. Then he had stopped and thought more calmly.

What was he trying to do? It was too late to do anything for Nancy. Now there was only his wife, his kids, and himself to think about. And once he went to the cops and told his story, that would be the end of his little family. Jessie would walk right out and take the kids with her. She'd told him as much the last time she'd caught him fooling with another woman. The smartest thing he could do was just forget about it. Meade was the only one who'd seen him with Nancy that night, and when the cops finally found him—he hoped—and blew him away, that would be the end of the whole mess.

Except that he couldn't forget about it. Couldn't forget Nancy, a gentle, decent person whose only flaw was a tendency to get mixed up with guys like him. He wondered why Meade had let him go in the first place and not shot him right along with Nancy. Was it some sort of sick game he was playing, a flaky way of amusing himself by waiting to see what he'd do? Had Nancy told Meade his full name and where he lived? Would the guy just show up at his house one night and do him, Jessie, and the kids all together?

The first night his family was home from Providence, he lay awake in the dark with an old army Colt .45 under his mattress while he listened for sounds. He felt Jessie's warm body beside him, imagined his children asleep down the hall, and went weak at the thought that he may have put everyone in the world he really cared about at risk. And for what? To get his rocks off? He should have his head examined. Yet who could have expected anything like this to happen?

The next day Lukens had called the Motor Vehicles Bureau, made up a possible hit-and-run incident involving a white Honda with the plate number he'd copied, and learned without surprise that the car had been stolen. It was then that he began his searching.

He sold paper products in the Hudson Valley area for a national wholesaler, and his time was pretty much his own. So fitting in an extra hour or so a day for his personal needs was no problem. He'd concluded that Meade had probably walked home from where he left the Honda, unless he used a bicycle stashed somewhere in the woods.

In either case, Lukens figured Meade to be holed up no more than a mile or two from where the Honda had been parked, and that assumption formed the basis of his search plan. Thinking of the Honda's parking spot as the hub of a wheel, he was simply following each of the wheel's spokes outward for a distance of two miles. If he hit what appeared to be a possible hideout for Meade, he'd make an anonymous call to the police with its exact location. Then if the cops didn't botch things up, Meade would be history.

This afternoon, with the sun just starting to slip from its zenith, Tommy Lukens was following his small pocket compass due north by northwest through a stretch of woods he had not been in before. He'd changed into jeans, a T-shirt, and hiking boots and left his business clothes in his car. He was comfortable in the woods and sometimes went after small game with a .22, although he rarely bagged anything. He enjoyed just being there. Carrying the small-bore rifle added a sense of purpose. Today, he didn't have the rifle, just the old Colt stuck in his belt under his T-shirt. He didn't expect to use the automatic. He didn't even have a license for it. But he liked the feeling that came from knowing it was there.

Tommy checked his watch and saw that he had been walking for twenty-three minutes. Which meant he'd covered about a mile. He would stay on this course for another mile, then if he saw nothing he'd go west for five hundred yards and head back toward his car. He had a factory account near Ellenville that he was due to call on at four o'clock and he needed time to change back into his good clothes and drive over there.

Ten minutes later he came out of the woods and onto a narrow blacktop running east–west. It was an old road, badly broken up and obviously little traveled. On impulse he walked west on it for a few hundred yards, feeling the warmth of the sun after the coolness of the forest. About to head back south, he noticed a rough opening in the brush to his right and pushed into it, seeing the opening widen slightly and the weeds and grass pressed down as though by the wheels of a car.

Once more Lukens was out of the sun and into the shade of the forest. This time there was mostly pine, with dried brown needles forming a cushion underfoot and the ground leveling out into a vague trail that traveled upward for a while, then crested and sloped downhill. It was an entirely different world, an older stretch of woods with the sun breaking up in the tallest tips of the ancient pines, so that only tiny speckles of brightness were able to reach as far down as the path. Lukens assumed it to be one of the many long-abandoned logging trails that crisscrossed the area. Yet there was definite evidence of more recent use in the flattened weeds and snapped-off tree branches on either side.

About half a mile farther on, he saw the glint of water through the trees, and moments later there was the roof of a house. His pulse suddenly throbbing, he edged forward until he had a clearer view. It was actually an old log cabin, well built and sturdy as a small fort, with a great stone chimney rising at one side and a sparkling lake close behind it.

There were no signs of life, no evidence of occupation or recent use. Tommy saw no power or telephone lines, no trash or clutter of any sort. Weeds and grass grew unchecked to almost window height. *False alarm*, he thought. And breathing more easily, he started around toward the far side. Still, there remained enough of a flutter in his chest to make him take the .45 out of his belt and flick off the safety.

What he had thought was the back of the cabin was actually the front, and there was a small porch with an overhang that faced the lake. He climbed the two steps to the porch and tried the doorlatch. It was unlocked. He quietly opened it, stepped inside, and felt something cold and hard press against the back of his neck.

"Don't move, Tommy."

William Meade's voice was quiet, easy, supremely matter-of-fact.

Lukens braced himself for the impact and shock of the bullet. It didn't come.

"Put on the safety."

His hand shaking, Lukens did as he was ordered to do. *I'm going to die right here and no one will ever find my bones or know what happened to me.*

"Now drop the gun."

For an instant Lukens considered taking his chances on a quick turn.

"Don't even think about it, Tommy."

The Colt hit the rough planking with a clatter, and Meade kicked it to the far side of the room.

"Sit down right where you are."

Lukens bent his knees and eased himself onto the floor. The fact that he was still alive and Meade was being so careful sparked a flash of hope. He had no idea why. There was just the feeling that if Meade wanted him dead, he would have killed him the instant he walked through the door. He could feel his heart going, yet he felt himself suffocating. He opened his mouth wide and took in air. He had a sudden fear of throwing up.

Meade walked around him, picked up the Colt, and put it

inside his belt. He was wearing cutoff, faded jeans and nothing else. His arms and upper body were lean, hard muscled, and bronzed from the sun, and he was holding the same si- lencer-lengthened revolver that Tommy remembered from their original meeting. Meade's movements seeming oddly slow and tired, he pulled up a chair and sat down facing Lukens.

"I guess you know who I am by now."

Lukens nodded. He was afraid to trust his voice.

"How did you know I was here?"

"I didn't. I've been looking for five days." Tommy swallowed dryly. "I just stumbled on the old trail and followed it all the way. Even when I opened the door, I thought the place was empty."

"How did you figure out where to look? I could have been anyplace. What made you pick this area?"

Tommy felt himself dripping sweat. He was trying so hard to think, to be sure he didn't say the wrong thing, that his mind went blank and he couldn't think at all. When he tried to speak, he stammered something unintelligible.

Meade took a bottle of scotch from a shelf, splashed some into a glass, and handed it to him. Then he sat watching him drink. "Easy, Tommy. Just tell me the truth and you'll be OK. Take your time. There's no rush. But please don't lie to me. Now let's try again. What made you pick this area?"

"I . . . I didn't go home that night when you told me. I hung around and followed you. Then I lost you but found where you left the Honda. After that I drove back and found . . . Nancy."

"And then?"

"And then I . . . well"—he fought to keep the trembling out of his voice—"then I figured you had to be holed up somewhere you could have walked to, so I just started looking."

"After first checking the plates on the Honda?"

"Yeah."

"Why didn't you go to the police?"

"You know why."

"Because of your wife?"

"I've got a couple of kids, too."

"Great." Meade wearily shook his head. "And what did you plan on doing if you found me? Blow my head off with your big forty-five?"

"Hey, I'm not that crazy. I've never shot that thing at anyone in my life. I don't even think I could. I figured I'd just make an anonymous call to the cops, say where you were, and leave the rest to them."

Meade was silent.

"It's the truth. I swear to God."

"I know."

Tommy Lukens stared blankly into his drink. "What I don't understand is why you let me go in the first place. When I heard on the news who you were, I couldn't believe you just let me walk away like that."

"I never expected you to be any kind of threat to me, Tommy. And no matter what you've heard or read, I don't just go around shooting people for the hell of it."

"Then why did you have to kill Nancy?"

Meade appeared to consider it a valid question. "I had my reasons. But it's too complicated a thing for me to go into right now."

Drinking his scotch, Lukens heard the glass rattle against his teeth. *Jesus, put the fear away and think,* he told himself. *The way he's talking, maybe he hasn't decided to do you yet. Maybe you still have a chance. Keep cool and goddamn think.*

"Anyway," said Meade, "you've just given us both a more

immediate problem. Now that you've done such a terrific job of finding me, what the hell am I supposed to do with you?"

Lukens groped for words but none came. All he seemed capable of producing at that moment was sweat and the smell of fear.

"Who knows you've been looking for me?" asked Meade.

Tommy improvised a kind of voice. "Nobody. Who could I tell?"

"Who knows that you were fooling with Nancy?"

"I couldn't tell that to anyone, either. Why would I even want to?"

"Because you're obviously a guy who likes to chase tail, and talking about it afterward can add to the kicks."

"Not if you're married and have two kids."

"Your wife and kids didn't stop you from screwing another woman. Why should they have stopped you from talking about it?"

"I guess I'd rather screw than talk."

Meade laughed and Lukens felt such a surge of hope at just the sound of it, that he almost went limp on the floor.

"What about our little Nancy?" said Meade. "Maybe she liked talking about it with her friends."

"No. She wouldn't have said anything either. She was engaged to another guy. They were supposed to get married next month."

"Ah, yes. So I read in the paper."

Wryly amused, Meade rose and poured himself some of the scotch. Then freshening Lukens' drink, he sat down once more.

"Let me tell you a few of the realities, Tommy. Right now the police know a bit more about what went on with Nancy than you might think. Semen tests have already told them there were two men inside her the night she died. They don't know yet that you were the other man, but they're very busy trying to find that out. They're doing this by bringing in every man who might have dated her these past few months to submit to a DNA test. So if just one of Nancy's or your friends even hints that you've been with her, you're going to be called in for testing. And once that happens, your little secret is out."

An overwhelming feeling of sadness mingled with Lukens' fear. He felt as if a great weight were pressing down on his chest.

"How do you know all this?" he asked.

"I know police procedures. But since you haven't been called in so far, I guess you did keep Nancy to yourself." Meade frowned. "Where did you leave your car?"

"Right where you left the Honda the other night."

Tommy looked at the gun in Meade's hand and saw his own death played out for him in full color. With his shirt running red, it suddenly became too much. "Please let me go," he begged. "I swear I won't tell the cops anything. I'm not rich but I'll give you whatever I've got. I give you my word. Let me go and you'll never have to worry about me again."

"I'm not worried about you, Tommy. I'm just sorry for you. I'm sorry for your wife and children, too. They don't deserve what you're bringing them. But it really wouldn't make any sense for me to let you go. Not now."

Meade finished his drink. Then he got up and started once again for the shelf where he kept his bottle of scotch. As he passed behind Lukens, he swung his gun in a short arc at the back of his head. The butt hit with a dull thump just behind his right ear. Tommy grunted once, went over on his side, and lay still.

CHAPTER
22

Canderro sat perched on the trunk of a fallen tree, watching the back of Meade's mother's house and shivering in the predawn darkness. About twenty yards to his right, a member of his regular stakeout team huddled in some brush, no doubt wishing he'd gone into another line of work. A short distance up the road that passed in front of the house, another plainclothesman sat, half dozing in a fake utility-company repair van with one-way windows.

The lieutenant was wearing a windbreaker, but it had rained earlier and he was soaked. The patch of woods where he was located crested a knoll about a hundred yards behind the house, and Canderro was able to see into several lighted rooms. But the lights had been on all night and the rooms were empty. Still, they didn't feel empty to him. There was a strange sense of invisible life, of people unseen yet still present.

What am I doing here?

As abruptly as that, expectation turned to doubt. If it ever got out that he'd conducted an unauthorized search. . . . Suddenly he felt like an actor trapped into playing a part intended for someone else, someone more experienced in lawlessness, in breaking and entering, and therefore better equipped for the role. Someone like William Meade.

Canderro watched the sky slowly lighten. He loved this time just before the rising of the sun, with the shadows fading to soft grays and the mists breaking. Growing stiff, he shifted to a standing position behind some brush. Things were clearer now, and he could see a bird feeder and a redwood table and chairs in the backyard, and a black automobile in the driveway. Then for the third time in the past hour he took out his service revolver, checked the chambers and slid the gun back into his holster. His rosary. Logic told him there was little chance of his finding Meade inside his mother's house, but logic had become so distorted for him lately that he found himself ignoring it. He certainly had paid no attention to rational judgment yesterday in following one of his own men who was already following Mrs. Lipton's big black Cadillac in the faint hope that she'd lead him to her son. A pathetic waste of time, effort, and manpower. But the worst of it was that he was becoming impatient, and that could be dangerous.

At 8:35 Mrs. Adele Meade, aka Dorothy Lipton, came out of the rear door of her house, got into her Cadillac, and drove off.

Moments later Canderro signaled to his man in the brush, left the woods, and approached the backyard of the house. He was out of sight of the nearest neighbors, who were about two hundred yards to the right and behind a line of tall hemlock. Using a plastic credit card, he slipped the latch on the back door and quietly entered the kitchen. He drew his revolver and stood in the center of the tile floor, listening.

Other than for the steady hum of the refrigerator, the house was silent. Then with his gun extended in front of him, the detective went down into the basement and began his search from there.

He did it slowly, carefully, moving upward from one level to the next. He didn't lower the revolver for an instant. This was still Meade's mother's house. As he probed every dark corner and, with a bracing movement, opened every door, Canderro wondered if Adele Meade had abandoned her son as she appeared to have done, or rather, given him comfort and shelter when no one else would. He hoped the house would offer him the answer.

It did.

It started in the closet of the second-floor bedroom with the discovery of an old Boy Scout uniform, cleaned, pressed, ready to wear, and complete with a sash-filled collection of merit badges that reached all the way up to Eagle Scout. Canderro wondered how many old ladies Meade was helping to cross the street *these* days.

But the uniform proved to be only the beginning. As it turned out, particles of William Meade were everywhere—in drawers, bureaus, cabinets, and attic trunks. Literally, the upper part of the house seemed to be a museum to his memory. There were awards, news clippings, letters, certificates of commendation, all meticulously logged in scrapbooks. Even school report cards were chronologically arranged from the first grade on. Every one. And there was nothing but *A* after *A* after *A*. Canderro wondered what would have happened if the kid had ever brought home a *B*, God forbid. The sky probably would have fallen. If his mother had, indeed, buried him, the one thing she obviously hadn't buried was everything he'd once been.

Kneeling on the attic floor, Canderro opened and stared

into the last of the storage trunks. He no longer saw individual items. It was more a sense of the whole that now pervaded him. Its effect was calming, as if this, finally, was how things were, and there was nothing that he or anyone else could do to change them. He had rarely known such calm. Yet he knew it was a false security in much the same way as the midnight quiet of a deep forest was false. Because if you ever stood alone in a wood and really listened, you'd find a whole world of screaming, living sound beneath the silence. You just had to adjust your ears to the new pitch.

Canderro made the adjustment. Wherever William Meade was at this moment, his mother knew about it. That fact was now established. Holstering his revolver, the lieutenant left the house the same way he'd entered it.

His two men remained in place, one in front, one in back. A third man was following Mrs. Meade's Cadillac.

CHAPTER
23

Sundays at home were the worst, so Garret left his apartment at about noon, had lunch at a local restaurant, then went to a light, throwaway movie on Third Avenue. When that was over, he spent an hour strolling through Central Park—until the sight of so many couples sharing the soft, glowing end of the day started to become too much, and he thought it best to go home.

He'd finished eating his frozen fish dinner and was just pouring a brandy when the telephone rang.

"Mr. Garret?"

It was a woman's voice. He thought he recognized it, but rejected that particular possibility as too remote. "Yes?"

"This is Jacqueline Wurzel. I hope I haven't called at a bad time."

"Not at all. How are you?"

"Just fine, thank you." There was a pause. "No, that's not true. I'm really not fine. Sometimes I answer in conditioned reflexes. As a matter of fact, I heard some unsettling news a few hours ago. That's why I'm calling."

Garret said nothing. It had taken him years to learn to handle silence, and it still required effort. The wire hummed as he waited.

"Would you happen to be free this evening?" she said. "I'd really like to talk to you and I don't enjoy the telephone."

"Where are you calling from?"

"Midtown."

Garret told her where to meet him in an hour. That would allow him at least forty minutes to let his brandy do its work.

They were in a small bar on East Seventy-fifth Street where it was pleasantly dark, no one knew or recognized him, and a middle-aged piano player sang the kind of vintage songs that made it possible to believe that people over thirty had once lived with love.

Their first drinks carried them past the initial uncertainties and polite, ritual sparring, and Garret began to feel like a shipwrecked sailor in the lull between storms. The heavens would soon tear themselves open again, but for now the calm was wonderful. Jacqueline had not yet gone into why she'd called, and Garret felt no need to press it.

Then as suddenly as that, she broke the spell.

"I had a phone call earlier today from a friend inside the State House," she said. "The governor is planning a news conference for tomorrow afternoon. He's announcing the suspensions of Benton, Reilly, Johnson, and me, pending an official inquiry."

Garret sat unmoving. He let go the faintest of sighs. "An official inquiry into what?"

"Into the poor judgment of the three commissioners in recommending William's release. And into my own obviously dangerous lack of perception as his parole officer. I know the governor's taking a beating in the polls and has to appease the voters, but it still hurts."

"I'm sorry."

"Why do you say that?"

He looked at her.

"You're not sorry," she said. "And you shouldn't be. I know you told me it was the system you wanted punished, not the four of us as individuals. But I'm afraid I don't really believe that."

"What *do* you believe?"

A waiter brought fresh drinks—straight vodka for Jacqueline and another brandy for Garret—and she waited for him to leave.

"I believe there's still a part of you that feels we're all personally to blame for William's murdering your wife and almost murdering you. Now you're back from the grave to extract payment."

She smiled, but it was forced. "It has an almost operatic ring, doesn't it?"

Neither of them spoke and the piano filled the silence with a warm, soothing ripple. For the first time in months, Garret felt himself capable of a positive human response. How long could you thrash about in darkness?

"There's something else I want you to know," she said. "Since all this started happening, I think about you almost constantly. And do you know what I think mostly? Of how jealous you've made me."

"Jealous? Of what?"

"Of all you've lost. Of your near obsession with it. Of the kind of feeling you and your wife must have had for each other."

Garret took some brandy. He glanced at Jacqueline's eyes, but they showed more than he felt he had any right to see, and he studied his drink instead.

"I'm thirty-six years old," she said. "I've had a fair number of relationships—even been married once. But I can't think of any man I've been involved with who would have carried on for me the way you've been doing for her."

"That's no great bargain, either. Do you know what it is to live with anger and take pleasure in nothing?" Garret paused. "I'll be honest with you. Sometimes I wish we'd never had all that much. The hole it left might have been easier to fill."

Her eyes flashed brightly. "Don't talk like that," she said. "You don't know what you're saying. At least you had it. All that joy was actually there. Everything you felt and remember can't ever be taken away from you. The worst, the absolute bottom, is never to have had it at all."

Jacqueline slowly circled the rim of her glass with the tip of a small finger. The act seemed to absorb her so totally that she might have been tracing her life.

"You may as well know something else," she said. "Along with a husband who didn't last, I also had a little boy who wasn't around very long either. I named him Max, after my father. Which turned out to be a mistake because all it brought him was my daddy's lousy luck."

Her eyes found Garret's and grabbed hold. "I had him just shy of four years, but I wouldn't trade those four with him for an extra fifty without him. You asked if I knew what it was to live with anger and take pleasure in nothing. Well, the answer is yes. I *know*. But I still wouldn't give up even a piece of what we had to cut my losses."

They sat there like two old prospectors, partners, going broke after a lifetime of searching. Garret was almost afraid to move or speak. It might throw off a delicate part of the mood.

Jacqueline evidently had no such fear.

"When we finish this drink, would you please take me home?"

"Is something wrong?"

"No."

Yet looking at her, he saw that the delicate, fleshy tip of her nose had turned pink and her eyes had a washed-out look that threatened to spill over the lids. Garret felt a new kind of emptiness in his stomach. Then, because he was neither a fool nor inexperienced in such things, he motioned the waiter for the check.

It was only a short cab ride to the converted East Side brownstone where she lived, and they covered the distance in silence. Ascending in the brownstone's tiny, brass elevator, Jacqueline stood staring straight ahead while Garret tried not to think of anything but the moment. At her door Jacqueline fumbled so long with her purse that Garret had to take it from her, find the key, and open the door.

She turned to him. "Thank you for seeing me. I appreciate it. Even though it's all so embarrassing."

"Why should you be embarrassed?"

"Because I guess I'm not nearly as liberated as I like to think."

"You mean, your calling me really bothers you that much?"

She nodded.

"Why?"

"Because when I think about it... well, there was an almost desperate quality to my calling that bothers me."

"That's foolish."

"I know." She smiled but it was forced. "But foolish or not, we can't help the way we feel, can we?"

"I guess not."

They stood looking at each other.

"How about if *I* call *you* next time?" he asked.

"That would be great."

"You wouldn't think I was desperate?"

"No."

"Well, you'd be wrong."

She was able to smile more naturally this time. "You're a nice guy, Paul."

"Not so nice lately, but maybe I'm improving," Garret said with a grin. He gave her a peck on the cheek and said good night.

Then Jacqueline went into her apartment, and Garret rode the tiny brass elevator to the ground floor.

He never left the building. Three minutes later, he was right back upstairs, ringing her bell.

Jacqueline opened the door almost instantly. "What did you forget to tell me?"

"That this whole thing is crazy. That we should both be long past the point of playing these idiotic mating games."

She didn't so much as blink or move. She glowed so brightly he felt the warmth pass right into him.

"Please," he said. "May I come in?"

"Of course."

He didn't even see the apartment. He saw nothing but her face.

"How much time, how much ritual do you need?" he asked. "Whatever it is, I'll try to give it to you."

"You don't have to give me a thing. Just your being here, just your needing to come back is enough."

Sudden doubts pressed him. "I could be cheating you.

Sometimes I feel like an empty goddamn husk. There may not be that much left."

"I'll be the judge of that," she said. She took one step toward him and stopped.

"Listen, I don't care if you do blame me for being blind to William, I don't care how much you despise our less than perfect system. All I care about is your being here. Sometimes I think every word I've said, every move I've made since we met was for no other reason than to make you want me."

He found her cheek against his, her body close, her scent out of a barely remembered dream. He had never believed in any mystic loyalty to the dead, and yet he felt a new and cold uncertainty. Emmy entered it.

"I want nothing from your wife." As though responding to his feeling, Jacqueline's whisper was directly to his ear. "She's part of you. What can I take from her?"

Not a thing, Garret told himself.

In bed, with his hands on her, life came back to him from a long way off. The past months had devastated him, left him all but dead. He'd felt, at times, without mind and heart. It was as though a clot of burned-out ash had formed in his lungs and made it impossible to breathe. But he was breathing now, taking the air from her lungs into his, feeling the separate parts of her body gather to match his own. Emmy was still Emmy; his loss, his anger, just as great. Still, he'd had enough of endings. If there was one last beginning left somewhere inside him, let it be used now.

Because they were in a rear bedroom and kept a small lamp burning, William Meade was able to see them from the fire escape. A part of him had expected all this to happen, but not this soon. It was the speed that was the big shocker.

The need, the fire, had been that great. That in itself was terribly exciting to him.

My Jacqueline.

He'd long imagined her body. He'd aroused and punished himself with his fantasies of how it would be. Yet he had remained unprepared for the reality. It was exquisite. From the sculptured perfection of her breasts, to the full, graceful curves of her hips, to the lamplighted sheen of her flesh itself, it was music. And Paul Garret had it all, every millimeter. He missed nothing. Why should he? It was a world without restraint. *His* world. And in a swift rush of emotion, Meade despised him for it.

How could she?

It shattered him because he knew then that he could never really have her. All such dreams were over for him. Of course he could have her sexually anytime he chose. But only once. Then she would be gone like the others. Which was how it would finally have to be. There was no other way. Yet he'd hoped for so much more. Hadn't she reached out for him? Hadn't she looked at him in a way that went far beyond words? Hadn't their spirits touched?

Or had he just been deluding himself? That was possible, too. It could happen if you wanted something as badly as he'd come to want her. But not with his Jacqueline. Never. Christ knew he'd gazed into the eyes of enough women in his life not to have been mistaken with the one he wanted most of all.

So she'd played him false, teased and cheated him. She had reduced him to this, to cowering in the dark on a third-floor fire escape, watching another man take joy and solace in her flesh. But the worst of it was that he no longer had any clear vision of himself, of what he was or even hoped to be.

He was like an eyeless apparition, groping blindly, changing form at will, but always wanting.

It was after midnight by the time Meade arrived home, but one of his lanterns was still on and its light shone warmly through the trees. He parked in his usual place behind a cluster of bushes and approached the cabin with a vague feeling of expectancy. For the first time something human was there waiting for him.

He opened the door quietly.

Tommy Lukens was asleep on the floor beneath the sink. He lay curled in the fetal position, with his left wrist handcuffed to one of the sink's cast iron legs. Everything that he might have needed during the more than twelve hours Meade had been gone was within easy reach. There were books and magazines, packages of sliced bread and luncheon meat, cans of beer and soda, a covered waste bucket, a lighted Coleman lantern.

Meade stood considering him. *And on simple earthly pleasures he was bent.*

Tommy opened his eyes, saw Meade standing above him, and groaned softly. "For a minute I thought the whole thing might have been some kind of dream."

"It was. It still is. At least that's what my father believed. He was always singing 'Row, row, row your boat gently down the stream. Merrily, merrily, merrily, merrily, life is but a dream.' That dumb little kid song was at the heart of his philosophy. Except that when he finally came out of his dream one day, he was just dead."

Tommy's eyes brightened. He seemed to find cheer in the mere fact of Meade's having once had a father. "Were you and your father close?"

"Sure. I was crazy about him." Meade picked up a can of

beer and popped it open. "You have children. Aren't they crazy about you?"

"Jesus, I hope so. But it's hard to tell with kids. They've got all this strange stuff going on in their heads."

Meade drank his beer. It was warm but felt sharp and clean going down. Everything inside him was still awash from before, and the talking helped quiet him.

"What's it like being a father?" he asked.

"How do you mean?"

"What does it feel like? When you look at your kids, what goes through your mind? Do you think, 'These little people are little pieces of me. They *are* me—we're one and the same'? Or do you think of them as separate? When they do something wrong, do you blame them or blame yourself for having made them that way?" Meade paused. "And what about death? How does being a father make you feel about dying? Does it make you feel better because you know you'll go on living in them, or worse because you'll have to leave them and never be able to help and love them again?"

Tommy Lukens stared at Meade in the lantern's glow. The sudden stream of questions seemed to have startled him, somehow added to his fear. "I don't even think things like that. I mean, my kids are just there. And there's no way I can see myself waking up one morning and their not being there. It would be like opening my eyes one morning and finding my arms and legs gone."

Meade's eyes were flat. "When I was a boy, I used to think a lot about having children. I couldn't imagine anything more important in life than being a father. Now I just thank God I never became one."

No one spoke for a while and there were just the soft night sounds coming through the windows.

"You know, I don't understand you," said Lukens. "You

don't seem like . . ." He struggled to phrase it. "Like you'd do the kind of stuff you've done."

"You mean I don't growl, spit blood, and carry a pitchfork?"

Tommy shook his head, sighed. "I've been here now— what?—a day and a half and I'm still alive. Which I never expected to be when I walked in and felt your gun on my neck. You even went and called my wife to tell her I was OK. You sure didn't have to do that."

"You promise to repeat those nice words when they bury me?"

Lukens' face was solemn. "You think they're going to get you?"

"Of course. It's just a question of when and how."

Meade's voice was quiet, without expression. He might have been discussing tomorrow's weather.

"Aren't you scared?"

"When I let myself think about it."

"How could you not think about it?"

"Hell, sooner or later everybody dies, Tommy. Birth is a terminal disease. But everyone doesn't walk around thinking about it all the time. With me it's just going to be sooner than later."

"Maybe they'll just send you back to prison."

"Not if I can help it."

"You mean you'd rather die?"

William Meade's smile was easy. "I look at it this way, Tommy. Dying can't be all that bad. So many have managed it and never come back to complain. It's our great equalizer, the most democratic act we have."

CHAPTER
24

At his desk, Canderro went over the seemingly unrelated sequence of events. Taken separately, they meant little, appeared to be just random bits of the general flow of information that entered any urban police headquarters. But pieced together, they obviously added up to something more.

First, there had been the young woman, a Mrs. Thomas Lukens, coming in to report that her husband, a local paper-products salesman, had left their house in Pleasant Valley early Saturday morning to call on several of his accounts, and so far hadn't come home. Late Saturday night, however, Mrs. Lukens did receive a telephone call from an unidentified male who told her not to worry, that her husband had not been harmed in any way, and would return home very soon. Before she could question the caller, however, he hung up.

The detective who'd questioned Mrs. Lukens reported her as having said the caller was polite and well spoken and kept assuring her that her husband was safe. Mrs. Lukens said, too, that her husband often kept irregular hours, but that nothing like this had ever happened before. If he did find he had to be away overnight, he'd always call himself. It was the anonymous caller who worried her most.

The second incident took place approximately twelve hours later when a couple of youngsters, out playing in a patch of woods near Stone Ridge, reported finding an over-turned sedan lying in a gully and covered by branches. There were no plates on the car, but the engine number identified it as being registered in the name of Thomas Lukens of Pleasant Valley, New York. The investigating officers found no particular evidence of foul play, nor were there visible signs of high-speed impact. According to the officers, the car appeared to have been eased into its present position in a deliberate attempt to keep it out of sight.

The day after these happenings were featured in the local news, a call came in from a man who asked to speak to Lieutenant Canderro.

"I've just heard about this Tommy Lukens thing," he said. "I think there's a chance I might know something about it."

Canderro switched on a recording device. "Who's this speaking?"

"I've gotta know something first, Lieutenant. Can my name be kept out of this?"

"You mean you want confidentiality?"

"Yeah."

Canderro signaled one of his men to get a trace going on the call. "No problem."

"It's not that I've done anything wrong. I just don't want people bothering my family with a lot of questions."

"I understand."

"If it's OK, I'll be there in about twenty minutes."

"See the desk sergeant when you come in. He'll expect you. Now what's your name?"

"Reams," said the man. "Fred Reams."

Canderro saw him approaching his glass-enclosed cubicle half an hour later, a still-young man with the build of a one-time athlete going to fat. There was perspiration on his forehead, and his palm was wet when they shook hands. The lieutenant was used to people being in that condition when they were in his office.

"I've never been in a police station before," he said.

"You're lucky. I have to be here every day."

Reams' laugh was nervous and Canderro got him some coffee to help settle him down. He also pressed a button in the desk drawer that started a tape rolling.

"Just relax, Mr. Reams. Now exactly what's your connection to Tom Lukens?"

"We work for the same company, Excelsior Paper. We sell, and every once in a while we have a few drinks together and talk. We're not real close friends or anything, but we've got stuff in common. Know what I mean?"

Canderro nodded.

"We're both married, got a couple of kids apiece, work hard, and take our paychecks home. Which doesn't mean we don't occasionally take advantage of opportunities that come up. Nothing serious, understand. No threat to wife and family. Just something new here and there to keep the blood pumping. Anyway, Tommy and I sometimes talk—compare notes, you might say."

Reams paused and mopped his face with a handkerchief. "One of those 'opportunities' I mentioned? Well, a few weeks ago she went and got herself murdered."

The lieutenant's eyes widened. "Nancy Palewski?"

"Yeah."

"What did Lukens tell you about her?" Canderro's pulses were racing but his voice was unchanged, his breathing steady.

"He said he was with Nancy in her car one night when this guy shows up with a gun, joins in with them for a threesome, then tells him to get lost."

"Meade let him go just like that?"

"Yeah. Except that Tommy didn't know it was Meade at that point. He didn't know that until he heard the news reports the next day. The girl didn't know either. In fact, she was so taken with the guy, Tommy said, that she seemed happy to be staying with him."

"And Tommy left and went home?"

"He left but he didn't go home. He walked to his own car and stayed hidden till Nancy's convertible passed. Then he tailed it until Meade dumped it a short distance away. The guy then took off in a white Honda and Tommy followed it down 684 and then off an exit. He lost sight of it for a while, but when he spotted it later, it was empty and there were no houses around. So he took down the plate number and went back to try and find Nancy. He found her, all right."

Canderro was hurriedly scribbling notes on a pad. His thoughts were so far ahead he couldn't keep up with them.

"Tommy called the registry the next morning and found out the car had been stolen. He felt like shit, but going to the cops wasn't going to accomplish anything but bust up his family. I was the only one he could tell and he made me swear not to say anything. But when I heard he was missing and his car was found in the ditch, I knew I had to call you."

"What do you think happened to him?" said Canderro.

Reams' beefy face was still pouring sweat. "I *know* what happened to him. He's lying dead in the woods somewhere."

"Why?"

"Because he couldn't leave the damn thing alone. It kept eating at him. He spent every spare hour tramping through the woods, looking for someplace where Meade might be holed up. I figure he finally found him and took a bullet for his trouble."

"How did he know where to look?"

"He had this theory that Meade was no more than a mile or two from where he left the Honda that night. So he used that as his starting point and each day headed out from there in a different direction."

"Where was the Honda left?"

"Damned if I know."

Canderro checked his notes. "When the Honda was on 684, was it traveling north or south?"

"I don't think Tommy ever said."

"Did he say how far or for how long he followed it?"

Reams shook his head. "I'll be honest with you, Lieutenant. I thought this whole search of his was so far off the wall I never really paid that much attention to the details."

"Did he take a gun with him while he was searching?"

"Yeah, he had a Colt with him. But he said he wasn't crazy enough to try to take Meade if he ever found him. His plan was to just make a call to you guys and tell you where he was."

"Anything else you can think of to tell me?"

"I wish there was." Reams' tone was depressed. "Are you going to tell Tommy's wife any of this?"

"No. She's carrying enough as it is. And there's nothing here to make her any happier." Canderro looked evenly at Reams. "Just make sure you keep a lid on your own mouth. I wouldn't want you becoming a possible target yourself. And if any more of those opportunities come up, spend a few bucks on a motel. You'll find it's a hell of a lot safer than the woods."

CHAPTER
25

The girl was alone in a booth at the rear of the cocktail lounge. She sat very still, reading a book and drinking. But it took William Meade no more than ten minutes to have her spotted as a hooker. It was nothing overt. He just knew. And he liked it. For some reason the whole concept of being a whore—a true, no-nonsense professional sex peddler—appealed to and aroused him tonight.

Standing at the bar, which was packed mostly with singles, he watched her so intensely with his pale, depthless eyes that he might have been trying to memorize her. She was blond, with the kind of pert, uniquely American good looks and full body that seemed to make her a combination of the legendary Marilyn and the girl next door. *Jesus.* Just straightening her skirt she did a little hip wiggle that carried enough built-in eroticism to run afoul of most state obscenity laws.

When Meade was certain she'd become aware of him, he ordered two double scotches and carried them over to her table.

"I hope you're drinking scotch," he said. "Because that's what I've brought you."

The girl had to lift her head to look at him. What she saw was a tall, lean, attractive young man with fair, sun-streaked hair, a carefully groomed beard and mustache, and wearing what conceivably could be the most expensive designer's slacks and sports coat in the place.

"You did fine. That's just what I'm drinking." She smiled at him with white, beautifully capped teeth and a plastic sort of cheeriness. "But what took you so long?"

"I was trying to figure out if I could afford you."

"What did you decide?"

"I'll sell my car if I have to."

That seemed to hit her perfectly and she laughed. Meade slid into the seat opposite her. He breathed her perfume and liked it. The scent was of crushed flowers.

"Since you can afford Ralph Lauren," she said, "you can afford me."

"Give me your most gentle price."

"Five hundred dollars."

"Is that for a week?"

"I'd kill you in a week. But you should be able to make it through a night."

"I'm a sucker for a woman with that kind of confidence."

"So?"

"So I guess you're all mine," he said. "I'll just have to cut back on lunches for a while."

She opened her mouth and showed him the tip of a moist, pink tongue. Then she slowly circled her lips with it until Meade felt his initial excitement starting to soar. A pro was a pro.

"There should be laws against you," he told her.

"Haven't you heard? There are. Probably the oldest laws

on the books. It's just that no one has ever been able to enforce them."

Then they just drank their scotch and locked glances. Her knees touched his under the table and Meade felt a thrill of anticipation travel to his groin.

She must have felt his eagerness because she said, "Would you like to go now?"

"Let's finish our drinks."

Meade enjoyed stretching it, drawing it out. It was part of the foreplay. He loved the ambience of the crowded singles place itself, the steady rock beat pumping from the speakers, the bursts of laughter rising above the bright chatter, the almost ritual mating dance of warm, nubile bodies.

"It might help me get rid of my shyness if I knew your name," he said.

Her eyes crinkled. "You're too much, lover. Just call me Bunny."

"*Bunny.*" Meade echoed the word. "A small, soft, warm-bodied creature noted for its ready affection, frequent mating habits, and lack of harmful intent."

"That's me."

"When did you turn pro?"

"A few years after getting tossed out of Bryn Mawr. I got sick of crawling to Daddy for handouts."

Meade gave a mock scolding look. "Hmmm, what would Daddy think of you now?"

She shot him a glance. "Hey, my mother's holier-than-thou society friends give it away more often and less discriminately than I sell it. I'm not ashamed of what I do. If I was, I wouldn't be doing it."

She took a sip of her drink. "But enough about *me*. What's *your* hangup?"

He said nothing but his stare cut straight through her.

"No offense," she said, "but young, good-looking types like you don't usually pay for it unless they need something special. So you might as well know right now, there are some tricks I just don't do."

"Like what?"

"Like bondage, beatings, ream jobs, or any of that sado-masochistic garbage."

"Don't worry. That's not what I need to turn me on."

"What *do* you need?"

"Just you."

At a certain point Meade suddenly found himself thinking of it as an exciting, totally involving ritual. He'd never considered it quite that way before, yet why not? If there could be ceremonial rites marking births, deaths, and anniversaries, why not ritual sex?

Their stage was the bedroom of Bunny's apartment, a veritable hothouse of living plants and flowered wallpaper, all breathing at them from wall, floor, and ceiling. An exotic, tropical jungle in the normally temperate zone of New York State. A minute after arriving, Bunny had come out of her clothing as though out of a chrysalis, and Meade marveled at her transformation from spoiled, rich-kid whore to accommodating nymph. She lent herself so naturally to the lewdest of acts that she became more and more innocent in his eyes as they progressed.

The thing was, Bunny was a girl who took genuine pride in her work. She was inspired and challenged, as if to be with him here was less a duty than a chance to display her erotic gifts. She had skills in abundance, jack-of-all-trades versatility, and that was how she finally made love to him: something from column A, something from column B, then a change of positions. She was a warm, perfumed, smooth-skinned animal, gliding from one feeding trough to the next and still coming back for more.

While at the same time and above and beyond it all, Meade remained dimly aware of the Mozart she had playing in the background. Hey, the kid had class.

With the room a warm grid of remembrance, they drank champagne and nibbled the caviar and crackers that Bunny had thoughtfully provided. Her mood was subdued, reflective, that of a good hostess whose own needs lay solely in providing for the pleasures of her guest. They sat in the glow of a bedside lamp, their still-naked bodies creating the only true sense of intimacy that remained. The sex itself, its sensations, could not be recalled. No mark of it was left in the brain. Only the fact that it had happened.

Meade felt a grudging and unexpected respect for the girl. She labored alone and without apology in an ugly, treacherous field, asking no favors, adapting herself to each new situation, doing her little erotic stunts on demand. He tried to imagine all those she touched so briefly and intimately, but they remained beyond his reach.

As he lay regarding her, he noted with approval her high, pointed breasts, narrow waist, and full, round bottom that seemed to move to a beat of its own when she walked. The lamplight was good for her, adding a tint of purple to her cheeks and turning the circles under her eyes to hollows of glamour.

"When did you first start realizing you were beautiful?" he asked.

"I'm not really," she said, meaning it. "I just happen to be your type."

He smiled when she said that. "Well, you carry yourself like a beautiful woman. It's what hit me when you first walked into that bar. Your bearing, the line of your back, the way you held your head as though you were two feet taller than any woman in the room. I wanted you right that minute."

"Before you knew you could buy me?"

"Before I even heard your voice or said a word to you. Which is the only true test of a man's response to a woman. Just that first sighting. The rest is nothing but trimming."

Consciously paying court to the girl, Meade saw her responding. Curious. A whore and a rapist-killer in a sweet little postcoital *pas de deux*.

As Bunny took him to her, he heard Mozart giving way to Brahms in the background. It was a soft mix of melody, with each note sounding so clear and appropriate to what was taking place on the bed that Meade was ready to believe the composer had written it with just this in mind.

Without losing a beat, he rolled over so that she was above him. Another small ceremony of possession. He saw their reflections in a mirror—hers, with the pale gleam of porcelain; his, with the deeper, warmer cast of bronze. They were beautiful together, a pair of classic sculpted pieces that Meade watched with the hard, concentrated stare of a voyeur at a live sex show.

Suddenly trembling with excitement, he reached over and switched off the only light in the room.

"You like it better in the dark?" she whispered.

"Right now I do."

There were blinds on the windows and the room was totally black. Meade groped for and found his automatic under the pillow where he'd placed it earlier. Just holding the gun added energy to his thrusts. He groaned and felt his heart flutter with anticipation.

"Come on, baby, come on!" Bunny urged.

Riding him, she might have been the lead jockey heading

into the final stretch. She was coming on rough and lewd now, her language out of the streets, her voice and body straining. Whore words, whore cries. But whether they were for her own needs or for what she thought were his, Meade neither knew nor cared. He was beginning his own run, his own slide to the edge. A high-wire balancing act. A little for her, a little for him, then more of the same with the tempo picking up and his gun in one hand and her wildly pumping butt clutched in the other.

Careful, not quite yet.

Steady.

She's yours but just hold it for a second.

Wait for her.

Wait or you've lost it.

Then he heard her cries become one long shout and he felt her taking him with her.

Now! he thought and brought the gun up under her chin and squeezed the trigger.

He heard the soft whooshing sound of the silencer and felt her go into spasm as the bullet rose through her brain. And along with it, he felt the exquisite godlike sensation of his own life pumping into her as she went. Then tracers of light shot through his head like pieces of sun and all he could do was scream.

She lay facedown on him, unmoving, the warmth of her flowing sweet and wet over them both. He saw nothing in the darkness, but he had no need for sight. Filled with the miracle of it, he knew it was *his* miracle, *his* creation. Every instant of it—from the perfect setting of the mood, to the split-second timing, to the final convulsive grasp of her inner musculature—was simply transcendent.

And the delicacy of the balance?

Jesus. If he'd fired even a fraction of a second too soon, he would have ended up cold and alone in a tomb. If he did it the same flashing measure too late, the heavens would be closed when he arrived.

Yet how to describe it when it all came out right?

To whom?

To yourself.

He doubted that it could be done.

Still, if you could believe a moment possible in which . . . if you were able to imagine all such things in combination, then maybe you could offer yourself at least some small idea of what this could be like.

He smiled. The poet of terminal sex. Or . . . the supreme joy of coming while killing.

But his wry humor didn't fool him for a second. The pride he felt was unassailable. In all the world he remained unique. Who else could ever have conceived, much less carried out and experienced such a thing? Who else but he would have dared? He was cutting his mark deep into the earth.

He was William Meade.

It took him no more than half an hour to shower himself clean, put on his clothes, acquire his usual small souvenir, and walk out of the ground-floor apartment. His car was just a short distance from Bunny's in the building's parking lot. He checked his watch as he drove away. It was 2:43 A.M.

Five minutes later he stopped at a roadside phone, dialed Paul Garret's number, and heard Garret's voice answer.

"Tell me something, Mr. Garret. When the phone wakes you at this hour of the night, do you know at once that it's going to be me at the other end?"

"Yes."

"How does it make you feel?"

"Like I want to throw up."

Meade laughed. "Isn't it nice that we can be so honest with each other?" He paused briefly. "I have another one for you, Mr. Garret. Tell Lieutenant Canderro she's in apartment one-C of a place called Kenmore Gardens. That's on Route Eighty-two, not far from Millbrook. I hope you believe me this time."

"I believe you." Garret's voice suddenly sounded hoarse, weary.

"Sorry I can't chat. But the seventy-second mean trace time is almost up, so I'd better get moving. Incidentally, I'm glad you're writing again. I never miss a column. Good night, Mr. Garret."

Meade hung up. The call had lasted exactly sixty-four seconds. Time to spare.

The phone still in his hand, Garret lay rigid and sweating in the dark. In his mind the new, still anonymous woman was lying on the bed beside him, her hair streaming blood onto the pillow, her eyes staring blindly at the ceiling. Somehow he could not get himself to turn in that direction. What he finally did manage to do was reach over and feel the sheets where he had her stretched out. The sheets felt cool. They were empty.

In need of something else to think of, he thought about Jacqueline. He pictured her face and body, imagined her voice, heard the sound of her laughing. It took effort not to call her. About ten minutes later he was composed enough to switch on the bedside lamp and dial Canderro's home number.

All he got, however, was his answering machine. So he tried Poughkeepsie Police Headquarters and was given Kate Venturi's number, where he did reach the lieutenant.

"Looks like Meade's done it again," Garret told him.

"I know. Trace and Tape beat you by seven seconds. I was just getting dressed."

"I should be able to get there in about two hours."

"Why don't you just take it easy, Garret. You don't have to put yourself through all that crap."

"Yes I do, Lieutenant."

It was close to 5:30 A.M. and still dark when Garret drove up to the scene of William Meade's latest murder.

He parked near the first barricade, behind the assorted police cars and vans with their revolving lights and crackling radios. Toy cops stood about like lead soldiers, the colored lights popping on and off their uniforms. People in nightclothes and various stages of undress leaned from windows of the apartment complex or stood outside in clusters. Their voices were hushed out of respect for the dead and this sudden reminder of their own mortality.

A uniformed sergeant motioned to him as Garret approached a wooden barricade. "Lieutenant Canderro told me to watch for you, Mr. Garret," he said.

The officer took him into a ground-floor apartment and left him there. Sensing his own nervousness, Garret struggled to remain still. In the bedroom police photographers were flashing lights and detectives were dusting for prints and taking measurements.

Garret stood in the living room. He saw Canderro through an open doorway and glimpsed a naked body on a bed. Blood was all over the body and bedsheets. It screamed at him and he wanted to scream back. He saw a bullet hole in the ceiling with red and gray matter spattered around it. The glare of lights was painful. He drifted into the kitchen and sat down at a table. Canderro found him there about half an hour later.

"Let's get some air," said the lieutenant.

They went out the back door and followed a path into a patch of woods. It was just getting light, with an orange sky showing through the trees. Canderro lit a cigarette and bent the match before tossing it away.

"Her name was Bertha Thompson," he said. "People called her Bunny. Meade picked her up in a singles joint a few miles from here. The barman said he was wearing a beard and hotshot designer clothes."

"Had he ever seen him there before?"

"He said no. Not looking like that, anyway."

They walked in silence.

"I'm afraid he's picking up steam," said Canderro. "This stuff builds on itself and he's getting real hot. This is his first shot at actually picking one out of a public place."

"I'm hoping it might also turn out to be his first mistake."

The detective looked at Garret. "How's that?"

"Maybe it'll pressure the governor to hit the panic button and go for the Harry Stover deal."

"Wishful thinking."

"Probably," said Garret. "But what else is there?"

CHAPTER
26

Once, in a heavy thunderstorm, Garret had watched the creation of a small flood. The rain had come down in sheets, forming rivulets on the hillsides. The rivulets rushed toward a stream that ran alongside a road. The stream swelled and gurgled as it poured over its rocky bed and climbed its banks. When it finally broke free and roared across the road, it had no idea it was not the Mississippi River.

Garret remembered this as the media first trickled, then gushed, then finally roared full blast with the news that William Meade had raped and murdered for the third time. The number itself appeared to add to the deluge. One rape-murder was a tragedy and two were doubly so. But when you hit three, you had entered the realm of the mythic. Unseen forces suddenly were at work, and this was something the waiting, watching public found irresistible. Also, because the number three automatically conferred on Meade the special status of a bona fide serial killer, there was the tacit promise of more to come.

The news stories themselves were handled in predictable fashion: banner, front-page headlines from the *News* and *Post;* smaller, more dignified print and headings from the *Times.* Much was made of Bertha Thompson's monied upbringing. The girl's father, one of the state's major developers, was supposedly in mourning at his estate in Chappaqua. Within hours of the tragedy the family had issued a statement decrying the senseless loss of a young, beautiful woman destined for a promising career in music, and calling for authorities to hunt down the vicious killer. Not even the *Post* speculated on how the unemployed Bertha had managed to make a living.

Later, Garret read with fresh interest about a roving *News* reporter who told of a rising tide of fear and anger among those he questioned: fear that their lives were becoming more and more vulnerable to random violence, and anger that a convicted rapist-killer with an unexpired prison term of up to thirty-two years had knowingly been set free to continue his raping and killing. There was little in any of the news reports that Garret didn't already know, but he read them with an addict's compulsion anyway, sensing in them the potential for an explosion that would somehow rebuild the world anew.

Garret woke from a sound sleep. It was the middle of the night and he saw his bedroom dark and felt Jacqueline beside him. He had no idea what had wakened him until he heard her cry out, then cry out again. He held her until she came out of it.

"Bad dream?" he whispered to her cheek.

"God, yes."

Her flesh felt cold and damp under the sheet and she was trembling.

"Well, it's over," said Garret. "Want to talk about it?"

"No. Not yet."

"How about a little brandy?"

"Just hold me. Please."

He pressed her closer, as if his role was to make them one. Maybe it was.

After a while the trembling stopped and he heard her sigh.

"I'm sorry I woke you," she said.

"That's why people sleep together. So there's somebody around to rescue them from their dreams."

"I can't seem to shake off what happened to that girl. Not even asleep. I just can't stop thinking about her."

Garret was silent. She was still carrying Meade on her back like a ton of rock. Each new victim added to her load.

"What the bartender told Canderro about the girl maybe being a hooker," Jacqueline said, "that's new for William. Do you think it means anything?"

"Sure. It means he's becoming an equal opportunity killer."

She groaned softly. "That's awful, Paul."

"You didn't know I was such a funny guy, did you?"

"There's a lot I don't know about you." She kissed him. "But I'm learning. Just give me time."

Garret lay there. In the dark the ceiling of air above his face seemed miles high. He held Jacqueline tightly but felt her moved by something beyond him, of which he was barely a whisper. Even together, they were alone.

CHAPTER
27

When the governor's phone call finally came, it came to Garret's office and surprised him, although he'd been thinking of little else for almost two days. It was a core moment. Just hearing Conway's voice, Garret saw every object in the room leap into suddenly heightened clarity. It troubled him that it should mean so much.

"Understand this," said the governor. "I haven't changed my mind. Long term, it's still against my better judgment. I'm still worried about Stover sticking it to me somewhere down the line. But I've decided to try for the quick fix anyway."

"I think it's the right move, Stephen."

"Right or wrong, I'm going for it. Even Helen's been on me." Conway paused. "What kind of timetable are you figuring on this?"

"Maybe four or five days. I can't be more exact until we get into specifics."

"Well, whatever authorization you need, you've got. I'll dictate something and fax it to you when we finish talking. Set it up with the warden, the state police commander, and whoever else you think necessary. I don't want any blow-by-blows. My blood pressure's not up to it. Just call me when the sonofabitch is either dead or in custody."

Conway sighed. "Preferably, all things considered, dead. Good luck, Paul. It's all yours."

The governor hung up and Garret stared thoughtfully at the phone.

It's all yours.

Stover's grim tales of death, Meade's unknowable responses. How many potentially lethal judgment calls?

Garret did some quick thinking, made the necessary phone calls, and set things up for that afternoon.

Then he took a noon flight to Rochester and arrived at Attica two hours later for a meeting alone with Harry Stover.

The lifer was waiting in their usual place. But this time Garret had arranged for a pot of coffee, no guards behind the one-way glass, and no hidden bugs or cameras. This time, too, Garret reached over and shook Stover's hand as he sat down.

"We're doing it, Harry."

Stover sat unmoving. "No shit?"

"The governor called this morning."

"He OK'ed it all?"

"Whatever you asked for, you've got."

The doe eyes glistened. "Thanks, Mr. Garret."

"Thank your Billy-Boy's latest. She's what did it."

Stover lit one of his Camels and blew smoke. Whatever was happening inside him stayed there.

"When do we go?" he asked.

"We started talking this afternoon. I just wanted a minute alone with you before we meet with the others."

"Which others?"

"The warden, Lieutenant Canderro, and the state trooper who'll be handling security, Captain Brentkoff."

"You mean the guy who's supposed to keep Billy from blowing me away?"

Garret nodded.

"And who's going to keep the captain from blowing me away if Billy doesn't?"

They sat looking at each other across the table. Garret searched for something in Stover's face that he could see into, but found nothing.

"Come on, Mr. Garret. We both know it's a lot simpler and safer for the governor to bury me than set me free."

"That's how much you think of Conway?"

"Hey. He's a fucking politician, ain't he?"

Garret refused to touch it.

"So what I'd like from you," said Stover, "is your word I don't get it up the ass from the guys in the Smoky the Bear hats."

"How do you know you can trust *me*?"

"Because I know."

"I won't be there when the shooting starts."

"You don't have to be there. Just tell 'em in advance you don't want the coroner digging any bullets out of me that's not Billy's. That'll take the piss out of 'em. Will you do that for me, Mr. Garret?"

"You can count on it, Harry."

"I don't really like the whole operation," said Captain Brentkoff. "There's no margin for error. If our security's too tight, Meade don't show. If we go in too loose, Stover gets hit. But since that's what I've been handed, here's how I see it."

Brentkoff shuffled his pages of notes, a wiry man with cold blue eyes and a voice like chipped stone. They were in the warden's office, each of the four men clutching his coffee like a steaming pacifier. *Without it,* thought Garret, *half the Western world wouldn't get through a day.*

"Since we'll be flying one of our own planes to La Guardia," said Brentkoff, "Meade's got just three possible strike openings. During the drive from the prison to our Genesee Barracks airstrip, on the trip from La Guardia to the body site, or he can be hidden and waiting on the burial ground itself. For my money, his best shot would be the last, using a high-powered rifle and scope sights."

He turned to Harry Stover. "All you've given us so far is that the bodies are supposed to be someplace on Long Island. *Where* on Long Island?"

"On the North Shore," said Stover. "Manhasset."

"Be more exact. I've got to have three sharpshooters in place hours before we get there."

"Billy said there's a deep stretch of woods on the west side of Searingtown Road between Northern Boulevard and the Long Island Expressway. You go into the woods at the entrance to a religious retreat... Saint Ignacius. From there you walk straight west for about three hundred yards till you see a giant oak, bigger than any other tree around. Billy said the kids are buried around the oak in a circle that's like the face of a clock. One kid is planted on every hour except twelve, where Billy put a cat so the kids would have a pet to play with. He said from the tree trunk to each kid is maybe twenty feet."

Brentkoff was writing everything down as Stover spoke. Watching him, Garret saw the trooper's mouth tighten into a thin line. Then the room was quiet and everyone sat very still, as if the lifer had been reciting some sort of black prayer that had invoked images too awesome and terrible to deal with.

"What I'm planning on," said the captain, "is three cars from the prison to the Genesee airstrip, and three cars from La Guardia to Searingtown Road in Manhasset. The lead and rear cars will be unmarked and manned by a plainclothes driver and two sharpshooters. The target car in the middle will be plainly marked as an official state police cruiser, and I'll be in it with Stover and two uniformed troopers. The intervals between all cars will be kept in the hundred-yard range."

"No helicopters?" said Lieutenant Canderro.

"I'm afraid of them, Lieutenant. No matter what fake markings we put on them, Meade would have to know they're ours and keep away."

"What about route coverage?"

Brentkoff consulted a penciled diagram. "There's really only one practical route from here to the airstrip, so Meade won't have to figure out which way we're going. He'll know. He'll also know there are seven stop signs and three underpasses along the route, and a gate check to halt us for a minute at the airstrip. We're planning on two hidden marksmen at each of these points. The routes from La Guardia to Manhasset are too many and too complex for reasonable coverage, so we're forgetting about them."

Just listening, Garret was fascinated, infused with the sharp sense of craft that was so integral to something like this. The secret joy of knowing one thing well.

But there were still things Garret did not understand.

"A couple of questions," he said. "Why do we assume Meade's going to know you'll be flying Stover from the Genesee Barracks airstrip? And how can Meade expect to get to Stover while he's squeezed inside a car with three armed troopers?"

Warden Gemson said, "Meade was here at Attica for nearly eight years. He knows our procedures. The Genesee airstrip is standard for us when we're transporting prisoners long distances."

Brentkoff took over to answer Garret's second question. "There are a lot of ways for a resourceful assassin to kill a man in a car. Even a well-guarded moving one. If Meade can get his hands on a few grenades, Molotovs, or tracer shells, he can blow up our nice shiny police cruiser and incinerate the four of us in seconds. More risky, of course, would be pulling alongside and spraying machine bullets or heavy-gauge shotgun charges at close range, with almost equally effective results."

"Are you using body armor?" Garret asked.

"We'll all be wearing Kevlar vests under our shirts. But they're not much good against head shots, explosions, or gas fires. Still, the odds are strongly in our favor, not Meade's. That's if he shows up at all. Which is another thing I'm not too hopeful about."

Again, the room was so silent that Garret seemed to hear it as a ringing in his ears.

Then Lieutenant Canderro spoke to Brentkoff. "I'm in regular touch with the New York and Nassau County police. What do you need from them at La Guardia, along the route, and at the site?"

"Not a thing. Just make sure they keep clear of all three areas. I don't want any patrol cars or individual cops blundering around at just the wrong moment. That's a *must*, Lieutenant."

The trooper looked at Garret, his ice-blue eyes almost luminous against his sun-browned skin. "The rest is in your hands, Mr. Garret. You're the one who has to suck Meade into this. You're pretty sure he'll be reading your piece?"

"I know he will."

"How can you be so certain?"

"The last time he called, he said he never missed a column."

"And you believe him?"

"He hasn't lied to me about anything yet, Captain."

Brentkoff considered the answer for a moment, then nodded.

"I'll put the piece together tonight," said Garret, "and make sure it's in tomorrow's editions. So if we allow Meade two full days to brood, work himself up, and plan his moves, that brings us to a Friday morning takeoff time."

He glanced around. "Anyone have a problem with that?"

No one spoke.

"Then one final point," said Garret. "If we do get Meade, Harry Stover here goes free. That's the deal. Which means I'll accept no hits on him by friendly fire as accidental, and I'll make sure it's prosecuted all the way as murder one. I suggest you pass that word on to each of your sharpshooters, Captain."

Brentkoff went red on top of his tan. "I resent the hell out of your implication, Mr. Garret."

"That's OK. Resent it all you like. As long as you don't forget it."

Harry Stover's eyes, being those of a mandatory lifer, showed nothing.

Garret initially thought of it as perhaps the single most difficult and important piece he'd ever written or would ever have to write. In itself enough to bring on a terminal case of writer's block.

Still, once he was at it he saw everything instantly, recognized how to spin this particular web of deception. It involved, of course, writing unsubstantiated reports of things that no reputable journalist would credit and that no newspaper with the stature of the *Times* would be likely to print.

Garret wrote that an anonymous but usually reliable source at the State Correctional Facility at Attica was promising shocking new revelations out of William Meade's past that would surpass in horror anything yet known about the serial rapist-killer.

He declared that the new information came from a convict, a lifer, with whom Meade was known to have shared the closest possible ties for more than seven years. Although never stated in so many words, the inference was clear that a long-term homosexual relationship had probably existed between the two men.

Among the more appalling aspects of these promised disclosures, Garret stated, were the tender ages of Meade and his victims at the time these crimes took place. The first of these killings reportedly had been committed when William Meade had yet to celebrate his thirteenth birthday.

Garret was careful to point out that to date, all of these statements were merely the unproven allegations of another prisoner. But Garret's source had reported, he wrote, that plans were currently being worked out to allow Meade's longtime prison confidant to lead authorities to a Long Island burial site.

When asked what had made him suddenly come forward with this grisly information, the lifer was alleged to have said that it had all finally gotten to be too much for him. He further claimed that the good Lord Jesus Christ came to him one night in a vision and said that if he didn't unburden himself of the terrible secret he'd held for so many years, even He wouldn't be able to save him, and he would burn in hell.

The religious reference was good, Garret thought. If anything would arouse Meade to the required killing rage, it would be Harry Stover's cynical faking of a holy visitation as an excuse for cutting himself an advantageous deal with the authorities.

Then to pour more fuel on what he hoped would be Meade's by-now flaming sense of betrayal, Garret threw in reports that the serial killer's Attica connection had already established his credentials as an informer by secretly directing police to the remains of two previously undiscovered bodies that Meade had buried years ago in a Dutchess County field.

He thought hard about the final question, which was whether to actually name the day that the informer would supposedly be brought to Long Island. He didn't want it too obvious. But neither did he want it to be so subtle that Meade might be late in figuring it out or miss it entirely. Yet why play games? Whom did he think he was fooling? Meade would know it was a setup regardless of how artfully the bait was camouflaged. So it didn't really matter. Meade was likely to make his move under almost any conditions.

"Rumor has it," Garret wrote, "that early this Friday morning will be the time chosen for the possible unearthing of the victims' bodies."

Reading the piece over, Garret thought it felt right. And it was strictly a feel effort. How else could it be done? Where would he find the journalistic precedents to draw on?

He edited and retyped it. Then knowing that Hank Berringer was working late that night, he walked into the editor's office and dropped the piece on his desk.

"This is for tomorrow," he said. "Would you read it, please?"

Berringer peered at him over his half-specs. "You mean now? This minute?"

"Exactly."

"You think it's that bad?"

"Just read the damn thing, Hank."

Garret eased into a chair. Then he watched the editor's face settle into its usual brooding lines as he picked up the cluster of pages and started to read.

My good friend.

He had none better. Yet he felt curiously strange around him lately, as if the central thesis of his life lay in so entirely different a direction these days that they barely spoke the same language anymore. How odd that he would feel a closer involvement with people like Canderro, Stover, and even William Meade than he did with this man who for years had been the next best thing to a brother to him.

Berringer finished reading and put down the four neatly typed manuscript pages.

"No wonder you wanted me to read it," he said. "I can almost hear Scott screaming in advance."

"And you?"

"Me? I'm just wondering when you decided it was OK to start playing God."

Garret was silent.

"What do you think you're fooling with, Pauly? People die at this sort of thing."

"People are already dead. All I want is to keep more from going."

Berringer got the Jack Daniel's out of his desk drawer, poured two good belts, and handed one to Garret. "Don't bullshit *me*. The only thing you want is to get Meade."

"Same thing."

"Not if a lot of cops and this Stover character get tattooed with bullets, while Meade goes dancing off into the sunset."

"That's not how it's going to be."

"You've got some kind of contract?"

"I've got the governor and the state police."

Berringer swallowed some bourbon, sighed, and slowly shook his head. "I must hand it to you, Pauly. You do have a way of getting things done. Even if they're the wrong things."

"What about the column?"

"What about it?"

"You going to give me problems?" asked Garret.

The editor looked at him with a kind of despairing reproach. "Why should I give you problems? You've already got double your fair share. And my gut feeling is that you're about to get yourself a lot more."

CHAPTER
28

William Meade picked up some groceries and a copy of *The New York Times* in Kingston that morning. In his paunchy, middle-aged mode, he wore his horn-rimmed glasses, iron-gray hair and mustache, and dark business suit with the easy certainty of a man who knew exactly who and what he was, and had no quarrel with any part of it.

As he drove home, the newspaper lay faceup on the seat beside him, but he did not so much as glance at a headline. He was saving it to read later, as he lay stretched out in the sun. It was one of the small ritual pleasures that he looked forward to each day. His stimulant. The excitement of seeing his name in print, of finding everything he did recorded in the most minute detail, seemed to grow rather than fade. Right along with the obviously equal excitement of the public, he thought, whose fascination with violent, sexually oriented death was clearly endemic to the species.

Meade hummed his favorite early-morning Vivaldi. It was

246

not a long ride from Kingston to the cabin, and even driving well below the posted speed limits he was home in fifteen minutes.

He parked behind some brush. Then he made his routine search of the immediate area and carried his groceries and newspaper into the cabin.

"Welcome home," said Tommy Lukens.

Handcuffed to the sink, Tommy nevertheless appeared happy and relieved to see his captor. And it was not an act. Each time he was left alone in the cabin, he suffered the very real fear that Meade might be shot to death somewhere in a police ambush, leaving him here to die undiscovered. In the worst of his visions, he saw himself as a forlorn cluster of bones surrounded by small piles of dried excrement. "Please," he'd beg whenever Meade left the area. "Take good care of yourself." Anchored in truth, the few words of caution had become a touch of dark humor they shared.

The remainder of Lukens' fears had been at least partially allayed by his not only still being alive and undamaged after three days of captivity, but by Meade's consistently thoughtful treatment. He was well fed, kept clean and shaved, allowed periods of exercise, given books and magazines to read, spoken to as if he were a friend. At moments he had the feeling that Meade actually enjoyed having him there and was keeping him more for his own needs than because he could think of no safe way to let him go. Who else did the guy have to talk to? Thank God he didn't seem in any rush to kill him. But how long would that last with a murdering crazy like this?

"Miss me?" asked Meade.

"Damn right. Couldn't wait to hear your footsteps on the porch." Tommy grinned at Meade's disguise. "No wonder nobody recognizes you out there. You look like a fat, sixty-year-old bank president."

"That's what I am inside. The *real* William Meade."

He began stripping down: gray hairpiece, brows, and mustache, shaped foam rubber that bulged his cheeks, jowls, and lower lip, a full undersuit of cotton padding that seemed to add fifty pounds to his body weight. Cleansing cream took away the dark circles under his eyes and the drooping lines edging his nose and mouth. In three minutes' time he was standing naked, glistening with sweat, and looking half the age he had looked before.

He picked up his *Times* and a towel and started out for his regular morning swim.

But he turned at the door. "I called your wife again, Tommy. I told her you were still OK, but I'm afraid she didn't believe me this time."

"What did she say?"

"That she'd gone to the police and reported you missing. She also wanted to know who I was and what I'd done to you. Then she just started crying and swearing at me."

Lukens swallowed dryly. "Poor Jessie. Did you tell her who you were?"

"No. That would really have scared hell out of her." Meade stood there. "If you'd like to write her a note, I'll mail it for you. At least she'll know you're alive."

"I'd sure appreciate that."

Lukens felt himself going all soft inside. He wanted to weep with gratitude. *Sonofabitch! The guy chains me to a sink for three days like a fucking dog, and all I want to do is kiss his ass for letting me write to my wife.*

Meade gave him a pen and a few sheets of paper and went out into the sun. There had been no phone call and he would not, of course, be mailing any note. But what did that have to do with anything? he thought.

Using an easy crawl, he swam a quarter of a mile to the far shore of the small lake, then turned in a tight circle and started back. He felt the power in his arms, and the water cool against his skin. The sun was high above him, diffuse and pale, and he had the sense that he could go on like this forever. When he stretched out on the grass in front of the cabin, he was breathing no more heavily than when he had entered the water.

Meade rolled over on his stomach and reached for the *Times*.

He was pleased to discover he had made the front page again. This time it was with a feature article that quoted a selection of noted psychiatrists, each of whom offered his own explanation of what might have created a psychopath, or sociopath—the terms were considered interchangeable—like William Meade.

One distinguished doctor said the condition was caused to a great extent by a lack of superego, that area of the brain that controlled self-criticism and enforced moral standards. Meade was like a psychological child in an adult body who simply did what he wanted to do when he wanted to do it without caring about the consequences.

Another expert was of the opinion that the condition was more likely to be brought about by environment than by genetics. This doctor, a woman, believed that most psychopaths were created, that a lack of bonding in infancy could mean there were certain nerves in the mind that just never hooked up.

Still another authority on the more-complex aspects of the human psyche talked of something he called the internal policeman, which normally developed in children of preschool age and helped prevent them from achieving pleasure for themselves at the expense of others. In someone like Meade, said this doctor, the inside cop somehow never materialized.

Meade read on, amused as always by the endless stream of psychological pap being ground out by the trained intellects in the field. He himself could quote every theory by heart. He'd spent much of his seven years in Attica studying every available text on the subject. If forced to, he was sure he could put together a scholarly, high-level thesis on it. Yet in the end the only thing he was absolutely certain about was that every psychological theory he'd explored to date was, at best, no more than an unproven supposition put together by some well-intentioned scholar. At worst, it was drivel.

Ladies and gentlemen, he wanted to say to them, *distinguished physicians one and all. I appreciate your considerable thought and attention. But I'm afraid the only reason I do what I'm doing is that there's really nothing in life I enjoy doing more.*

What Meade did approve of, however, was the article's final paragraph. One psychiatrist was quoted as saying that there was something inside murderers that was inside everyone, and that people wanted to know about them so they could learn more about themselves.

William Meade was pleased to agree. At least they understood that much. Whatever was in him was in them.

The sun baked his body. It stamped its warmth into his head. He felt best at the height of the day. This was when he heard only the truest of his thoughts and saw no ghosts or shadows.

He turned straight from the feature article to the op-ed page at the back of the first section. On the days when Paul

Garret's column was carried, it was always in the upper right-hand corner of this page. It was there today.

It was titled "Rumors and Allegations." And from the opening paragraph, whatever warmth and brightness the day might have held for Meade a moment before was suddenly no longer there.

He lay with it, barely moving, for almost an hour. By that time everything he felt was like an old injury. And the anger was reduced to a cold resolve.

The worst of it was that he felt used. It was as if he'd learned everything there was to know about betrayal except the way it worked. Yet without the wisdom of hindsight, if he had it all to do over, he knew he would do it no differently. Whatever he'd gotten from Harry, he'd needed and wanted, and it would never have been there without the trust and sharing. Not to mention his own compulsion to tell, to have someone other than himself know everything, in case he never made it out of Attica. Back then it had seemed more likely than not that he would die there. Cons were always leaving in boxes. And he was facing a possible forty years. So he figured this was his life and what the hell.

But *Harry?* It was still a shock.

Harry, Harry. . . . You were never really as smart or tough as you thought. Mostly, at your best, you were lovable. Now you're not even that.

Naturally, he understood it all. In essence it was like one of those old English drawing-room comedies, in which everyone knew what everyone else was thinking and plotting, yet pretended not to so that the pure ritual of the performance could be preserved for all to enjoy.

In his mind, with the initial shock and anger gone, his own enjoyment of it had already begun.

CHAPTER
29

Garret woke at 6:00 A.M. in a standard, cookie-cutter motel room a few miles from Attica. He stared dimly at a white ceiling and had no idea where he was or what he was doing out there. Then he remembered it was Friday and jumped out of bed so quickly he had to hold on to a wall and blink away a sudden rush of vertigo.

Hoping it was not raining, he opened the blinds and stared out at a green landscape under a lightening pink sky. There was no rain and no visible threat of it. Somehow, it seemed a good sign. Yet shaving, moments later, Garret looked in the mirror and saw his face drawn and his eyes too bright. He felt edgy and uncertain and found himself wishing Canderro had come up with him. But the detective had thought it better to stake himself out at the Long Island site to forestall possible problems with the locals. Considering all the units involved, it made sense. Still, Garret missed him.

There was an instant-coffee maker in the room and Garret boiled some water and sat with it. He wished there was something more for him to do. The whole procedure at this point was beginning to feel too passive. It was gnawing at him. Captain Brentkoff had not even wanted him up here, but to hell with Brentkoff. Sitting around in New York would have been worse.

The last two days had flown by, but now the minutes dragged. At exactly 6:45 he left the motel, got into his rented Cougar, and headed for the prison.

Less than fifteen miles to the northeast of Garret's motel, William Meade parked the Jeep he was driving behind an old clapboard farmhouse and walked up to the kitchen door. His hair and mustache were a mix of gray and brown, but he was otherwise undisguised. He wore jeans and a T-shirt and was carrying the same small olive-drab canvas bag he had with him the day he stopped at the Garrets' house in early spring.

Through the screen door he saw Ralph Deagan, his wife, Marie, and their baby daughter, Cissy. They were sitting at the kitchen table, having breakfast. Marie was feeding the baby, who was in a high chair making happy baby sounds. Deagan was an airplane mechanic who worked as a civilian service chief at the Genesee Barracks airstrip, and Meade knew he'd be leaving for the field in less than half an hour. Meade knew a lot of things about Deagan. Which was why he was here.

The mechanic saw Meade approaching and rose and opened the screen door before he had a chance to knock. He was a young muscular man with his hair pulled back in a short ponytail.

"Whatever you're selling," he said, "you're gonna have to do it fast. I'm leaving for work in about fifteen minutes."

William Meade gave him his best smile. "I'm not selling a thing, Ralph. Just stopped by to see you and the family."

Deagan looked closely at him. "Do I know you?"

"Name's Meade. William Meade."

He might have said, "Name's Christ. Jesus Christ." The effect on Deagan was the same. It went from shock, to disbelief, to wonder. The fear didn't show until seconds later. But by that time the automatic was out and pointing.

Meade heard a sharp intake of breath from Marie Deagan at the table, then a complaint from the baby at the interruption in her feeding. He motioned Deagan to move back from him to discourage any sudden leaps at the gun. He needed this one alive.

"Oh, God," whispered Deagan's wife.

"It's all right, Marie," said Meade quietly, soothingly. "I'm not going to hurt you or your husband or the baby. All I want is a small favor from Ralph. Then I'll be on my way and the Deagan family will be fine."

Deagan just stood staring. The coffee mug he'd been drinking from was still in his hand, and there was a tightness to his jaw that whitened the skin around his mouth.

"What the fuck do you want?" he said.

Meade saw all the signs he'd not seen in time with Paul Garret. In another moment this one, too, would be ready to die going for him.

"I'll tell you what I *don't* want," he said. "Which is for you to make any asshole moves that'll force me to blow you, Marie, and little Cissy away for no damn reason at all."

Meade allowed several seconds for the light to go out of Deagan's eyes. "So just walk carefully around to the other side of the table, sit down next to your wife and baby, and we'll talk for a few minutes."

The mechanic did as he was told, and Meade moved a chair into position and sat down ten feet away, facing him.

His wife took his arm and held on to it. She had started to cry. The baby was screaming for more food.

"Please keep feeding her," said Meade. "Daddy's going to have to concentrate very hard on what I'm about to tell him, and we don't want any distractions."

He waited until the child had quieted. Then he held up the small canvas bag that was still in his left hand.

"I'll make this quick and simple, Ralph. All I'm asking is for you to place this little bag in the luggage hold of Captain Brentkoff's flight just before takeoff. You do that and we'll all be happy."

The mechanic stared coldly at the bag. No one had to say what was in it. Everyone knew. And this way, the whole thing somehow seemed less terrible.

"What about the poor bastards on the plane?" he said. "They gonna be happy, too?"

Meade's smile was gentle. "Maybe happiest of all. God's arms are warm. His night is sweet."

"And if I say no?"

"Why would you do anything as stupid as that?"

"Because I'm no murderer."

"You'll learn. It's not hard. And you may even learn to like it. I did."

Meade sighed, his patience wearing. "There's not much time, so I'll be blunt. Say no, and I kill you and Marie right here at the table and leave Cissy to finish her breakfast alone. Say yes and it's over in two hours, no one but us ever knows what happened, and you've all got your lives ahead."

A master of timing, Meade allowed fifteen seconds for silent consideration.

"There it is, Ralph. I can't make it any plainer than that. Would you rather destroy yourself and your family, or kiss off a few strangers who don't mean shit to you?"

Sobbing loudly now, Marie was still spooning cereal into her baby's mouth. "For God's sake, Ralph!" she said. "Can't you see he means it?"

No one said anything, and for a moment there was such intimacy among them in the drab, dimly lighted country kitchen that when someone so much as stirred or took a deep breath, the others felt it.

"What the hell do you want me to do, Marie?" asked Deagan.

His wife glared at him. "What the hell do I want you to do?" Her voice rose shrilly, half hysterical. "What the hell do you *think* I want you to do? Get our heads blown off?"

Deagan sought Meade's eyes rather than his wife's. "Why did you have to pick *me?*"

"Because you're chief mechanic, have access to every plane on the strip, and have a wife and baby I can pressure you with. Who'd have been better?"

Meade checked his watch. It was 7:13. "What time are you due at work? Eight?"

"Yeah."

"And Brentkoff's flight is set for nine?"

Staring dully at Meade's automatic, Deagan nodded.

"Which plane is he using? The Lear or one of the two Grummans?"

"The Lear. Jesus, how'd yuh find out all this stuff?"

"By asking questions."

Meade watched the baby open her mouth for a spoonful of cereal, swallow, then open her mouth for the next load. A perfect little eating and shitting machine.

"Okay," said Deagan. "Let's get the thing over with. How's it gonna work?"

"Couldn't be easier. You take this little bag in to work with you, and I take Marie and the baby for a little ride in my Jeep."

"A little ride to where?"

"Not far. Just someplace where I'll be able to watch the Lear take off into the sky, and you can't send cops after me."

Meade's flat eyes held the mechanic. "Now listen to this part carefully. I'm using a barometer trigger. It works on altitude. It's set to close an electric circuit at two thousand feet and activate a timer. Exactly one minute after that, the device goes. Which means I'll be able to see and hear the explosion. You follow me?"

"Yeah."

"I'm explaining all this so you won't try to con me and just end up killing Marie and Cissy."

"How the hell could I do that?"

"By spilling your guts to Brentkoff and rigging a bunch of phony news reports of the plane exploding somewhere in flight."

Meade saw the mechanic's eyes waver. The poor fool had already been groping along this very path. God, people were predictable. Not an original thought in a million. That was more pathetic than anything. A bunch of third-rate clones.

"So don't disappoint me, Ralph. If you do, I'll shoot your wife and little girl without blinking an eye, and come back to finish you later. Play nice, and the minute I see and hear that thing go off up there, I'll send your family home."

Gently, William Meade placed the green bag on the kitchen table. "It's all set, so be nice and easy with it. I want it in the forward luggage hold, as close as possible to the cockpit. That's sure to knock out all flight controls and set off the wing tanks."

Everyone sat looking at the bag, including the baby. Deagan's expression was pained. His face shone with sweat.

"What if the fucker don't go off?" he said.

"You'd better pray it does, Ralph."

"Yeah, but what if it don't?"

Meade shrugged. "Then I guess it's just too bad for poor Marie and the baby."

"That's unfair as hell."

"I know."

Marie spoke between sobs. "Why . . . are you . . . doing this?"

"There's a man I knew in Attica who'll be on the plane," Meade said softly. "We were good friends. At least I thought we were good friends. Until he disappointed me."

The State Correctional Facility at Attica stood tall in the early sun, a strangely beautiful fortress with red-brick pointed towers and off-white walls. At 8:10 A.M., exactly on schedule, the small, three-car convoy was forming in its outer courtyard. The fourth and final car present, Paul Garret's rented gray Cougar, had been included only after much argument with Captain Brentkoff.

Five minutes before departure, Garret himself had begun to wonder what he was doing there. At best he was merely a spectator at a carefully planned, minutely detailed paramilitary operation in which lives would be at risk and to which, at this point, he'd contributed nothing.

Yet he was there. And he was armed. And he was wearing the same high-quality Kevlar body armor under his shirt as everyone else.

At 8:15 Brentkoff gave the signal and they got into their cars as originally arranged . . . three troopers in each vehicle except Garret's, and all carrying high-powered automatic weapons.

At the last moment Captain Brentkoff approached Garret's car.

"A final word," he said. "Be especially watchful approaching stop signs and overpasses. That's where the grenades and gasoline bombs are most likely to be tossed. And if one of us in front of you takes a hit and starts burning, for God's sake don't leave your car and try to help. Don't even stop. Just pull around, speed up, and keep going. Emergency fire equipment will never be more than a few minutes away."

Garret nodded and watched the captain walk away, a tall trooper, resplendent and well pressed. *My protector*. Still, the man took his job seriously and did it well. And *he* was the one who would be sitting right beside Harry Stover every foot of the way.

The prison gates swung open. Then the four cars drove out of the courtyard and immediately assumed their prearranged, hundred-yard intervals.

It turned out to be a nonevent.

Twenty-two minutes later, all four cars of the small convoy entered the Genesee Barracks airstrip, drove directly onto the tarmac, and parked less than fifty feet from the waiting Lear jet.

Ralph Deagan was checking the Lear's wheels, tires, and landing assembly when he saw the cars arrive. Captain Brentkoff and the eight troopers with him were locals, out of the Genesee Barracks, and he knew them all. They weren't his buddies. But sometimes they'd have a few beers and talk and he knew them, for Christ's sake. What he didn't know was exactly how many of them would be on the flight.

Hey! How the fuck many of you guys am I gonna kill?

He thought it angrily, bitterly, as if they were the ones making it happen, not he. But he knew better. It was Meade who was making it happen—Meade who was in control. That he might have a choice was just an illusion. You don't weigh your own against numbers. There was just this woman and little baby and him. Then there was the whole rest of the world.

Oh, Christ. Oh, sweet Jesus Christ.

Then just thinking about his wife and baby being with Meade, the panic was on him again, and the sweat was cold on his back and in his armpits. What if Meade killed them anyway? He said he wouldn't, but what the hell did that mean with a creep like that? He didn't need a reason to kill. He shot women like they weren't even people.

The panic came in waves. In between the waves he was calm.

He had to stop thinking like that. If he panicked bad enough, he'd go sniveling to Brentkoff and blow it for sure. Then Marie and Cissy would really be gone. This way, maybe they had a chance. Meade didn't talk like he was crazy. He was damn smart . . . smart enough to figure out what he was thinking with the fake crash reports. Maybe it was really like he said. Maybe he just wanted to get this one guy who'd screwed him in some way, and that would be it. Even crazy people weren't nuts all the time.

I have to believe that.

He finished checking the landing assembly. Then he glanced over at Brentkoff and his men. Two troopers and a guy in handcuffs had already boarded, and others were preparing to follow. He hadn't yet loaded Meade's bag. If he was going to do it, now was the time.

What did he mean, *if*. There was no fucking *if*. There was just Marie and Cissy and God. And right now, maybe not even God.

"How many troopers are you taking?" Garret asked Captain Brentkoff. He had to raise his voice to be heard above the crackle of radio traffic from the open hatch of the plane.

"All eight. These are my best and I know how they'll react. I don't want to have to worry about a bunch of strange cops in New York."

The trooper looked closely at Garret. "I have to insist on your not coming. It's nothing personal. But from here on we're tight and stripped down, and anyone not absolutely needed just adds to our exposure."

Garret was no longer in the mood to argue. He understood all right. He'd been feeling like an unnecessary appendage for much of the past hour.

"I assume the plane itself is secure," he said.

"Damn right. This whole area has been under twenty-four-hour guard for the past three days. No one but authorized personnel has gone anywhere near the hangars and planes."

"What about packages or luggage? You carrying anything in the baggage hold?"

Brentkoff's eyes crinkled. "You think Meade's slipped a bomb in on us?"

It was the closest Garret had ever seen the trooper come to actual amusement. "I know it's farfetched, but I think it's worth taking a minute to check out."

"Sure. Why not? It can't hurt."

Garret felt himself being humored. But Brentkoff did call over one of his men and tell him to grab the groundcrew chief and look through the luggage hold for anything that might be labeled suspicious.

In the cockpit the pilot and copilot started up their engines, and Garret stood in the rush of sound and air. He suddenly felt let down. The only kid on the block not going to the party. And it was *his* party.

"Hey, Ralphy!"

Deagan turned. One of the plainclothes troopers, Pete Breslin, was coming toward him.

"Open up the luggage hold," said the trooper.

Deagan felt his stomach churning. "I just closed it."

"Too bad. Old Iron Ass wants it opened."

"What for?"

"So we can unload all the frigging bombs Meade's got ticking away in there," said Breslin.

The mechanic stood staring at him. Less than two minutes before, he'd deposited William Meade's little bag as ordered. Now it was all over. His wife and baby were gone.

Deagan found his voice. "He's kidding, ain't he?"

"That prick never kids. I mean he looks for bombs and killers under his bed. Come on, Ralphy. Open the crate up so we can get the hell out of here."

Numbly, Deagan walked over to the plane, worked open the luggage hold, and climbed inside.

Behind him, the state trooper stuck his head through the hatch and glanced briefly at the few boxes and cartons he saw there. "How about it, Ralph? Everything look kosher to you?"

The mechanic inhaled deeply. "I loaded every piece myself."

"What about that little canvas bag up front there?"

"Loaded that, too. That's the one Meade gave me personally."

The trooper was laughing as he turned away, but not when he reported back to Brentkoff.

"Luggage hold secure, Captain."

On the tarmac Paul Garret and Ralph Deagan stood no more than ten feet apart, watching, as the Lear roared down the runway, took off, and climbed steeply into the cloudless sky. They were able to see the flash quite clearly at slightly above two thousand feet. The explosion came exactly five seconds later.

CHAPTER
30

William Meade and Marie Deagan saw and heard the explosion from the crest of a hill about ten miles due north of the airstrip. Because they were that much closer to it than Garret, there was only a three-second difference between sight and sound.

Good-bye, Harry, thought Meade.

"Oh, Lord," whispered Marie.

They sat together in silence in the front of the Jeep. The baby was asleep in her mother's lap and Marie rocked her gently. They were parked in a clearing about a hundred yards from a dirt road, and the only sounds were those of birds.

"How do you feel, Marie?"

"Sick."

Meade looked at her. She was a slovenly dark-haired woman with blotchy skin who was rapidly going to fat. The only thing in her favor was youth, and even that was passing.

"That's all?" he said. "No joy that they were the ones dying up there, and not you and your baby down here?"

The tears, which had been intermittent for the past hour, started again.

"Are you really going to let us go?"

"I said I would, didn't I?"

She could barely manage a nod.

The fear was still all over her. Each time Meade breathed, he caught a whiff of it . . . sour and heavy.

Christ, she's even worried about my raping her.

The thought amused him. Here she was, this pathetically unappealing woman who'd probably never be physically desired by any man other than her husband, and not too much longer even by him.

"And I'm not going to sexually assault you, either, Marie." Meade's voice was softly reassuring, his expression sincere. "Though I admit I'd love to have you."

Meade dropped mother and baby within walking distance of a gas station. Then he got rid of the Jeep, jumped the wires on a gray Dodge sedan, and started the long drive home.

In his mind he could still see Marie almost starting to glow at his final compliment to her desirability. He mocked himself. *My good deed for the day.*

It was a while before he realized there really had been no need for him to abandon the Jeep. Somehow he'd imagined Marie giving the police a description of the car he was driving. It was a groundless concern since there'd be no way for her to mention his presence without indicting her husband as the person responsible for the destruction of the Lear and all those aboard.

This mental lapse on his part was so atypical he found it disturbing. No harm done here. Yet at another time, such a break in concentration could easily have proved fatal.

Think, for God's sake. Stay alert.

Meade focused on the plane itself. He had no exact count of the number of people who'd been on the Lear. But between the crew and the state troopers, he figured there had to have been at least eight or nine men he had killed in order to get Harry. The sheer number of dead, along with the reasons for their dying, were new experiences for him and he thought about them.

Until now he'd killed only single, specifically targeted individuals, and then just for the thrill of it. And the thrill itself was mostly sexual. This morning, except for Harry, he'd killed eight or nine faceless men who simply happened to be in the wrong place at the wrong time.

So how did he feel about *that?*

Damn good, he decided.

Which was exactly how God must have felt last week when he knocked those four hundred and twenty-nine pilgrims out of the sky and into a mountain. And while they were on their way to pay their devotions to *Him,* no less, at Mecca. Oh, how He had loved that. He must have loved it. Wasn't He doing that sort of thing all the time? Like those hundred thousand Pakistanis He'd drowned last year in a single typhoon across the lowlands. Or those sixty thousand Armenians He'd crushed under that earthquake in early spring. Not to mention the countless millions of less dramatic, less publicized incidents in which the death tolls were not nearly as impressive.

Meade smiled through the windshield at the road ahead. Compared to God, I'm just a piker. Really small time.

Somebody . . . it may even have been Shakespeare himself, said it a lot better:

> *As flies to wanton boys, are we to the gods;*
> *They kill us for their sport.*

CHAPTER
31

It was early evening and almost nine hours after the bombing when Garret reached the wooded Long Island burial site of William Meade's earliest victims.

By that time all but two of the alleged eleven sets of remains had been recovered, and the newly opened graves and piles of fresh dirt formed a huge circle about the great oak at their center.

"Like the face of a clock" was how Harry Stover had quoted Meade as describing it, with one kid buried at each hour except twelve, and a cat buried at twelve to give them all a nice little pet to play with.

How could a human mind ever think up this kind of stuff?

A small army of police—some in plainclothes, some in uniform, and some in coveralls—were still digging and working over the area, and Garret spotted Canderro leaning against a tree, smoking. The inevitable batteries of cameras flashed and clicked, perpetuating their own small parts of the scene. There was little remaining daylight to break through the trees and everything was heavily shaded. Darkness was on its way, and Garret could almost feel an extra rush toward night in the roll of the earth.

The lieutenant saw Garret and came forward to greet him.

"I'll tell you this, Garret. You gave me a couple of real bad minutes earlier. I thought maybe you'd talked Brentkoff into letting you come along on the flight."

"Thanks for caring."

They stood looking at each other. If there was an odor to such things, the space between them would have smelled of desperation. The failing light deepened the hollows in their cheeks and around their eyes.

"How do you figure Meade managed it?" said Canderro. "Wasn't the plane checked out?"

"Brentkoff almost laughed when I suggested it. He was that sure of their security. But he did send a trooper and a mechanic to look through the luggage hold."

"Did you see them doing it?"

"I saw them." Garret's voice was flat. "I also saw twelve men walk onto that plane who'll never walk off."

Jacqueline Wurzel opened her door, looked at everything on Garret's face, and just held him. It was shortly after 10:00 P.M.

"When did you eat last?" she said.

"I had coffee at about six-thirty."

"This evening?"

"This morning."

Jacqueline put together some pasta and salad. Then she sat watching him eat.

"I guess you've heard it all," he said.

She nodded. "It's been a real media blitz. You've had yourself quite a day."

"Not as bad as those on the plane."

"I know."

"No, you don't," he said, and told her some of the things he had avoided telling her before.

She reached for his hand.

"You could have been on that plane, too."

"Sure," he said. "But I wasn't."

Hours later, after they'd held each other and made love, a ringing broke in on their sleep.

The phone was on Garret's side of the bed, and he reached out for it without thought before he was fully awake. The room was dark, but a luminous dial read 3:12.

"Hello?" he said.

"My apologies for the uncivilized hour, Mr. Garret. But I'm rather restricted in my calling opportunities these days."

Garret bolted to a sitting position, gripped the receiver fiercely.

Jacqueline switched on a lamp, saw his face, and knew instantly who was at the other end.

"I must say I'm glad about you and Jacqueline," said Meade. "It has an almost classic symmetry that I find irresistible. You can't keep focusing on the dead."

A pause and a soft sigh.

"And speaking of the dead. The twelve in the Lear were all yours, Mr. Garret. It was you who set the whole thing up for poor Harry. How does it feel? Exciting? Sort of like blowing away those little guys in 'Nam, I'll bet. No one admits it, but there's an unbelievable feeling of potency in taking a life."

Garret could no longer hold back. "OK. How the hell did you do it?"

"You weren't listening, old friend. *I* didn't do it. *You* did."

There was a sound that might have passed for a laugh.

"Incidentally," said William Meade, "I'm very glad you weren't one of those on the plane. Good night, Mr. Garret. My love to Jacqueline. Please tell her I still admire her more than any woman I've ever known."

The line went dead and Garret slowly put down the receiver. He fell back on the pillow and stared up at the ceiling.

Jacqueline pressed close to him under the sheet.

"It was really William?"

"It sure was."

"I can't believe it. How could he have known you were here?"

"He probably tried my place and got no answer."

"But how did he know about *us*?"

Garret said nothing.

"Do you think he's been watching me?" she asked.

"Or me."

"Oh, God." A short pause, then: "I don't believe he means either of us any harm. If he did, it would have happened long before now. What was he saying to you?"

Garret told her and she lay with it.

"If it'll make you feel any better," he said, "I can call Canderro and get you protection."

"What about *your* protection?"

"I can't live that way."

"What makes you think *I* can?"

"It's not the same thing."

"Why? Because I'm a woman?"

He touched her cheek. Either his fingers were cold, or she was running a fever.

"I'm a parole officer," she said. "I carry a gun and I've been trained to use it. If you want to go down to the range with me in the morning, I'll outscore anything you shoot."

He kissed her. "Pretty tough broad, aren't you?"

"When I have to be. But just the idea of William out there someplace, watching, gives me the creeps."

Garret felt the same way. And when he finally turned out the light, the sudden darkness made it worse.

CHAPTER
32

Lieutenant Frank Canderro sat in a rear booth of the Clover Bar and Grill, waiting for Kate Venturi. She'd already called twice to say she might be delayed by as much as forty minutes and maybe they'd better just forget about having lunch this afternoon.

Canderro had told her not to worry about it, that there was nothing he'd rather do anyway than just sit around drinking on duty, and that he'd be there whenever she arrived. He was used to Kate being late. She had an extended history of emergency cases that absolutely could not be walked away from without anguished, counselor-dependent students suffering the most dire psychological consequences.

In the meantime he waited and drank in a cool, pleasantly dim corner of the restaurant. He reflected mostly on the wet, tiring, thoroughly depressing morning he'd had. A solid five hours of tramping through woods and from one house to another under a steady summer rain to get the feel of what some of his men had been doing now for days. Unable to reduce the potential search area to anything less than a twenty-five–square-mile tract, he'd nevertheless squeezed all he could out of Reams' secondhand story, plus the more specific location of Tom Lukens' abandoned car. The rest had been pure conjecture. An additional handicap had been the need to keep the search low-key, using no more than half a dozen plainclothesmen operating under the thin cover of government surveyors. Anything larger and more overt would only alert Meade long before they could get within striking distance.

It was an admittedly frail effort with not much chance of success. But after yesterday's plane disaster it was the only aggressive effort they had going.

Of course, there were still the surveillances on Jenny Angelo, Natalie Bingham, and Meade's mother. But in his present mood these were much too passive for Canderro. More than anything, he wanted to talk to Mrs. Meade, or Mrs. Lipton, or whatever she chose to call herself these days. If nothing came out of the stakeouts soon, he decided he'd question the woman directly.

A cable news channel was flickering at the far end of the bar, and Canderro caught a glimpse of his face and heard his voice trying to explain how and why twelve men had somehow been killed in a failed attempt to put an end to William Meade's reign of terror.

The detective was immediately followed on-screen by the governor himself, who proclaimed thirty days of official mourning for the nine state troopers who were killed. He also pledged "the full resources of the state to bringing the cold-blooded killer to justice."

Me and the governor. So say we.

Canderro saw Kate enter the restaurant and scan the tables. He waved and she came down the aisle, her cheeks flushed with hurrying, her eyes bright with pleasure at seeing him. She pecked his cheek and slid into the booth.

"I'm so sorry, but this poor little eight-year-old has this pair of idiot divorced parents who've managed to give him every complex imaginable and I absolutely couldn't leave until—" She took a deep breath and smiled. "Thank you for waiting, darling."

He ordered her usual gin and tonic. "OK," he said when her drink arrived. "Now tell me all about the kid with the idiot parents."

He just sat there drinking and listening, enjoying the warm eagerness of her face and taking pleasure in the short fluffy style of her hair and the way her breasts lifted against her blouse. Looking at her, he became aware of how much he'd come to take her presence for granted. It was suddenly impossible to imagine that whatever days and nights remained to him would not in some way include her. *Better be careful*, he thought. There'd been another relationship he'd taken for granted. . . .

"But enough about me," she said. "What have you been doing all morning?"

"Wandering around in the rain, Meade hunting. That's what I do these days, hunt a lousy rapist-killer." He sipped his Kentucky sour mash. "I also talk to radio and television reporters, explaining why I haven't caught him."

"Stop complaining. You're suddenly famous. I like that part. I like people coming over to me at work and saying they saw your picture on TV or in the paper." Her expression suddenly fell. "Of course, I do worry about you. Worry that one day Meade or somebody like him will take you away from me." Her eyes glistened.

"Hey, what's this sad stuff all about?" he chided. "You'll always have me to kick around."

"Will I really? Do I even now?"

"Why not?"

"Do you want me to tell you?"

Canderro motioned to the waiter for another round of drinks. "No."

"I'll tell you anyway," Kate said, her voice slightly taunting now. "I don't really have you because you still carry around that dumb, thirty-year-old picture of your wife like a mooning kid. Because you still won't admit you love me as much as we both know you do. Because you still refuse to live with me on a sensible, continuing basis. And especially because you're still scared half to death of committing yourself to a relationship that threatens to make life reasonably and permanently pleasant for you."

"Well, now I know."

"You knew before. It's just that every once in a while, I have to get it all properly stated and laid out."

"Okay, Madame Psychologist. So how would you diagnose me? Acute fear of joy? Manic-depressive? Or maybe just plain old-fashioned death wish."

"I love you, Frankie."

"I can't imagine why."

The pale Irish eyes from her mother's side tore straight through him. "For a lot of silly reasons. But mostly, I suppose, because you're probably the most decent, moral man I've ever known."

"Jesus, could you get arguments on that."

The lieutenant reached his desk at 2:45 P.M. and found that day's pile of messages and memorandums waiting. Among the red-flagged flimsies was a message asking him to call Paul Garret. It had been logged in at 9:12 that morning. He took care of a few can't-wait situations, then dialed Garret's direct line at the *Times*.

"Canderro," he said. "What's up?"

"I just wanted you to know that Meade called last night."

"Oh, shit!" The detective leaned forward slightly in his chair and pressed the record button. "Another body?"

"No. It wasn't that kind of call."

It came to Canderro in a delayed reaction. "We've got a tap on your line. I don't understand how we—"

"He didn't call me at home. I was in Jacqueline Wurzel's apartment."

It took Canderro a moment to respond. When he did, there was surprise, even a little shock in his voice. "You were with Meade's parole officer?"

"That's right."

"What time did the call come in?"

"A bit after three this morning."

"How the hell did Meade know where to find you at *that* hour?"

"I don't know. Unless he's been watching me."

"Either that or watching Wurzel."

The line was silent.

"Sorry to pry into your personal life, Garret. But exactly how many times have you met with Miss Wurzel?"

Garret took some time to time about it. "About six or seven."

"Where have you been with her?"

"In her White Plains office, in an East Side bar . . . in her apartment and mine."

"Where's her apartment?"

"In a converted brownstone on East Seventy-fifth."

"Did she answer the phone when Meade called?"

"No. I did."

"What did your friend have to say?"

Canderro shouldered the phone and lit another cigarette as Garret repeated everything Meade had told him. Listening, he felt a deepening depression. But when he spoke, he was careful to keep it out of his voice.

"Were those Meade's exact words? 'My love to Jacqueline'? 'Please tell her I still admire her more than any woman I've ever known'?"

"Yes."

"But he didn't ask to speak to her?"

"No."

"As far as you know," said Canderro, "did Meade ever come on to her sexually while she was his parole officer?"

"If he did, Jacqueline never mentioned it." Garret paused. "You think his comment last night had sexual overtones?"

The lieutenant rolled his eyes. "You mean you don't?"

Garret said nothing.

"This whole thing scares me shitless, Garret. The son-ofabitch is too close to you both. So what I'd like to do is put some people on your backs."

"You already know how I feel about that. And when I simply mentioned the idea of protection to Jacqueline, she climbed on her feminist high-horse and challenged me to a shootout on the firing range."

"You care anything about this woman?"

"Yes."

"Glad to hear it. Then let's not horse around with what Miss Wurzel wants or doesn't want. Starting tonight, there'll be someone watching her twenty-four hours a day. And she won't know a thing about it."

Garret's sigh came across the wire. "I feel better already."

Sure you do, thought Canderro. *That's why you called me.*

CHAPTER
33

William Meade had conducted a trial run the night before so he had the stakeout on Jenny Angelo's house clearly spotted. The front watcher was parked about fifty yards up the block in an unmarked car with darkened windows and a high antenna. The man in back had set himself up in Jenny's garage, keeping the doors partly open so he could sit a short distance back and look out without being seen. Meade expected no problems from either man. In his mind he still hadn't decided whether Jenny knew they were there. A small part of him knew she did.

Still, he felt his hope rising as he crouched in the dark. It was close to 3:00 A.M., with just a thin crescent of moon and nothing in sight moving. The house itself was an old-fashioned Cape Cod, well set back from a cul-de-sac and surrounded by trees. There were no sidewalks or street lights, and high privet hedges sheltered the house from the front and sides. He'd once known this house as intimately as his own and could still picture every detail of every room. He could feel Jenny and her family, along with everything else, coming to life and stirring inside him. The other Angelos were no longer in residence. Jenny's brother, Pete, had died in Vietnam, and her parents were currently drifting through Europe on an extended sabbatical from their teaching jobs at Post College. Only Jenny was home.

All right.

Meade headed for a side basement window, dropped down into the dry well, and made sure there was no wiring. Then using a glass cutter and suction cup, he opened a hole just large enough to get a hand through and slip the latch. Three minutes later he was inside and climbing the cellar stairs to the foyer. He stood there for a moment, listening for sounds. He heard none. Along with his other concerns, he was worried about frightening Jenny.

He slowly climbed the stairs to the second floor, drawing air into his lungs and feeling it go out fast and burning. No surprises here. He'd expected to feel no differently. Out of prison for more than eleven months, he'd thought about and put off this moment for all of that time. The thing was, it made no sense, was totally without logic. Considering his present dire circumstances, there was absolutely no reason for him to be here. That is, other than the single reason that had finally brought him. He *wanted* to be here.

Just don't let me bring her harm, he thought. Then he silently eased open a door and was in the same room with her.

Pausing, he heard her breathing and recalled the hundred times he'd lain beside her, hearing the same soft, regular sound. The moon brought a faint, translucent glow through the windows and he saw the outlines of her body on the bed. Until all the old uncertainties came back to punish him and he was afraid to make a move.

He knelt on the rug beside her bed.

She slept curled under a light sheet, facing him. Her face, soft in sleep, was vaguely puzzled, frowning. *How young she looks*, he thought. In seventeen years she hasn't aged five minutes. If there was a plan to anything, she'd been preparing all these years for this moment of sleep beneath his eyes, and he'd been preparing for her. *If there was a plan.*

As gently as possible, Meade slipped one hand behind Jenny's head on the pillow, placed his other hand over her mouth, and leaned lightly across her body. Her eyes opened and her body stirred, then stiffened as she came out of sleep in a rush. She managed a muffled gasp. That was all.

"Don't be frightened," he said, not whispering, but wanting her to hear and recognize his natural voice. "It's me, William. It's all right. Please don't be frightened."

Above his hand her eyes stared wildly. Not knowing how much she was able to see in the darkness, he said, "I look different. I have a mustache and my hair is longer and darker. But it's still me. My voice is still the same. Don't you recognize my voice?"

Slowly, he removed his hand from her mouth. His throat ached and his palms felt clammy. Jenny's mouth was open but she made no sound. She just lay there staring up at him. Not knowing what to do, how to reassure her, he stroked her hair, her face. Emotion blinded him. Wiping his eyes, he said, "It's me," and kept saying it. "It's me . . . it's me. . . . "

Jenny tried twice to speak and failed.

She tried again. "Aah, William . . . "

It came from her in a soft groan. In the dim blue glow of the moon, she looked fully into Meade's face, at his tinted hair and new mustache, at what time and disaster had done to his eyes. She tried to say more and again failed. All that happened was that her eyes blinked and her mouth trembled.

"I know, Jen," Meade said. "What more can I say? I know."

"You look so thin . . . so different."

"And you haven't changed at all."

"What did you do to yourself? How could you do all those terrible things?"

There was anguish in her voice, not fear, and Meade gently drew her head to his chest. "It's never a giant leap, Jen. It's always one step at a time. One morning you wake up and you realize what you've become."

"I'm sorry," she said, weeping.

"For what?"

"For running away from you."

"It was the best thing you ever did."

"No. It was the worst thing I ever did. But you were beginning to frighten me, and I didn't know how to get you to change." She separated herself from him, wiped at her eyes. "Maybe if I'd stayed with you, all those people would still be alive."

She found his hand and held it, pressing hard. "I came back here almost a year ago," she said, falling back on the pillow. "I was hoping that when you got out—"

"It was too late, Jen. Too much had happened."

"Not then. You'd done your time. You were free and clear. We'd have still had a chance. Why didn't you come to me then?"

"It was so many years since you'd left. And in all that time you never sent a word. Not that I blamed you. Whatever you thought I was, I knew I was worse. I didn't want to infect you all over again. How could I have come to you then?"

"The same way you've come to me tonight."

Jenny's voice had turned flat. Her eyes, even in the dark, were suddenly fierce.

"If you couldn't come to me then," she said, "how can you come to me now—after all this killing? I'd like to know."

There was long-buried anger in her voice now and Meade let it enter and sift through him. He was rising out of a dead calm.

"I just wanted to see you one more time, Jen."

"You mean for a final kiss before dying?"

Once, in college, Meade had tried peyote. He had a similar reaction now. His hands tingled and everything seemed to quiver in a pale blue light. "What do you want from me?" he asked her.

"Not your death. Or is that really all you've got left to offer me?"

Meade felt himself mentally and emotionally stunted. *I'm living in my own time warp. Not a molecule in me has changed since I was twelve years old.*

"I'll tell you something," Jenny said. "These past few weeks, even after all you've done, I've still had these crazy fantasies. I pictured you showing up here one night and . . . I don't know, my being able to change you, I guess."

"What are you trying to say, Jenny?"

"That I don't consider you beyond all hope. If you'll let me, maybe I can give you a reason to stop all this."

He felt only a terrible sadness for her.

"And there's this, too," she said. "I love you. I've never stopped. And there's nothing you've done or could ever do that will change how I feel."

Jenny pushed herself up so that she sat facing him. She wore a red T-shirt with LONG ISLAND HEALTH CLUB written across her chest. In her lap her fingers were entwined like spikes.

"Aren't you ever going to kiss me again?" she asked.

She had the look on her, Meade thought, of a soldier who

has filled his canteen with a rare vintage wine and dived into a fox hole to drink it. In a minute he'll have to start shooting and getting shot at again.

He leaned forward and touched her lips with his. It was a light, tentative kiss made leaden with memory and regret. Yet something in it lifted him out of himself for a moment and he needed another moment to work his way back.

Suddenly, a bright light split the darkness.

"Police!" cried a voice. "Don't move!"

William Meade stopped breathing.

How?

He looked into Jenny's eyes, saw a hint, a sign of something.

"Now hands over your head. Slowly. Nice and easy."

It was another voice . . . hoarse, very nervous. There were two of them. Both watchers had come in. The beam of light wavered. Meade didn't move. Neither did Jenny. Except her eyes. Which suddenly glanced down, then quickly came up. She had to do it again before he understood, before he looked where she had looked and saw the butt of a revolver barely visible beneath her pillow.

"Get those fucking hands up!"

The voice was excited and even more nervous. The flashlight was shaking badly. This was real big-time for a couple of Long Island cops.

Now, Meade thought. And taking a deep breath he grabbed the gun, rolled across Jenny's legs and heard their shots exploding before he hit the floor. Then he was firing himself, getting off his rounds in clusters of two, aiming slightly above the flashlight until it fell, his ears blasted by the sound in the contained space of the room, and the smell of powder stinging his nostrils. He kept firing until there was just the click of the hammer on empty chambers. His own automatic was under his shirt and tucked inside his belt, and he had to struggle to work it free as he lay on the floor.

But suddenly all was quiet and there was nothing to shoot at. Automatic in hand, Meade crawled toward the open door. The powerful police flashlight was on the carpet, its beam brightening a section of flowered wallpaper. The cops lay like two sacks of rumpled clothing, and they were dead.

Tiredly, Meade rose and turned back toward Jenny on the bed. "Jen . . ." he said, and at that instant he saw her.

She'd been hit three times in what must have been their first, wild, opening burst, and there was a great deal of blood. But not on her face. Her face was clean, untouched, and just as lovely as it had been only moments before.

"Oh, Christ," he said, and lay down on the bed and held her.

Her eyes were open and she was still conscious. "Don't worry," she told him. "I'll be all right."

"Sure you will."

He pressed a handkerchief to the worst of her wounds, the one in her chest, and rocked her. He might have been trying to put her to sleep.

"It was their gun," she murmured. "They gave it to me . . . made me sleep with it in case . . ."

He tried to quiet her. "Shh . . . . Don't talk, Jen."

"I was supposed to shoot you. Imagine. *Me . . . shoot . . . you.*" She flinched suddenly, spit up blood. "Button," she said after a moment, "under the pillow."

He held and rocked her. "What button?"

"Under the pillow," she repeated.

It seemed very important to her. So he moved the pillow and saw a rubber switch on an extension cord. It was the kind used in hospitals to signal for a nurse.

"The lights go on outside. That's how they knew."

A trickle of blood came from her mouth, and Meade wiped it away.

"I'm sorry," she whispered. "But I was better at the end, wasn't I?"

He nodded.

She drifted off then and he knew she must be hemorrhaging badly. By the time he heard the first sirens in the distance, she was gone.

He left moments before the Nassau County police arrived.

CHAPTER
34

Garret woke up to the early reports of it on the radio. It had happened too late to make any of the morning papers but was carried as the lead item on every newscast, with special bulletins breaking in on the regularly scheduled programming.

One of the network commentators had referred to the killings as *Meade's Manhasset massacre,* and the bleak alliterations had caught on and spread. Garret listened to the confused jumble of reports, then called the teletype room of the *Times* for clarification. What he finally was left with was that a police stakeout had evidently backfired, with Meade raping and killing his former girlfriend, Jenny Angelo. Two Nassau County detectives had been shot to death trying to capture him, and Lieutenant Canderro was reputedly now at the scene but had so far refused to comment pending further investigation.

Garret was about to leave for his office when the doorman appeared with a messenger-delivered letter. It read:

Dear Mr. Garret,
I neither raped nor shot Jenny Angelo. Ballistic
tests will show it was police bullets fired from one
or both of the dead officers' service revolvers that
killed her. Also, forensic examination will find no
evidence of my semen anyplace on or in her body.
This is just to keep the record straight. I really
don't need any extra credits.

It was unsigned.

Garret sat holding the message. He felt a curious numbness, a sense of futility overtaking him. People were dying while he sat at a typewriter tapping out his words of pain and protest. This was among his worst moments. The frustration alone was becoming corrosive.

Instead of going to the Times Building, he drove out to Manhasset.

There were police barricades blocking the approaches to Jenny Angelo's house. But Garret told a sergeant he had official information for Lieutenant Canderro and was allowed through. Because two of the victims had been cops, the street was crowded with top brass, political as well as police. As Garret neared the house, the air seemed to him to thicken with piousness.

Neighbors and residents of the surrounding area stood a distance away, waiting. They wouldn't be disappointed. Three green body bags were carried out of Jenny Angelo's house and loaded into a coroner's wagon. The cops carrying them moved slowly. No one ever rushed with the dead. And certainly not civil servants.

Garret stopped where he was, feeling a familiar sickness. He'd never known or even seen the woman and two men who'd just died. But because William Meade had played a part in their deaths, he could feel their weight on his chest. Suddenly they were his familiars.

Lieutenant Canderro came out of the house surrounded by a cordon of gold braid. This was a Nassau County police operation, but Canderro seemed to be doing most of the talking. William Meade had evolved into his area of expertise. Some specialty, thought Garret, catching his eye. A moment later the detective separated himself from the group and came over.

"Hello, Garret."

His voice sounded cold, or maybe just tired, and Garret didn't think he looked well. There were dark circles under his eyes and his color was bad. Yet what reason did he have to look any better?

"A big night for our boy," said the detective flatly. "I figure you should be able to squeeze at least three police incompetency columns out of this one."

Garret allowed him his cutting edge of sarcasm. He had a right to it. "Was it you who cleared the releases to the media, or was that all Nassau PD?"

"I don't clear anything on Long Island. They run the show here. Why?"

"I was just wondering whether you agree with the official version that Meade raped the woman, then killed her along with the two cops."

"What's there not to agree with?"

Garret took out Meade's note and gave it to the detective. "A messenger delivered this about an hour and a half ago."

Canderro read the note. When he finished, he swore softly. "Sonofabitch. We could have lived without *this*."

"Was there any visual evidence of rape?"

"I don't know. There was a lot of confusion by the time I got here. Give me a few minutes."

Canderro rejoined the group he'd just left, and drew aside a tall lean man in plainclothes. Then Garret saw them go back into the house together.

It was a while before they came out. Then they went straight to Garret. Canderro introduced the tall man as Chief of Detectives Bernhardt, and they shook hands.

"We have a bit of a situation here, Mr. Garret," he said. "Can I talk to you off the record?"

Garret took a moment. Anything he agreed to in advance as being off the record, he would be morally committed not to use in print. Which could make things difficult for him at some future time. Nevertheless, he nodded.

"To begin with," said Bernhardt, "does anyone besides the three of us know about this note?"

"No."

"Good. That makes things a bit simpler. Now here's what we've got. I must admit the rape announcement was premature. It was released by an overeager officer who figured that because Meade was the perpetrator, sexual assault was included with the killing."

Bernhardt paused, a soft-spoken man who obviously had experience in presenting clear-cut police errors in their best possible light.

"The assumption that Meade killed the woman," said Garret, "was evidently premature too."

"Well, we don't really know that yet, Mr. Garret. And we won't know it until ballistics matches up guns and bullets. All we know for sure right now is that two of our most outstanding police officers, with twenty-nine years of experience between them, were shot to death by a rapist-killer. And

I'd rather you made no mention of this note to anyone until the necessary tests are made and we have the results."

"I have no trouble with that."

"I appreciate it," said Bernhardt.

"How many bullets did the woman take?"

"Three."

"What if the tests show they came from one or both of the officers' weapons?"

The chief of detectives shrugged. "Then that's how it'll be. But knowing the caliber of the two officers, I don't expect that to happen."

An instant later Chief Bernhardt was called away by one of his men. Garret stared after him. "He'll make sure it doesn't happen, won't he?"

"Probably," said Canderro.

"And you'll accept that?"

"It's not my job here to accept or not accept."

Garret said nothing.

"Don't be so superior, Garret. I wasn't in that bedroom last night, but it's not hard to put together what might have happened here. A lot of bullets were flying in a dark, enclosed space, and some of them might have ended up in the wrong place. It's too bad, but these things sometimes happen in firefights. Who can it help if it comes out that these two cops accidentally shot this girl while dying in the line of duty? And who can it hurt if it's blamed on Meade? The sonofabitch already enjoys full credit for killing seventeen people. One more victim added to his list can't change a damn thing for him."

Canderro lit a cigarette and blew smoke. "Besides, if anyone's to blame for this disaster, it's me. I was the one who found the woman and called for the stakeout in the first place. So if you were hoping for some new cops to bash in your next piece, I'm afraid you're just going to be stuck with me again."

"This Jenny Angelo—was she still seeing Meade?"

Canderro thought about that one. "In her daydreams, maybe. She told me she loved the guy when she was nine years old and never stopped. Looks like she finally died from it."

His eyes were steady on Garret's. "Let's get out of here. We're due for a talk." There was no smile as he added. "Off the record."

They drove in separate cars to a diner on Northern Boulevard and settled down with black coffee in a corner booth.

Canderro began bluntly. "Do you think I'm some kind of asshole, Garret?"

"No."

"I don't think you're one either. As a matter of fact, I like you. So let's cut the bullshit for a while. At least as much as we can. Okay?"

Garret nodded.

"The thing is, I think I've made a mistake in not telling you everything I've been doing. You may be able to help. So I'm going to tell you now."

Canderro started off being cool and matter-of-fact, then his heart took over. He talked of becoming involved—on some level—with all the principals in the case: Meade and his mother; Jenny Angelo and Natalie Bingham; the missing Tommy Lukens and the once-sexy but now dead Nancy Palewski; even the frail, elderly Reverend Mr. Cantwell, who still considered vengeance to be solely the Lord's. For the first time Canderro revealed how much he wanted this one, taking him through all the theories he'd concocted to explain

Meade's methodology and laying out every connection he'd been able to turn up.

Garret listened in a solitude of his own, saying nothing. What could he say? The lieutenant needed to unload, and he was more than ready to be a sounding board. After weeks of floundering, it felt good to be a full partner in this hunt that had become a cause for both of them.

When Canderro finished, he ordered fresh coffee and they sat brooding over it.

"What happens now?" Garret asked.

"I have to talk to Meade's mother. After last night there's no point in waiting any longer. Meade obviously knows we've got her under surveillance." He paused a moment. "I think it's important you come along."

"Why?"

"Just your presence will help. I'm the enemy, the guy who's hunting her son. You're the guy he almost killed. What do you say?"

"When do you want to do it?"

"Right now."

"All right."

"Good," said Canderro. "I'll just call my stakeout to be sure she's home."

She was.

They drove upstate in two cars with the lieutenant leading the way. When they reached the general area of Wallkill, Garret parked his own car and rode the last few minutes with Canderro.

As they neared the house, the detective alerted his surveillance crew by car phone, although Garret wasn't aware of any watchers. Canderro parked in the gravel driveway and they climbed three steps to the porch.

The door opened on Canderro's second knock, and a tall, slender woman with dark hair, cut stylishly short, stood looking at them.

"Mrs. Lipton?" said the detective.

"Yes?"

"Lieutenant Canderro. Poughkeepsie Police Department." He showed her his shield and identification but she didn't so much as glance at them. "I'd like to talk to you if I may."

She stood there, unmoving, no longer young but still an exquisite woman. One whom you knew instantly would sooner suffer real pain than reveal her age to a man. William Meade had her high cheekbones and pale eyes.

"And you, of course, are Paul Garret." She spoke quietly, without emotion. But this seemed less a lack of feeling than a mark of iron control. Stepping back, she let them in. "I've been wondering how long it was going to take you people to show up."

The porch kept the house cool, but sunless and dark. She had to turn on a lamp in the living room, which was lined floor to ceiling with books. This was not the house where William Meade had grown up, but Garret couldn't help wondering which of the books he might have read as a boy and young man. The furnishings looked old, well cared for, and quietly expensive and carried an air of people and times long gone. Above the fireplace was a formal oil portrait of a distinguished-looking man in a business suit who must have been Meade's father.

They settled into a group of chairs arranged in front of the fireplace. Sitting there, Mrs. Lipton's back was straight, her chin high. "Just to save time and set the record straight," she said, "I haven't seen my son, he hasn't called, written, or tried to contact me in any way, and I have absolutely no idea where he is." She paused. "Now if you gentlemen have any questions other than the ones I've just answered, please go ahead and ask them."

Canderro took a fresh pack of cigarettes out of his pocket. But he held the pack in his hand without opening it. "When *did* you last see your son?"

"When he was sent to Attica—about nine years ago."

"But you must have visited him in prison," said Garret.

"No, I didn't."

He just looked at her.

"Please understand," she said. "I've never had, nor do I have now, the slightest interest in either seeing or talking to a convicted rapist and murderer."

"Not even if he's your son?" said Garret.

"Especially if he's my son. I absolutely couldn't bear the sight of him."

Canderro said, "I find that a bit hard to believe."

"That's your problem, Lieutenant, not mine." She looked evenly at Garret. "I think of your wife often, Mr. Garret. You've made me know your wife through your writing, so she's the one who stays with me the most. I feel as if I have an obligation to her."

"Obligation?" Garret noticed the creamy quality of her complexion, the total absence of wrinkles. "In what way?"

"In a very real way. I brought William into this world. I gave him his life and he took hers. I guess that makes me an accessory of sorts."

She gazed coldly at the two men facing her. "Lord knows, I've tried to separate myself. I left my home of thirty years, changed my name, cut all ties to my son, my relatives, and the friends of half a lifetime."

Other than for the sound of some crows, it was quiet, and Garret tried to imagine how these past nine years—taken one hour and one day at a time—had been for her. He couldn't.

There was no way he could conjure it. He saw the lieutenant was studying the pack of cigarettes he still held unopened in his hand.

Abruptly, Canderro stood up. He put the cigarettes back in his pocket and took out a folded paper. "This is a warrant to search your house, Mrs. Lipton. I have some men outside. They won't take long and nothing will be disturbed."

"Do you think I have William hidden in the attic?"

"Not really."

"Then why must we go through all this nonsense?"

"Because you're still his mother."

Mrs. Lipton rose. Standing there, she was the same height as the chunky detective. "You don't believe a word I've said, do you?"

"No, ma'am. I don't."

"Why?"

"Maybe because I had an Italian mother."

It was beyond her. "Is that meant to be a joke?"

"A poor one. What I really meant is that it's hard for me to imagine a mother, any mother, abandoning her son because he's in trouble."

"There are varying degrees of trouble, Lieutenant."

"You mean there's some sort of sliding scale for measuring these things? At what point do you turn your back, Mrs. Lipton? After grand-theft auto? Maybe manslaughter? Not rape, but rape and murder in combination?"

She was silent. Watching, Garret found her eyes offering as little as her son's.

"All I'm trying to say," said Canderro, "is that if my mother had ever discovered that her beloved Frankie was actually Jack the Ripper, she'd have wept, prayed for my immortal soul, assured me of her undying love, and wondered what she could have done wrong. What she definitely wouldn't have done was write me off as dead and disappear from my life forever."

"Then you think I'm a cold-hearted mother?"

"No, ma'am. A warm-hearted liar."

Their eyes locked for what seemed a long moment.

"Tell me this," she said finally. "If I *am* lying, why didn't I go to see him in prison all these years?"

"I have no idea," said Canderro. "My business is with your son's aberrations, ma'am. Not yours."

He went to the front door. Moments later four detectives in utility company overalls came in and spread through the house. The lieutenant went with them.

Alone together in the living room, Garret and Mrs. Lipton heard the clump of heavy footsteps overhead and the sound of drawers being opened and closed.

Mrs. Lipton glanced at the ceiling. "I suppose you think I've been lying too."

"Did you listen to the news this morning?"

"Yes, unfortunately." Sitting there, she seemed to have disappeared inside herself. "Each day I swear I'm going to smash every radio and TV set I own, but I never do."

"You're the only one who might have a chance to save him, you know."

"No one can save my son. He's gone. I've already said my final prayers for him." She looked at him then with a new intensity. "The sooner that God and you and Lieutenant Canderro can arrange for William to die, the better it will be for him and for all those living in fear."

It was pouring as the lieutenant drove Garret back to where he'd left his car, one of those sudden summer storms that seems to come out of nowhere and disappears the same way. The drops hammered the steel roof, the wipers clicked back and forth, and Canderro sucked on his cigarette and frowned at the black, rain-slick road.

"All performance," he said. "She should get a damn Oscar. The truth is up in the bedrooms and attic. I saw it all before, but I did it legally this time, with a warrant, and took pictures, hair and fiber samples, and possible prints. She worships her golden son. She's built him a shrine. All that's missing is the incense."

Canderro glanced at Garret. "Don't tell me you believed her."

"Hardly. Certainly not what she told me while you were upstairs—that she wanted him dead." Garret gazed past the wipers and saw the sky starting to lighten in the distance. "But I do keep wondering about the rest. Why *didn't* she visit him in Attica all those years? Why did she change her name, cut herself off from everyone she knew, and just disappear? I know there are people who simply can't handle the shame of something like this, but she doesn't strike me as the type."

"She's not," said Canderro. "This lady can handle whatever she has to. So there has to be another reason for all this crap."

"There is. It's called mother-love."

"Exactly. So whatever she did, it had to be done in the hope of helping her William. And since the jewel in her crown was in jail at the time, the only way I can imagine her trying to help him would be in getting him out of there as fast as possible, in any way she could."

There was a moment of silence, and Garret saw bits of sunlight suddenly glitter like coins in the road ahead. Then the detective turned his head slightly and they looked at each other.

CHAPTER
35

It stormed again during the night, but Paul Garret, finally lost in sleep, didn't waken.

In Poughkeepsie thunder pounded Frank Canderro's head as he clung to Kate on her rumpled sheets.

Outside of Wallkill trees swayed and hissed in the woods behind Mrs. Lipton's white, clapboard house, and lightning broke in jagged streaks. Briefly, William Meade was illuminated. He stood unmoving between two tall maples, his face lifted heavenward, his eyes tightly closed in what might have been an attitude of prayer. But he was not communing with God at that moment. He was simply absorbing the rain, letting it come down over him, breathing deep, long slow breaths as the water poured off his head and shoulders.

There was no great rush tonight, no pressing need to worry about the backyard watcher, at this moment taking refuge from the storm in his partner's van out front. There really was no need to worry here at any time, but worrying was part of his nature. And after last night's trauma with Jenny, he was being doubly cautious. It was all just too depressing. You planned and planned, and you were as careful as could be, yet there were still surprises. And somehow they were never good ones.

When he felt his teeth starting to chatter, he left the woods and slipped into the house through the back door.

His mother was waiting in the leaden dark of the kitchen.

"Take off those wet clothes," she said. "The one thing we don't need at this point is you coming down with double pneumonia."

Without a word Meade stripped to his skin and stood there shivering, his body wraithlike in the darkness. His mother had an oversize bath towel ready and she rubbed him as if he were a child, while he huddled before her with his knees pressed together and his arms crossed and hugging his chest. She rubbed his shoulders and back, his thighs, genitals, and buttocks. What she couldn't reach and render warm for him was the layer upon layer of ice forming inside his chest.

"Come up to bed," she said after she'd dried him.

But even in bed, under the covers, his teeth were still chattering. Until his mother took off her gown and lay down beside him, pressing him with her flesh until its warmth broke through, holding him with her body while he just felt weak and pliant and a little sick in his heart. He needed her so badly that it spread all through him, making him want her all the way up from his toenails and down from the roots of his hair. Then he could feel himself disappearing back inside her where he had begun—and sometimes still felt sure he should have remained—disappearing back into infancy and prenatal blindness and finally into utter dissolution.

"Ma!" he cried, and kissed his mother's face, and she kissed him and wildly stroked his flesh as though something very bad had happened to him and she was desperately trying to make it better.

"It's all right," she whispered. "I'm here. It's all right."

Then his mind and heart collapsed and he felt himself lost somewhere without hope of return.

But of course he did return, and the pain came right back with him, along with his mother's voice, soft in the darkness.

"They were here today, William," she said. "Paul Garret and Lieutenant Canderro. They came with a search warrant and a whole bunch of detectives who had a fine time going through the house. It was last night that finally did it. Dear God, I can't believe you shot three people this time. And one of them Jenny."

"It wasn't like that. It wasn't that way at all."

Then he told how it really happened, feeling, even in the telling, as though he were losing his wits.

"I sent Garret a note, explaining it," he said after he'd finished.

"That hardly matters, William. Don't you know that all anybody cares about is that three more people are dead because of you?"

"I just wanted to see Jen one last time."

"Well, you saw her, and all she did in return was betray you to the police."

"She did change her mind in the end."

"That's lovely. It almost breaks my heart. I'll send her a medal so she can be buried with it."

Lightning streaked the room a brilliant silver-blue. Then thunder rolled in, rattling the windows.

Meade curled himself along his mother's side. His arm was around her and his face was pressed to her breast. "I'm sorry," he said.

"Of course you are, sweetheart. Don't you think I know that? You're always sorry. That's what makes it all so pathetic. Then the next one comes along and it starts all over again."

"You know I'm trying, Ma."

"That's not good enough anymore."

All he could do was hold her then. He felt chastened, and foolish, and fearful, as if she was finally tired of waiting for him to grow up. The shivering inside him started its icy slalom and he rode it almost gracefully, knowing she had to feel it and hoping it would soften her as always.

Not this time.

"Listen to me, William. I've done all I can but it's just not working. I can't be your keeper. I can't be with you every second. I can't—"

"You're right!" His sob broke through and cut her off. "I've made a mess, Ma. I know it. Jesus, did I ever make a mess."

She sighed and stroked his face. "Not alone, darling. You didn't do it by yourself. I started it for you. I just loved you too much. I never really gave you a chance."

She needed a moment to take hold, and there was only the rain drumming against the windows.

"But that's all history now," she said. "We can't do anything about that anymore. The only thing we can do something about is the future ... if we're to have a future. Because as things are going now, you'll soon be dead or in prison, and I'll be put away for aiding and abetting."

She kissed him as though this would in some way make the whole thing easier. "So I think it's time we put the plan in motion—get the new names, IDs, and passports. I'll have to wire the rest of our cash and negotiables into the numbered accounts in Switzerland and the Cayman Islands. Then we can start new lives in a part of the world where all this will be behind us."

In the dark Meade closed his eyes and found only greater blackness. Muffled thunder sounded in the distance.

"Why are you so sure things will be any better for me someplace else?" he asked.

"I'm not sure. But what I do know is that they've become utterly impossible for you here. If I had any doubt about that before last night, your shooting of those two policemen removed it."

"They would have shot me, Ma. I had no choice."

"Oh, you had a choice, all right. You never should have gone into that house in the first place. You have a brilliant mind, William. It's your emotional lapses that have put you where you are."

He remained very still. It seemed important right then not to move. He was absolutely certain that if he moved just the slightest bit, it would somehow make him start flying to pieces.

"Why don't you just go without me?" he said.

"Do you really think I could do that? Do you really think I could simply go off and leave you here alone? You're my life, William. If you died, whatever good is still left in me would die with you. Don't you know that yet?"

He took a long slow breath and let it out in a whispered sigh. "I know it, Ma."

"Besides, we've been preparing for this for nine years. All those elaborate disguises I wore to the prison. All that cash handed out to your jailbird friends. It's been a lot of work, but it's finally achievable. Ten days at the most is all we need. You *must* hang on."

Meade remained silent. His mind whirred, considering all

the options. Should he try for a new life? He still wasn't sure.

His mother hugged him to her. "Cheer up, darling. It's going to be better for us this way. You'll see. We'll live new lives in a new place. My first life really ended when they took you away nine years ago. I was dead inside the whole time you were gone. I'm not going to let that happen to me again.

"Not ever," she said fiercely.

CHAPTER
36

Garret flew up to Rochester for Harry Stover's funeral.

He was surprised by the large size of the crowd before he realized it was made up almost entirely of plainclothes police and the media. Someone had to have figured Meade would show up for a final farewell to his old cellmate, and spread the word accordingly.

But the only person Garret spoke to was Stover's mother, a fragile, ailing woman who accepted the governor's promised $100,000 check from Garret with shock and an embarrassing show of gratitude.

I get her son killed, he thought, *and she can't thank me enough and offers to pray for me.*

They had drinks at Jacqueline's place that evening. Then they walked to a nearby Italian restaurant for dinner. Along the way, Garret tried to spot the NYPD watcher that Canderro had arranged to tail Jacqueline. But he came up with four possibles and no certainty. He knew that when they were good, you never saw them. Even so, not being able to spot the tail made him a bit uneasy.

Funerals always made him feel lonely, and Harry Stover's was no exception. During dinner he could not get enough of looking at and touching Jacqueline. The sweet scent of life came off her and he needed it badly this evening.

Still, when she asked about the funeral, he told her, and she saw its effect on him.

"You really didn't have to go," she said.

"Of course I did."

"It couldn't have been guilt. The whole scheme was something Stover thought up himself."

"Yes, but I was the one who set it in motion. And there's always a certain accountability."

Her eyes were mocking. "To whom?"

"To myself." He looked at her. "But you of all people should be able to understand that."

"I understand it, but it doesn't make me happy."

Later, the love they made seemed particularly intense, as if each were making a declaration.

"My God, I love you," she said when she was able to form the words.

Garret held her close. He felt the support she gave him, and still wondered at the miracle of it.

He smiled. "It's just lust."

"That was *before,* dummy. When there's something left afterward, when you simply don't want to let go, it's love. Don't you know *anything?*"

"Less and less."

His hand stroked her breast.

"I think we're going to be very good for each other," she said.

"We are already."

"And lucky, too."

"Can you guarantee that?"

"Only if you stay with me."

"Nothing could tear me away," he told her.

He was faintly surprised to find that he meant it.

The ringing broke in on Garret's sleep.

But he came out of it so slowly this time that Jacqueline had already picked up the phone and said hello before he was fully awake. The clock said it was 12:53 A.M. A bit early for Meade to call, yet who else could it be?

Garret switched on a lamp so he could see Jacqueline's face. The phone was to her ear and she was simply staring at the ceiling, her expression so absorbed that she seemed to have forgotten Garret was beside her.

Her end of the conversation was almost nonexistent. Just an occasional yes or no, and even these were spoken in a dull monotone. Then, turning to Garret, she handed him the receiver.

"William wants to talk to you."

"Yes?" he said into the phone.

"Hello, Mr. Garret. The police are still saying I raped and murdered Jenny Angelo. Didn't you show them my note?"

"I did."

"Who read it?"

"Lieutenant Canderro and Nassau County's chief of detectives."

Meade's laugh had a hard edge. "Then I guess they're hanging poor Jenny on *me*."

"You're William Meade. Why should one more body bother you so much?"

"Because I loved her. Because these lies trivialize her death and reduce me to an unfeeling monster."

Garret's own false civility suddenly became too much for him. "You fucking bastard! You *are* an unfeeling monster."

There was a long silence. When William Meade finally did speak, his voice had lost none of its carefully controlled calm and politeness.

"You're wrong, Mr. Garret. I do feel. And sometime soon I hope to be able to make you understand just how deeply. Good night to you both."

The connection was broken.

Garret hung up the phone. An odd sensation, a stiffness, seemed to have dried on his cheeks, and he touched it with the tips of his fingers. Nothing was there.

Jacqueline huddled close beside him as if suddenly in need of warmth. "What did he say?"

Garret told her.

"What a strange man," she said.

"That has to be the understatement of the century."

"Do you believe what he said about the police and Jenny Angelo?"

"Yes."

"Are you going to do anything about it?"

"Am I going to *do* anything about it?" Garret looked at her curiously. "What do you expect me to do? Champion the cause of justice for William Meade?"

She was silent.

Absorbed until now with his own involvement with Meade, Garret suddenly remembered Jacqueline's one-sided conversation with him.

"What was he going on about with you?" he asked.

A faint breeze drifted through the window. It carried something sharp and salty off the East River. Jacqueline breathed it in.

"Just some ruminating," she said.

"About what?"

"Himself, naturally. And a bit about me."

Garret waited.

"He just told me how much he appreciated what I'd given him during our sessions together, and that I shouldn't blame myself for what's happened." Jacqueline paused. "He also said the hardest part of being with me for all those hours was trying not to ruin everything by letting me know how he felt about me."

"Did you know?"

"Of course."

"Didn't it bother you?"

"It did at first. I wasn't sure how far it might go. But it never came out in the open, and William was doing so well that it seemed a positive force. I mean, if his caring about me as a woman inspired him to stay on track ... Well, how could it hurt?"

"If a man is a compulsive demon, it could do more than just hurt. It could kill."

"Yes, but who knew that then?" said Jacqueline. "And William has great social skills. Especially with women. He knows about us. In one way or another he's made us his life's work. You feel it when he simply looks at you. And it's not that he's overtly carnal. That's not how he comes on. It's his interest and caring that you feel. The fact that he's finally driven to rape and murder us has got to be the ultimate irony."

Garret lay there, wordless. He was aware of a sudden tension in him that was like the tightening in a muscle before it cramps.

He reached over and turned off the light.

CHAPTER
37

"Y our mom still alive, Tommy?"

Surprised by the question, Tommy Lukens stared dully at William Meade.

"My mom?" he said. "Yeah. She's alive."

"You love her?"

"I guess so. Sure." Lukens' laugh was nervous. "I just don't think about her all that much."

"I love my mom, too," said Meade. "Only I do think about her all that much."

At near two in the morning, with four double whiskeys pumping through his blood and the cold residue of depression chilling his brain, Meade was about as far into himself as he could get. He and Tommy Lukens were alone in the cabin. Yet he could all but feel unseen presences, dead as well as alive, stirring in the wavering kerosene light.

"Remember how your mom used to bathe you when you were a little kid?" Meade asked.

"My mind don't reach that far back."

"Mine does. And I especially remember the bathing. My mom used to get right in the tub with me." He paused a moment, thinking. "I can still feel how soft she felt. I loved that. I loved everything about her body. My mom nursed me longer than most kids are nursed—long enough to remember being wild for her breasts. I guess I was just never really weaned."

Looking faintly amused, Meade sipped his whiskey.

"Christ," he laughed, "I was still sucking at momma's sweet tits when they sent me to Attica."

He gazed evenly at Lukens, waiting for his reaction. It was a while in coming.

"You really mean it?"

"You think I'd make up stuff like that?"

Lukens was being cautious. This was so crazy it had to be dangerous.

"I know these things happen," he said. "I just never could figure out how it gets started."

"It's gradual. You start out with love and closeness. Then because my dad was away so much, Mom had all this empty space to fill. Which was OK for a while. Until her own needs began to push her over the edge."

Meade's voice had gone flat, his pale eyes blank.

"But it really began when I was about twelve . . . the beginnings of puberty. Mom suddenly couldn't stand my being out of her sight. If she saw me with a girl, she'd be miserable, stretched out tight for days. Understand. At her best she was the most loving person you could imagine. I adored her. I thought she was more beautiful than any movie star. And when she smiled at me, when I had her approval, I was a giant."

Meade gulped whiskey and gazed at Tommy Lukens' rapt face.

"Yet at the other end," he said, "she could be a witch. I was scared to death of displeasing her. Whatever I did, I felt it had to be the best or I'd lose her love and be cast out. And remember. This was before our real beginning together. This was nothing but fucking foreplay."

Rising to get a fresh bottle of whiskey, Meade saw his eyes in a mirror and found them empty as air. He added to their drinks and sat down.

"Then one Saturday night," he said, "when my father was out of the country, I came home late from a church social and Mom was wild. She said she'd been worrying herself sick while I was probably busy tickling some filthy little tramp. She said I was worthless, nothing but dirt. It devastated me. At the age of twelve my goddamn life was over.

"I ran to the bathroom and began swallowing aspirin. Let her see. Let her know what she'd done to her son who loved her. And it worked. Mom was after me in a flash, grabbing and holding me and sticking her fingers down my throat until I was spewing vomit and aspirin. By now she was as hysterical as I, with the two of us blubbering like babies and clutching each other and finally stripping off our puked-up clothes and huddling together in the shower."

Meade sat brooding over his whiskey.

"This was twenty-six years ago last week," he said, "and my insides still go soft just thinking about it. Mom held me and I held her and the water was pouring down over us and all sorts of terrible yet wonderful things were happening inside me. And it was Mom who was making them happen. It was Mom who was touching me in places I knew she shouldn't be touching me. It was Mom taking my hands and making me touch *her*.

"But, oh, sweet Jesus, how it felt. And there was my own mom doing it, kissing me all over like when I was a baby, and sucking and licking me until I was sure I was going nuts. I was twelve years old, for Christ's sake! I'd had a grand total of two wet dreams and one masturbatory disaster that felt as if someone was prying open the hole with a pair of pliers. And here was my sexy, naked, thirty-two-year-old momma, with a body straight out of a *Playboy* centerfold, driving me out of my fucking skull."

Biting his lip, his face glistening with sweat, William Meade stared at Tommy Lukens in suddenly sightless remembering.

"By now Mom had us on her bed, and I swear, if she wasn't holding me, I'd have dived through the window. That's how crazy scared I was. But there were Momma's lips going at me again, whispering their messages into my brain, while she slid my stiff little dong back into that same warm place she'd once squeezed me out of."

Meade's eyes closed. Rocking gently, he softly recited a fragment out of Sappho.

> *Evening star, you bring me all things*
> *Which the bright dawn has scattered.*
> *You bring the sheep, you bring the goat,*
> *You bring the child back to its mother.*

"Jesus Christ," said Tommy.

William Meade's pale eyes opened.

"And that was our first time," he said softly. "Though not our last. How I loved and loathed that woman. How I lusted for her body and despised my own for wanting it. Goddamn it! She was stealing my fucking soul.

"Let me tell you something, Tommy. There'd be times when I'd place my hands on my mother's flesh and feel everything good in me draining away. Yet it was easier for me to be gutted than have to give it up. I lived in my own black hole. Away from Momma my life was a fraud, a constant lie. Who could I share it with? I was sick to death, and not even Mom could cure me. How could she? She was my damn disease."

Meade sat motionless.

"Sometimes I was sure I was going crazy," he said. "But that would have been too easy. God and I had something much worse in store. We'd be partners in my atonement. We'd bathe me in blood.

"And we did it, He and I. We butchered all these kids, taking them one at a time every couple of months until I had eleven little pink bodies planted around a tree. Then we topped it off by doing my dad just before I turned seventeen."

Manacled to the sink, Lukens sat on the floor gazing at Meade in disbelief.

"You killed your father?"

"Blew him and his plane clean out of the sky. I still dream about it. Hardly a night goes by that my father doesn't come to me. And I was crazy about that man."

"Then why did you...?" Lukens could not complete the question.

"Kill him?" Meade said. "Oh, I had all sorts of terrific reasons. I was jealous of his sticking it to Momma. I was scared green he'd found out about us. I had the hots for this gorgeous black piece he was keeping at the time. Who the hell knows why? The reasons keep changing. The only thing that stays the same is that I did him."

Meade watched Lukens struggle with it, a simple halfdrunk guy with little true understanding of what was being unloaded on him.

"I'm sorry," he heard Tommy say. "I guess you've had your own rough time of it."

But Meade saw no true sympathy in his face. Only terror. If this man could kill his own father, said Tommy's face, then what chance have I?

"I've decided something," Meade said. "I'm letting you go. I'm sending you home to your wife and kids."

Tommy's lips worked but no sound came from his mouth. A deep red flush stained his cheeks, his ears.

"When?" he finally asked.

"Right now."

Meade put down his drink and opened Lukens' handcuffs. Then he helped him to his feet.

Tommy clutched the sink to steady himself. His legs were wobbly. They had lost much of their strength.

"I don't understand." His voice was thick and hard to follow. "Aren't you worried I might tell the cops where you are?"

"Is that what you're going to do?"

"Jesus, no. Hey...you're giving me my goddamn life. I won't tell anyone a thing. I'll say I was blindfolded the whole time. I'll say you brought me someplace I never saw."

Panic turned his speech shrill. "Please. You've got to believe me."

"I believe you, Tommy. But I'll be leaving here soon myself, so it doesn't matter what you say."

It finally broke through and tears started from Lukens' eyes. "I thank you," he whispered. "I can't tell you how—"

Then his tongue froze between his lips, his eyes stared blindly, while no further words came to tell this strange man—this tormented killer who, by some blessed order of God, was giving him back his life—that he, Thomas Lukens, would be grateful to him for the rest of his days.

William Meade walked outside with Lukens. The killer felt good. He felt purged, atoned, somehow answered for.

A half-moon hung high over the lake and reflected a bright path on black water. Tommy Lukens breathed deeply as he stared at it.

"I never expected to see a moon again," he said. "Never. Jesus, I'm happy."

"I'm glad," Meade told him, and meant it about as much as he had ever meant anything.

Then dropping a step or two behind Lukens as they walked, Meade lifted his revolver with its attached silencer and shot him once in the back of the head.

Soundlessly, Lukens fell forward on his face.

What a lucky man, thought Meade. *How many of us ever manage to die happy?*

CHAPTER
38

After a restless night spent brooding about the implications of Meade's conversation with Jacqueline, Garret got up, breakfasted, and took a taxi directly to the Times Building.

Entering his office, he saw a small, neatly wrapped package on his desk with the mail. It was unstamped. Which meant it had probably been delivered by messenger.

Garret's first instinct was to leave it there unopened and run. As if by so doing, he could magically resurrect a life that he knew in advance was gone.

Must I really live with insanity in every breath?

He slipped on a pair of the latex gloves that Canderro had given him and carefully opened the package. Something wrapped in white tissue lay on top of a pale blue envelope addressed to Mr. Paul Garret. Unpeeling it, Garret exposed a small circular piece of what appeared to be dark meat. It was approximately an inch in diameter, was tapered to a rounded, acorn-shaped tip, and had a small opening through its center.

Staring at it, knowing what it had to be, Garret sank into what felt like a terminal fever.

Of course. The ultimate sexual mutilation. Except that the source of this particular *hors d'oeuvre* had been male rather than female.

Garret reached for the blue envelope and took out a handwritten note on matching stationery. It said:

> *Dear Mr. Garret,*
>   *Please tell Lieutenant Canderro that Tom Lukens can be found not far from Alligerville, about a hundred yards west of the intersection of routes 209 and 213. His wife may find some small comfort in knowing he died happy in the belief he was about to return home to her and the children.*
>   *The enclosed grotesquerie is a small token of what really caused his death. That pathetic thing is what gets us all in trouble. Without my own I would not be where I am today. Partially deprived of his, perhaps Tommy will do better in whatever new life awaits him.*
>
>   *Your friend,*
>   *William*

My friend, William, Garret thought.

He took a fifth of Jack Daniel's from his desk, tossed off a good, full shot straight from the bottle, and sat staring at a leather couch across the office. He stared until his last remembered sighting of William Meade took shape there...a lean, handsome man gazing pleasantly at him over the barrel of a 9-millimeter automatic.

All right, enough, he told Meade in the faintest of mental whispers. *Why take it out on all these others? Come after* me. I'm *the one you really want. I know you're close. I can feel you sniffing around. Come on, friend William. Here I am.*

Garret did feel he was getting closer, that there was a subtle narrowing of spaces. He had an almost psychic awareness of his presence and he was not normally big on such things. He just wished he could know Meade better. He was trying very hard to slide inside him, to hear and feel his breathing, to conjure up the twisted images that haunted him.

This was what Garret wanted. But as of now, the most he could do was pick up the phone and call Lieutenant Canderro.

CHAPTER
39

Unwilling to assign the unhappy task to anyone else, Canderro took it on himself to drive Tommy Lukens' wife downtown to formally identify her husband's body. Earlier, having taken on the role of death messenger as well, he had brought the news that deprived the same woman of her husband, and her two young children of their father.

At the morgue there was a long, terrible walk through corridors smelling of antiseptic and embalming fluid. An attendant led them to a room with refrigerated bins, and pointed to a wheeled stretcher where Tom Lukens' body lay covered with a sheet.

The lieutenant uncovered Lukens' face.

Meade's bullet had entered the back of Tommy's head, angled upward and exited at the top, leaving his face undamaged. His eyes were open and his lips were drawn in what might have passed for the barest suggestion of a smile. Canderro glanced at his widow, a pretty young woman with trendy, deliberately frazzled blond hair and dark, hurt eyes. She had said very little since Canderro had appeared at her door with the bad news, and whatever she felt was well controlled.

"That's him," she said in a flat voice. "That's Tommy."

She turned away and Canderro brought the sheet back with a professional turn of his wrists. After a certain number of years, you became accomplished even at things like this, he thought.

The detective walked beside her under the naked glare of fluorescent tubes. The light was a sickly white, the silence as dead as a stretch of desert.

"Are you all right?" he asked.

"I'm OK," she said. "You don't look too great, though. I guess all this is getting to you, huh, Lieutenant?"

Canderro said nothing. It wasn't the response he'd expected.

"I just want you to know I appreciate your kindness," said Mrs. Lukens. "I mean, never mentioning anything about Tommy and that Palewski girl."

She saw his face and shrugged. "Not everyone's like you. People are always looking for angles. I don't know how they find out these things. Just yesterday I was offered a lot of money by one of those supermarket rags for my story. 'What story?' I asked. 'The story of not knowing about your husband's cheating until after his body showed up,' they said."

Mrs. Lukens stopped walking and Canderro stopped with her. He breathed deeply and felt his nostrils burn from the stricken air.

"What do you think, Lieutenant? I've got two little kids to raise, piles of unpaid bills, and no husband. Would it be so terrible if I took the money?"

"Hell, no. Who can it hurt? Not your husband."

"That's how I'm starting to figure it. And I swear I think Tommy would even like the idea of our being paid money for what he did, and for what finally ended up happening to him because of it. I think he'd feel he deserved it."

They started down the corridor again.

Whatever Lukens might deserve, thought Canderro, a bullet in the head, a sliced prick, and a slab in the morgue were definite overpayments. He had a sudden fantasy of his own death then, with his spirit struggling to tear itself loose and lift off, and Kate weeping and kneeling in prayer and wondering how much *she* might be able to get for *her* story.

Back in Canderro's car, they rode without speaking.

"I'd like you to understand something," the widow Lukens finally said. "I know Tommy did his share of tomcatting around, but I also know he loved me. That's just how he was and one thing never had anything to do with the other. I caught him once and he was so afraid I'd leave him that he cried like a baby and swore he'd never touch another woman again. And I know he tried not to, Lieutenant. But for some married men, chasing women is like alcohol is for others. And there's not a single chapter of Adulterers Anonymous they can go to for help."

Canderro needed Kate badly that night. Another one for the morgue always made him feel the weight of his own limitations—left him wanting to escape himself.

And escape himself he did, letting an old excitement take him up and then down, all the while thinking, *Jesus, I'm lucky,* because he knew even while it was happening that it didn't have to be anywhere this terrific.

They were adrift in the following quiet, but not asleep, when the telephone rang. Kate answered it, then handed

Canderro the receiver. "It's one of your men, Detective Vaughn."

He saw it was not yet ten. In his mind it was well past midnight. "What's up, Danny?"

"There's an outside chance we may have spotted him."

Canderro's knuckles went white on the receiver. "You're sure?"

"We're not sure of a damn thing, Lieutenant. That's why I'm calling. We don't want to take a chance of screwing this up."

"Who's with you?"

"Eagan."

"Where?"

"Half a mile south of Ashokan. On a two-lane blacktop running west of Route Twenty-eight. It may be nothing, but you'd better approach dark. Not even parking lights."

"What about backup?"

"Please, Lieutenant. No mob scene. We're shit-deep in the woods here and every fucking sound carries. Also, we haven't that much to go on and don't want to look like ass-holes if it turns out to be nothing. If we're on target, the three of us should be enough anyway."

"Give me twenty minutes," said Canderro.

In what seemed a single motion, he tossed the receiver back to Kate and was out of bed and started to dress.

"Frankie?" she said.

He was pulling on his pants. "Yeah?"

"Be careful."

It took him seven minutes longer than he'd expected. It was a black, starless, moonless night and he had to inch along the last few hundred yards without his lights. He never saw the two figures in the road until he was ten feet away from them. Even then they were no more than silhouettes, Eagan's tall and thin, Vaughn's broad and chunky. They slid into the car with Canderro.

"Here's how it is," Vaughn said. "We'd been checking the area all afternoon and found nothing. But when it was just starting to get dark and we were finishing up, we saw lights cutting through the trees about a quarter mile west. Our fucking maps don't even show a road there, so we hiked down and checked it out."

Vaughn licked his lips and swallowed dryly, a solemn man who seldom smiled. "We found what must have been an old logging trail. So we followed it a pretty good distance and finally spotted a small cabin on the edge of a lake. There were no lights and we didn't see anyone around. But we were being cautious. We never got any closer than a few hundred yards."

"That's it?" Canderro felt let down. "A cabin and an old logging trail?"

"No," said Eagan. "We saw the car too. It was parked away from the cabin and covered with brush. If we hadn't been searching, we'd never have spotted it. We got the plate number. Then we made it back here to our car and called in for a computer check."

Eagan paused for effect. "Listen to this. The goddamn car was reported stolen an hour before."

Canderro looked at his two detectives and they stared back. But they suddenly seemed uncertain.

"What do you think, Lieutenant?" said Vaughn.

Canderro shook his head. "I don't know balls about whether you've stumbled on Meade. But you've sure as hell scratched us up a car thief."

• • •

Crouched in the darkness outside his cabin, William Meade had to deal with his own uncertainties.

Less than two hours ago, his warning buzzer had gone off in the cabin. With no regular electric power he'd improvised a simple, battery-operated photoelectric beam to cover the trail and give him a few minutes' notice when someone was headed his way. It had worked well enough with Tommy Lukens, but it was also sometimes set off by foraging deer and raccoons. This time he didn't know who or what it had been.

Still, taking the buzzer seriously, he'd remained on full alert. His night-vision goggles bulged grotesquely over his eyes, his infrared light was in his lap, and a fully loaded automatic with attached silencer was in his hand. He was ready. He also was on edge. His senses told him there was something different about this, and he trusted his senses.

For the third time in the past half-hour he checked his equipment. He turned on the invisible infrared beam, adjusted his goggles, and saw the woods glow green around him. Insects trailed pearls of green fluorescence like the contrails of high-flying planes. He was in a luminous, eerily beautiful world but found himself too skittish to enjoy it.

Meade focused the infrared on the trunk of a nearby tree, aimed his automatic at a finely textured section of bark, and imagined himself squeezing off a dry round. *Whoosh*. A kid playing cops and robbers. But when had he gotten to be the bad guy?

The thought depressed him. *Think about something important*, he told himself. *Think about what set off the buzzer*.

He tried to believe it had been an animal. But his mood was such that it didn't work. He was at one of his low points and from there he thought only the worst. And the worst right now was that it had been something more than an animal, or someone hiking or hunting small game, or young lovers looking for a place to lie down. This intruding unknown had disappeared very quickly, which in itself was disturbing. As if having discovered something suspicious, he or they had hurried off to take some sort of action.

Or am I just getting paranoid?

William Meade waited:

If I have to, I can wait this way all night.

I can do anything.

I can be a tree, grass, part of the earth.

I can be all that I really am and can ever be ... dust.

The night and the woods, in combination, were so dark that it was nearly impossible for the three detectives to follow the overgrown trail. They walked slowly, single file, Vaughn and Eagan taking point and second position because they had been here earlier when there was still a bit of light, and at least had some idea of where they were going. At the rear of the column, Canderro was aware of a black bulk moving in front of him, and that was all. It was easy to stumble, so they walked with their weapons holstered and no more than four-foot intervals between them. At moments the lieutenant felt utterly foolish—three professionals performing a night problem in futility. At other times some instinct waiting in his head told him they were marching straight into a pit and that if they had any brains at all, they'd get out of there this minute and come back in the morning when they could see something more than a wall of night.

He remembered Kate telling him to be careful, and wondered how you were supposed to be careful in this line of work. And if you could be careful, would you? And if you would, how much of a cop could you finally hope to be?

When they had been walking for about twenty minutes,

Vaughn stopped and indicated a dark, formless mass at the side of the trail.

"The car's under there," he whispered.

Canderro saw only a black abstraction. "Where's the cabin?"

"A few hundred yards straight ahead," said Eagan. "If there were any lights, we'd see them from here."

They stood clustered in silence.

Breathing the pine-laden air, Canderro felt the tightness in his throat that came from knowing that this near-total darkness gave the edge to the guy who was dug in—not the guys who were trying to flush him out.

Fifteen yards away, William Meade knelt in the brush with his night-vision goggles in place and focused. He shone his infrared light on the faces and bodies of the three detectives, rendering them a luminescent green. He recognized Lieutenant Canderro but had never seen the other two men. More lying cops who just wanted to blow his brains out. His heart was going fast enough to shake his chest, yet his hands were steady and dry.

He had heard them talking and it was all becoming clear. It was the other two cops, not the lieutenant, who had set off the buzzer earlier. They were explaining things, so they'd probably called Canderro afterward. They were still only guessing. They'd never gotten close enough to the cabin to know for certain that it was his. The car seemed important so they may already have checked out the plate number. Because there were only the three—and they were all but sightless—he felt he had a better than fair chance of controlling the action.

Dear Jesus be with me now.

The silent prayer was automatic, a half-forgotten reflex. In truth, he was starting to enjoy the situation. Suddenly, *he* wasn't the prey. *They* were. And they didn't even know. He watched them, letting the hate build, despising them more each second. Insects. What were *their* lives compared to *his*?

Three blind mice.

The three detectives were still huddled together, their whispers now so soft that Meade no longer could make out their words.

See how they run.

His mouth twisted into a grimace. No time for freaking out. If he was going to do this right, he had to get all three of them. If just one got away, the cabin and all it meant would be finished for him. Again, he could feel his heart going very fast and he kept yawning, dryly, nervously. He brought his gun up.

Then he stopped and thought about it. Was he being foolish? It was all in his favor but he'd still be facing three armed cops and anything could happen in a firefight. If he simply left them alone, he could just fade off into the dark and get away clean.

Yes, but get away to where and to what purpose? To hell with that. The top of his head was lifting, coming off. *I love this place, damn it! It's Dad's and mine. They have no right, no right.*

The detectives' discussion seemed to be over. Having broken apart, they were preparing to move on toward the cabin. Meade again brought up the automatic, his finger gentle on the trigger. He aimed at the nearest detective, seeing his chest glow green in the infrared light. But he hesitated a second time. He blinked rapidly over the gunsights, immobilized. Then he thought, *Hell! Whatever happens, it'll be worth it. Just blow the vermin away.*

Meade fired.

Squeezing off his shots quickly, in clusters of two, he heard only the soft whooshing sounds made by the silencer. He felt the gun bucking in his hand and saw the first detective go down. Then the second man went and finally the third disappeared from sight as well.

Meade crouched there, holding very still. He quieted his breath to keep it from rasping in his throat, but something was laughing and singing inside him. He'd done it. He'd gotten them all. His home—his life as it had come to be—was preserved. Not a shot had been fired in return and he'd heard no movement, no sound other than those of a summer night. When a full five minutes had passed, Meade began slowly circling toward the bodies.

He stayed close to the ground, snaking along on elbows and knees. His automatic was in one hand, his infrared was in the other. His bug-eyed goggles made him look like an earthling's latest vision of an extraterrestrial. Then cautiously peering out from under a bush, he saw them.

They lay in so confusing a jumble of arms, legs, and bodies that it was hard to sort things out for an accurate count. When Meade finally accepted the fact that there were no more than two bodies, and that the third cop was unmistakably gone, a sharp pain thrust into him. It was replaced instantly by a slow burning. *How could I have missed?* Then still flat out on the ground, he searched for possible pulse beats and found none. He learned, too, that the missing man was Lieutenant Canderro.

I should have killed him long ago.

It had all been so fast.

One moment they were standing in the dark, preparing to move on toward the cabin. Then the next instant there were the sudden whooshing sounds of a silencer and all three of them going down—Canderro out of pure reflex and some black prayer of salvation, Vaughn and Eagan grunting and gushing blood. Canderro felt their warm wetness on his hands and against his face. If they weren't already dead, they had to be close to it.

He crawled off the trail and into the brush. The urgency of life was in his throat and in the almost frenzied speed of his movements. He felt a dizziness, a loss of balance in the dark. How could the guy shoot like that in such blackness? He had to have night glasses. And how had he known they were coming? Another stupid question. *He had known.*

Canderro stopped behind some brush, drew his revolver, and lay there listening. If he couldn't see, he would have to hear. But what? He hadn't even seen a muzzle flash. All he knew was that the silenced shots had come from somewhere to the left of the trail and he was now somewhere to the right. With Vaughn and Eagan down and spewing blood in between.

Two more deaths. And he had a clear sense of his own on the way. I shouldn't have listened to Vaughn. I should have called in for backup. He was disgusted with himself. All these years in the job, then making a blunder like this.

It occurred to him only then that he didn't even know for sure that it was Meade out there. Yet who else could it be? A car thief? Bullshit. A car thief would have just taken off, not tried to murder the three of them. It was Meade.

His brain seemed to be working with difficulty but his choices were clear enough. He could stay where he was, let Meade come looking for him and hope for a quick lucky shot with surprise in his favor. Or he could try to slip back to his car in the darkness and belatedly call in for support. Or he could take a chance on instant suicide by trying to blindly hunt down Meade while the killer watched him approach through his night glasses and neatly picked him off. Of course his final option was to simply stay hidden for five or six hours until daylight evened out the odds. Then he could go after him.

Having worked through his own options, Canderro tried to imagine what Meade would be planning for himself. He pressed his cheek to the ground as if to feel the texture of the killer's thoughts. *Speak to me, you sick fuck.* But all he was left with was a face full of dirt and eyes crowded with night.

Meade still lay with the dead. His flesh was smeared with their blood and his heart seemed to have gone awry. When he breathed, the air smelled burned. Why not? The hot barrel of his automatic was under his nose. And it was all for nothing. Two dead cops, and because the third was still alive out there, he was homeless, a desolate. He would have to leave here, leave this place, leave the heart of his only good memories.

He thought of trying to hunt down Canderro, of killing him and thereby changing everything. But with the forest so impenetrable and far-reaching, it seemed a forlorn hope, and he quickly gave up the idea. There also was no way of knowing whether the lieutenant or one of his men had called in the cabin's location before starting toward it themselves. It was all over for him here.

He lay in the dead silence.

Then his mind slipped into gear and put him in motion. Not knowing where Canderro was or whether he might be watching the stolen car, he decided to keep away from it. Instead, he took several bunches of keys from the two detectives' pockets and circled off through the trees.

He moved carefully, stopping every few moments to listen. His brain still seemed to be working in fits and starts and he was just making one move at a time. He couldn't trust his judgment for any more than that. In losing his spiritual shelter, his one true home, he felt as though he'd lost his core.

Meade reached the narrow blacktop and saw the two unmarked police cars parked about fifty yards away. He checked the keys he'd taken, found one that fit an ignition, and drove off without lights.

It was then that he knew where he was going. Only then. And it came to him as quickly and simply as that. *Of course,* he thought, and smiled. It was enough to make him believe in a benevolent God after all.

But first he stopped at a nearby parking area, broke into and jump-started a suitably inconspicuous-looking gray Toyota and dumped the police car into a handy ravine. From there it took him no more than twenty minutes to drive to the house.

It was a strange feeling to come back. Not unpleasant. The fact was, it felt good. Positive and hopeful. Almost as if it were part of some grand design. Like closing a circle.

He parked the car out of sight in a garage that had once been a barn. Then he walked around to the front door and picked open the lock. Inside, he turned the switch on a lamp and found the electricity still working. Having established that fact, he cut off the light, put on his night goggles, and started up the stairs.

Steps, walls, and ceiling quivered with tones of iridescent green, and at the outer fringes of his vision was the graceful arch of a rainbow. His flesh tingled. It felt renewed in a way he could not recall it ever having felt before. When he put his hand on the banister, the polished wood was alive against his palm. He was ready to remain on this single flight of steps for the rest of the night.

Then he was off the stairs, across the bare, wood planking of the upper hallway and facing the bedroom where it had all started. *My memorial.*

The door was closed and the stenciled police placard proclaiming the room a crime scene was still hanging across it. Garret had, of course, been back for his brief visit the day he'd left the hospital, but Meade was sure he hadn't returned since. Self-inflicted pain was not his style. *That's more my thing.* Meade opened the door and went inside.

He stood there, slowly moving his infrared about the dark room. The calm he felt was very fine, very delicate in its balance. It was enough for him to just stand there and look. He looked at the chalk outlines of Garret's body on the floor where he'd fallen and should have died, yet somehow hadn't. He looked at the dark bloodstains reaching out from a still-darker core. And he looked, finally, at the chalk marks and bloodstains on the rumpled sheets of the bed where he'd left Emily Garret's body.

It was all there. A quiet scene. *Like an empty glade,* he thought.

A framed mirror hung on the wall above a dresser and Meade approached it in the darkness, focused his infrared directly on his face and considered his reflected image.

What stared back at him might have been a gargoyle carved in green stone, and his bulging goggles only added to the illusion. Overall, it was perhaps the most threatening face he'd ever seen. It was the truth. It was precisely the kind of truth one discovers by walking into a room and seeing a beautiful and, until then, virtuous woman engaged in the most degrading sexual act imaginable.

Meade removed his gargoyle's popping eyes and cut off

the infrared. But even in the darkness, the dreadful image stayed with him.

Then numbly, feeling the last of his strength and will beginning to ebb, he groped his way to the bed and lay down with the dried blood and welcoming ghost of Emily Garret.

CHAPTER
40

It was early, seven in the morning, and they were at Jacqueline's place.

"Paul! Come fast!"

Jacqueline's words were shouted.

Garret was in the shower but there was enough in her voice to bring him out dripping, half-blind, and groping for a towel. He dug soap out of his eyes and stumbled into the room. Jacqueline was sitting up in bed, naked, staring at the television. Her face was pale, with two round spots of color high on her cheeks.

"I'm not sure," she said. "I just tuned in. But I think they've found William."

Garret was instantly beside her. His stomach was in his throat and water was running from his ears. He saw the familiar face of the news commentator for the "Early Show," heard the professional smoothness of his voice, but could make out only bits of what he was saying.

Then as if driven by a will of its own, the camera was all

333

over the place, an erratic, fluttering eye blinking at a cabin in the woods, and patches of early morning mist, and a lot of uniformed and plainclothes police milling about. There were voices shouting, and a siren in the distance and the flashing party hats of patrol cars. Finally, in the midst of it all, Garret was able to pick out the two green body bags being carried toward a van, with an unshaven, disheveled, and almost equally green Canderro solemnly escorting their passage like a combination mourner and guard of honor.

Was it possible? Was William Meade really lying dead... a corpse, a piece of inert meat, in one of those bags?

Garret couldn't believe it. Or if he did believe it, he didn't want to. And even if he wanted to, there was an insane rage tearing around inside him that said this wasn't how it was meant to happen, not this way, not off somewhere in the middle of the night while he, Paul Garret, slept peacefully through it, unaware and unknowing. It absolutely couldn't be.

I'm crazy.

But then the commentator's voice broke through and he heard the facts as they were then known...with the only conclusive truths being that the beast's lair had finally been uncovered, two more police officers were dead, and the killer himself had once again flown away.

At the end, like a fox run to ground and surrounded by baying hounds, Canderro stood facing clusters of reporters, photographers, and minicam units. They made sharp, stabbing attacks, their strobe lights ripping the fog, their shouted questions flying, their faces greedy with false friendliness.

"Hey, Lieutenant," one called. "How did you finally find him?"

"A lot of routine pick-and-shovel work," said the lieutenant. "Then detectives Vaughn and Eagan spotted head-lights where there wasn't even a road."

"Why didn't you have more backup?" shouted another reporter.

Canderro stared blankly into the camera. "We didn't know it was Meade when we went in."

"You mean it takes two dead cops to find out something like that?"

The lieutenant's eyes were cold. He started to speak, then changed his mind and said nothing. Watching, Garret could almost feel the anger and frustration fly out of his face.

"Do you have any idea where Meade may have gone?" someone else asked.

"I'm not free to answer that." Canderro started to walk away.

A tall, heavyset reporter stepped in front of him. "Before you leave, Lieutenant, how do you explain this mess?"

Canderro gave him a long, slow look. *"Mess?"*

"Yes, *mess*," said the man. "You went in after Meade in the middle of the blackest night of the year, used only two cops, and got both of them killed. And Meade got away clean in one of your own cars. Who's to blame for all that?"

The lieutenant did not so much as blink. *"I am,"* he said and walked away.

That was the heart of it.

Jacqueline cut off what remained with the remote, and they sat with the following silence.

It was Jacqueline who spoke first.

"It was so strange," she said. "For a few moments back there, when I saw them carrying those body bags, I thought William was in one of them."

"I thought so, too."

She looked at him then. "How did it make you feel?"

A lie started in his brain but never left his mouth. She deserved better. "Angry," he said. "Cheated. As if an important part of me had been left hanging somewhere."

"Not happy?"

Garret shook his head. "Not really. What about you?"

Jacqueline was silent for so long that Garret knew she had to be fighting back her own collection of lies.

"I didn't feel happy, either," she finally said. "But it wasn't just because it involved William. I'd have felt the same way about any life being ended."

"I don't think that's entirely true."

"Why not?"

Garret rose tiredly from the edge of the bed, leaving a broad wet mark on the sheets. His towel trailed limply from his hand.

"The thing is," he said, "we both want Meade's rampage to end, but we each want it on our own terms. You'd like him alive and seeking redemption. One of your poor black sheep returned to the fold. While I'll take him either alive or dead, but I still want to be part of the taking. That's my monkey right there. So I'm afraid we've still got our own little needs to satisfy."

Garret called Canderro from his office. The detective wasn't yet at headquarters, though, so Garret tried him at his home number.

"Yeah?" Canderro's voice was hoarse with cigarettes, whiskey, and sleep.

"Paul Garret, Lieutenant."

"What the hell time is it?"

"About nine."

Canderro groaned. "Shit. I just got to bed at seven."

"I'm really sorry about your two men."

"This a fucking condolence call?"

"There's something I want to check with you."

"OK," the lieutenant said, yawning. "What's up?"

"Do you think Meade's mother knows he murdered his father?"

"Never thought about it."

"Well, think about it now."

Canderro took a moment. "Hard to tell. But all things considered, I can't really see the guy sharing something like that with his old lady."

"Unless she hated her husband and talked Billy-Boy into getting rid of him for her."

"You're starting to think like a cop, Garret. But I can't buy that either. What's your point?"

"I want to go over there tonight and try hitting her with it. Alone. Just the two of us. No cops present. In a sense, both of us victims of her son. Maybe I can reach something in her. Especially after last night. Christ! You almost had him there. Now her boy is out in the cold, running, with no place to go."

The line was silent.

"What do you say, Lieutenant?"

"Sure. Why not?" Canderro's tone was suddenly flat. "I really did fuck it up last night. I mean, I *had* the sonofabitch. And all I ended up with was two good guys dead and a pile of crap."

Garret stood on the porch of Meade's mother's house in Wallkill, breathed the sweetness of the honeysuckle and knocked on the door. It was close to one in the morning. According to Lieutenant Canderro people were most vulnerable when torn from sleep at this hour, so why not operate under the best possible conditions.

About a hundred yards up the block, Garret spotted the car that Canderro had told him would be part of the continuing stakeout. With no place else to go, maybe Meade would finally become desperate enough to try to sneak home to Momma.

A yellow porch light went on and Mrs. Lipton's voice called from the darkness above. "Who's there?"

"It's Paul Garret, Mrs. Lipton."

Other than the crickets, there was only silence. Garret considered it to the woman's credit that she had enough confidence, sensitivity, and understanding not to have said anything more at this point.

Moments later Mrs. Lipton came down in a short summer robe. Then still without speaking, she led Garret into the kitchen where she seemed programmed to instantly put up a pot of coffee. It was that automatic.

She sat down at a breakfast table and lit a cigarette, making a small ritual of the act so that her presence was all the more enlarged in the light of her two more obvious addictions. Sitting there, Garret felt a curious intimacy between them in this nighttime kitchen under its sterile, white fixture.

"All right, Mr. Garret," she said, now that she apparently was ready to deal with him. "Exactly what is it you need so desperately from me at one in the morning?"

"I'm sure you know that a lot better than I. You're his mother."

Her hand rose and fell in a weary gesture that held more resignation than annoyance.

"Please," she said. "We've been all through that. Why must we repeat everything? Nothing is different."

"Wrong. Things are very different for Tom Lukens and detectives Vaughn and Eagan. All three were murdered by your son since I was here last. Or doesn't that mean anything to you?"

Garret watched her face as he spoke. He hoped it would tell him more than anything she might have to say with words. The world in which she lived was not one of normal responses.

"It means something to me," she said. "I care about human life. But that still doesn't help me know where William is."

"Canderro's been all through this house. He's seen your shrine to William. You adore him. So stop this crazy playacting and help us save lives. His included."

Mrs. Lipton folded her hands about her coffee mug and said nothing. At this point she wore an expression that Garret had learned to recognize as belonging to those in the criminal trades. It was a tough look, the kind worn by those who followed their own paths. She would have made one hell of a gangster.

"We're not enemies," he told her. "We've both been hurt. I've lost a wife and you've lost a son. But your loss is worse because William is still out there killing. Please..."

Garret stopped. It was useless. There was a remote little glow in her eyes that put her so far beyond him that he might as well have been out of the room.

"I'm going to have to tell you something," he said. "I don't like having to do it, but you leave me no choice. Your husband's death was no accident. William murdered him. He put a bomb on his plane. Just as he did upstate the other day."

The quickest and truest reaction to shock always came from the body. It couldn't protect itself with thought, as the brain could do. To Garret it was as though Mrs. Lipton had taken a jolt of electricity. It turned her back rigid, made a pale mask of her face, and set her hands trembling. But she recovered quickly, and when she spoke, her voice was normal.

"Where did you ever pick up such a story?"

"Lieutenant Canderro got it from a woman named Natalie Bingham. And she got it from William himself."

Mrs. Lipton's mask slipped. "And who is Natalie Bingham?"

"Your husband's longtime mistress. They had four children together. Mr. Meade left a trust for them in his will. That was how Canderro found her in the first place. You can check the facts yourself. The trust was called the Phoenix Children's Center to keep you from learning about the bequest."

Mrs. Lipton groaned softly. But no words followed to explain what she was feeling or ask the questions that needed to be asked. Nevertheless, Garret gave her the answers.

"Your son found out about them and decided to play avenging angel. Unless he just wanted the woman for himself. Because he did become her lover afterward."

"But dear God. William *adored* his father."

"That can change in an instant with someone like William. Remember that. Because one wrong move and you could finally be in danger too."

Mrs. Lipton sat with it, and Garret could almost feel his chest fill with what she had to be experiencing. What takes place inside a mother's heart at the thought of being murdered by her own son? This mother was tough, but how tough would it finally be possible for her to be?

"I'll be honest with you, Mr. Garret. Nothing William may have done, or may still do can surprise me too much anymore. So in a crazy sort of way, what seems to hit me hardest at the moment is this woman and the four bastard children you tell me my husband fathered."

Mrs. Lipton shook her head in slow wonder. "Good Lord. How could I have lived with a man for almost a quarter century and known so little about him?"

"It all happened a long time ago."

"Not to me it didn't. It happened to me less than five minutes ago. Do you think there's a statute of limitations on that kind of hurt?"

She looked at Garret. "What other glad tidings do you have in store for me? So far, you're really making my night."

Garret was silent.

"Not that I blame you," she said in a voice soft enough to make all conversation seem remorseful. "You're simply an angry man whose wife was murdered by my son. If you put a gun to my head, I'd understand it. But not even that could make me tell you something I don't know."

CHAPTER
41

illiam Meade lay stretched out under a cluster of

William Meade lay stretched out under a cluster of
bushes at the back of his mother's house.
Through the lighted kitchen window he was able
to see his mother sitting alone over coffee and a cigarette.
Garret was no longer there. But Meade had arrived in time to
see him and his mother talking earlier.

Interesting.

Finding Garret in the house had been a surprise, but easy
enough to understand. Garret was frustrated and the body
count was getting to him, so he was putting more pressure on
Momma. No problem there. Mom could handle him. She
also could handle Canderro, his cops, and anyone else they
might throw at her. A perennially capable, self-contained
woman. Sometimes maybe even a trifle too much so. But
that was something else entirely.

When the kitchen finally went dark, Meade checked the
back surveillance man and found him dozing at his usual
post among the trees. Then he snaked through the shadows to

a dry well at the side of the house, slid open a silently moving window, and slipped into the basement.

Moments later he entered his mother's room and saw her on the bed. In the dark, lying there, she looked very tall and slender, almost elongated.

"Mom?"

She neither moved nor spoke, and he thought she was asleep. Then moving closer, he saw that her eyes were open and she was staring at him rather strangely.

"I'm OK," Meade told her, because this was their first contact since the police had stumbled on his place and she had to be anxious. "The fools never even got off a shot. It's just too bad Canderro had to slip away and wipe out the cabin for me. But I have another place. A real brainstorm. Listen to this. I've moved into Garret's house."

He grinned. "Could you imagine anything more beautiful? *I'm living in Paul Garret's house.* They'll never figure that one out in a million years."

But his mother failed to respond as expected. She just lay staring at him through the dark, a stretched-out figure in a pale, luminous gown. A silent ghost.

Meade eased down on the edge of the bed. "You all right, Mom?"

"No. I'm not all right."

Even her speech seemed strange to him. It sounded stilted, blurred, as though she was having trouble forming the words.

"What is it? What's wrong?"

"What's wrong is that Paul Garret was here to see me again. This time, alone."

"I know. I saw him through the kitchen window. And I'm sure he's still putting pressure on you. But why should that bother you? He's harmless."

"Not so harmless."

Mrs. Lipton closed her eyes. When she opened them a few seconds later, they glistened.

"He told me about Natalie Bingham and her lovely little family. He also told me what you did to your father. I thought I was finally beyond pain where you and your father were concerned. I was wrong on both counts. Obviously the worst was yet to come."

William Meade's first instinct was to perform... to claim ignorance... to deny, deny. But that was too much even for him. His entire insides seemed to have gone into reverse, to have broken down and reconstituted themselves backward. He ached. From the top of his head to the little bones in his feet, he simply ached.

"I never wanted you to know," he whispered. It was all he could manage.

"And that's supposed to make everything all right?"

"I'm sorry."

"Again?" Her voice broke. "What are you sorry about? That you murdered your father? That he was betraying your poor, dear mother? That he was making a fool of her for years with another woman and an entire new family?"

She paused, pressed down by the weight.

"Or are you just sorry," she said, "that I had to find out about the whole miserable business?"

Meade said nothing. He reached for her hand where it lay on the bed, held it in both of his, and began to weep. Emotion blinded him. He tried twice to speak and could not.

Then the cold anger came. It started slowly but grew fast. Soon, it began freezing the tears and turning the rest of him to a thing of ice.

"Come to sleep," said his mother.

Meade took off his clothes and lay with her. But the anger kept him awake, and he spent most of what remained of the night thinking about and planning the chronology and more salient details of what he now knew he was going to have to do.

It was not yet 6:00 A.M. and still mostly dark when Meade was up and gone from his mother's house and well on his way to Manhattan.

He had allowed himself less than three hours' sleep, but he needed no more. He was still pumped up with more energy than his veins could contain or his nerve endings could handle. He felt so hyper that there was almost exultation in it. When had he eaten last? It didn't matter. He was running fine on empty.

He reached East Seventy-sixth Street at shortly before seven and left his latest car, a Volvo, in a metered parking space just off Lexington Avenue. Then he walked around the block to Seventy-fifth Street and spotted the watcher immediately.

The detective was sitting in a teal blue Plymouth about fifty feet west of Jacqueline Wurzel's converted brownstone. He was reading a newspaper and smoking a cigarette. His elbow rested on the open window beside him.

It was a quiet residential area with little traffic moving at this hour. Meade counted five pedestrians on the street, but they were all a good distance away and none was headed in his direction.

Meade quickly walked toward the surveillance car. He had on the same jeans and sport shirt he had worn the night before, and he carried a folded newspaper in his hand. With Meade approaching from the Plymouth's rear, the detective was unaware of him until he bent and leaned across the car's open window.

"Excuse me, sir. Do you have the time?"

The detective glanced at his watch without turning. At that moment Meade lifted the folded newspaper, held it level with the detective's head, and fired through it. There was only a single, soft, whooshing sound and the detective fell over sideways on his seat and lay still.

Meade looked up and down the block. The traffic light had just changed to green at the corner of Lexington, and a cluster of three cars was approaching. No problem there. They'd simply drive past. But a man and woman had just come out of a nearby brownstone on his side of the street and were headed his way. This was possible trouble.

Meade quickly opened the car door, shoved the dead man's legs and torso out of the way, and sat down behind the wheel. He closed the door as the couple passed. They were arguing and were not even aware of him.

All right.

Meade slowly rolled his head to ease the tightness in his neck. He had to relax. He was too tense. This was all his—he was in total control and there was nothing to be uptight about. He just had to keep his head on.

There was a clipboard on the dash and he looked over the attached sheet. The watcher evidently called in every hour on the hour and he'd already completed his seven o'clock check-in. Good. By eight it would no longer matter whether he made any more calls or not.

Meade spread sheets of newspaper over the detective's body in case some passerby happened to glance in. Then he rolled up the open window, got out of the car, and locked the doors behind him.

Jacqueline Wurzel left her building at 7:30 A.M., her usual time, and walked a long block east to the big underground garage where she kept her car.

It was a clear, sunny morning, a perfect summer day, but she was unaware of it. Her thoughts these days had little to do with the weather. She found her bright, happy-looking red Mustang in its usual space and waved to an attendant washing a car as she drove past him to the street.

Traffic was heavy going north on the Franklin D. Roosevelt Drive, but it began opening up by the time Jacqueline neared the city line.

Heading for her White Plains office, she was having a hard time concentrating on her morning's work schedule. So far, her suspension was turning out to be strictly public relations. She still worked her regular caseload. The only difference being that she had to put up with the irritating attentions of a supervisory officer sent down from Albany to peer over her shoulder. Another annoyance was everyone's almost juvenile fascination with the fact of her having been the famous William Meade's parole officer, and their compulsion to keep questioning her about him. That in itself marked her for stardom. And these were allegedly sophisticated professionals.

Jacqueline drove mechanically, as if on automatic pilot. She'd traveled this same route for more than five years and had learned to make the most of the approximately one-hour commute. Once you were able to accept the traffic, it was good thinking time. A kind of buffer. You prepared yourself on the way out and had a chance to decompress before reaching home. Right now, approaching the exit to White Plains, she swung into the right lane and began braking to the posted ramp speed.

"Don't exit, Jacqueline. Just stay on the parkway."

His voice was right behind her ear and so soft it was hardly above a whisper. Jacqueline sucked air as she heard it, a sharp gasp that filled her throat with something bitter.

The wheel quivered in her hands but the car remained steady. Once, as a child, she'd been knocked under by a huge wave, and now she was experiencing the same shock and fear as when that breaker had rolled over her.

"I need you for a while," Meade said in the same soft voice.

Then he added, "I've missed you."

Jacqueline had not said a word. She had no idea whether she could. She was just concentrating on keeping the Mustang in lane.

"Did you hear me, Jacqueline?"

She swallowed the bitter thing in her throat.

"Yes, William."

CHAPTER
42

Paul Garret was at the *Times*, butchering a page of copy, when Lieutenant Canderro called. It was 10:15 A.M.

"Listen," said the detective. "The New York Police Department just phoned me. One of the detectives they had watching Jacqueline Wurzel was found dead in his car about an hour ago. He was parked right across the street from her house."

A crater opened in Garret's stomach. "What about...?" He could not even say her name.

"Nothing on Miss Wurzel. A garage attendant saw her drive out at around seven-forty, but she never got to her office. I take it you haven't heard from her or Meade."

"No." Garret's voice was rasping.

"Okay, don't go imagining stuff. If he just wanted to do her, she'd be done by now and we'd know it."

Garret swallowed, forced himself to focus.

"What do we do now?" he asked.

"We wait to hear from him. And you're the one who's gonna hear. So the New York cops got a court order for a tap-and-trace on your office line. They're doing it now."

Garret sat staring at the walls. The whole of his life might have been contained in this room. And if he had a future, that was here, too.

"What happened with his mother last night?" Canderro asked.

"Not a damn thing.".

"Did she know her darling boy blew up his old man?"

"No. But she still wouldn't budge an inch when I told her."

They were both silent.

Garret put his head back, closed his eyes.

"God," he whispered.

By 3:00 P.M. Garret had received six calls. None was from William Meade. Yet each time the phone rang, his palms turned wet and his mouth went dry. It had become a conditioned reflex.

The telephone rang for the seventh time at 3:47 and Garret picked up the receiver.

"Garret," he said.

"Listen carefully and don't interrupt, Mr. Garret. Because of your tap-and-trace, I've got just sixty seconds."

Meade's voice was angry, hard ice.

"You have only yourself to blame for this," he said. "What you did to my mother last night was cruel and unforgivable. What you did to me was even worse. How *dare* you intrude in my personal life? How *dare* you? You're not God. And I'm going to make you walk eye-deep in hell for it. With Jacqueline leading the way. So just think about that until you hear from me again."

Meade ended the call and Garret slowly put down the receiver.

How dare you intrude in my personal life?

The question had to be either the ultimate in *chutzpah* or the most telltale sign yet of pure madness.

Imagine.

The sonofabitch rapes and murders my wife, leaves me with two bullets in my head, kills two more women and eighteen men, and rages at me for daring to intrude in his personal life.

Garret began dialing Canderro's number. The New York Police Department tap would be reported to the lieutenant almost immediately, but Garret had his own need to talk.

"Canderro."

"Meade just called," said Garret and repeated the brief, one-way conversation pretty much word for word.

"Any outside sounds or noises in the background?"

"None that I heard."

The detective took a long moment, and Garret could almost feel him trying to think of something comforting to say.

"At least we know she's alive," Canderro told him.

Garret had not even considered the possibility of Jacqueline being dead. Obviously the detective had. Thinking of it now, Garret felt even worse.

"How do we know she's alive?" he asked. "Meade never said anything about it."

"No, but that bit about Jacqueline leading the way to hell for you was about future action, not past. He wants to use her to punish you, Garret, and he can't use a corpse for that. Just as he never talked about killing *you*."

Canderro paused.

"It's not that simple for him, either," he said. "The crazy fuck has to be all twisted up with his own feelings about her too. Didn't he once say he admired her more than any woman he'd ever known?"

"That's right," said Garret, and surged with such a rush of hope that he felt pathetic.

"What I really can't figure is where he could have taken her. He can't stay in the woods or go to Momma's, and motels are sure as hell out."

"Whose cabin was it that he was in?"

"We traced five generations of deeds in his mother's maiden name. But that was it. Nothing else was registered. Anyway, I've still got men combing the area. Maybe we'll get lucky again."

Canderro thought about what he'd just said and grunted. "Some luck. Two dead cops and Meade flown."

Garret could feel his brief rush of hope starting to leak out of him.

"One more thing," said the detective. "Whether you like it or not, the NYPD is putting watchers on you for your own protection."

"You mean like they did for Jacqueline?"

"Have a heart. One of their guys died at it."

"I just meant it didn't help her any."

"You got complaints," said Canderro, "call New York headquarters. Or your lawyer. If you want to spring for an invasion of privacy writ."

Garret thought it best to leave that one alone. He could always take care of it later. Right now, he didn't trust his own judgment.

"The way I figure it," said Canderro, "you should be hearing from your friend before the night's over. If I'm not here, you know where to reach me. In the meantime, just take it easy."

"Sure."

• • •

Garret was back at his typewriter. But he couldn't complete a page in three hours, and what he did squeeze out he didn't believe for a minute.

Canderro had advised him to take it easy, yet how was he supposed to do that? Might as well try to leap the miles of darkness to the moon.

At moments he could barely get himself to move. Simply sitting in his office and breathing required enormous effort. Staring at the phone itself for long periods, he tried to will it to ring. And twice he called the operator to give him a test ring to make sure the instrument was working.

For one particular stretch he thought about Jacqueline herself and things she had said. Had he fully absorbed and appreciated all she'd told him during that brief time together? What had she tried to pass along that he may have failed to take in? Part of her sat with him now, keeping him company as he waited. There was a pitiful sort of comfort in simply this.

Whatever became of the thoughts and feelings of a woman who loved you after she was gone? Did they stay with you in a kind of afterglow that kept you from feeling alone and unloved? Or did they disappear with her?

Garret hoped he could keep whatever Jacqueline may have left for him.

No. To hell with that. He didn't hope anything. He just wanted *her*.

The telephone stayed silent.

At 9:00 P.M. he left his office so he could watch the telephone at home.

CHAPTER
43

Something in Meade responded to the old house. He hadn't lied to the Garrets that first day. He *had* envied them their living here. He *had* felt an almost mystic bonding from the start. With his cabin gone, there was no place he could think of that he'd rather be. And having Jacqueline here with him, however briefly, was calming and pleasurable enough to soften his anger.

They sat in the living room with a bottle of the Garrets' best brandy, only a single small table lamp burning, and the windows blacked out with blankets. The nearest road was a good distance away and there were no visible neighbors, but Meade was still being cautious about light. He also was wary enough of Jacqueline to keep her handcuffed to a radiator valve beside her chair.

So far, all seemed to be going well. Details were important in something like this, and he was trying to be meticulous about them. Apart from the planning, logistics, and security required, there were the problems of timing and control, of keeping a number of balls in the air at once, of gauging and preparing for the kind of emotionalism that was rarely predictable under stress. His own, above all. With the level of anger he was feeling, he knew he needed constant restraint, or everything would fly to pieces.

Yet he was doing fine to this point—and most important, with Jacqueline, who had a key role to play in what lay ahead. Treating her gently, he'd calmed her initial fears and given her the feeling that things were nowhere near as desperate as she'd originally thought, and that if she and others just behaved sensibly, some sort of reasonable accommodation would evolve.

Poor Jacqueline. His lovely, all-knowing, former keeper, who really knew nothing at all about what was happening and would happen...not even that she was at this moment sitting in her lover's house, sipping his vintage Remy Martin, and awaiting any number of rare, exciting, once-in-a-lifetime experiences. The final one of which she would not, sadly, be able to fully appreciate.

He was almost ready to feel some small pity for her. Until he pictured her naked body, until he remembered all that sweet vulnerable flesh entwined with and entered by another man, until he imagined her cries and experienced once more the pain of her betrayal. Then all he felt was icy, carefully controlled rage. Still, it was mostly out of this feeling that he decided to open up. If there finally was a time for everything, what better time than now to speak of this?

"How could you have done that to me?"

Jacqueline looked at him. He'd spoken to her as if she'd been inside his head, listening to his thoughts, and her eyes were blank.

"How could I have done *what* to you?" she said.

"Betrayed me with *him*."

She could only stare, a frightened woman doing her best not to panic. His face and voice were no different than they'd been just seconds before, yet the sudden, irrational question seemed to turn him into something else.

"Do you have any idea what it was like for me?" Meade asked. "What it did to me to watch him having you? To see his hands on your body and you opening up to him? To kneel out there on your fire escape like some pathetic beggar while you gave another man all you'd promised me?"

Her brandy in one hand, Jacqueline's other hand started toward her mouth before the cuffs grabbed and held it.

"I *promised* you?"

"Maybe not in so many words. But it was always there, always implicit in everything you said and did. It was in the way you looked at me, and in the faith you showed. You were my friend, Jacqueline. The only one I had. And with the unspoken promise of more to come. I couldn't have just imagined it. That hour a week with you was the only thing that kept me straight all those months."

"So what happened, William?"

Meade looked around the room, and then at the ceiling, and finally back to Jacqueline.

"I went for a hike one spring day," he said flatly, "ran into a woman I wanted, and indulged myself."

"Just like that?"

"No. Not just like that. I had a long history of that kind of thing. Not that you or anyone else ever knew, but it was there. So it was only a matter of time before I started again. If it hadn't been Emily Garret, it would have been someone else."

Meade's pale eyes picked up a torch of lamplight as they considered Jacqueline.

"You can't imagine how hard I had to work to keep it

from being you. God, how I wanted you. At moments I'm almost ready to believe I did Emily Garret to keep from finally
doing you."

"Then why didn't you *do* me?" she asked, mocking his eu-
phemism.

"I couldn't bear the idea of losing you."

They just sat there until an owl, perched somewhere near
the lake, broke the silence.

Jacqueline drank her brandy for courage. "Did you really
watch us from my fire escape?"

"Every last bit. Everything."

"If it hurt so much, why did you watch?"

"Because it also was exciting." Meade shrugged. "Who
knows? Maybe the pain helped make it exciting."

They stared at each other.

"Even now," he said, "just sitting here talking about it, it
still excites me."

Then seeing a new fear enter her face, Meade suddenly
felt driven to frighten her even more. He stood up, unlocked
her handcuffs and put them in his pocket.

"Let's go upstairs," he told her. "I think it's time I showed
you a few things."

She did not move. "What sort of things?"

"Nothing dangerous. Just some interesting bits of memo-
rabilia that should do no more than add to your education."

When Jacqueline still failed to move, Meade took her arm
and lifted her to her feet.

Then holding her elbow, he walked her up the dark stairs
and onto the pegged planking of the upper hallway. They
might have been two soldiers, buddies, crossing enemy territory. No lights were on there, but Meade picked up a flashlight and focused it on the police notice taped across the
bedroom door.

Jacqueline stood reading it: CRIME SCENE. DO NOT DISTURB.

"Is this some sort of joke?"

"Why? Do you think it's funny?"

"No."

"Then I guess it's no joke."

Meade opened the door and walked Jacqueline into the room itself. She saw it all then: the blackened bloodstains and chalked body outline on the floor, and the exact same kind of thing on the bedsheets. So that she finally stood there like an observer on the moon, with the full message reaching her at last.

Meade watched it freeze her face.

"My God!" she said. "You're actually *living* in the Garrets' house?"

"Why not? It's a beautiful old house. I love it. They'll certainly never think of looking for me here. Besides, I have no place else to go."

Her shock amused him.

"You think my living here is worse than my shooting Mr. Garret and raping and killing his wife?"

She had nothing to say. It was that far beyond her.

"I also sleep on the bloodstained sheets," he said softly. "I find it comforting, as if I've finally been located dead center in time and place."

Meade smiled. "That should disgust you even more. Or does it just frighten you?"

Jacqueline faced him squarely. "Why have you brought me here? Why do you hate me so much?"

"I don't hate you, Jacqueline. I love you. I thought you understood that."

"I seem to understand less and less."

"As for why I've brought you here?" he said. "Well, it's really to punish your lover boy. He's been viciously cruel.

He's hurt my mother and turned me ugly in her eyes. And that's something I can't let him get away with."

"How are you going to punish him? By raping *me?*"

Meade smiled above the level beam of his flashlight. "Is that what you want me to do?"

"The only thing I want you to do is let me go."

"I had to kill an inoffensive New York police officer to get you, Jacqueline. It would be a horrible waste for me to just let you go after that."

Meade stroked her hair, fondly, almost absently, as one would a child's.

"No," he said. "I'm afraid there's no rape on tonight's program. We have something else we're going to have to do."

CHAPTER
44

Paul Garret slept fitfully through the night.

He awoke twice in a sweat, dreaming the phone was ringing and he somehow was unable to get to it.

When he awoke for the third time, it was daylight and the ringing was real. But it was Lieutenant Canderro on the other end, not William Meade.

"Tap-and-trace reports nothing," said the detective.

"I know."

"Hang loose. Something's gotta come soon."

"Not if he's killed her." Garret found it to be almost a catharsis to say it.

"He won't do that, Garret. It's not his style. At the end, maybe. But not now. Not so soon. He's gotta work you first, make you sweat."

"He's doing that part fine."

"Listen," said Canderro. "There'll be nothing in the news about it. We're blacking the whole abduction out. It saves us a couple hundred crackpot calls and maybe even bothers

Meade a little. His kind likes attention. So if you go to the office, keep it covered."

"I'm not going to the office. I'm staying right here."

"Whatever's best for you."

It was exactly 7:14 A.M. when Garret hung up. It was his habit to take notice of such things. As if at some arbitrary time in the future he would be called upon to pinpoint the exact moments when certain events in his life took place.

At 9:18 the doorman brought up a small, rectangular package that had just been delivered by messenger. Garret looked at it. Instant holes began opening inside him like geological faults.

Then feeling himself about to enter some far-gone state, he placed the thing on a foyer table, went into the bathroom, and splashed his face with cold water.

In the mirror over the sink, he looked pale and gaunt, his eyes ringed with dark, his scars red against the leached-out whiteness of his skin.

Take hold. This is exactly what he wants.

Steeling himself, he went back out to the foyer and began to undo the wrappings from the package. "Please," he whispered aloud. "No body parts. Not that shit. Not for her."

He went weak.

It was an ordinary videocassette. Just that. A roughly scrawled label read FOR YOUR EYES ONLY.

Garret picked up the telephone to call Canderro. Then he changed his mind. Better wait and see what he had.

The VCR was in the wall unit in his study. He slipped in the cassette, pressed the play button, and sat down in the old swivel chair he used when he wrote. He was trying to prepare himself for the worst, but how was he supposed to prepare? And with someone like Meade, what was the worst?

The tape was running now but there was only darkness

and flickering colored dots. Then the screen turned bright, and Garret saw what looked like a bedsheet tacked over a wall. There was no sound.

A moment later, William Meade's voice broke the silence.

"Are you frightened, Mr. Garret?" he said. "Since you care for Jacqueline, you should be. Caring for someone makes you vulnerable to pain and loss. When that person suffers, you suffer. When she dies, pieces of you die with her. You learned that when you lost your wife. But you were lucky with Emily. You were unconscious while it was all happening. This time you won't be as lucky. With Jacqueline I'm making sure you see everything."

Meade paused.

In the sudden silence Garret quickly got up, hit the eject button and yanked out the cassette.

He stood there holding the thing in his hand. What sort of resolve could he summon when the situation seemed so futile?

Yet even with all that seemed on the edge of happening, he could not imagine it. Not even Meade would do something like that, would actually kill her on camera just to punish him. Except that he knew perfectly well that Meade would not only do what he liked with her, but would undoubtedly savor every last moment.

Garret had never taken a drink this early in the day in his life, but he took one now, belting the whiskey straight from the bottle in heavy swallows until at least some of his brain cells seemed anesthetized.

The cassette was still in his hand. Even while pouring the whiskey, he had not put it down for an instant.

What should I do?

Watch it, you gutless wonder.

Watch her die?

If she can die, you can see her do it.

He knew himself then and he was not all that courageous. Still, whatever had been required of him he had always done, and he knew he would do this too.

Eyes burning, he could barely see to put the cassette back in the VCR and start the tape rolling. Cheap, useless sentiment. That alone infuriated him.

Then the hanging bedsheet was back on the screen.

"Just so you understand," said Meade's voice. "Jacqueline knows nothing of this. She can't hear me speaking. She's frightened but could never really believe I would terminate her. But you know better, don't you, Mr. Garret? So pay close attention. This is entirely for your benefit."

The screen went dark.

When it brightened a moment later, Jacqueline was standing in front of the bedsheet. She was naked.

She stood with her hands at her sides, gazing off somewhere. Then a shadow crossed her face, a flinching as though she had been slapped, and everything changed.

Suddenly, she looked terrified. Her mouth opened. Her lips moved. She formed words. Garret tried to read the truth of what was happening to her in her eyes, but her face suddenly turned away and she crumpled to the floor. She sat on the floor, shaking.

"A little lesson in fear, Mr. Garret," said the videotape's narrator. "Strip even the bravest woman naked. Show her a slender metal rod running live current. Let her imagine it making contact with certain of her more sensitive erogenous parts. And that's all there is to it. Whatever she may have been before, she won't be afterward."

Garret closed his eyes.

Then he forced them open.

Watch, you sonofabitch.

"Let me tell you about electric power, Mr. Garret. It undoes you. You scream and don't know it. You drip mucus and soil yourself like an infant. You see parts of yourself moving and the movement has nothing to do with you. You beg to die and stop feeling, but you live and you feel. You howl like an animal for God's help, but He's either too busy to hear you or He's left early."

Garret felt a terrible dread of will and control failing him. All his concentration was focused on staying with her. As long as he stayed, she was not alone.

"Look at her," Meade said quietly.

Like an obedient robot, Garret stared mutely.

Jacqueline still sat huddled on the floor, hands to her face. Weeping now, she was, as she wept, a frail, delicately made woman. Who would have thought so frail?

"Are you hurting, Mr. Garret? I certainly hope so. Yet I've barely started. I haven't actually touched her yet, have I? But I will. Just be patient. In the meantime, think about it. Try to imagine what's coming. Though I honestly doubt that you can."

The screen went dark.

CHAPTER
45

Garret drove up out of his garage and headed crosstown toward the West Side Highway. Watching his mirror, he saw a dark gray sedan pull away from the curb and follow about fifty yards back. By the time he was across Central Park, he was certain it was his brand-new police protection. It made him feel no safer. What he mostly felt was foolish.

He rode with Meade's videocassette on the seat beside him. Every once in a while he glanced at it, as if hoping to find it gone. He smelled the fear it gave off. When he put his hand there, he was sure he could feel it, too.

Still, it was only fear. It was not hard pain and it certainly was not death. He'd been so prepared for one or both of these that simply their absence generated a kind of joy. The fact that pain and death probably remained no more than a day or two away was still a bonus to him. As of now, Jacqueline lived.

He stopped at a Tenth Avenue gas station and called Canderro at his office number. Listening to the ring, he saw the gray sedan parked at the curb, fifty yards down the avenue.

"Canderro," said the detective.

"I have a videocassette I'd like to show you privately—*not* at your office," Garret told him.

The lieutenant took a moment to work it through. "That's instead of a phone call?"

"Something like that."

"Where are you calling from?"

"New York. Just off the West Side Highway."

"Come to my house," said Canderro, telling him the fastest way to get there.

"I'm carrying a tail. Should I try to lose him?"

"No. It'll just start a fuss." Canderro paused. "As a matter of fact, drive real easy."

The lieutenant lived in a small, brick row house near the old center of Poughkeepsie. As Garret climbed the stoop, he was able to see his watcher parking up the block. What a way to earn a living.

Canderro opened the door as Garret rang the bell, and took him into a neatly furnished living room with lace antimacassars on the arms and backs of the sofa and chairs. A dozen well-cared-for plants were clustered in the best of the light, and Garret had the feeling that nothing in the house had been allowed to change as much as a hair since the detective's wife and little girl had been blown up instead of him seven years ago.

Canderro glanced at the videocassette in Garret's hand and sniffed once, like a bird dog, at the whiskey on his breath.

"Straight Irish?"

Garret nodded.

The lieutenant poured them two good stiff ones. Then he

took the cassette and read the FOR YOUR EYES ONLY on the label.

"When did the damn thing come?"

"Nine-eighteen this morning. The doorman brought it up."

Canderro looked at him. It was now midafternoon.

"I wanted to run it first myself," said Garret. "Then I guess I needed some time."

"Sure."

There was a television set and VCR in a breakfront between two windows and Canderro plugged in the cassette and started it rolling.

Unable to sit, Garret sipped his whiskey and slowly circled the room. He heard William Meade's voice but tried not to listen to what he was saying. Not that it made any difference. He could have recited every word from memory.

There were framed pictures of Canderro's late wife and daughter all over the place. It was hard to avoid looking at them. They were both fair haired and blue eyed and had the same open smile. Seven years. There were any number of clichés about time being a great healer, and every one was so much garbage. Certain things never healed. If you were lucky, maybe after a while you just stopped bleeding.

Meade's voice went silent as the videotape ended.

Canderro sat crouched forward on a hassock, elbows on knees, staring into the empty screen. He pressed the rewind button and didn't move until the click sounded. Then he punched out the cassette and slowly turned to Garret.

"You think you've seen the worst," he said, "then a sadistic fuck like this comes along...."

Their eyes met and stayed together. If Garret had not known the detective before, he knew him now.

"How much time do you figure before he kills her?" said Garret.

Canderro drank his whiskey and remained silent. His eyes shifted to some of the pictures of his wife and little girl.

Garret answered his own question. "I give him a day," he said. "Two, at most. After that it's over."

He spoke thickly because of the whiskey. His tongue felt double its size.

Canderro just crouched there, looking at and adding up his losses. He might have been listening to organ music.

"At least we know one thing for sure from the tape," Garret said. "He's in touch with his mother."

Canderro turned his head as if it weighed a hundred pounds. "So I guess you want another shot at her."

"What else is left, Lieutenant?"

Meade and Jacqueline were enclosed in an upstairs bedroom of Garret's house. It was not the room in which Emily Garret was raped and murdered. It was the one down the hall where yesterday's videotaping was done. The same bedsheets hung across the wall, and blankets still blacked out the windows.

There was no light on in the room now. Whatever light filtered in came from a small night lamp out in the hall.

Meade and Jacqueline lay naked on the bed. It was a warm night, made even warmer by the blankets over the windows. But the heat had nothing to do with their being nude. Their bodies were exposed because that was how Meade wanted them. It was not just a whim. Like everything else he was doing now, it had a purpose, was part of the prelude to what lay ahead.

Jacqueline's eyes were closed, but Meade knew from her breathing that she was not asleep. The small pretense had become her way of briefly escaping his attention. Not that he'd molested or even touched her to this point. And other than for the abject terror deliberately drilled into her by the mechanics of the videotaping, he'd pretty much eased up in the psychological department. But all she had to do in this house was breathe and she inhaled fear.

Meade raised himself slightly to look at her. In the dim, reflected light from the hall, her body was so exquisite, so erotically disquieting that he had to congratulate himself for his forbearance.

Still, there could be diversions.

He reached over and lightly palmed her breast.

Jacqueline's eyes opened but she did not move. Nor did she look at him. She simply lay there, waiting.

Her left wrist was handcuffed to a length of steel chain and the chain was padlocked to a brass headboard behind them.

The room and everything in it was so still that Meade was almost afraid to move. He felt just the faintest sensation in the center of his palm as her nipple rose and stiffened.

A simple reflex. A fly lighting there would have produced as much. He needed more.

Abandoning her breast, Meade sought his diversion farther down. He had a fine, sensitive touch there. He knew that place and its soft terrain well. Soon he would know *her*.

But she offered him nothing. He might already have pumped his final bullet into her head. He was poking inside a corpse.

Even her juices were cold.

Meade lay back and left her alone. Oppression wandered through him and dug at his chest. When he looked at Jacqueline's face, it was as frigid and without welcome as her body.

It was too much.

"Look at me," he said.

She refused.

Meade grabbed her by the hair, lifted her head toward him, and positioned her eyes inches from his own. He stared into them and showed her parts of himself that he'd been careful not to let her see before. Then he slapped her in the face and let her head fall.

Blood trickled from her lip.

"What are you waiting for?" she said quietly. "Why don't you just shoot me now and get it over with?"

CHAPTER
46

S hortly after 8:00 P.M. Garret brought down to his car the few things he thought he might need, and headed upstate toward William Meade's mother's house in Wallkill. This time a dark blue Pontiac was following at a respectable distance.

His fear for Jacqueline rode with him. He was still trying to work out how much time she might reasonably have before Meade took action.

Reasonably?

His sense of violence insisted it was very little. Why else had Meade rushed so quickly to send him the tape? He had to feel himself mortally wounded, his appetite for revenge strong and growing stronger.

The bastard's intellect and polished cover could sometimes make you forget the deadly glitch that pressed him to kill, then kill again. And he was starting to need his deaths more and more quickly. He needed one now.

It was a fine cloudless night, and once he was out of the

371

city, the air smelled clean and fragrant. Yet driving along the Hutchinson Parkway, Garret's eyes just seemed to conjure up again and again the naked body of a terrified, weeping woman, and as his foot pressed down on the accelerator, all he could smell was her scent.

Mrs. Lipton opened the door and looked at Garret, looked at the large brown leather suitcase in his hand. She gave a long, full stare to them both. Then she sighed and stepped back.

"I half expected you to show up here again one of these nights," she said. "But I never expected you to bring a suitcase and move right in with me."

Meade's mother did look as though she might have been expecting company. It was past eleven, but everything about her—hair, makeup, clothing—seemed fresh and perfectly put together. Yet Garret did not think she looked well. There was nothing specific. It was rather as if each of her near-perfect features had slipped slightly out of focus and somehow become blurred by the increasing weight of events.

Garret brushed past her without a word and put down his suitcase in the center of the living room.

"Do you own a videocassette recorder, Mrs. Lipton?"

She just looked at him.

"I thought not," he said. "So I brought my own. It's in this suitcase. I got a short videotape from your son this morning that I want you to watch."

Carefully, holding to his false air of calm, Garret opened the suitcase, took out his VCR and a few tools, and set to work making the necessary connections to a portable television set he'd noticed previously.

He worked quietly and efficiently yet nothing seemed here and now. Connecting wires, he no longer felt connected to himself. His mind brought too much dread to each possibility. He spoke with cold certainty, yet he felt anything but certain. He had a loaded gun strapped to his body, but he might as well have been unarmed. In his heart he knew he was that helpless.

At one point he sensed rather than saw Mrs. Lipton rise from where she was sitting.

"Where are you going?"

"To put up some coffee."

"Stay where you are. I don't want you leaving this room."

Garret's tone was such that she sat down without a word. If a chair could hold a field of force, she was gripped by it.

Moments later Garret started the cassette rolling.

He sat watching and listening with her. If possible, he was more affected, more damaged this time than the first. Now he knew what was coming, and anticipation added to the horror. It was as if each image had been so consecrated by the fact of being preserved on film that it was rendered doubly powerful.

When it was over, they sat like two mourners, strangers to each other, at a third stranger's wake. They might have been wondering what they were doing there together or even why they had come.

Garret knew why.

"As you've just seen and heard," he said, "this is my punishment for telling you about William and his father. So please. No more of your comedy about not knowing where your son is. This woman is dead unless you do something to prevent it."

Staring at her, Garret wondered what he could possibly expect from this mother of a rampant killer. Whatever feelings she might still have for her son, they were nothing if not haunted by visions of blood and terror.

Her hand rose and fell in a weary gesture that held more resignation than anger or concern.

"Do you really think this videotape shows me anything about William I don't already know? I've even survived the killing of his own father, my husband. Why would you think I'd betray him now because he's threatening the life of a woman who doesn't mean a thing to me?"

"Because you've been warned about her in advance. Because her death can be prevented. But only by you. No one else knows where William has her. So if you refuse to help and she dies, you've made yourself an accessory to murder."

Mrs. Lipton was silent and it made Garret a little sick, knowing how much he needed her to speak.

"We're running out of time," he said. "I can't afford the luxury of being civilized about this any longer."

"Meaning what?"

"Meaning," Garret said slowly, "that if Jacqueline Wurzel is going to have to die a hideous death merely because you refuse to prevent it, then I'm going to make sure that you die, too."

Mrs. Lipton stared at Garret with the same wryly amused expression she seemed to have passed on to her son. "My God, I can't believe you're actually threatening to kill me."

"That strikes you as funny?"

"The thing is, Mr. Garret, you hardly project the generally accepted image of a cold-blooded killer of helpless women."

"Neither does your son. But that hasn't seemed to slow him down one bit, has it?"

Garret reached inside his jacket, drew his gun from its holster, and held it out for Mrs. Lipton to see.

"This is a 9-millimeter, semiautomatic pistol," he said quietly and evenly. "It's exactly the type of weapon William used to murder my wife and a lot of others, and pump two bullets into *me*. It's also the weapon he'll probably use to blow away significant portions of Jacqueline Wurzel's skull unless you do something to stop him."

Mrs. Lipton's carefully made-up face seemed to have lost much of its color, and her features might have blurred even more. To Garret, it was like seeing a face painted on a banner suddenly stir in a strong breeze. Without changing expression, it seemed to shiver.

"I know what you're trying to do," she said, "but you're going about it all wrong. I don't care beans about your lady friend. And your threats are so much foolish grand opera. You should know by now that all I really care about in this world is my son. Yet I haven't heard one word so far about what my saving your woman can do for William."

"What do you want done for him?"

"The same thing you want done for Jacqueline. I want him saved."

"He's beyond saving."

"If he is, then so is your lady. But I don't believe he is."

Garret felt something stir and they stared at each other. Mrs. Lipton showed nothing. Her discipline was steel. It would have to be. How else would she have been able to live with this for so many years?

"Still," she said, "you're the one who has to decide."

"Decide what?"

"What you want most. Jacqueline alive or William dead. You can't have both."

Garret felt her eyes flat on his face. He sat wordless.

"I'll tell you what *I* want," she said softly. "I want William alive. I want to take him out of the country. I want to give him one last chance to live like a human being. With your help I can do all that *and* save this Wurzel woman. If you're interested, I'll explain how. If you're not interested..."

Mrs. Lipton shrugged. "Then Miss Wurzel dies in a day or two, and my William probably soon after that."

Garret just looked at her. He felt something near to awe. Glancing up, he found Richard Meade's portrait gazing down at him from over the mantel. Poor guy. Between his wife and son he never had a prayer.

She accepted his silence as interest.

"Here's how it would work," she said. "I'll take you there myself. I have a key and we'll go in during the early morning hours, when William is asleep. You'll have a gun at his head as he awakes, so there'll be no problem with that. Then you'll leave with your lady friend, and I'll take my son. All I ask is twenty-four hours' lead time before you tell the police."

"I don't understand. Why do you need me at all? Why don't you just leave with your son?"

"Because I know William won't go unless he's finally forced to. I've had everything ready for days and he keeps stalling, putting me off with one excuse or another. But if this works, he'll have to come with me. His safe harbor here will be gone. I'll be gone. There's no way I can stay here after this. And William needs me, Mr. Garret. He's dependent on me."

Garret felt parts of him being sealed in by the smooth flow of her words. Other parts still tried to fight their way free.

"How do you know I won't just shoot William or hold him for the police?"

"Because I'll be with you every second and I'll have a gun, too." She showed him a hint of her son's most disarming smile. "Besides, I'll expect your word that you won't try anything that foolish."

"My *word?* That I won't shoot a mad-dog killer who's murdered my wife?"

"Exactly. You suffer a major handicap in something like this, Mr. Garret. You're a decent, honorable man."

Garret's thoughts flew about, chasing loose ends. "We're both under police surveillance. There are watchers outside right this minute and I was followed here myself."

"They're fools. They won't be a problem. The only problem I see right now is you."

Garret was silent, trying to consider all the angles.

"Yet why should you refuse?" she said. "You'll have what you want most. Your woman alive, not dead. You may have to give up some of the joys of vengeance, but those are empty joys at best. As for justice, how much of that can anyone over the age of puberty realistically expect?"

Garret waited while it settled inside him. He was like a debater suddenly robbed of all argument. The big surprise was the amount of relief he felt.

Still, he needed to fix on something else for a moment, gain some distance.

"What I've never understood," he said, "is why you disappeared for all those years. Why you never once visited your son in prison. Why you never wrote or contacted him. Why you sent through that whole elaborate fiction of changing your name and abandoning him."

"I was preparing."

"For what?"

"To get him out of prison."

Despite all the intimations he'd had, Garret looked incredulous.

"I started preparing the day William was arrested," she explained. "I thought about nothing else. I was obsessed. Whatever it would take, legal or illegal, I was going to do it. Everything has its price and I was ready to pay it."

Garret said nothing, considering the implications.

"But even with him out," she said, "I was still preparing. I wanted to stay ready in case he lapsed."

"Then you expected it?"

Her eyes, like her son's, were flat. "Not like this. Who would have expected anything like this?" She almost smiled. "Still, I did manage to see him from time to time in prison. William had some inmate friends who were valuable to us. I never went as myself, of course. But it was simple enough to assume other identities for my visits. Where do you think William got his talent for theatrics?"

Silently, they went on circling each other.

"So what about your lady, Mr. Garret?"

A moment was lost, and then the next.

"I don't want her to die," he said.

Driving home an hour later, Garret stopped at an all-night diner to call Canderro at the number he'd given him. It was close to midnight. He saw the dark blue Pontiac edge into the parking lot and stop. No one got out.

The lieutenant himself answered. "Yeah?"

Garret heard a woman's voice in the background. It had a faintly complaining sound.

"I left her about ten minutes ago," Garret said.

"And?"

"It was like screaming into the wind. As if she were stone deaf."

"What about the fucking tape? Or is the bitch blind, too?"

"She said she already knew all about her son. And what made me think she'd betray him now to save a woman who didn't mean beans to her?"

"So what happened then?"

"I made a complete ass of myself. I threatened to shoot her

if she just sat there and let Jacqueline die. I even showed her my goddamn gun. Wasn't that terrific?"

"I once told you what frustration can do to a cop. Now you know."

"I swear to God, Lieutenant. I think I really could have killed her at that moment."

"No, you couldn't. But cops sometimes do."

Garret was silent. Everything he had said was true. His lies, so far, were only lies of omission. When he felt less than great about it, he just pictured Jacqueline with the top of her skull blown out and he felt better. Because he liked and respected Canderro, it was not exactly a state of grace for him. But neither was it all that bad.

Looking outside, he saw a trail of smoke drift out of the watcher's window as the surveillance man lit a cigarette.

"Don't worry," said the detective. "You'll hear from him again. He's not doing anything fast. He likes dragging it out, sticking it to you good. In the meantime we've got a lot of people out there beating the bushes. We stumbled on his first place, we'll hit this one, too. Now just go home, belt a few, and get some sleep."

He grunted softly. "Hey. Like Yogi said, it ain't over till it's over."

CHAPTER
47

Garret fell asleep sometime in the early morning and jumped up in bleary-eyed panic three hours later.

Nothing had changed.

At nine-thirty he called Hank Berringer at the *Times*.

"I'm not coming in until later," he told the editor, "but I'll need to talk to you when I do. You'll be around all day?"

"When am I not? What's wrong with your voice, Pauly? You hitting the sauce this early now?"

Garret cleared the morning thickness from his throat. "I'll see you later."

He was so certain there would be something from Meade that he was staying home to wait for it. But he had a time limit on it. He would have to leave by four.

It was 2:26 P.M. when the doorman brought up the package.

Garret carried it into his study. He felt nothing he could name, just cold nausea and something in his brain that had come to expect the worst.

It seemed to him that he was learning nothing from all this. Except perhaps that there was no bottom to anything. Only more and darker space.

Garret opened the package, took out the cassette, and put it into the videocassette recorder. He pressed play and sat down to face whatever was waiting for him.

Whatever I have to do, I can do.

Then Jacqueline appeared, sitting naked on a sheet-draped chair, her hands locked together behind her and her ankles taped to the chair's legs. She was gazing off to the right somewhere, as if none of this had anything to do with her. She might have been a princess at a royal ball, awaiting her prince. Someone, not herself, was sitting tied to a chair, nude, while a rolling camcorder bore silent witness.

"Welcome to episode two, Mr. Garret," said William Meade's voice. "This episode is mostly to let you know that your beloved Jacqueline is not nearly the martyred innocent she may seem to you in all this. Because the truth is, she has done as much damage in her own betrayal of me as you've done in yours. But I'm going to let her tell you about that herself."

There was brief silence, then Meade spoke again.

"Jacqueline?"

She slowly turned toward the camera.

"How did you feel about me when you were my parole officer?"

She stared blankly.

"Was I just another case to you, or did you feel something different, something more?"

"Something more," she said.

"In what way?"

"I cared about you."

"You mean as a man?"

"Yes."

"Did you know I cared about you as a woman? That I admired and wanted you?"

Jacqueline slowly nodded. "I knew."

"Did you ever do anything to discourage me from feeling that way?"

"No."

"Even though you knew this was becoming more and more important to me and could be dangerous to someone with my history?"

"Yes."

"Did you at times encourage, perhaps even provoke me to want you sexually? By a word? A glance? By wearing a particularly provocative perfume or article of clothing?"

Jacqueline licked her lips but did not answer.

"Did you?"

"Yes."

"Why did you do that? Did you hope it would draw us closer together? Lead to a deeper feeling between us? Perhaps even to something that might be called love?"

"No."

"Then it was just a titillating little game you were playing? Like teasing the big, bad rapist-killer? Like seeing how far you could go with him before the poor dumb animal lost control, came after you, and forced you to blow him away with your gun?"

Jacqueline sat staring into the camera. Her head drooped. But her torso and breasts, supported by the position of her hands drawn behind the back of the chair, were held erect.

"Was *that* how it was?" Meade insisted.

She shook her head. "No. It wasn't like that at all."

"Then what in the goddamn hell was it?" he shouted.

Jacqueline's head jerked up. She was startled as much by

Meade's sudden show of anger as by his equally unexpected use of profanity.

"I don't know what it was," she said.

"Yet you knew very well what it was doing to me," said Meade softly, his voice once more controlled. "You knew how much I looked forward to that one pitiful hour a week with you. You knew the things I had to be imagining, thinking, feeling. You knew what you were dangling in front of me every minute we were together. But worst of all, you insidious cock-teasing bitch, you knew you were never going to let me have it. Didn't you?"

She sat dumbly.

"Answer me!"

Garret saw Jacqueline slip into a deeper level of resignation. Her voice became even more monotone.

"Yes. I knew."

"And you also knew what your jumping into bed with Garret would do to me, too, didn't you?"

"Yes. I knew that, too. I knew everything."

"And now?" said the invisible Meade. "What do you know now? What do you know sitting there tied to a chair naked, with those incredible tits staring at me, and Garret's own personal little playpen all juiced up and waiting between your thighs?"

"I know how wrong I was," she said, as if reading from a script.

"What else do you know?"

"That I did cruel and unforgivable things to you."

"What else?"

"That I deserve to suffer for it."

"What else?"

"That I want to suffer for it."

"Suffer how?"

"As terribly as I've made you suffer."

"And when would you like all this to happen?"

"Now," she said.

"Were you in any way pressured to answer as you have, or did you do so willingly and on your own?"

"Willingly and on my own."

With the catechism apparently over, the camera left Jacqueline and focused on the bedsheet draped over the wall behind her.

When the lens picked her up again a moment later, the camcorder must have been on automatic because William Meade himself suddenly appeared alongside her. He wore cutoff jeans and a T-shirt and carried a slender metal rod that was attached to an electrical extension cord.

Garret's first reaction was to eject the cassette as he had the first time. Then he just braced himself. Yet he could feel the mutilation going on inside. Remembering Jacqueline crumpled and weeping yesterday at merely the suggestion of electric shock, he had to wonder what Meade could have done to make her so pliant and controlled today.

Just don't kill her. Just let her live through the night. Just don't do anything permanent. Just give me until three tomorrow morning. That's not being too unreasonable, is it?

Meade faced the camera. The great god Zeus in cutoff jeans and T-shirt, with lightning in his hand.

"Please pay close attention, Mr. Garret. This is as much for you as it is for Jacqueline."

The gentleman killer was back. Garret preferred him angry and profane. At least it showed him as he was.

Then William Meade turned to Jacqueline and touched the electric rod to the center of her breast.

Her piercing cry simply blew Garret's mind. It put him beyond pain. It closed off the light and all further sound. It shook him loose from his bones. It made him forget who he was and that she was someone separate and apart from him.

He told her this. He let her know that this was his best, that he was capable of nothing better, that he was with her and would stay that way. He said he was no hero, and showed her his tears to prove it.

He looked back at the screen, saw her slumped, unmoving, and tied to her chair. Mead had stepped out of the picture to allow him a clearer view.

Just let her not be dead.

Moments later she stirred and moved. Then he allowed himself to breathe.

"I'm sure you absolutely can't wait to catch episode three, can you, Mr. Garret?" said Meade's voice. "But don't be impatient. It will be there before you know it."

Jacqueline, the picture, and William Meade's voice all cut out together.

Garret sat with it. He had to put himself straight. Everything he wore was sweated through and began turning cold against his skin. When the chill hit him, he stripped and went in for a hot shower.

He was not normally fussy about what he wore, but this time he dressed with care. Even to the point of changing his shirt twice because he did not like the way the collars felt against his neck.

At one point, belting his trousers, he almost began to feel like an aging bullfighter, going through his ritual preparations to face a final rendition of death in the afternoon—except that he had neither the history nor the tradition of the bullring on his shoulders. Only the threat.

Because he was going into the *Times* first, he was careful to choose a jacket loose enough not to bulge too conspicuously over his hip holster. He checked his automatic, briefly considering taking along a few extra rounds for an emergency, then decided against it. If a full clip was not enough, nothing would be.

He took a last look around. He had left lights on in his study and bathroom, and he switched them off. He went into his bedroom, saw that the bed was unmade, and carefully straightened the sheets and a light summer blanket. Although he hardly ever bothered putting on the bedspread, he somehow felt the need to put it on today.

Emmy's picture was on a bureau, and he glanced at it in passing. He saw a lovely, fair-haired woman with an incredible smile. It was getting harder each day to remember anything else.

Garret left the apartment.

The doorman whistled him up a cab with a Hungarian driver and they started crosstown toward the Times Building. Glancing back, Garret saw his NYPD watcher pull away from the curb and settle in fifty yards behind them. Whoever was on shift today was driving a three-year-old silver-gray Plymouth.

Paying off the Hungarian fifteen minutes later, Garret watched the Plymouth trying to park in front of a fire hydrant. It took the cop three tries before he made it.

Just before 5:00 P.M. Garret walked into Hank Berringer's office and closed the door behind him.

The editor was talking on the phone and showed no change of expression as Garret settled into a chair. He spoke quietly and seriously, which was how he always spoke. Yet Garret felt himself freshly aware of it.

My solemn friend.

Berringer hung up and looked at the darkness circling Garret's eyes.

"So what's your problem today?" he said. "Other than Meade and lack of sleep."

"I need a favor."

"Who doesn't?" The editor chewed an unlighted cigar and waited.

"I assume you still park your car in that underground garage across the street."

Hank nodded.

"And it's there right now?"

"Unless it's been stolen."

"Here's what I'd like you to do," said Garret. "In about fifteen minutes I'd like you to walk across the street with me to that Italian restaurant right above your garage, Vinny's."

"I've eaten there. The scampi's terrific. But isn't it a bit early for dinner?"

"We're not going for dinner. We're just grabbing a quick shot at the bar. Then we'll take the lobby elevator down to your car and you'll drive me a few blocks west and uptown. At which point you'll get out and leave me the car for the night."

Berringer sat staring. "And that's the favor?"

"Yes."

The editor slowly, deliberately, lit his cigar and leaned back, puffing smoke.

"What's going on, Pauly?"

"Right now," said Garret, "there's a detective in a gray Plymouth waiting out front to follow and protect me when I leave the office. And tonight, I just don't want to be followed and protected."

"They're worried about Meade?"

"Evidently."

"Has he threatened you?"

"Not really."

"What the devil does 'not really' mean?"

Garret breathed deeply. He needed to stay calm, but his friend was not about to make it all that easy for him.

"Meade's made no direct threats," he said. "He's still just fixated on me. That part is no different than it's been right along."

"Then what's different?"

"The body count...the mass hysteria...the need to do something, anything, even if it's foolish and irrelevant."

"You think the police's effort to keep this psychopath from killing you is foolish and irrelevant?"

Garret said nothing.

"How long have the cops been following you?"

"A few days."

"What's going on tonight that you suddenly have to lose them?"

"I can't tell you that, Hank."

"Can't or won't?"

Garret shrugged. It was impossible to start explaining now. No. He was afraid to. He absolutely could not trust Hank with something like this. Under the pressure of love, friendship, whatever, he could easily see him calling Canderro and ruining everything.

"It doesn't matter," he said.

"And what if I said I can't or won't do what you're asking? Would *that* matter?"

"You're just going to have to trust me."

"It's a funny thing," said the editor. "But the minute somebody tells me I'm just going to have to trust him, that's exactly when I know trusting is probably the last thing I should be doing."

"That's up to you."

"Like hell it is. It's not up to me at all. We both know

there's no way I can possibly turn you down. That's the worst part of it."

"Why the worst part? Why not the best?"

"Because I've got a terrible feeling about this whole thing."

"What *haven't* you ever had a terrible feeling about?"

Berringer brooded over the ash building on his cigar. "Nothing," he said. "And I've—goddamn—never been wrong."

They left the editor's office at 5:30 and walked out of the Times Building together a few minutes later.

Garret saw the silver-gray Plymouth still standing in front of the fire hydrant. The detective had the *Daily News* open across the steering wheel and appeared to be reading. Crossing the street, they passed within ten feet of him. Hank Berringer did not even glance in his direction. He walked looking straight ahead.

Vinny's was in an office building and had two entrances, one from the street and the other from the building lobby. Garret and Berringer entered from the street, went straight to the bar, and ordered bourbon and soda. From where they were standing, they were not visible to the watcher. But Garret did see him walk past the restaurant window once and peer inside to make sure he was there.

When they finished their drinks, they left through the restaurant's lobby entrance, moving quickly now and taking the elevator straight down to the bottom level of the multi-story underground garage. They got into Berringer's six-year-old but still glistening Mercedes, and with the editor at the wheel and Garret slouched as far down as he could get in the passenger seat, they drove out of the garage about a hundred yards up the block from where the Plymouth was parked, and turned left at the next corner.

After a few blocks Berringer pulled over to the curb and got out. Garret slid behind the wheel.

"Thanks," he said and shook his friend's hand through the open window. "I appreciate it."

"Just take care of my goddamn car," Hank said fiercely. "I swear to God I'll never forgive you if anything happens to this car."

"I love you, too."

Garret was sitting in the front section of the Marriott Hotel parking lot on the outskirts of Newburgh when Mrs. Lipton's black Cadillac slowly passed in front of him and parked in an empty space thirty feet away.

It was shortly after 8:00 P.M. and just about dark.

A blue Grand Prix followed her into the lot almost immediately and parked a short distance farther down. There was only one detective in the car.

When the watcher was set and in place, Garret saw Meade's mother leave her car and walk toward the hotel's main entrance, about seventy-five yards away. The detective stayed where he was until she disappeared into the lobby. Then he got out of the Grand Prix, paused to light a cigarette, and casually strolled after her.

At that moment Garret started his engine and drove quickly in the opposite direction from the detective. He pulled up in front of the hotel's northside entrance just as Mrs. Lipton came hurrying out of it.

The Mercedes was off and gone before the detective discovered that his subject was no longer in the lobby.

CHAPTER
48

Near to euphoric, Meade sat quietly rocking in Paul Garret's bedroom, sipping the celebrated journalist's brandy while watching his helpless and desirable lover stretched out nude and asleep on his bed.

It was a moment to be savored.

Apart from everything else, Jacqueline's body alone fascinated him. He had desired it for so long, had indulged himself in so wide a variety of erotic fantasies that at times he was afraid he might have priced himself out of the market. How could reality ever match the ultimate in creative fancy?

Which was exactly what had put him into such a funk of a mood last night. Because there was that exquisite, long-awaited moment of finally lying beside her, of touching her for the first time, and he might as well have been touching a corpse. There was simply no response. He himself might have been no more than a piece of rotting meat. It diminished him. It made him feel like nothing. It enraged him to the point where he lost control of himself and actually hit her. And this, of all things, he considered unforgivable.

He'd never struck a woman before.

The thing was, he cared about women. He *more* than cared. He adored them. But only for the pleasure he was able to take from them. And he took no pleasure from giving them pain. Others did, of course. But he'd never been, nor was he now, one of those. What he did was for his own delight, not for their torment. The fact that they would finally die of it was not at all its purpose. It was just an unfortunate side effect. It was the price that had to be paid for his rapture.

Was it worth it?

Of course.

He watched the soft rise and fall of Jacqueline's breasts with her breathing. Each movement sent rosy pictures to his brain. Then his brain passed them on to his body.

He smiled.

As if it could have been possible for him to abuse such perfection with the jolting agony of an electric prod. Still, it had all been convincing enough, he was certain, to tear Garret apart. Jacqueline's shrill, prolonged screams, her faked writhing, her body convulsing with shock, had been the ultimate charade. She had performed her assigned role to perfection, not understanding its true purpose, but obeying his directions faultlessly, because not to would have meant putting up with the real thing. Or so he'd told her.

A carefully rehearsed *Grand Guignol* designed to give the illusion of pain when none existed. And he was sure it had worked, sure it had forced Garret to scream and writhe right along with her. Yet it was all as false, as counterfeit, as most of life. The only true reality was death. In the end that was what it all came down to. And it was what he would finally offer them both.

But no pain, he thought, and wondered dimly if perhaps there would not be some small hope of redemption for him in simply that.

Jacqueline stirred but did not awaken. She hadn't slept in almost thirty-six hours and was exhausted. Meade ached to lie with her, to touch her, but after last night's disappointment he was holding off. He knew now that it was not going to be any good for either of them this way, so why fool with it? Better to wait for the perfect time, and not nibble away at her in advance simply because she was here and available and he was getting impatient.

At times his feelings about her confused him, and he was not used to being confused. He knew that she would be dead before morning, and that this was how he'd planned and wanted it. Yet with all his anger he still felt things that did not make sense. Part of him still could not abide the idea of letting her go, still refused to accept the thought of her not being here to gaze at, to speak to, and to touch. Not tomorrow, nor the next day, nor the day after that.

Suddenly, she seemed to have given a different meaning entirely to death.

CHAPTER
49

Lieutenant Canderro was supposed to pick Kate up for dinner at seven. He called to say he'd be late. When he finally arrived, it was well after eleven.

As Kate went to kiss him, he gave her his cheek. "Better let me get some scotch on my breath first."

"Did you eat?"

"I wasn't hungry."

She fixed him a sandwich along with his drink. But he had a cigarette going by then and it was no contest.

In the kitchen, sitting across the table, Kate watched him draw deeply and hold the smoke inside a long time. Then the smoke drifted out of his nostrils and hung there in a small cloud.

"Something's going on," he said.

She saw the smoke and saw him drink his scotch. Just before the glass touched his lips, she saw the slight shaking in his fingers. There was a clicking sound as the glass hit his teeth.

"Just before seven," he said, "the New York police called to say they'd lost Garret. He just walked into some restaurant with another man and neither of them ever came out."

An electric clock made a soft whirring sound over the sink. Otherwise, the room was quiet.

"About an hour and a half later, the Wallkill police called to tell me they'd just lost Meade's mother. It was the same kind of thing. She drove to the Marriott Hotel near Newburgh, went into the lobby, and disappeared."

"What about her car?" Kate asked.

"It's still there."

"You think it's coincidence?"

"I'm a cop. I don't believe in coincidence."

Kate felt the warmth of the kitchen. The room caught the afternoon sun and held on to it for a good part of the night. She waited for Canderro to go on. But he was studying the color of his scotch, and she knew he could sit that way for an hour.

"Then you think they're together?"

"Come on. I *know* they're together. Or will be before the night's over. And that means he's worked out some kind of crazy deal that doesn't include cops. Which scares the fucking bejesus out of me because the poor sonofabitch doesn't stand a chance between those two."

Kate poured herself a short one. She didn't really want a drink, but it bothered her to see him drinking alone. Besides, she liked having some business to do with her hands when she was nervous, and she was nervous now. She knew too much not to be nervous. He had made Garret's loss his own from almost the first day, and the feeling had only gotten deeper since.

"What should I do?" he said.

She looked at him, gave a strained smile.

"Finish your drink and come to bed."

"Help me, Kate. Tell me where the murdering fuck's holed up."

She drank her scotch.

"Come on, Kate. Talk to me. You got more good sense than anyone I know. You got all these psychology degrees. Creeps like Meade—you know how they think and feel, what kind of things they might do."

Canderro paused to brood.

"I mean, how could the guy find another safe house so fast?" he said. "How could he even begin to think where to look?"

Kate's face was perfectly still. "You serious?"

"What do you mean, serious? Do I look like I'm laughing?"

"I mean, do you really want to try talking it through and seeing what comes out?"

"Isn't that what I've been saying?"

It was quiet in the room.

"Why not?" Kate said.

She did know pretty much the whole thing. But because it had come to her in bits and pieces over the course of many months, she had him go over it all again.

They took it from the beginning, from the first moment of William Meade's appearance at the Garrets' country house, from everything that was said and done that day, to everything that was to finally follow. Nothing that Canderro knew, nothing that he had seen or had been told to him, was left out.

When the recounting was finally over, Kate sat with it for a while.

"The thing we have to remember," she said at last, "is that

the Garrets were the real beginning for Meade. They were what set him off. He'd been out of Attica all those months and behaving. So what was so special for him here? What suddenly lit his fuse with these two?"

They'd moved into the living room, not bothering to put on the lights, but just sitting there in the dim glow from the kitchen. At the opposite end of the couch, Kate could make out Canderro's eyes, deep set in the angled square of his face. She felt his exhaustion in the dark. He made no response, but none was required and she knew he was listening.

They were on their third round of drinks.

"As I see it," she said, working the answer herself, "there had to be more than just one thing that got him going. Emily Garret was certainly an attractive enough woman, but hardly the kind of Barbie doll that sets men panting at first sight, right?"

"Yeah."

"So what's left is the place, the situation, and the woman's husband. And each of these had to enter into it. The place was this big old house that Meade instantly loved, and that gave him a handy excuse to get inside. The situation was warm, friendly, and isolated enough for the needed privacy. But most important, the husband was Paul Garret. That was what really tipped the scales and pushed Meade into it."

Kate paused. She sipped her scotch and waited for either agreement or disagreement.

Canderro continued playing straight man. "Why Garret?"

"Because of who he was . . . a famous journalist. I think the minute Meade recognized the name, he was bitten by the virus. To rape a woman was one thing. But to rape her while forcing her famous husband to sit there helpless and humili-

ated—and to know how he was responding—had to be an irresistible turn-on for him."

"OK, OK. So?"

She tried not to let his impatience get to her.

"So nothing. You asked me to talk it through, so that's
what I'm doing. And knowing why it all began with Garret's
wife has to be an important part of it."

"Go on."

Kate was pacing now, unable to just sit. Canderro drank
and fought his need for sleep.

As she paced—smoking, drinking, thinking, picking up
random bits and pieces—Canderro's eyes followed right
along from the couch. In the faint glow from the kitchen, he
saw her in sections: a mass of dark hair, the lines of her
breasts, the fullness of her hips. She had long legs. Sometimes he was sure that if it were not for the floor stopping
them, they'd go on forever.

"Everything seems tied to Garret," she said. "He's Meade's
only continuing relationship in all this. Everyone else he's
touched is dead."

"Garret'll be dead after tonight, too." The detective's
voice was flat, drifting.

"Maybe," Kate said, "but look at Meade's behavior up to
this point. Maybe there'll be more fun and games, more
tapes, more stretching it out."

"From your mouth to God's ears. But I don't believe it.
Whatever his old lady's up to is changing the whole damn
thing."

In the semidark, Kate seemed to glow with excitement.

"It's not just to punish Garret."

Her words caught Canderro on the edge of dozing. "What...?"

"What Meade said he's going to do to Jacqueline. On the videocassette you told me about. That's not just to punish Garret. He wants more than that. Anyway, I don't buy it. If he really was going to torture the woman, he wouldn't have talked about it on a videocassette. He would have shown himself doing it. That was only to scare Garret, get him all charged up."

"All charged up for what?" Canderro said.

"I don't know."

Kate thought about it. "Maybe for whatever Garret is trying to do tonight with Meade's mother. But I'm remembering what you told me Meade said on that videotape. He said Garret was lucky with his wife because he was unconscious when she was raped and murdered. But that with Jacqueline he was going to make sure Garret was aware of everything."

Kate had stopped her pacing. She was planted in the middle of the room. Her eyes glinted.

"Don't you see?" she said. "Meade never finished it. The bastard never really got what he wanted. He never had Paul Garret, never had this big famous journalist sitting there helpless and impotent, watching him, William Meade, screw his wife. And I swear I think that's what this whole thing is all about."

The detective sat straighter on the couch. He rubbed his face with both hands, squeezed the tiredness from his eyes. He leaned toward Kate slightly but remained silent. He did not want to interrupt whatever kind of roll she might be on.

"Except for one thing," Kate said slowly. "Meade has to want more than just having Garret watch him rape and probably murder Jacqueline on videotape. Half the excitement would be lost if he couldn't actually have him in the same room while it was going on, actually have him there, watching. That has to be it. I swear that has to be what he wants."

After almost an hour of talking, Kate's voice was so soft it might have been coming from another room.

"And that's what Meade's mother is doing," she said. "She's helping her son."

"How?"

"Who the hell knows? How can a normal mind follow that kind of thinking?"

Kate had put up some coffee and they were back at the kitchen table, huddled over steaming mugs. The overhead light made her cheeks paler, her eyes darker.

"This is crazy," she said. "I can't think straight anymore."

"I don't want you to think straight. I want you to think like William Meade."

She stared at him.

"Don't stop, Katy. You're doing great."

"Sure."

"Go back to Meade's mother. You were onto something there."

Kate drank her coffee. Then she sat rubbing hands on her arms as if she were cold. Her eyes were bleary.

"We know Garret and Meade's mother are together," said Canderro quietly, encouragingly. "We know they had to go to a lot of trouble to lose their watchers. So they've got to have some kind of deal going. Something for each. It's not hard to figure out what Garret wants. That's easy. He wants his Jacqueline back. But what does Meade's mother want?"

They sat there, the question between them.

"No," said Kate. "It's not what his mother wants. It's what *he* wants."

"OK. So what does he want?"

"We already know that. He wants Garret there, watching him do whatever to Jacqueline."

"So he gets his mother to bring him?"

"Exactly," she said.

Canderro shook his head. "Garret's desperate but not stupid. Why would he stick his head in a noose like that?"

"Because he wouldn't know it's a noose. Not until it was too late anyway. Whatever kind of deal he thinks he's got with Meade's mother, you can bet Meade somehow has him faked out."

"So we've figured out everything except what matters most," said Kate. "Where Meade is."

She was walking again, circling the kitchen in bare feet. Then she took a corn broom from a closet and began sweeping the floor. Canderro leaned back in his chair and stared at the ceiling. The only sound was the broom on the linoleum.

Kate finished sweeping.

"You did see where he was, you know," she said. "At one point you had the place right there in front of your eyes."

Canderro stopped staring at the ceiling and stared at Kate instead. He studied her as if he'd forgotten who she was.

"The videocassette," she said. "Garret showed you the tape Meade had sent him of Jacqueline. She was standing someplace, wasn't she? Then you said she was sitting down. You had to see walls, a floor, some kind of furniture. You had to see *something*."

"No."

"What do you mean no?"

"I didn't see a thing. All I saw was a bunch of white bedsheets. They were over everything."

"Even the walls and floors?"

Canderro nodded.

Kate sat down at the table, facing him. "Didn't that strike you as kind of strange?"

"Not at all. The guy's smart. Something in the background, some dumb little thing, could be picked up and identified. He just played it safe and covered everything."

"Yes," she said. "But an ordinary wall and floor? Who would remember anything different in them? I've been in your house a hundred times over the last few years. Do you think I'd be able to recognize one of your walls or floors if I saw it on a videotape?"

"Maybe not, but I would."

"Why you and not me?"

"Because it's my house. I'm the one who lives there and knows it."

Then they just looked at each other.

CHAPTER
50

It was a long time for two people not in love to have to spend together in a parked car.

Following Mrs. Lipton's directions, Garret had driven Hank Berringer's Mercedes from the Marriott Hotel, where he'd picked her up, to the dark wooded spot outside of Hopewell Junction where they had been sitting for close to four hours. And they had another two hours to go.

Still, there had been enough to talk about.

Their plans were complete. Meade's mother had drawn a simple diagram of the house, a two-story Dutch Colonial, showing the exact layout of the rooms. Most important, the placement of the bedrooms in relation to the front and rear entrances.

Like the cabin on the lake, Mrs. Lipton had told Garret, the house was hers, but with the deed recorded in another name. She refused to say where the house was. Her plan was to drive Garret there herself to forestall any possibility of his changing his mind en route and calling the police.

At her best, he thought, she was not an especially trusting woman. But then she had no reason to be.

As she described it, the house itself was set near a lake, in the middle of a large wooded tract. Allegedly, it could only be reached by a long, dirt driveway that ran down from a two-lane country road. They would leave the car at a reasonable distance from the house to keep it from being heard, and walk the rest of the way. Once William was asleep, she said, he slept heavily and rarely awoke. But the sound of an automobile engine carried a long way in the country quiet.

He had listened gravely as this dignified, sophisticated woman described how she would silently unlock the rear door of the house with her key and lead the way about fifteen feet to the right, where her son would be asleep in a downstairs bedroom. Garret would follow a short distance back. Should William unexpectedly awaken at that point, he would see only his mother and not be alarmed. Garret would then move forward and cover him with his automatic.

If William did not awaken, so much the better. Garret would place the gun to his head while he was still in bed, manacle him to a radiator with a pair of handcuffs that Mrs. Lipton had thought to bring with her, and drive off with Jacqueline Wurzel.

As for Mrs. Lipton herself, with the twenty-four-hour grace period Garret had promised her, she would then be free to carry out whatever arrangements she had made for her new life with her son.

With the hours pushing forward, Garret had begun to feel a strange, almost unshakable faith in this woman. Or maybe not so strange. Because she did inspire faith. She accepted her beatings. She hung on. She lied. She schemed. She was less than choice in her methods. She did whatever had to be done.

And what about my obligations?

The only one he had that was worth a damn right now was to Jacqueline. And he was not about to start second-guessing himself there. Still, there had, admittedly, been other possibilities.

He might have shared it with Canderro, of course. He certainly would have felt more comfortable knowing he had backup. But it would have been too dangerous. The lieutenant would have had to follow them all the way without being seen, and that would have been impossible along the twisting, turning, mostly empty back roads along which Mrs. Lipton had directed him. He'd seen her watching their back all the way, and it would have been good-bye Jacqueline if she had so much as suspected a tail.

Something else had occurred to him: a radio beeper.

Planted somewhere in Hank's car, the signal would have allowed Canderro to stay out of sight without fear of losing them. But the idea had hit Garret too late for him to be able to do anything about it, and then he was just grateful he hadn't. Because no more than ten minutes after Mrs. Lipton got into the car, she had him pull over and park while she checked the Mercedes from bumper to bumper with a flashlight and an electronic meter, searching for just such a homing device.

Talk about trust and survival. The two were antipathetic.

So he sat beside her in his friend's Mercedes, listening to plans, trying to concentrate on too many things at once, wondering what it would be that would finally go wrong and undo him.

Think positively.

Mrs. Lipton lit a cigarette. She was a chain-smoker and had gone through almost a full pack just sitting there. Garret had been keeping track. She didn't need her gun. She could kill him just as effectively with lung cancer.

"You have to understand something," she finally said. "It's not William's fault. It's mine. I did it to him."

Garret looked at her. With the help of the moon she might have been twenty years old.

"I destroyed him. I loved him too much. I twisted him all out of shape. There was no getting away from me. I carried him inside me as if he'd never been delivered. Unless he kills me first, the poor thing will die there . . . unborn."

At 2:30 A.M. they changed places. Mrs. Lipton slid behind the wheel, and Garret got into the passenger's seat.

She started the engine.

"How far is it from here?" he asked.

"About twenty minutes."

Through the trees Garret took a last look at the fragment of moon. A delicate pattern of leaves was silhouetted against it, unmoving in the still air. Only later would he remember how beautiful it was.

CHAPTER
51

The moon stayed in sight all the way and Garret's eyes barely left it. He'd taken it as his personal talisman. As long as it remained visible, he and Jacqueline were protected from harm.

I'll be wearing voodoo amulets next.

It was only when he saw Hennessy's barn and silo that he realized where they were. Still, there were any number of places they could be headed for from here, and it meant little.

But five minutes later they turned left at Old Indian Rock, then right at the dark silhouette of Pickett's farm stand, and finally left again at the great oak, and there was no longer any doubt in his mind as to where they were going.

"I don't believe this," he whispered.

Mrs. Lipton drove in silence. Her hands were firm on the wheel. Her back was straight. Her eyes were steady and unblinking on the road ahead. She might have been on her way to a nocturnal picnic.

Garret closed his eyes and opened them, a suddenly unstrung man expecting a host of fearful apparitions to disappear. They did not. His face blank, he felt successively stunned, sick, angry. And through it all was the beating of his heart...so strong, so insistent, that he wanted to quiet it with his hands.

"William had no place else to go," she said. "And the house was there. It was safe. And to his somewhat less-than-rational way of thinking, there was even a kind of symmetry in his coming back and finding shelter there."

Garret left it alone. They were approaching his place and there were other things to think about.

But God.

He checked for the moon. It was off to the right now, above a dark mass of trees. But it was still there.

Then his mailbox appeared in the headlights and Mrs. Lipton turned into the driveway, which was really only a dirt trail. And long. It was almost a quarter of a mile to the house.

I'm back, he thought, and was close to feeling the air actually circling in on him.

Unused for all these months, the driveway was grown over and covered by weeds and brush, a black trail in the lesser darkness of a patch of woods. Insects rose in the headlights. A rabbit bounded off in a blur of movement.

The car inched slowly along for several minutes. Then it stopped.

"We'd better walk from here," said Meade's mother.

She cut the motor and switched off the lights. For a moment it was like being blind in a deep pit. Then he picked up his fragment of moon and some stars through the trees.

Mrs. Lipton placed a hand on his arm, and they walked side by side, weeds clutching at their legs. There was no breeze, and other than for the crickets and cicadas, the woods were still. Garret kept his eyes on the trail ahead and tried not to think of the wrong things. He felt like a novice being initiated into the secrets of a new order.

With the watchers on her, she could not have been here before. Yet even this place, *his* woods, seemed to be familiar to her—as were the farthest reaches of her son's depravity. Right now, she appeared as serene as if she were taking an afternoon stroll through Central Park.

Garret himself needed calming. His brain brought too much dread to every possibility, almost made him feel that Meade had been gifted with secret powers, a special grace. It was hard to imagine him asleep and unaware of what lay in store for him. It was undeniable. Meade's closeness alone gave off signals, created its own psychic warning in the woods.

Then they rounded a bend in the trail and Garret saw his house, a great, two-chimneyed bulk of rising darkness among the trees. And it was suddenly the absolute center of the universe.

His breath became clogged in his throat. He groped for his automatic, felt it snag inside his jacket, and finally yanked it free. He was breathing heavily. His own puffing was the only sound he heard.

Mrs. Lipton squeezed his arm.

"It's fine," she whispered. "There are no lights. William is asleep. So please try to relax. I don't want you shooting him out of sheer panic. Are you sure you're all right?"

Garret nodded. He suddenly felt ridiculous. "Let's do it," he said, and flicked off the automatic's safety.

A narrow slate path circled around to the back door and he stayed close behind Mrs. Lipton as she followed it. She had her key out and ready.

Garret's hand tingled on the butt of his automatic as though the gun itself carried an electric charge. He heard the faint metallic sound of the key turning in the lock and saw the door open inward.

Then he followed Meade's mother into the heavy darkness of his own back hallway, and silently closed the door behind him.

Something pressed against the back of his neck. At almost the same instant a light came on overhead.

"Bring your gun straight up."

Meade's voice came from close behind Garret's head.

Garret stood frozen.

"Do it!"

He raised the automatic until it pointed at the ceiling.

"Now flick on the safety and hand it back over your right shoulder. Slowly."

Moving like a mechanical man, Garret did as he was told and felt the weapon lifted from his hand.

Mrs. Lipton had turned the moment the light went on and was gazing past Garret at Meade. Her eyes blinked against the sudden glare. She nodded at her son, a slight tip of the head, no more. Then she looked at Garret and smiled.

It's always those who smile when they shouldn't, he thought, and wondered if her white, even teeth were really going to be the last things he would see in his life.

Garret stood listening to Meade's breathing. He still had not seen him. He slowly turned. It seemed important at that moment to at least get a look at him.

Meade, too, was smiling. But not as naturally as his mother. His smile was staged, that of a not especially convincing actor. He was not nearly as cool as he looked and sounded. Apart from the fake smile, his breathing gave him away. It was rushed. He was wearing cutoff jeans and a T-shirt and held a gun in each hand, Garret's automatic and his own.

This man.

Garret was afraid to move, afraid to leave this instant. As long as he stayed like this, nothing would happen. A moment was lost. Then two. It hit him that everything was lost.

With that, he was able to speak.

"What have you done with her?"

"Nothing. Don't you know I've been saving our Jacqueline for you?"

Garret felt a numbness all through him. The hallway, the entire house was numb.

"But right now you'd better come with me, Mr. Garret."

Lightly prodding him with his automatic, Meade walked Garret past his mother and into a dark bedroom off to the left. He sat him down on the floor and handcuffed his right wrist to the leg of a radiator.

Then without another word, Meade left the room and closed the door behind him.

Garret sat alone with it in the dark.

At this moment he could almost sense it all sliding into place. Everyone lived with his own fantasy of the way things worked, but his was crude and graceless next to William Meade's arabesque. For Meade seemed to share with Hans Christian Andersen a childlike sense of the grotesque, that wild mixture of joy, miracle, and death in which all things were possible if only you were crazy and ruthless enough to reach for them.

The people in Meade's magic landscape, like Andersen's woodland spirits, rode the same beasts and blew wet kisses to cheering crowds. And if they died, their deaths were less than tragic because they were less than real.

They would come alive in some other story and live happily ever after.

All you had to do was wait, thought Garret.

Then die again.

CHAPTER
52

Kate lay on her back, making the soft sounds of sleep that Canderro was too loyal to call snoring. It was really more of a gentle puffing sound than a true snore anyway. What it meant mostly was that Kate had entered the deepest part of her sleep and was not likely to awaken until first light.

He leaned over and kissed her. It was in the nature of a final test, as well as his own real need to make contact. She did not stir.

Canderro eased out of bed, gathered up his clothes and holster, and began to dress.

Forgive me, Kate.

The thought was as close to an act of contrition as he could allow himself. But he knew even that was unnecessary, that Kate would understand. Jesus, would she understand. Who in his world knew him better?

Which was exactly why it had not been easy to fool her, why he had played it so carefully from the start. From the moment they had groped, worked, and stumbled their way into it, a part of him had been preparing.

He had tried to create doubt with his first words.

"It's too crazy," he said. "The sonofabitch wouldn't be that stupid. Christ. To actually go back and try to hole up in Garret's own house?"

Kate shook her head. "But it's *not* stupid. It's the smartest thing he could have done. Who would ever think of looking for him there? Did *you*? Until we pressed and pressed and finally just blundered into it?"

Even as he went through his performance word by word, Canderro was planning every move he intended to make. He was that sure Meade was there.

"Okay," he said, pretending to finally give in to Kate's insistence. "If it'll make you feel any better, I'll call downtown and give it a shot."

He had picked up the kitchen phone, dialed his own home number, and made certain Kate overheard his fake, one-way conversation with only a steady ringing at the other end.

"Lieutenant Canderro here, Sergeant. How yuh doing? Good. Listen. Who's on shift in the Ardonia area? Who? OK. Here's what I want done. Tell them to check out the old Garret house off Route Two Ninety-nine. Yeah. That's the one. I just got this crazy bug up my ass says Meade might be holed up there. Yeah, I know it's wild as all hell. But anything's possible with that fruitcake. Just tell 'em to go in real easy and call for a backup if they see anything suspicious. They can also get me at the eight-eight-four-three number. If I'm shooting blanks, just forget I ever called. No point waking me up to tell me I'm wrong."

Canderro laughed into the receiver. "And don't fucking spread it around, Sergeant. I don't like looking like any more of an asshole than I have to."

When close to an hour had passed without the phone ringing, Kate had made him call back.

"Canderro again, Sergeant. Couldn't sleep anyway. I guess it's nothing, huh? OK. What the hell. Can't shoot a guy for trying. I owe yuh one."

He had hung up, looked at Kate, and shrugged.

It was a big disappointment for her.

"Damn it, Frankie. It seemed so right."

It was *right,* he had thought.

Canderro finished dressing and checked his revolver. He stood in the dark room for a moment watching Kate sleep. He listened to her soft sounds that he refused to call snoring. He thought about kissing her again but was afraid to take the chance of possibly waking her.

Then he walked out to his car and strapped on the ankle holster he kept in his glove compartment for emergencies.

This one was all his. He had been waiting a lot of years for it. When you waited that long for something, there was no way you were going to share it.

The detective was determined not to repeat his old mistake. He was not going to depend on the system. The creaking machinery of justice had failed with his wife and child and had already failed once with William Meade by turning him loose in the first place. And now, given the chance and twenty deaths later, it would stumble through a six-month legal circus, with platoons of opposing lawyers and psychiatrists having a field day, and Meade copping an insanity plea and coming up for reevaluation in a year's time.

No way, Billy-Boy.

I'm coming, Canderro told him. *Don't go getting impatient. You just wait for me, yuh hear?*

CHAPTER
53

William Meade opened the door and switched on the light. Less than ten minutes had passed since he left the room.

"We're going upstairs now," he said.

Garret heard the lilt in his voice and saw his face. There was excitement, expectation, in both.

Meade had an automatic in one hand and a key in the other. Moving deliberately, he pressed the gun muzzle to the back of Garret's head and unlocked his handcuffs.

Garret breathed Meade's after-shave lotion and recognized it as his own. Apparently not wanting to miss anything of his, Meade was sucking up everything in sight. Then Garret felt his own shirt sticking to the sweat on his back and realized just how frightened he was. Not at all the response, he thought, of a man with great hopes for his future.

Meade followed him out of the room and up the hall stairway. A single light was on in the hall. The other rooms were dark. Meade's mother was nowhere in sight.

This is my house.

Knowing he was about to see Jacqueline, Garret tried to prepare himself. But how did you prepare? His last sight of her on the videotape had been a nightmare. And what had William Meade done to her since?

The yellow police tapes were still in place and a crack of light showed under his bedroom door.

He listened to Meade's footsteps on the stairs behind him.

What if I dive straight back and take him down?

You will die right here.

So?

So while you're alive, there's still always a chance. And you're not dead until you die. Besides, you can't leave her alone with him. Not until you absolutely have to.

"Open the door," said Meade.

Garret obeyed.

Jacqueline was sitting straight up in bed.

With Garret's first glimpse of her she seemed to be nothing but eyes, those huge eyes, staring at him with so clear and poignant a look that he felt something struggling to roll over in his chest.

"Paul."

She spoke his name softly, as though testing it on her tongue.

One wrist was handcuffed to the brass headboard, the other hand rested in her lap, and she looked beautiful. Her hair was brushed and shining, her eyes were accented by makeup, and her lips glowed a rich, moist pink. As for the glamour hollows under her cheeks, they might have been inspired by Dietrich at her best.

For the barest of cover, she wore a sheer, lace-trimmed nightgown that Garret remembered his wife wearing on special nights. Now it just tore small pieces of him. Still, Jacqueline looked lovely in it.

Meade, the ringmaster, the consummate impresario. All this careful preparation and setting up. And for what?

But where were her burns, the signs of the torment he had watched on the videotape? Her eyes told him nothing. All she seemed able to do was look at him and slowly shake her head.

It was Meade who did the explaining.

"What you saw on the cassette was just a performance, Mr. Garret. I don't really inflict pain like that."

Garret was silent. Did the man expect some sort of humanitarian award at this point? Still, a part of him had to be grateful for at least that.

Jacqueline sat very still on the bed. Her eyes shifted between the two men as if she were trying to decide something. Yet at moments her eyes carried the same blank, hundred-mile stare that Garret had seen on grunts coming out of the line. The only word she had spoken so far was his name.

Meade closed the bedroom door and it seemed like a signal.

"Sit down, Mr. Garret."

Garret settled into an old ladder-back chair that Emmy had found at the Salvation Army for fifteen dollars and paid an additional hundred to fix up. He saw his own black blood on the plank flooring, and Emmy's juices still staining the bed. He felt as if particles of some sort were bombarding him—his hands, his cheeks, the tip of his nose. In the space of silence, he seemed unable to gauge things, to measure exactly what lay ahead. For the moment he stopped trying.

Meade stood on the chalk outline the police had made of Garret's body, and from the look of him it might have been the tip of Mount Everest.

His automatic was held casually at his side. The handcuffs he had taken off Garret dangled half out of a pocket. Exuding an air of quiet well-being, he was in the best of his exaggeratedly polite, mildly amused modes.

"I've gone to a lot of trouble to arrange this little get-together, but I know it's going to be well worth it."

Meade looked at Garret. "Forget what I said on those tapes. That was strictly for effect, part of my way of getting you here. You and Jacqueline act sensibly, and the deal you made with my mother still holds. With perhaps a few refinements. You have my word on that."

Garret sat with his hands in his lap, everything squeezed shut like an eyelid. This was a man who could get his mouth to swear to just about anything.

"My mother and I are leaving the country tomorrow," Meade said. "She's arranged it all ... money, passports, identities. Everything we'll need for our new lives. Of course you and Jacqueline will have to be locked in here until we're safely away. Which should be less than twenty-four hours. Then I'll let the police know where you are."

Garret looked into William Meade's eyes. "That's if we act sensibly?"

Meade nodded.

"And what's acting sensibly?"

"Nothing too awful. Certainly nothing terminal, or even painful. At most a few small indulgences."

"I can imagine your small indulgences."

"No. You can't imagine them at all. And you really shouldn't be quite so superior, Mr. Garret. Certainly not sitting where you are now."

Meade addressed Jacqueline. "Have I hurt you in any way since you have been here?"

Jacqueline hesitated. "No," she said.

"Have I abused you sexually? Have I raped you?"

She was silent.

"Please tell him, Jacqueline."

"I haven't been raped."

"Thank you." Meade smiled. "A somewhat less-than-en-thusiastic testimonial, but you do get the point, don't you, Mr. Garret? I could have done anything I wanted with her, but I chose to do nothing. Would you like to know why?"

Garret did not say a word.

"I'll tell you why. It was because *you* weren't here. Be-cause as much as I want Jacqueline—and that may be more than I've ever wanted any woman—it wouldn't have been anywhere near complete for me without you."

"I couldn't be that important to you."

"But you *are* that important to me." Meade shrugged. "The trouble is, we live in a strange time, Mr. Garret...the age of Sigmund Freud. We think we have to be able to ex-plain and understand everything down to the last molecule or it doesn't exist. But that's just not so. There's more going on inside us than we'll ever know."

He made an impatient gesture with his gun. "Well, you're here now, so none of that matters, does it? Anyway, we've done enough talking."

Meade glanced toward the bed. "Jacqueline, I think it's about time for you to take off Mrs. Garret's pretty little nightgown."

"I can't." Jacqueline's voice was flat. "Not while I have these handcuffs on."

Meade tossed her a small key.

Moving as through programmed, she opened the lock, re-leased her wrist, and left the handcuffs hanging from the brass headboard. Then she swung her legs off the bed, stood up and lifted the gown over her head. Her breasts tugged upward with the movement, fell back, and stayed alive as she stood staring at a far wall.

"Now you can take off *your* clothes, Mr. Garret," said Meade.

Garret sat in silence for a long moment. When he did speak, his voice had a dry sound. "I guess this is one of the small indulgences you mentioned before."

"It's a start."

Of course, thought Garret. He was beginning to see a bit more of the picture. Debasement. That was the core of it. Humiliate him. Rob him of all dignity. Demonstrate his helplessness. Demean his woman. Make him feel less of a man. It was a time-honored technique. He had underrated Meade, hadn't credited him with this much style.

But at least this was something he could handle.

Garret got up from his chair and undressed, letting his clothes fall to the floor piece by piece until he stood naked.

Meade stared at the clusters of scars scattered across his body. "What are those from?"

"Small arms. Some rocket and mortar fragments."

"I didn't know you were such a big military hero."

Garret looked at Jacqueline, but she was still staring at the far wall. "I'm no hero."

"Well, we'll soon see. Because what you're going to have to show us right now is a little sexual combat with Jacqueline on the same bloody battleground where I took your wife."

Garret stared at William Meade and found something reptilian staring back at him.

"No," he said.

"No, what?"

"I won't do it. I won't let you turn us into a couple of dogs in the street."

At that moment Garret was ready to risk another dive at

the gun. He felt death flail about him like echoes from an old nightmare. Its guts clotted his lungs and he had to open his mouth to breathe.

Meade felt it too.

"Haven't you learned *anything*, Mr. Garret? Please. Don't go trying it again. Don't you know it's still not worth dying for? Maybe you'd better explain it to him, Jacqueline."

She came over and touched Garret's hand but he refused to look at her. At that moment he would look only at the creature holding the gun, feeling its pulse as if it were his own. A raw heat gusted between them in waves.

"Paul," she said. "It shouldn't matter that much."

He looked at her then.

"Please," she begged. "Take it one step at a time. We'll just make believe he's not here."

"You can do that?"

"I can do whatever I have to. So can you."

A practical woman. But he was less than sure about himself. Yet what, after all, was he being asked to do? Make love to a woman he loved? She was right, of course. You just had to take it one step at a time. And debasement couldn't be inflicted. It had to come from inside. Maybe Meade would be disappointed.

"All right," he said.

Meade smiled.

He turned the lamp so that it shone on the bed. Then he drew up a chair and awaited his pleasure.

CHAPTER
54

William Meade's mother was in the room directly below Garret, Jacqueline, and her son.

It was a comfortable, pine-paneled family room, with scattered bookcases and shelves, simple country furnishings, and a pleasant air of well-being. A brass, green-shaded student lamp was lit, with blankets draped over the windows as a blackout precaution. The house was so isolated that only squirrels and raccoons were likely to see any light. But William was always meticulous about such things. Which was just as well, she thought dryly, considering his life-style.

It was quiet upstairs. From time to time she would hear the faint sound of a voice and an occasional step on the bare flooring. But that was all.

Not that she had any great interest in what was taking place up there. A key part of her survival technique was to remain as aloof as possible from such details. It was a method of operation she had adopted almost two decades ago in dealing with some of her son's more sociopathic leanings, and it had helped her to maintain at least a reasonable measure of balance ever since.

Yet there was a core difference in what was happening here tonight. For the first time ever, she had allowed herself to become involved in one of William's projects, to actually play a key role both before and during the fact. So much for her allegedly clean hands.

She had her reasons of course. Most important, it had given her leverage. William had wanted and needed her help so desperately in getting Paul Garret to the house that he had been willing to promise anything she asked. And she had asked for two things. One, that he would finally quit stalling and leave the country with her. And two, that he would not make her a publicly revealed accessory to murder. "Play whichever of your erotic little games you like," she had told him. "But I want Paul Garret and that Wurzel woman alive and in good shape when we leave here."

They were finally going.

She had waited so long and been disappointed so often that she still found it difficult to believe. Yet the corroborating evidence of their going—the details, the hard facts—were all right here in the room with her, right here in a single, oversized, leather shoulder bag.

Sitting there, she lifted them out one by one, an embarking pilgrim checking the physical trappings of her pilgrimage just before departure.

It was like being reborn. Everything was new: names, passports, credit cards, driver's licenses. The bank drafts and money transfers all carried their new identities, of course. As did certain negotiable securities. Some of it had been months in preparation and cost a small fortune. But every forgery was a masterpiece of its kind and utterly undetectable. There was also an additional fifty thousand in cash for possible emergencies.

They would be going unencumbered by possessions. Whatever they needed for their new lives, they would buy. In approximately eight hours, all they had to do was leave this ghost-ridden house, drive straight to Kennedy Airport, and be gone from everything in their nightmare past forever.

Most significantly, she'd taken it on herself to make absolutely certain they would be leaving no tracks, no loose ends behind. It had not been an easy decision for her to make, and she'd agonized long and hard before making it. But in the end she knew it was the only way to be sure they couldn't be traced. So she'd personally terminated the one individual who could have connected her and William to their new identities.

I shot a man to death. I disposed of his body. I didn't leave a single trace.

Once the decision was made, what surprised her most was how easy it all was. Which did not spare her the requisite guilt and self-loathing that followed. But these were things she had lived with and been schooled in for so long that they were part of her.

So here she was.

She poured herself some vodka from Paul Garret's liquor cabinet, lit a cigarette, and settled in for a review of things to date.

She felt no fear or excitement, only a peculiar apathy, and this bothered her. She considered it a symptom of emotional disintegration. During the past nine years of her new life and identity as Mrs. Lipton, she'd been given to frequent reflections on her old life and identity as Mrs. Meade and rarely found them enjoyable. Making a judgment now, she felt forced to admit that she'd mismanaged just about everything.

Her life was a mess. But since it had never really been too great at any time, there was not that much to mourn over.

Taking a long-delayed inventory, she wondered whether she was a smart woman or a fool. Well, at this point she could hardly claim to be brilliant. Perhaps at one time she might have considered her intelligence to be equal to the top of the line, but not anymore.

Intelligence without discipline was like a fast thoroughbred without a rider. And for a long time now her brain had been galloping without true reason or control. Certainly her behavior with William, from that first searing time when she'd indulged herself with him in a frenzy of blind lust, could be classified as neither reasonable nor controlled.

Now, sipping her vodka and waiting, she thought of what lay ahead and wondered whether even this would work. Not that there was any real choice. Surrounded by battalions of police, they were all but finished here. If there was still some small hope for William, it had to be someplace else. The only thing she could do at this stage was give him a final chance at it.

Sitting there, hearing the occasional sound from upstairs, she silently prayed it worked. Cautiously, she was still able to pray. God, she did pray it worked. She had killed a man to ensure it.

If she had to, she would kill again.

CHAPTER
55

It had taken Lieutenant Canderro no more than seven or eight minutes to exit Kate's apartment, adjust his ankle holster, and settle himself behind the wheel of his car. But during that brief period his feelings toward what he was about to attempt had gone up, down, and around at least half a dozen times.

Now he just sat in the driver's seat, stared dumbly through the windshield, and found himself without any clear idea of where he was supposed to be heading. His mind an empty sack, he watched a small slice of moon break out from behind a cloud.

And the weather reports had all called for rain, he thought irrelevantly.

Then he looked at his hands on the wheel and suddenly remembered every detail of every road he would have to take.

There was almost no traffic in the downtown area and he was able to make good time through the city. The moon was fully clear of the clouds now and threw long paths of purple shadow across the road. Once out of town, there were only scattered houses with no lights visible in the windows.

The houses slept, neat and lifeless in the dark. Between them was forest, mostly pine and maple, looking black against the sky. Canderro envied the people sleeping in their neat, dark houses. How safe they felt in their beds, behind their locked doors. As though no notion had ever crossed their minds that anyone in America would dare take it into their heads to do them harm.

He made his left turn onto Route 299, a rutted blacktop that wound through woods and farmland. The moon flickered in small blue stains among the leaves, and the air was as piney and aromatic as if it had just rained. When Canderro began to catch glimpses of far-off lake water through the trees, he cut his speed.

Moving very slowly now, he was watching for the mailbox and dirt opening that marked the drive to Garret's house. The woods were thick here and they'd be easy to miss in the dark.

Finally, he saw them. The driveway was almost completely grown over and the mailbox leaned halfway to the ground. It didn't take long. Another few months and they would be hidden.

Instead of turning in or stopping, Canderro drove for another five hundred yards. Then he pulled off the road and parked in the brush. He was not about to make the same mistake that he and his men had made at Meade's last burrow. He was not going anywhere near the driveway, which Meade had probably festooned with more of his early-warning devices.

If you were lucky and lived long enough, he thought dimly, you could sometimes learn one or two things before something completely different surprised and killed you.

He checked both his holsters, ankle and hip, and slid quietly out of the car. The ankle holster always made him feel like a bit of a cowboy, but it had proven useful over the years on some of his less predictable assignments. Better to have it than not.

Canderro stood there for a moment, feeling his heart going, breathing slowly and deeply until the tightness in his chest began to ease. It was always that way with him when he felt he was going to have to shoot a man.

With his breathing easier, he started circling wide and to the right through the woods.

If everything was as he'd figured it, there would be four of them in the house: Garret, Wurzel, Meade, and Meade's mother. Depending on Meade's twisted compulsions, Garret and Wurzel could be either tied up, under the gun, or dead. Though he tended not to think dead. Not so soon, anyway. If Meade had just wanted them dead, he could have finished them off with a lot less hassle than he was going through now, with this whole business in videocassettes and using his mother and Christ only knew what else.

No. This had to be more complicated than just a couple of quick shots in the head. And since everything with Meade was centered between the legs, it was a fair bet that some fancy sex would be at the heart of things. Which could mean that all three might be involved. And Meade's mother? Probably off in another part of the house, letting her Billy-Boy do his thing.

Jesus, how does a woman let herself get like that?

Then there was the matter of the house itself.

Having headed the original investigation, he knew the place top to bottom, along with the old barn, used now for cars and storage. He went over everything in his mind: layout of rooms, front and back entrances, attic, apple cellar.

What he wanted most was for Meade to be downstairs, somewhere on the first floor where he could be seen through a window. Everything sweet and simple then, with a nice clear field of fire and the whole business finished fast and safe with two or three well-placed rounds.

Exactly.

Well placed where? In the back?

If necessary. In fact, so much the better. Why not?

Because, asshole, you couldn't do it.

How many did he do it to?

Sure, but you're not him.

Canderro just wished he was faced with that kind of problem. Because that was only his best-case scenario. What was much more likely was that Meade would be in one of the upstairs bedrooms, and nothing would finally be that simple for any of them.

What the lieutenant did not even consider was that Meade might not be in the house at all.

Then he emptied his head of all such thoughts and pushed through the dark wood.

According to his estimates of distance and terrain, he still had another twenty minutes of walking to do.

CHAPTER
56

Garret lay with Jacqueline, their bodies naked and touching, and felt like nothing so much as a failing performer in a sex show.

He thought at first it might be better with his eyes closed. He hoped that shutting out all sight of the bed and the room, all sight of William Meade sitting there with the gun in his lap, might make it easier. But he was wrong.

Jacqueline was there for him. Her flesh was soft and familiar. Her touch was warm and skilled. But for all the physical effect she was able to have on him right now, she might as well have been clay.

Garret touched, fumbled, struggled against his thoughts and, not surprisingly, stayed soft.

"Paul?" she whispered.

He opened his eyes and found hers.

I love you, her eyes told him.

Yes. But what had love to do with any of this? His need at that moment was for lust, not love, and no such erotic nourishment came off her. Not for him, anyway. Certainly not with Meade sitting ten feet away and holding the same automatic with which he had killed his wife.

All rosy and scented, Jacqueline was feeding him a sultan's feast of flesh, but he had no appetite for it.

A part of him wished he did. For both their sakes. Given his choice right then, he would have chosen to go into her with all the deliverance of a man who has had to climb twin mountains to get there. But another part of his brain told him they were both suspended over the abyss, and he could not block out the fear.

Had Meade been a cat, his back would have been arched and he would have been making high nasal sounds. As it was, all that came out of him was his breathing.

He was darkness, this one.

But failing still, Garret met Meade's flat stare and held it. *Up yours, brother. And if I die, I die. But you can't make me do what's not in me to do.*

He disengaged himself from Jacqueline and sat up. He moved slowly, tiredly.

"I can't," Garret said.

Meade kept looking at him with his eyes. He suddenly seemed very sad. It was as if he found Garret's inability to perform a great personal loss and was trying his best to distance himself from it.

"You're sure?"

"Yes."

Meade sighed. "Considering the conditions, I can understand it. I'm sorry."

Garret was silent.

"Then I suppose it's up to me," said Meade.

Garret slowly drew himself to the edge of the bed. He sat there with his legs hanging loose, fear gripping him, turning his legs to jelly and rendering him incapable of articulate speech. Like a terminal patient whose faculties were failing one at a time, he was sure his voice had left his throat—just as, at that moment, he felt he had left his life behind him.

All right, he thought, *I guess I'm ready to die.*

And he understood the final moments of a man condemned to die in the electric chair. Except that he had a certain envy of that man, who knew his death was at least part of an orderly process, that it might even carry a measure of justice. His own projected end seemed so utterly senseless.

Jacqueline spoke behind him, her voice soft, pleading. "Paul...please don't—"

That was all Garret heard.

He was off the bed then and going for the automatic.

The second time.

He had learned nothing.

His brain packed with blood, he sailed free.

Then the butt of the automatic slammed into his skull, and he saw that same dark opening, like a crack in the earth that went down forever.

Garret's head ached and he was unable to move his right hand. But he knew he was not dead. You could not be dead and feel this awful.

Seconds later he blinked open his eyes and found he was sitting naked on the floor, handcuffed to a radiator.

"Not a bad try, Mr. Garret. If I hadn't felt it coming, you might have made it."

Jacqueline kneeled, white faced, on the bed. Her left wrist was again manacled to the brass headboard. Meade was busy taking off his clothes.

"I've been waiting for you to come back to us," he told Garret. "I didn't want you to miss anything."

As Meade undressed, he piled his clothes neatly on a chair. His lean, muscular body shone a deep bronze in the lamplight. He almost seemed to preen as he moved. Evidently he was that vain about his physique. To Garret, it was his only obvious vanity. When his clothes were all off, he carefully placed his automatic on top of them.

Meticulous, thought Garret, and found himself settling into a curious calm, just as a man, in dying, might have a moment when, though helpless, he knows he is already in death and so can wait without anger and fear.

Not so Jacqueline. Crouched naked on the bed, she was suddenly like some sort of expensive animal, all fangs and claws, ready to spring.

"Come near me with that miserable thing," she told Meade, "and I swear I'll tear it off by the roots."

He laughed.

"I mean it, William. I'll cripple you."

"No, you won't, Jacqueline. All you're going to do is join me in some of the happiest lovemaking that either of us has ever enjoyed."

"The hell I will."

Meade reached into a pocket of his folded jeans and a switchblade came out of his palm like a snake's tongue.

"We'll just have to set up some ground rules," he said. "Behave, and we'll all be fine. Act up, and..."

Bending, he drew his knife lightly across Garret's chest. A delicate line appeared, widened, let go a tiny red bead.

"Act up," Meade repeated, "and I'll carve our mutual friend into small pieces for you."

Oddly, there was little pain in the touch of the blade, but the act itself was so careless, so impersonal and indifferent, that Garret felt of no more importance than a side of beef in a butcher shop.

"Please," he said, willing to try begging. "Leave her alone. She never did anything but try to help you. Why do this to her?"

"It's not just for Jacqueline, Mr. Garret. I'm doing this for all of us. There's something here for each. I thought by now you understood that."

Meade looked at Jacqueline. "I've worked and waited for this moment a long time. Don't spoil it for me."

He placed his knife beside his gun and went to Jacqueline on the bed.

Once again, Garret had to watch. Except that this time the performance would be live, not on videotape. And if he had not been sure before of exactly how it was going to end, he was sure now.

Jacqueline.

They would both have to die, of course. No matter what Meade said and promised. But she would go first so that he, sitting here, would see and know. That was a very important part for Meade.

Pain rose up in Garret, seemingly out of every nerve. Good. He wanted the pain. But it was not enough. He bit his lip until he tasted blood. Better. He strained against the hand-cuffs so they cut his flesh. Nothing. Everything was nothing. Only dying was something. The final disaster, the waiting cliff. And they dangled love like a carrot to keep you walking toward it.

He watched.

The worst of it was that the mind kept working. You couldn't stop it. Whatever you felt, you neither fainted nor went into a coma. In fact, you remained lucid to the point of detachment. Unless that only applied to this particular type of rape. Which hardly seemed like rape at all. The thing was, there was no screaming, no blood, no violence, no sign of forced entry. To be honest, all it really looked like was two people having sex. And despite the unquestionably intense feelings of those taking part, there wasn't a single bit of visual drama or tragedy attached to watching a man and woman engaged in sexual intercourse.

If you could somehow stay separate from the entire act, what it was mostly was ridiculous, and pathetic, and stripped of all human dignity. You looked at frantically waving body parts, at spastic limbs and clutching hands. And you felt yourself watching less an act of human passion than the final stages of a violent terminal disease.

Which, first for Jacqueline and then himself, he knew it would ultimately prove to be.

CHAPTER
57

anderro went cold with disappointment when he saw the house. He was making his final approach from the lake side, the rear, and the house loomed tall and dark against the sky, its two chimneys catching the moon, and not a sign of lights, cars, or human occupancy anywhere.

In fact everything had become so overgrown that there were some bushes that partly covered the first-floor windows. It looked as though no one had been anywhere near the place in months.

No. I couldn't have been this wrong.

Gun drawn, the detective crouched in the shadows. Then because he was close to the barn, he decided to try there first. He moved lightly and quietly for a man of his bulk, carefully easing one of the big doors open just enough to let him squeeze inside.

It took several moments to adjust his eyes to the almost total darkness. Then he was able to make out the shape of a light-toned car, and a curious joy came to him. The feeling was so intense that he wanted to shout.

Jesus Christ, he thought, and if he had not known before just how important this had become to him, he knew now. But there was only the one car and he had been figuring on at least two. One for Meade, and the other for Meade's mother and Garret. Unless the second car was parked somewhere along the driveway, or simply wasn't there yet.

He would know soon enough.

He quietly raised the car's hood and groped around until he found the rotor. Then he removed it, carried it out of the barn, and tossed it behind some bushes, just in case.

There was a fog drifting in off the lake, and everything beyond twenty-five yards wore a shroud. Walking toward the house, Canderro could feel the excitement in his stomach and taste it in his mouth. Instinctively, he reached for a cigarette, then he just patted the pack. Later, he promised himself. If he was alive later. Fine. Then he'd die a full cigarette healthier.

The thought of dying made him think of Kate.

Maybe he should have left her a note. What kind of note? He never left notes. Still, he suddenly wished he'd said more to her, wished he'd been better able to let her know he understood all she'd tried to do and that, everything considered, he was grateful. But who ever really managed to say such things? If you did manage somehow, it was usually too late to make any difference.

Still, the note could have said a few words about his loving her. He'd never written the words, never actually put them down on paper. It was something he felt she would have liked.

Sorry, Kate.

Never mind being sorry. Sorry don't help.

What then?

Just don't fucking die.

It's a deal, he thought.

Nearing the house, Canderro wondered whether the fog was rising or was falling. He saw the tops of bushes cut off like dead men's markers. He felt mist on his face, sweat on his back, and the remains of the night's whiskey in his stomach.

The house was totally black. At least from the two sides he was able to see as he approached. Where were the lights? Everyone couldn't be goddamn asleep. Or maybe he was wrong. Maybe the car wasn't Meade's after all and the house was empty.

He walked, stopped, listened. Nothing but forest sounds. Silently, he crossed the slate patio at the back of the house, turned a corner, and caught his first glimpse of light. It came from a first-floor window and was no more than a half-inch crack of bright yellow, but it was there.

Clutching his revolver, Canderro carefully slid between a bush and the house and pressed one eye to the opening. A blanket was hung over the window, but at one spot Canderro was able to peer past it into the room.

At first he saw only a wall of books. Then angling his head slightly, he saw Mrs. Lipton.

She was sitting beside a lamp, studying some papers and smoking a cigarette. He saw the point of the cigarette glow red and the smoke rise like a curtain. A bottle of vodka and a half-filled glass were on a small end table at her elbow.

Canderro strained to see if anyone else was in the room, but his field of vision was too narrow. From the woman's total attention to what she was reading, he figured her to be alone. Then as she shuffled through a few papers, he saw the passports.

That alone seemed to stop his breathing. He stared at the two small, square booklets as if there were something vital in each of them that he absolutely had to see. When Mrs. Lipton finally slipped them into her bag with several other official-looking papers, he began breathing again.

They're leaving, he thought furiously. *They think they can just walk away from the whole thing...from* me. The moment passed, but the cold gust of rage remained.

Where were the others?

Canderro stepped back and looked at the other ground-floor windows on that side of the house. They were all black. Even from out here, he felt the emptiness of the rooms. Then he leaned way back, lifted his head, and saw another crack of light on the right-hand side of a second-floor window. The window was directly above the room where Mrs. Lipton was sitting.

The detective walked completely around the house to be certain there were no other lights. He saw none.

He stood again with his eye to the crack of light. Mrs. Lipton had put all her papers into a big leather pocketbook and was just sitting there now, smoking her cigarette and drinking her vodka. She was waiting. But for what?

Canderro stayed exactly where he was. He stared inside as though trying to memorize the woman and the room. He stayed that way, thinking...his gun in his hand and a pulse beating in his temple, He remained that way for three full minutes.

Then he left the window. Treading softly, he started toward the back door.

CHAPTER
58

For Paul Garret, the continuing act was interminable, quiet anguish without end.

Still, sitting naked on the bare plank flooring, handcuffed to a radiator, his assigned role was to watch. So he watched.

My contribution.

A curious point. Yet it could not be denied. There was a subtle but gradually rising concern about what the woman he loved might be feeling.

Slightly insane? Of course. But who would be foolish enough to swear for his own sanity at such a moment?

He knew Jacqueline had had no choice, that if she resisted in any way he'd be sliced like an orange. Still, the basic fact remained. She was engaged in an act of sexual intercourse. She was *getting laid*, for Christ's sake!

Was she repulsed? Sick inside? Broken? Or, accepting what not even God was able or willing to prevent, would she be making the best of the situation? Perhaps even squeezing some small hint of excitement from it. She had to have had a fair number of men before he knew her. What difference could one more make? Especially if he was as physically attractive as Meade.

Might the body simply feel the touch of a man, not know or care that it was not him, and respond out of pure reflex? Would he rather she suffered? No. But neither did he care for her enjoying it, he told himself, and searched for signs of pleasure in her the way a cancer patient searched for new tumors. An extra torment. But he was unable to stop, and he clutched this new psychosis as closely as an embrace he could not bear to leave.

What were her arms doing? he asked himself. One was manacled to the brass headboard and the other was doing nothing. Good. And her face? Turned aside, averted. Fine. And her lips? Tightly drawn, a battle line. Excellent. And her eyes? Steel darts aimed at the ceiling. Wonderful.

Finally Jacqueline's thrashing brought her face around to him and he saw a little look of woe. It was the face of a frightened child, fearful of getting a licking for something she did not do. And as quickly as that, he put aside any crazy notion he might have had that there could be anything here for her but increasing hurt.

There was a stab of pain in his head where the gun butt had caught him, but he wished it could be more—as if his hurt could in some way atone for the hurt she was receiving now. It was lunacy, of course. If the two bullets he'd taken in his head had in no way been able to help Emmy, not even his dying would help Jacqueline. If anything, it would have hastened her own end.

It was all too clear. The only death that could bring salvation to either of them was Meade's. *But how?*

• • •

Rape, ravishment, sexual assault, Meade was thinking, were all the wrong terms for it. The true mood of what he was doing, of what was really taking place here, was too cool to fit any such descriptions.

It was more as though they were two professional dancers come together in a series of long, slow, carefully rehearsed moves. It took effort, but he was avoiding any sense of urgency, any wild rush to pick up speed and climax. He wanted this one to last. It had to last. There would never be an encore for the two of them. When it finally ended, it would be over and that would be it. Whatever reprise he might conjure up sometime in the future would only be in his mind.

He glanced at Garret through hooded lids, watching him as if from somewhere else, absorbed in this moment that suddenly seemed to hold all the pieces of his life. Strange, that this man should have reached him as he had. There were still things there that he could not understand, and he'd always enjoyed thinking he could finally understand anything of which he was a part.

At that moment Garret was studying him as if he could not quite remember who he was. This was not the reaction Meade had either expected or wanted. Where were his pain and anger? If they were there, as they surely should be, he couldn't see them.

That was what he wanted now...*to see them.*

What was wrong with the man? Meade had raped and murdered his wife, had fired two bullets into his head, and now he was raping another woman he loved.

And he just sat in silence.

And he remained soft and disinterested where it mattered most that he be otherwise.

Meade picked up the pace a little, driving harder now,

hoping to see something more from Garret for his extra effort.

But he saw nothing. Until he had the feeling that Garret was not going to see or hear anything he said or did anymore. It was as if Garret had suddenly decided to be blind and deaf, and that was the end of it.

The man knows, Meade told himself. *He knows everything that's going to happen. He's figuring it all out. He's picturing the whole thing right now, seeing that single perfect moment being reached, and the first bullet taking the top of her head off exactly on schedule, and the second round coming for him just thirty seconds later.*

Not even my mother knows. But he *knows.*

William Meade liked it that they knew each other's thoughts.

Then he just thought about Jacqueline.

CHAPTER
59

Lieutenant Canderro carefully tried the latch on the back door and found it locked.

He stood on a heavy slate step, smelling the woods. The door was old and weathered and the paint was peeling in spots. The lock appeared to be just as old. It was the spring type and was easy to open if you knew how. Canderro had known how since he was fourteen.

He holstered his revolver and took a plastic card from his wallet. He slid the card between the lock and the door jamb, felt the latch slide in, and gently eased the door open. There was no sound. Then he closed the door the same way.

The detective was in a back hallway. To his right was a pantry and kitchen. Straight ahead and to his right was the stairway leading to the second floor. The only light came from the left, from the open doorway of the room where Meade's mother was sitting. There was no way Canderro could reach the stairs without walking past the doorway. And that was the direction Mrs. Lipton was facing.

There it was.

Canderro stood as though anchored in a tub of concrete. He breathed the air of the house, and it was old and mildewed. He shifted his weight and a floorboard squeaked. It was a small sound but it went off in his head like a shot.

Great.

Are you going to goddamn stand here forever?

He took a moment to get his breathing in order. Then he drew his .38 from his hip holster, gripped it with both hands, and extended it, stiff-armed, in front of him. He estimated the distance to the doorway. Five long strides and a quick rush in. He wanted surprise but not startled outcry.

He wanted.

Canderro moved lightly and quickly.

He counted one . . . two . . . three . . . four . . . five . . . long strides. Then he whirled left and followed the .38 into the room. His momentum carried him deep, almost as far as the chair where he had seen Mrs. Lipton sitting.

"I have a gun on you, Lieutenant."

Somehow she was behind him.

He stood staring at the empty chair.

"If you move, I'll shoot," Mrs. Lipton said. "Just toss your gun on the chair."

Canderro stood there, weighing the odds against a quick turn and getting off a few quick rounds.

"Don't force me to kill you," she said.

The cold flatness of her voice decided him. This one was pure ice. And at less than seven feet, there was no way she could miss. Bending slightly, he dropped his weapon on the chair as ordered.

"Put your hands on your head and turn around slowly," she told him.

Canderro obeyed and faced her.

Mrs. Lipton was standing with her back to the wall, pointing a bright, nickel-plated revolver at the center of his chest. Her bag hung from a shoulder strap. The gun was just as steady in her hand as he would have expected it to be.

"I guess it was the squeaking floorboard," he said.

"You weren't that quiet with the latch, either."

Canderro sighed. He listened for sounds from above and heard nothing.

"You've got good ears," he said. "But I've got ten men waiting out there, so it all evens out."

Meade's mother stared at him. Nothing changed in her face, but Canderro saw a tiny pulse flutter in her neck.

"I don't believe you have anyone out there, Lieutenant. But if you do, why are you in here alone?"

"To save lives."

"Whose?"

"Everybody's."

They stood looking at each other as if trying to search out each other's thoughts.

Mrs. Lipton hesitated and the detective sensed an emptiness in her mood that he felt he could enter.

"Get me with your son," he said. "Let me talk to him. The worst that happens is you'll shoot me thirty minutes later."

Canderro listened to himself . . . the way he spoke, what he said. He tried to think it through from the other side, tried to imagine how it would sound if *she* were the one telling it to *him*. Not too bad, he decided. The important thing was, she was still standing there letting him talk, listening to him. And he was still standing there, six feet away, his two hands on top of his idiot head, moving his lips, opening and closing his mouth.

"I was out there looking in the window before," he said. "I saw your passports and papers."

The detective paused, letting the fact of it hang there, waiting to see how she might respond.

Mrs. Lipton did not respond at all. She just considered him with her flat eyes.

"If you and your son really mean to get out of the country and stay out," he said, "maybe we're not all that far apart."

"I'm not sure I know what that means."

"It's simple. It means right at this minute getting Garret and Wurzel out of here alive is a hell of a lot more important to me than getting your son back in jail or killing him." Mrs. Lipton stood with her back pressed straight against the wall, wordless. Her shining, nickel-plated revolver was still absolutely steady in her hand. Not a hair on her head was out of place. Her makeup appeared freshly applied. And it was somewhere between three and four o'clock in the morning. Canderro had the feeling she never allowed herself to look even a hair different.

"Unless Garret and Wurzel have already died," he said. "In which case—"

"They're not dead."

Canderro briefly closed his eyes. "I'm happy to hear that. Then there's hope for us all."

The room was silent while the words themselves, and their implication, settled.

"I find what you're saying hard to believe, Lieutenant."

But the detective saw how desperately she was trying to believe it, and this encouraged him.

"I'm just a cop," he said. "There are things I can do and things I can't do. I can't bring back those your son's killed. But if I can keep him from putting away two more, I wouldn't be one damn bit ashamed of it."

Meade's mother fixed on the detective for a long moment. She might have been trying to distance herself from him and what he was saying and offering, trying to find a place further away where she could see and judge things in better perspective.

Standing there, Canderro tried to read it all in her face. Might as well try to read Mount Rushmore.

Then her eyes blinked and something seemed to change.

"Let's go upstairs," she said.

Canderro wondered if she could hear his heart going.

"OK if I drop my hands?"

She barely nodded.

Going up the stairs, she kept the detective six full steps ahead of her. She was being that careful.

Canderro counted thirteen steps in all, as if picking up this particular point of information was about to play a key role in his ability to survive the next half-hour.

Then he saw the yellow crime scene tape across the closed door and tried to imagine what was going on in the room behind it. He could not. He heard murmurs, soft sounds coming from inside, but he could not identify these, either.

"Knock on the door," Mrs. Lipton told him.

She had stopped halfway up the stairs and was carefully aiming her revolver at his head. She held the piece in the officially prescribed two-handed grip that was taught on most firing ranges, and Canderro had the sense she was hoping he would try something so she'd have an excuse to practice on a living target.

"Knock on the door," she said again.

This time the detective did it.

"William, I have to talk to you."

Meade's mother's voice was raised enough to be heard through the door.

There was no answer for several beats.

Then Canderro heard a muffled, "Later."

"Now!" said Mrs. Lipton. "Get yourself in order and come out here. We have a visitor."

Again, there was nothing but silence from the room. But a half-minute later, the door opened.

It hit Lieutenant Canderro that he'd never seen William Meade in the flesh before...only in official police photos and a few snapshots.

Meade was very different in person. To Canderro, he was bigger, more imposing, more wholesome-looking, with a straightforward, boyish, ingenuous look that said he expected only the best from life and had not yet been disappointed. At the moment, he was barefoot, stripped to the waist, and wearing only a pair of cutoff jeans that he was still fumbling to zip with one hand. In his other hand he held a 9-millimeter automatic.

His eyes, barely moving, went from Canderro to his mother, who was still standing halfway up the stairs, then back to Canderro. His face and upper body glistened with perspiration, and he gave off a strong odor of overheated sex.

"I'm surprised," Meade said to Canderro. "I didn't think you'd be smart enough to figure this out."

His voice was soft, gentle, almost girlish in tone, and hearing it, Canderro found it hard to imagine him as someone who would deliberately cause the deaths of twenty people.

"The lieutenant claims he has ten men waiting outside," said Mrs. Lipton.

"Really?" Meade looked no more than mildly interested. "Do we believe him?"

"Offhand, I'd say no." Mrs. Lipton allowed herself a moment. "Yet it's not impossible."

Meade shifted his position in the partially open doorway, and Canderro had his first glimpse into the bedroom.

It registered in quick flashes, almost surreal in impact, images of two nude bodies, one male and the other female, that the detective saw, yet did not see, with Jacqueline stretched out on a bed and Garret squatting on the floor and each anchored in place with what had to be handcuffs. It might have been the fastest of lenses clicking out freeze-frames at fractions of a second. Then Meade shifted back to his original position, and the lunatic camera clicked off.

Oh, Jesus.

Canderro's legs were suddenly water. He stood floating on them. He looked deep into Meade's eyes and saw the worst of it reflected there. *This fuck can shoot me before I even have a chance to open my mouth.*

"Like I told your mother," he said. "You've got maybe twenty minutes left to deal. Then they start lobbing gas grenades and coming in. So it's up to you. You want to sit down, talk a little, and walk out free? Or shoot me and get carried out?"

Meade smiled. It was as soft, gentle, and pleasantly accommodating as his voice.

"I don't mind sitting down and talking a little."

"First I got to see they're OK," said Canderro.

Meade weighed the request. Then he stepped back into the room and motioned with his automatic for the lieutenant to follow. There was a touch of grandness in the gesture, the irrepressible pride of the devout collector pleased to show off a few of his most prized collectibles.

Of course. He wants me to see them.

Canderro went inside.

With the windows closed, the air was heavy with the same odor of overheated sex given off by Meade himself. No one said a word and the room was tight with the silence.

Canderro looked at Jacqueline on the bed. She met his

glance, and there was a fever in her eyes that put her beyond such paltry luxuries as humiliation and embarrassment. He saw a lace-trimmed nightgown on the floor, and he picked it up and draped it over her nakedness.

"You all right?"

Jacqueline nodded.

"It'll be OK," he said. "I've got men outside. I'm sure we'll arrange something."

She lay there, chewing at her lower lip. Canderro had no way of knowing whether she believed him or even understood what was taking place.

He swung around to where Garret sat handcuffed to the radiator. Neither of them spoke. Feeling himself pressed from four sides, the detective had absolutely no idea where he was heading. All he was doing was pushing things one step at a time. If he ever got anyplace worthwhile, he hoped he would know it.

He picked Garret's pants up off the floor and dropped them in his lap. The nakedness bothered Canderro. It was somehow dehumanizing. It robbed them of an essential human defense. Concealment.

"I'm sorry," said Garret. "I never should have tried it alone. I made a real mess."

"Hey. You had plenty of help."

Garret was silent.

The detective turned and faced William Meade, who was standing behind him watching with his usual mix of mild interest and wry amusement.

"OK, let's talk," said Canderro.

CHAPTER
60

They walked the lieutenant no more than ten feet away to another bedroom—Meade's mother still carefully aiming her nickel-plated revolver at her prisoner's back, Meade himself with his 9-millimeter automatic off safety and ready.

Mother and son, thought Canderro.

A white bedsheet covered part of one wall and the floor, and the detective knew that this was where the videotaping had taken place. The usual blankets blacked out the two windows in the room.

Canderro entered the room first and seated himself on the edge of a large double bed. The bed was in a corner, which gave him one wall protecting his back, and another wall covering his left side. There were only two chairs in the room and they both faced where he was sitting. What mattered most to him was that he could look at both chairs at once without having to turn his head.

Mrs. Lipton dropped heavily into one of the chairs. Meade

remained standing. He stood close beside his mother, one hand resting on the back of her chair. The curiously old-fashioned pose reminded Garret of every family picture-album he had ever seen. Some family.

"Go ahead," said Meade. "You wanted to talk, so talk. Tell me why any cop in his right mind would walk in here alone if he really had backup out there, waiting."

"To keep you from either killing those two or holding them hostage with a gun at their heads."

"You expected to do this by yourself?"

"How else? If we attacked in force, they'd be dead right off. Alone, I at least had a chance at surprise, with nobody getting hurt. If your mother didn't have such good ears, or if I was only a little quieter coming in, I'd have had it too."

Meade nodded slowly. "And now that you can't have it?"

"I can still put a damn good deal on the table."

"Good for whom?"

"Everybody. I explained it all to your mother."

"Now explain it to me," said Meade.

The lieutenant went through it all again. He spoke slowly, stretching it out. He needed time to plan ahead. Not so much plan as arrange in his head. He was figuring it as more of a string of football plays than anything else. He'd do this, and they'd do that, and one would follow the other. Parts of it were still blurred, but he felt it would clear in time. It had to, he told himself.

Then no longer hearing the drone of his voice, he knew he'd finished explaining his collection of life-sustaining lies for the second time.

William Meade and his mother were silent. They watched him sitting on the bed, and Canderro had the sense of walking a high wire in a wind. Everything was so delicately balanced that any sudden change could send him crashing.

Meade glanced at his watch. "I count about fourteen minutes left to your deadline."

The detective nodded.

"Let's suppose we buy it," Meade said. "How does it work? What happens next?"

"You break the blackout," said Canderro, improvising one projected move at a time. "You get the blankets off the windows and turn on every light in the house."

"That's the signal we've got a deal?"

"That's it."

"And then?"

Canderro sucked air. "OK if I have a cigarette? They're in my left side pocket."

"Very slowly," said Meade, leveling the automatic.

The lieutenant lit up and dropped the pack and the matches on the bed beside him. He saw a network of cobwebs swinging in the glow of the old overhead fixture. He looked at Meade's mother sitting straight-backed in her chair, eyes fixed on his face and barely blinking. A tough lady. He listened for sounds from the next room. There was nothing, and he wondered how much of what was being said they were able to hear.

"And then," Canderro continued, "you release Wurzel and Garret and send them out the back door. Where I came in."

"What do we get in return?" asked Mrs. Lipton.

"You get me. I stay with you as your insurance."

"How long?"

"Until you feel you're clear. Their orders are to let us drive out without following. You can always lose a tail anyway. And if you're worried about beepers being planted, you can switch cars someplace."

Canderro looked at Meade. "We all know how good you are at that."

"What's to stop me from putting a bullet in your head when we don't need you anymore?" asked Meade.

"Nothing."

Meade had been standing the entire time, but he sat down now in the chair beside his mother.

"You don't mind dying?" he said.

"Sure I mind. Who doesn't? But that's the chance I took the minute I walked in here."

Canderro pulled on his cigarette, blew smoke, and watched it drift up to the light.

"Anyway," he said, "what's my choice? You either kill me now for sure, or maybe decide to let me go later on account of you've gotten to love me so much."

Meade laughed.

Not his mother. "You talk too easily about dying, Lieutenant. That worries me a little."

"Why?"

"Because anyone who loses all normal fear of death can be dangerous."

"You don't have to worry. I'm still afraid."

"You have a strange way of showing it," Mrs. Lipton said.

She half turned to her son. "What do you think, William?"

"I think we've been grossly underestimating our good Lieutenant Canderro."

Meade sat quietly considering the detective. He seemed to be looking for something he had yet to give a name.

"I've been wondering," he said. "How did you figure out I was here?"

"Garret showed me a videocassette you sent him. I saw the bed sheets covering the wall and floor."

"So?"

"So why would you take the trouble to hide a wall and floor unless you were sure Garret would recognize them?"

Meade's grin was slow and easy. "I told you we've underestimated him, Mom."

Mrs. Lipton was silent. Along with everything else, thought Canderro, she had to be less than happy with her son's need to send Garret the videocassette in the first place.

Meade took another look at the time.

"Just nine minutes to go, Lieutenant."

Canderro sat casually smoking his cigarette.

"So here's how it's going to be," said Meade. "What we're *not* going to do right now is turn Jacqueline and Garret loose and send them out there. If your promised attack does start on time, we can always switch on the lights, let you get the attention of your men, and do your deal then."

There was a long silence that had a coldly familiar feel to Canderro. It was very much as if he had been here before and knew exactly what was coming.

"But if it turns out you've been lying all along," said Meade, "and nobody turns up for the big attack other than a few crickets and cicadas..."

He shrugged and offered the detective one of his sweeter, gentler smiles. "Then we'll just have to figure out what to do about that."

CHAPTER
61

The two bedrooms shared a common wall as well as an old-fashioned heating register. Also, both of their doors had been left open, so that Garret and Jacqueline were able to follow just about everything that was being said in the next room. Other things, further understanding, came to them from within themselves, and often without their knowing exactly how.

Separately manacled, they remained together yet physically apart. Their hopes rose and fell, changing direction by the minute. They exchanged fragile, easily shattered glances, and understood that in these looks there was something very near to dread.

Perhaps worst of all, they were unable to touch. And at moments they needed that more than anything. Yet that part did not change. It was a constant. The space between them remained an unalterable seven and a half feet.

Only their eyes could meet and make contact.

At rare moments that was almost enough.

In between the listening and the exchanging of glances, they whispered things. These were meant to comfort, to reassure. They did not. Mostly their effect was pretty much the opposite.

The things they did not whisper, their true thoughts and fears, lived with them like uninvited guests.

Canderro had become the biggest enigma of all. Garret did not believe him for a minute, and he doubted Meade and his mother did, either. The detective had no ten-man backup waiting for him out there someplace in the dark. Garret knew this with as much certainty as he'd ever known anything. Yet he couldn't entirely accept the idea of Canderro's placing his own and their lives at risk by coming in here alone. Not unless there was more to it. There *had* to be more. The man was a professional, for God's sake. And a good one.

So he told himself.

Still, it nagged.

He gazed at Jacqueline lying on the bed, and she had never looked lovelier to him. With Emmy's gown loosely draped over her body, she projected an unconscious grace that defied where she was, what she faced, and everything that had been done to her.

"You're beautiful," he whispered.

Her lips tightened and she said nothing.

"I mean it."

"I know you do," she said, and for the first time began to weep. "I'm sorry. This is so dumb. I just suddenly wished you could have known me ten or fifteen years ago. I looked better then."

"Maybe younger, but not better. Never better."

She managed to smile as she wept. "My God, you really do love me, don't you?"

"Don't ever doubt it."

"Even now? Even after seeing William doing everything he did to me?"

"More than ever."

"I just wish I could hold you."

"You will," he told her with all the confidence he wished he could feel but did not feel at all.

"Do you really believe that?"

"I do," Garret lied.

He heard Canderro's voice going again in the other room. But it was not coming through very clearly at that moment, and he did not feel like straining to hear what the detective was saying. *Enough of his goddamn bullshit*, he thought, and suddenly found himself furious with him.

How could he?

It would have been different if Canderro had not found them. That could not be helped. But this was something else. This had to be nothing less than criminal. To have finally been able to figure out where they were and then not to have surrounded them with an army was surely beyond excusing.

It occurred to Garret that this was not the first time. Hadn't the lieutenant done pretty much the same thing when he spotted Meade's cabin? Except that then he'd taken two men with him, gotten them both killed, and finally ended up losing Meade besides.

So what was it with the man? Ego? A need to play God and do it all himself? The thing was, he'd liked and respected Canderro. He still did. And what if it *was* a matter of ego? Sometimes it was only ego that got you out of bed in the morning and kept you from blowing out your brains before dark. It was not a dirty word.

Unless, of course, he thought, *it ends up getting me and someone I love killed.*

"Four minutes," said Jacqueline.

Garret saw her studying her watch.

"This is worse than waiting for water to boil," she said.

He was silent.

"If I ask you a question," Jacqueline said, "will you answer honestly?"

"Is it an important question?"

"Yes."

"I'm sorry. I never answer important questions honestly. It's a journalist's one unbreakable rule."

"Are you afraid of what might happen after the four minutes are up and no police are out there?"

"I sure am."

"I'm glad. Because I'm absolutely terrified. And it's worse to be frightened alone."

"You're not alone."

"When I was a little girl," she said, "I had my own private angel to look after me whenever I was afraid. But I seem to have lost her somewhere along the way."

Garret found himself nodding in agreement and understanding. But also with regret. He had taken his best shot at looking after her and here he was, sitting naked on his bedroom floor, chained to a radiator valve, waiting for them both to die.

"I just wish we could be touching," she said.

He sat there.

"We are," he finally told her, and was surprised to find that he meant it.

Yet he had lied to her about being afraid. The fear had been replaced now by regret and anger. Regret that he had not been able to do more and better for Jacqueline. Anger that William Meade would be getting away with every last goddamn bit of it.

You should have brought your army, Lieutenant. Alone, I'm afraid we're nothing.

Toward the end of the waiting, sliding into the final minutes, Garret mostly watched Jacqueline's face. In a curious way he seemed to find there an almost exact reflection of his own feeling.

Did love finally create its own emotional clones? At times, it almost seemed so. She might have been a mirror image of the way he felt.

Attached through the heart?

An incredible feeling.

Finally, what else was there?

CHAPTER
62

Not one of them appeared to have changed position as much as two inches as the deadline arrived and passed.

Lieutenant Canderro sat on the edge of the bed, smoking his third cigarette.

William Meade and his mother were still in their two straight-backed chairs facing him. Their faces were drained of all expression. Whatever they might have been feeling seemed to have leaked out.

"It looks as though nobody is coming to your party, Lieutenant," said Meade.

The detective was silent. He felt a familiar tightness in his toes and calves and knew they were going to start cramping soon if he did not start moving a little.

"I still find it hard to believe he was foolish enough to try something like this alone," said Mrs. Lipton. "But apparently he was."

"No," said Meade. "There's nothing foolish about the lieutenant. He's rock solid. A twenty-year cop. If he came after me by himself, he had a good reason."

Canderro concentrated on Meade's eyes, on their light gray color. Whatever was inside the man was in his eyes. And every last bit of it was held by a single thread.

"It doesn't matter now," said Meade's mother. "It was all just a bluff. And it's over."

"Nothing is over, Mom."

Meade smiled, squinting slightly. "As it happens, I have my own theory as to why he did it." He looked at Canderro. "Want to hear it, Lieutenant?"

Canderro did not say a word. He was busy watching Meade's eyes. Narrower now, everything in them seemed compacted, pressed together, and more intense. Two tiny pinpoints of light were reflected there, one for each eye. They danced.

"You did it so you could have me all to yourself," said Meade.

The detective stirred himself as though just waking. "You think I was that hot to make myself a hero?"

"No. You were that hot to make *me* dead."

Canderro sat there smoking. He glanced at Mrs. Lipton and saw her eyes shift briefly to her son. When her eyes came back to him, there seemed to be something in her face that had not been there before.

"I'm a police officer," he said. "My job is to arrest criminals, not murder them."

"I know what your job is, Lieutenant. But this time you weren't doing your job. You stopped acting like a police officer the minute you decided to come after me yourself instead of calling for backup."

Canderro knew, then, what was building. What he did not

know was precisely where it was heading or the exact moment it would arrive.

Studying the detective's face, Meade seemed pleased by what he saw.

"The truth is," he said, "I understand what you did. It's my kind of thinking. In fact I'd have done the exact same thing in your place. So we're not all that different."

Meade nodded consideringly. "With my current body count, it makes a lot more sense for you to shoot me than to arrest me. What are they going to do? Rehabilitate me?"

William Meade smiled. "You've made me respect you, Lieutenant, and that's something I never really expected. I certainly haven't respected many in your line of work. It's just that..." His smile was at its warmest now. "It's not in my nature to simply wish you well and send you on your merry way."

Canderro had no advance warning. There was just the sound of the gunshot filling the room, along with the bullet catching him in the upper part of his left arm. For all practical purposes they took place at the same instant.

The bullet's impact knocked him back on the bed, and he lay there, blinking at the ceiling. It took him several moments to understand what had happened. Not so much the shot itself, but what it was likely to mean for himself and for those in the next room.

Then he heard Mrs. Lipton's voice.

"My God, William! What did you do?"

"Why so shocked, Mom? I've done a whole lot worse than shoot a cop in the arm."

"Never in front of *me*."

"That's why I did it," said Meade quietly. "I decided it was time you knew exactly what I do."

"I *know* what you do."

"No, you don't. You've just heard about it, all sanitized, on the six o'clock news. You have to see it for yourself to really know and understand."

Canderro lay listening and sucking air. He was trying to collect himself. He thought about going for the one move he had left, but it had to be at just the right moment and this was not it.

"Please sit up, Lieutenant," said Meade. "Let my mother have a good look at you."

Slowly, the detective worked his way to a sitting position on the bed. He was wearing a short-sleeved shirt and the wound itself was visible and running blood. There was little pain. But he knew that would start increasing as the shock wore off. The one good thing was that the bullet had missed the bone and passed through.

"See this man?" Meade said to his mother. "He came here with a gun tonight to terminate us both. Not just me. But you, as well. Because there was no way he was going to leave you around as a witness to his premeditated murder of *me*."

Meade paused. "So what you're going to do now is simply return the favor."

There was silence in the room and a moment was lost.

"Me?" said Mrs. Lipton, and Canderro saw the sudden lifting of her brows.

"Who else? It's a new age for us, Mom. When we leave here in a few hours, we'll be starting fresh, sharing new lives in a new place. Sharing everything. Even this. So just lift your pretty revolver, aim at the left side of the lieutenant's chest, and gently squeeze the trigger."

"I can't do that."

"Of course you can," said Meade softly. "It's the easiest thing in the world. And the most exciting."

She shook her head.

"It's true," he said. "If I feel it, you feel it. That's how it's always been."

Mrs. Lipton sat with her revolver half raised.

Watching her as intensely as he'd ever watched anyone or anything in his life, Canderro prepared to move.

"There's no other way," said Meade. "He knows too much about our plans."

"So do those in the next room."

"Don't worry about them. You just do the lieutenant."

Mrs. Lipton looked at Canderro's face. Then she looked at his arm. Then she looked at the thin trail of blood flowing onto the bedsheet.

"Why is my doing it so important?"

"Because it will finally put you with me."

"I've always been with you, William."

"Yes. But on a different level. More like my keeper. I don't want that anymore, Mom. It lessens me."

She let a long moment go by. When she finally spoke her voice was harsh. "You'll be happy to know I shot a man to death last week. I couldn't leave him behind. He got us our new passports and papers and knew our identities. I hated it, but I did it. It didn't excite me. It just made me sick."

"This one will be easier for you."

"I'm not doing it."

"Yes, you are, Mom. From now on we're equals. We share in everything. The lieutenant is yours."

Canderro sat absolutely still. He knew it was coming very soon now, but not from which direction. He watched them both. Then he felt the pain beginning.

William Meade slowly bent and placed his automatic on the floor beside his chair. Then he carefully slid the gun across the room to the far wall.

The small, dramatic act hung in the air, numbing the room. It seemed dreamlike and slow. Meade's voice, following it, sounded like part of the same dream.

"It's all yours now, Mom. So you'd better decide. Fast. Is it the lieutenant or us?"

Canderro was not fooled. Earlier, he had noted the bulge of what had to be another weapon in Meade's back pocket. Still, it would take him at least a few seconds to reach around, grab the gun, bring it to bear and fire. Which would be about as much of an edge as he could hope for. Meade was still his first thought. Momma was the big question mark.

His arm would slow him a bit, but every nerve-ending was screaming for him to go for it.

Then with a faint sniff of a new grave, Canderro went.

Watching Meade's eyes until the last second, he swung off the bed sideways and landed on the floor rolling away from them. He had the snub-nosed special out of his ankle holster before he stopped rolling, and got off two quick shots at Meade over the edge of the bed. He saw him go over in his chair as though slammed by a two-by-four, his mouth wide and calling out, but no sound heard because of the exploding gunfire.

Die, you lousy murdering bastard.

Another shot exploded, not his own, and he felt the sudden fire in his gut and thought, *Oh, shit,* as the next one took him clean in the leg.

He looked up then and saw Meade's mother sitting there in her chair, calmly aiming and pumping bullets as though he were no more than a tin target in a shooting gallery.

Gripping her revolver with both hands, she was going for his head this time, an avenging angel of death with blood in her eyes and malice in the tight line of her mouth. But Canderro moved before the finishing shot went off and the bullet splintered the flooring beside his cheek.

Now, he thought, because she was impassively aiming again and there was no way the next round was going to miss. He felt the burning all through his stomach and he was sliding and slipping in blood.

Do it now or you've bought it.

Half on his side, Canderro got the snub-nose up and saw her face over the two gun barrels...his, blued steel...hers, nickel-plated. Her eyes were glassy with rage.

Good God, he thought, and fired an instant before she herself squeezed the trigger.

Her shot went into the wall behind him.

The detective blinked into the sudden silence and the acrid smell of cordite. Mrs. Lipton was no longer sitting in her chair.

Moving torturously, sliding on his own blood, Canderro slithered and crawled around the edge of the bed. He saw floating white spots and everything else was going from red to green and then back to red.

Jesus, don't pass out. Not now.

William Meade was not in the room. Some blood was on his chair, but it went nowhere else. The automatic he had slid across the floor was still lying against the far wall. The gun he had evidently taken from his back pocket was next to his overturned chair.

Using one arm and one leg for traction, the detective drew himself farther around the edge of the bed.

Mrs. Lipton lay on her back beside the chair. Canderro's shot had left a small dark hole in her forehead, just below the hairline. Her eyes were still open, looking past him with a hundred-mile stare.

Even dead, she was a beautiful woman.

The detective lay there, pumping blood onto the floor. He was starting to feel cold inside and knew that the gut shot was bad. The other two hits, arm and leg, just hurt like hell. The gut shot could goddamn finish him.

Christ! Where's Meade?

Never mind Meade. Get to Garret while you still can.

He had a moment then. He was nothing but open raw depths, and he could feel lights shifting inside himself along with the blood.

Hold on, he told himself, *or it all just turns to shit.*

He picked up Meade's automatic and shoved his other gun under the bed. Then dragging his shattered leg, he crawled toward the door like a dying snake.

CHAPTER
63

Hearing the shooting was a thundering nightmare. The explosions jarred their brains. The silence that followed was worse. It dragged them beyond remembered fear.

They looked at each other and waited.

Closer to the open doorway and down on the floor, Garret heard the sounds first. Rasping breath...something softly sliding...an occasional faint groan. Whispers, carrying their own sickness. Garret felt ill in a way he had never felt before.

A single bloody hand appeared on the floor. It was followed an instant later by the rest of Canderro.

"God," said Jacqueline.

Garret swallowed dryly.

The detective crawled into the room and collapsed, face-down, gasping.

Canderro lifted his head. "Listen...I got a couple into Meade...but couldn't finish it. He's around somewhere. His mother's dead."

He pushed Meade's automatic toward Garret's free hand. "Shoot the cuffs...off."

Garret picked up the gun and aimed it at the chain that anchored his other hand to the radiator.

"Wait..." said Canderro, and looked at Jacqueline on the bed. "Toss him...a...pillow. Bullets can...ricochet."

Garret wrapped the pillow around the chain and carefully fired through it. As easily as that, he was loose. He did the same for Jacqueline where she was manacled to the headboard. Each was left with a bracelet and half a chain still attached to one wrist. But they were free to move.

Garret quickly slipped on his pants and shoes. Jacqueline put on the only covering she had available...Emily's nightgown. There was an extra vulnerability in being naked, Garret thought. It came to him that it made you feel very different to wear pants and hold a gun in your hand. You felt strong and angry, instead of weak and frightened.

When he turned to Canderro, the detective was unconscious on the floor.

Garret rolled him onto his back. He listened to his breathing and heard it rasping in his throat. He pulled up the detective's blood-soaked shirt and looked at the small, round hole in the right side of his stomach. It oozed only a thin trickle of blood, but he knew the worst of these gut shots was always on the inside. Because he felt compelled to do something, he covered it with a clean folded handkerchief.

Garret crouched there. *Hang tough*, he told himself in the faintest of mental whispers. Then he took the snub-nosed police special out of the detective's belt and slowly stood up.

He checked the revolver's chambers, found three unspent cartridges still left, and handed the revolver to Jacqueline.

"Watch him," he said and his voice was hard.

"Where are you going?"

"To look for Meade."

"How do you know where to look?"

"I don't. But I'll find him. Or he'll find me."

"He may have gone off somewhere."

"No. Where could he go with a couple of bullets in him? Besides, we're here, his mother is here, and Canderro is here. Even if he could, he would never leave us. He has no one else."

They stood listening to Canderro's shallow, erratic breathing. *Just keep doing it,* Garret silently told the detective.

He looked at Jacqueline, slender and incongruously seductive in his late wife's nightgown for special occasions. Was there some sort of metaphysical planning that went into such things?

"Please," she said. "Hold me. Just for a second. William will wait for you."

Pressed close, he felt her heart going very fast. But all he could think of was Meade.

"Listen carefully," Garret said. "When I leave this room, I want the light out, the door closed, and you flat on the floor with your arms propped on pillows and your revolver aimed straight at the door. Understand?"

"Yes."

"If I want to come back in, I'll knock three times and say 'It's me' before I open the door. Anyone else coming in has to be Meade. Which means you start squeezing off shots at once. Rapid fire and without stopping. He'll be against the hall light at a range of seven feet, so you can't miss."

Garret stood thinking. He ejected the ammunition clip from the automatic Canderro had given him, saw that it was full, and clicked it back into the grip. Then he gave it to Jacqueline and took her revolver for himself.

"You've got a full twelve rounds in this piece," he said.

"If you have to use it, don't stop firing until either the gun is empty or you're sure Meade is dead."

Garret looked at Jacqueline again, stalling, putting off the moment of leaving.

"Have you ever shot anyone?" he asked.

"No."

"Any qualms about being able to do it if you have to?"

"No."

"You're sure?"

"Absolutely."

"Even if it's Meade?"

"My God, Paul," she said fiercely. "*Especially* if it's him. What kind of person do you think I am?"

"The best kind," he said. "The kind that can't ever kill easily."

"Maybe a few months ago, but not anymore."

Garret got the two pillows and settled her into position on the floor next to Canderro. He kissed her. Then he turned off the light, left the room, and closed the door behind him.

His starting point was the next room. He went in and saw Mrs. Lipton lying on the floor, her nickel-plated revolver beside her. The gun glinted in the overhead light and threw small pieces of brightness on the ceiling. Looking at her, Garret felt nothing. Yet this in itself somehow bothered him. Her feet were apart and appeared awkward and disconnected, like those of a rag doll. He thought of her great dignity as a woman.

He saw the trail of blood Canderro had left as he dragged himself out of the room.

He saw, too, the blood on Meade's overturned chair.

Then he left the room and started down the stairs.

CHAPTER
64

William Meade slowly eased open the closet door. He heard Paul Garret's footsteps going down the stairs and the sound of his own labored breathing. The rest was just silence.

At least his hearing was still good. Other parts of him were less than good.

Then the faintness and the dizziness took over again and he had to lean back against the hanging clothes and the shelves, while he breathed the smell of camphor and waited for the worst of it to pass.

An ankle holster, he thought dryly. *Who would have expected anything like a gun in one of those gimmicky little ankle holsters? The silly cop sitting there, waiting to be finished at their leisure, and then he's suddenly off the bed and on the floor, pumping bullets.*

Never underestimate the enemy. Good advice. Only a little late.

Meade breathed with difficulty. He had been hit once in

the chest and once in the shoulder. Although there was little visible bleeding, things felt broken inside.

He inhaled and exhaled as though the bullets had torn away most of his lungs and what remained was clogged with fluid. In his mind he was struggling through deep sand that stretched to a limitless horizon. Then he closed his eyes for a moment and somehow found the will to go on.

A few seconds later he was able to leave his closet.

Meade went over and knelt beside his mother. But he was very careful not to look at her face. He was not quite ready for that. He just stared at her skirt, which was hiked up over her knees. Then he pulled her skirt down and adjusted it more modestly.

He had the feeling that whatever had happened here was something that he was not likely to ever understand, so it would be foolish of him to try. Yet everything in the room, everything inside his mind and heart, was sad and bitter. He thought that perhaps his mother had this same terrible feeling before she died.

Meade noticed the awkward way his mother's legs were placed, and he carefully straightened them out. His hands had begun to shake and he put them to his head, trying to hold himself and his hands still.

He stayed motionless. Yet he felt he should be moving, should be taking some sort of positive action. It was as though there was something important outside of this room that he should be doing to make things better.

It came to him then that his mother should not be lying on the floor alone, that maybe he should be lying beside her. He began to get the idea that the two bullets in him might not really be enough to buy him the necessary salvation, that the pain and the sadness and the not being able to breathe might only be a very small part of his required atonement.

Meade looked around, as if seeking answers somewhere in the room that he'd so far been unable to find within himself.

He gazed at the walls and the ceiling and the bed and the two chairs ... one, upright; the other, on its side. He studied the closet he had stumbled into, helpless and in shock, and the long trail of blood left by Canderro as he dragged himself out, and the nickel-plated revolver that he had badgered and cajoled and finally tricked his mother into firing, when he should have done the firing himself.

There was no need, no need other than my own.

He wished there was some way for him to change it. He thought of the way it had been, with the lieutenant sitting there on the bed facing the two of them, and nothing left to do but give him what he deserved. He imagined himself quickly and safely doing it, imagined Canderro lying there on the floor instead of his mother, imagined their flying off together with fresh hope and only the best of everything ahead.

And in the imagining, he was stirred.

Finally, he was able to look at her face.

Her open eyes entered his heart like a *coup de grâce,* and he reached over and gently closed the lids. The dark lashes curled over her cheeks, giving her the vulnerable look of youth. Her color was pale but otherwise fine. Had it not been for the small hole in her forehead, Meade might have convinced himself she was asleep. But when he kissed her lips, they held no warmth.

I'm sorry, he silently told her.

He sighed and a sudden rush of blood came from his mouth.

When the hemorrhaging stopped, he picked up his mother's revolver and walked uncertainly and with great care out into the upstairs hall.

He stood near the stairs for a moment, listening for some sound of Garret on the floor below. He thought he might have heard a door being closed, but he could not be sure. Then there was not even the thought.

Meade walked the few steps to the next bedroom. He could see himself. He moved like something held together with strings.

He knocked three times.

"It's me," he said in a voice that sounded to him very much like Paul Garret's.

Then he opened the door and walked in.

He saw Jacqueline lying on the floor in Emily Garret's nightgown. She was aiming an automatic at his head. Canderro lay, unmoving, beside her, either unconscious or dead.

William Meade stood there with the light behind him. His mother's revolver was in his hand, pointing loosely at the floor.

It occurred to him that he had been waiting most of his life for this moment.

He opened his mouth to speak, to tell Jacqueline, wryly, that he was not really Paul Garret. But no words came... only blood. She lay there aiming her gun and staring at him and at the blood. He wondered why she was waiting.

Meade tried again to speak. This time he wanted to let her know that within his limitations and as best as he was able, he had tried not to hurt her.

Within my limitations and as best as I was able.

Epitaph.

A mouthful at any time. With a tongue drowning in a pool of blood, impossible.

He offered his favorite amused smile, but he knew it had to be merely grotesque.

From a long way off he once more wondered why she did not shoot. But of course he knew. In these things you either can or you cannot. Not that it mattered. It was only a question of a few seconds now. He felt he could handle a few seconds.

"William..." she said.

Taken altogether, he thought, not the greatest of final conversations. Yet what was there to say?

He heard what had to be Garret's footsteps.

First, they were in the downstairs entrance hall. Then they were climbing the steps.

Meade turned and left the room to meet them.

Garret looked tired. He moved slowly, his head bent. He carried Canderro's snub-nosed police special in his hand like a flag of defeat.

William Meade silently watched him as he neared the top of the stairs.

"Paul!"

Jacqueline cried out the warning, and Garret lifted his head and saw Meade looking down at him.

Meade offered his own greeting. It came out garbled by blood and unintelligible. But the bizarre, red-toothed smile that accompanied it was nothing if not friendly.

Garret shot him twice in the head and once through the heart. He stopped firing only because there were no more bullets in the gun.

Jacqueline came out of the room and they stood there, holding each other. Her flesh was damp and cold and she was shaking.

"I couldn't do it," she whispered.

"Couldn't do what?"

"Shoot him."

Garret drew back slightly to look at her. She was dry eyed, but her lids were blinking rapidly and she seemed to be on the edge of something.

"He heard your instructions before," she said. "He knocked three times, said 'It's me,' and came into the room. He stood there, right in front of me, and I swear I couldn't even squeeze the trigger."

Garret held her and said nothing.

"He *wanted* me to shoot. He was just waiting for it. He could have shot me six times over and he never even lifted his gun."

Garret nodded. "He could have gotten me on the stairs, too. I never saw him until you yelled."

"But at least you didn't freeze. You were able to do it."

She was still half in shock.

Garret took her back into the bedroom. He wanted to see if Canderro was still breathing. He was. But with the same frightful, gasping sound as before.

"We'd better get him to a hospital fast," Garret said.

He ran, gasping, all the way to where he and Mrs. Lipton had left Hank Berringer's car. Having gratefully accepted the mere fact that the detective was still alive, he was in a near panic at the thought of driving back to the house and finding him dead of waiting.

But when Garret got back to him, Canderro appeared no more dead than before. If anything, he looked slightly less spectral, with Jacqueline having cleaned away some of the blood and bandaged him with strips of bedsheet.

They half dragged, half carried him downstairs and out to the car. He regained consciousness as they stretched him out on the backseat.

"Damn," he whispered.

"You're OK," said Garret.

"Sure ... I'm great." Canderro's eyes closed. "What ... about Meade?"

"Dead."

The detective sighed. "Thank Jesus."

"Thank *you*," said Jacqueline.

Garret was behind the wheel and driving now, gliding the car carefully around the worst of the ruts. Jacqueline was kneeling on her seat and facing the rear to watch Canderro. In the east the sky was just beginning to lighten.

"Where ... you taking me?"

A froth of pink bubbles came with the words.

"Poughkeepsie General," said Garret. "It's closest. And they did OK with me."

"Two calls...." The detective's voice was starting to fade. "Chief ... Reagan and my ... Kate."

Canderro went out again.

Garret listened to his breathing and it seemed fainter than before.

Don't let him die, he thought. Which was about as close to a prayer as he seemed able to allow himself these days. He thought it hard, with both hands strangling the wheel, as if intensity alone would be enough to get it accomplished.

But then he decided, *What the hell* ... and went all out, using his old childhood mental whisper and asking for a break for his new friend, Frank Canderro. No. More than a break. Because what was needed here was a nice, old-fashioned miracle like the one he himself had been granted just a few months ago.

If I deserved it, Garret whispered inside his head, *this cop who walked into my house and saved Jacqueline and me deserves it a hell of a lot more. Because at his best he showed more heart and courage than most of us ever show, making no big deal of it but just doing what he felt had to be done.*

CHAPTER
65

It took them twenty-three minutes to reach the hospital in Poughkeepsie, and Lieutenant Canderro was in the operating room seventeen minutes later.

Garret and Jacqueline had stayed close beside him for as long as they were allowed. He had regained consciousness only once, as they were sticking all the needles and tubes into him. He stared blankly at Garret, tried a ludicrous wink, mumbled something about Kate, and went under sedation as they were wheeling him down the corridor.

It was only then that Garret went to make the two calls he had requested.

Chief of Detectives Reagan said, "Holy shit," and told Garret he would be at the hospital as soon as he finished with the bodies and whatever other forensic procedures had to be taken care of at the scene.

Kate whispered, "Sweet Mary, Mother of God," and said she would meet him in the emergency room in twenty minutes.

She was actually there in fifteen.

Garret saw her approaching, a pretty, obviously distraught woman who was already searching his face for possible bad news at a distance of fifty feet. Jacqueline rose with him and took her hands.

"He's going to be fine," Jacqueline told her. "I feel it in my bones."

Kate looked at Garret for confirmation and saw just the opposite. She slowly sat down.

"He completely fooled me," she said, and told them everything that had happened earlier.

"But if you tell us he called headquarters about it," said Garret, "how...?"

"That's just it. Frank never made the call. He faked it to throw me off. The smart-ass knew I'd never let him try anything that crazy alone."

"How could you have stopped him?"

"By calling headquarters. By telling them where he was going and what he was trying to do."

"You'd have done that?" said Garret.

Kate's eyes were fierce. "You're damn right I would."

They were still in the waiting room an hour and a half later when Chief of Detectives Reagan came in with a horde of reporters and photographers trailing after him.

Garret swallowed and got the bitter taste of his mouth.

Flashbulbs and strobe lights went off, minicams whirred, and reporters began tossing questions like grenades with their pins pulled.

Garret ignored them.

The chief motioned to a couple of detectives who started pushing everyone back. Then he took Garret, Jacqueline, and Kate down a corridor to an empty conference room and closed the door.

"What's the latest on Frank?" he asked.

He was looking straight at Kate as he spoke, but it was Garret who answered.

"He's still in surgery."

"How bad is he? Where'd you say he got hit?"

Garret had never said. "He took hits in the arm, leg, and stomach."

Reagan shook his head, quivering his jowls. He lit a cigarette despite the No Smoking signs.

He looked again at Kate.

"Would you mind telling me what the hell Frank was doing in that house alone?"

"Why ask *me?*"

"Because it was your bed he had to slide out of in the middle of the night to get there."

Kate met his stare without blinking.

"Well, Chief," she said, quietly, "as far as I've been able to tell so far, he was in that house saving the lives of two innocent people, while terminating a mad-dog killer and his equally psychotic mother. Which was something neither you nor any other cop in the state was anywhere near doing."

Reagan sat considering Kate through a haze of smoke. He wore a scornful expression.

"And in the meantime," he said, "he's maybe inside there right now, dying of it."

Like an unexpected slap in the face, the statement brought her close to tears.

Reagan decided to leave it alone. He turned to Garret and Jacqueline. For the first time he seemed to notice the single handcuff and dangling fragment of chain that each of them wore.

"What the hell happened in that house?" he said. "We'll take your formal depositions later, but in the meantime I'd like a quick run-through. How you all got there, and why. How the lieutenant found out. Who did what to whom. Whatever you want to tell me."

The chief saw Garret and Jacqueline exchange glances.

"Understand," he said. "You're both victims here, not suspects. And if you want to remain silent for now, that's your right. But I'd still like to know more than just the bare bones I got from you on the phone."

"I think it might be better if we waited awhile before going into all that," Garret said.

"Waited for what?"

"For the lieutenant to come out of surgery, for one thing."

Reagan sat there, frowning.

"I'll be honest with you," said Garret. "I don't really like anything I've heard from you so far. I don't like what you said to Kate, and I sure as hell don't like you coming down on Lieutenant Canderro because he neglected to call you in advance about his plans."

"There are certain standard police procedures that we—"

"To hell with your standard police procedures," said Garret quietly. "Jacqueline and I would be lying dead in my house this minute if we'd been depending on your standard police procedures to help us. So don't dump that garbage on me. And if you want to be really smart, don't let me hear about your dumping it anywhere else, either."

It was more than three hours before the head of the surgical team finally appeared. Kate, Jacqueline, and Garret were alone by then, and the doctor approached them directly, a thin, tired-looking man in rumpled operating greens.

"You're immediate family?" he said.

Garret stood up. Kate and Jacqueline appeared incapable of any such move.

"Immediate friends," said Garret.

The surgeon removed his glasses. "Yes. Of course. You're Paul Garret. I should have recognized you."

He shook Garret's hand. "I'm Tom Kendall, chief of surgery here. I enjoy reading your columns."

Dry-mouthed, Garret waited. He took the pleasantry as a good sign. Not even a bloodless surgeon would be cold and insensitive enough to be making small talk if the news were bad. Unless Kendall himself needed more time to deal with it. There were human qualities in everyone, even those who chose to spend their working lives slicing people open. But Garret's fear for Canderro was getting to him now, and he had to hold himself in check.

Speak, you icy sonofabitch.

"Well," said Dr. Kendall, "your friend got through the surgery. He wouldn't have if he hadn't been as strong as he was."

"Meaning exactly what?"

"That with three bullets in him and the loss of so much blood there was a better than fair possibility we were going to lose him. The son of a gun held on, though."

"And his prognosis?"

"My least favorite word," said Kendall. "It assumes I have a crystal ball, which I don't. The most I can offer you at this point is that he's holding his own."

Garret stood there, suddenly feeling frustrated, wanting more certainty than the doctor was willing to give him. He was aware of Kate close beside him, felt her fingers digging into the flesh of his upper arm.

"I want to see him," she told the doctor.

Kendall looked at her. "I'm afraid that's not possible right now."

"I must see him now," Kate said. "It's important. He got

out of bed in the middle of the night. I never knew he was leaving. I never even had a chance to . . ."

Her voice was quiet. Her manner was controlled and reasonable. But her fingers were ten spikes driven into Garret's arm.

"Are you Lieutenant Canderro's wife?" asked the doctor. He was obviously confused by Garret's previous identification of them as friends.

Kate stared at him, shook her head slowly.

"It's simply not permitted, Miss. He's still not awake. You'll have to wait and see him at the proper time."

"What if he's dead at the proper time?"

The surgeon just looked at her.

As he turned to leave, Garret stopped him.

"Excuse me, Doctor," he said. "Lieutenant Canderro got three bullets in him while serving others. Couldn't you bend the rules a little to serve the needs of someone he loves?"

"There are no exceptions."

"That's too bad," said Garret. "Because there are about a dozen reporters and photographers waiting for me outside. Would you really want me to make a big, ugly media event out of what you're saying?"

"Is that what you would do?"

"You can count on it."

Kendall sighed. "I'll send someone to take the lady."

Moments later a nurse appeared and Garret went down a corridor with her and Kate. Jacqueline stayed behind.

Kate held tightly to Garret's arm. They walked through air heavy with drugs and sickness.

The nurse took them to a large postoperative recovery room where Canderro lay unconscious. Things ran in and out of him through a network of tubes. The detective's eyes were closed and his mouth was set. His expression was as calm and controlled and as stubborn as ever.

Kate wept.

Garret took her hand and held it. He wanted to share what she was feeling, if such a thing could in any way be possible.

"I hate him," she said with quiet fury. "If he dies, he'll have thrown his life away and mine with it. And there was no need. That bird-brain Reagan was right for once. If you're a cop, you act like a cop. You don't go in business for yourself."

Garret was silent.

"And don't think Frank went in there alone just for you two," Kate said. "That was all for him. He didn't want any army of cops arresting Meade. He didn't want him back in Attica or in some mental hospital. He had to kill him. He had to personally blow him away. Even if it finally meant you and Jacqueline dying with him."

Kate covered her face with her hands.

"I swear to Christ," she wept through her fingers. "If he doesn't come out of this, I'll never forgive him as long as I live."

"Yes, you will," came a whispered voice.

Startled, Garret turned and saw the detective's lips moving awkwardly. Kate rushed to him, kissed him on the forehead.

"Frankie, I'm here...I'm here," she said, repeating the words over and over again. She took his hand, and Garret saw the lieutenant's fist close on her fingers.

Another soft murmur, this one unintelligible.

Kate bent her head to listen. "You were right, Kate," he got out, the words coming in slurred fragments. "Right about Meade...right about me."

Kate wiped at her eyes. She reached over to brush the hair from his forehead, and when she did, he raised his lips to hers, holding the kiss before collapsing back in exhaustion. For what seemed a long moment, Kate stared down at him. Then Garret saw the corners of the detective's mouth lift in the faintest of grins.

Feeling like an interloper, Garret nonetheless felt his spirits lifting. What had the big cop once said about rage keeping a man alive, willing him to go on? He had a feeling that the lieutenant had a different kind of emotion working for him now. And as only one who has risen from the dead can know, Garret had a sudden certainty that Canderro would be all right.

CHAPTER
66

It was late afternoon by the time Garret and Jacqueline finished taping their depositions at Poughkeepsie Police Headquarters. Then they left the building and got into Hank Berringer's car for the drive back to New York.

Garret saw Canderro's blood all over the backseat and thought, *Hank's not going to be happy about this.*

But then, who *was?*

He started the car and drove out of the police parking lot. The wheel was all that kept his hands from shaking, and he held onto it like a drowning man.

Jacqueline leaned over and touched his cheek with her lips. "Are you all right to drive?"

"I'm fine."

"You must be made of iron. I'm exhausted."

Moments later, she was dozing.

Once out of the city, the trees and hills shone a warm, misty orange in the late sun, and Garret thought he'd never seen anything more beautiful. He found his eyes near to flooding.

Naturally.

No great mystery. There had been moments during the past eighteen hours when he'd never expected to be seeing anything like this again. Which was exactly how he used to feel in Vietnam coming out of a bad stretch in the line, under heavy fire, with everything looking brand-new and unexpectedly moving because he had already written himself off going in.

He thought then of Meade, recalled the killer's last moments, tasted the blood in his mouth, felt the pain of his chest wound, imagined his thoughts before all thought was finally gone.

My private demon.

And how was he finally supposed to exorcise *that?*

Moments later Garret made a sudden turn and drove in another direction entirely.

Jacqueline awoke an instant after he'd stopped the car and turned off the motor.

Half-dazed with sleep, she blinked her eyes and straightened beside him.

"Where are we?"

Garret let her discover it for herself. He saw her glance around at the trees, then at the grassy field sloping down to the lake, then at the driveway leading to the entrance.

Lastly, he saw her staring at the house itself.

But even then, it took another moment to register.

"You've come back *here?* To the *house?*" The disbelief raised her voice a full octave.

Garret nodded.

"Why, for God's sake?"

He said nothing. He just sat there, looking at the house and remembering how much he'd always loved being in it.

"I don't understand."

"I just have to go inside for a few minutes," he said.

"Did you forget something?"

"I'm not sure."

She looked at him and remained silent.

"It shouldn't take long," he told her.

"Would you like me to go with you?"

He saw her eyes and almost had the sense that she had caught him at something. He shook his head. "No."

Garret could feel her watching as he walked to the front door and opened it with the house key he still carried with his other keys after so many months.

Then he was inside and the door was closed and Jacqueline could no longer see him.

He shut his eyes and stood there breathing the smell of gunpowder. It was sharp and bitter and burned his nostrils. He felt the emptiness of the place and that was almost worse than anything else. It was as though the house itself had died along with those who'd been shot inside it.

Garret envisioned William Meade as Emmy and he had first seen him on that day in early spring, an almost startlingly handsome young man who moved across the grassy knoll with an easy graceful stride. He pictured again his boyish face with its friendly open quality that didn't seem to go along with his eyes, which were pale and flat in expression. *Flat eyes*, he remembered thinking.

He remembered, too, what appeared to be the young man's unique and genuine love for the old house, love for what had stood up against time and abuse because it was simply the best.

Meade had killed that as well. Now there was no more here than dried blood and the memory of death. There would never be anything more.

Garret stood there until his brain quieted. *All right...* he thought, *easy, nice and easy.*

He opened his eyes and slowly climbed the stairs to the second-floor landing and the rooms beyond.

Bloodstains, old and new, cried out to him from floor, sheets, chairs, walls. The air itself might have had cries dripping from it. He wanted to cover his ears against what rose out of the silence. He wanted to stop breathing to keep the smell of death from his lungs.

I'm getting to be grotesque.

He opened closets and took careful inventory of what was in them. Bits and pieces of another life. Everything was exactly as it had been on the day of Meade's first visit. He had touched nothing since.

In Emmy's closet he stood against the feel of her clothes and was unable to leave. The closet still held her fragrance. He stood there breathing it, soaking in her absence. When he felt it choking him, he pried himself free.

Yet as he left the room, Emmy stayed close beside him.

As did William Meade.

Although he, finally, was as dead as she.

Both gone, yet not gone.

He suddenly felt ill, struck down, as if something of him were passing through unseen disasters. His chest clogging again with the worst of his thoughts, Garret opened a window and breathed deeply.

The air came in sweet, clear, and tinged with the aroma of pine. It was the kind of air he'd always thought of as quite possibly being the final resting place of the soul. About which he admittedly knew nothing. Yet who knew more?

Hearing the window open, Jacqueline leaned out of Hank Berringer's Mercedes and waved. Garret waved back.

Jacqueline was smiling and Garret felt his heart stirred by simply her smile and her wave.

Imagine. She could still do that.

What was wrong with him? There were still miracles. Something pure always survived. For every Meade there had to be a million Canderros. And like it or not, even Meade had to be granted a measure of grace for deciding to go out without malice or further killing. He could just as easily have taken them both with him.

He could have.

He had them.

And he had chosen not to.

"I'll be right out," Garret called to Jacqueline, and carefully closed the window.

Then he considered what he was about to do. Even now, it was not easy for him.

Everyone will think I'm crazy, he thought. But another part of him argued: *You'll be twice mad if you don't.*

His last doubt gone, he started down the stairs.

Vista Ridge was no more than three miles from the house, but it had good elevation and offered a dramatic view of the valley immediately to the west and the distant hills beyond. It was on the route back to New York, and it had always been a kind of ritual for Garret and his wife to park there for a few moments to enjoy a departing glimpse of their house in the rich fullness of its setting.

Even their dialogue, as they sat on the pull-off, carried something of the ceremonial.

"My God, look at it," Garret would say. "Did you ever in all your life . . . ?"

"Never," Emily would reply.

"Never what?"

"Never expect us to have anything like this."

"It is superb, isn't it? I'm not just being silly, am I?"

"Yes, it's superb," she would assure him.

"How did we ever get so lucky?"

"It wasn't luck. We worked for it. We deserve it."

"You're absolutely right."

Then they would look at each other and grin.

But Garret had never really believed the part about deserving it. If you were gifted with something that good, there had to be a fair amount of luck in it, too. Either that, or God was smiling. The idea of getting exactly what you deserved in life had been worrisome to him even then. Since William Meade, it had become a nightmare.

Garret thought of all that as he parked now on Vista Ridge.

"Why are we stopping?" Jacqueline asked.

"For a last look at the house."

With the sun low and tinged with orange, *superb* was still the best word Garret could think of for such a sight. It was all a single tinted blaze; yet its form and mood might have been two separate phenomena, each with its own appeal. Had there been a jeweled tower rising from that one distant house, with golden spires reaching for the sun, Garret could not have been any more moved.

Then he saw the smoke.

At first it did not really look that much like smoke. What it looked like mostly was just another of those soft purple-gray mists that come up out of the earth at dusk and finally turn into darkness.

Until it grew deeper and heavier and eventually rose in a billowing cloud that trailed across the sun and removed all doubt as to what it really was.

Jacqueline clutched Garret's hand. She tried to speak, but

for a moment there seemed to be a partition between her brain and her tongue.

Then she broke through.

"My God, Paul!"

He was silent.

"Paul!"

"It's only a house," he said. "It doesn't breathe, or bleed, or feel pain."

A hawk flew out of a tree just below the ridge line and glided in lazy circles.

Jacqueline looked at Garret. He sat solemnly watching the smoke grow thicker and billow higher.

When it had covered the sun like a giant shroud, he whispered a silent *kaddish* for the dead and started the car.

"All right," he said. "Let's go home."

**IF YOU ENJOYED *IMPULSE*,
DON'T MISS MICHAEL WEAVER'S
NEW NOVEL!!!**

DECEPTIONS

(coming in hardcover from Warner Books,
January 1995)

Bet you can't wait . . .